ROSE EDWARDS

The
EMBER DAYS

uclanpublishing

The Ember Days is a uclanpublishing book

First published in Great Britain in 2021 by
uclanpublishing
University of Central Lancashire
Preston, PR1 2HE, UK

978-1-91297915-8

1 3 5 7 9 10 8 6 4 2

Set in 10/16pt Kingfisher by Nicky Borowiec.

A CIP catalogue record for this book is available from the British Library.

Printed and bound in Great Britain by Clays Ltd, Elcograf S.p.A.

To my Best Boys,
Tom and Devon

🌿 CAST OF CHARACTERS 🌿

THE TELLERS

Torny Vafrisdota: survived possession, lost in the mist

Ebba Rathnasdota: survived martyrdom, looking for her place

THE REGNA: VELLSBERG, MERZEN & LUGHAMBER

Berengar of Vellsberg: a young nobleman, happy to be home

Bilhildis: Berengar's mother, concerned about the company he keeps

Theogault of Vellsberg: Lord of Vellsberg, has plans for Berengar

Rosamund of Merzen: pretty and promised, all part of the plan

Neklaus of Merzen: too pretty to trust, has his own ideas

Gisla: Abbess of the Hekateran Order, knows where the power lies

Raiders/Rus: marauding seafarers, destructive but useful

THE QESAR

Aisulu of the Blue Wolf Clan: a Carrier with her own burdens

Kizmid: a Captain of Water Qesar, knows Aisulu

Varkha: Negotiator of the Lughambar Concession, decisive

Serke: healer from the Stahranid Empire, many things at once

Uryz: Negotiator of the Ban Granis Concession, on his own side

Tsomak: a boy with a burden

The Kagan: spiritual ruler of the Qesar, lives in secret Izoloh

The Noyan: commander of the Qesar Horde, military leader

THE CORDA: THE GOLDEN WAY & BAN GRANIS

Seargent Hadric: a mostly good man

Ceol, Lotho: Merzen soldiers, unlucky bystanders

Ormund, Bishop of Corvennes: knows what he wants

Emperor Merovec: a ruler with a story to sell

Various villagers, guards, raiders, priests, children, Water Qesar, horses, judgy old women, hapless merchants, servants, and suspicious cart drivers.

BACK IN ARNGARD

Aud, Kelda, Sorleyson: old friends from the wayhouse in Frithberg

Jarle: the stable hand, hidden depths

Fetch: Ebba's wolfhound, too recognizable

Berger Dagomar: a merchant with a demanding patron

Rathna: Ebba's mother, now living in Birchhold

Rafe: Ebba's cousin, back in Eldinghope

Erland of Hellingap: Captain of the Bearskins

King Kolrand: pays tribute to the Southern Emperor

The Bearskins: the king's personal guard, known for their discipline

GHOSTS

Prester Grimulf: priest of the White God, killed by the Harrower

Galen: Torny's companion, had his wish granted

Fenn: Torny's guide, died protecting her

Uncle Ulf Berrson: Ebba's uncle, got what he deserved

Lana: a casualty of war, helped across by Ebba

Arf Berrson: Ebba's father, murdered by his brother Ulf

Brenna: raised Torny grudgingly, then forced her out

Vigdis: Torny's birth mother, a staffbearer, died on Far Isle

Staffbearers: magic-workers of the Arngard gods, wiped out

GODS & SPIRITS

White God: only god of the Southern Empire

Blessed Hekatera: a martyred saint in the White God's religion

Harrower: ancient goddess of destruction, set free by Ebba

Taghr, the Daylit King: sky god of the Qesar

Sarik, the Sunlit Queen: sun goddess of the Qesar

Gamlig: god of death, lives in the Dark Earth, land of the dead

Ai Nakota: genderfluid god of the moon (they/them), guides spirits
between realms, called upon by Qesar shamans

Needlemouths: the Hungry Ones, ghosts of the despairing dead

❧ AUTHOR'S NOTE ❧

The names of people and places in Arngard are loosely based on the Norse language. The letter 'j' is pronounced as a 'y', so the name Jarle is pronounced 'Yarle'. People are known by their first names, while their second names are patronymic, meaning 'son/ daughter of X'. So Torny Vafrisdota is Torny, daughter of Vafri (her father). In rare cases, maternal names are used: Ebba and her brother Stig are called Rathnasdota and Rathnason, after their mother Rathna.

Part One:
REGNA

"To Merovec, most pious Patriarch, great and peace-giving Emperor, crowned by God, against whom all enemies break like waves against a bastion, life and victory.

Fruit of the *Corda*, defender of the *Regna*, son of an unbroken empire, unity resides in you. One God, one soul, one reign, eternal and indivisible."

Oath of the *Imperium Infractum*

"What are the three souls of all living things?
The breath that moves the body,
The shade that passes between realms,
And the self, without which we are empty of ourselves."

Qesar catechism

One

POOL

TORNY'S TALE

The Borderlands

I wake up choking, my hands covered in dried blood.

In my dreams, they're always bloody, and my eyes are failing, and the mist is all around me. But now I'm awake and the blood is still there, even though the spring sunshine comes streaming through the barn door.

My heart kicks.

What have I done?

I lie still, trying to remember. Outside I can hear swift water and birdsong. We came here late last night, whispered through the dark by unfamiliar voices. I search my memory, feeling for the nothingness I've come to fear worse than discovery.

But it is all complete, and I know where I am, and I am alone. No one lies near me, no horrible stillness spoils the morning.

I can't feel any pain, other than the ache in my side, and even that is fading day by day.

I sit up, my nearly-healed ribs grumbling, and that is when I feel the wetness between my legs. I touch myself there, and my fingers come back covered in fresh red.

Even though I'm alone, I can feel my face burning.

Cursing, I kick away the blanket from my legs. Hero, my horse, is tethered by a manger. She snuffs at me as I fly past her. I stumble outside, drop to my knees beside the mill pool and plunge my hands into the clear water. I scrub the blood from them as best I can, then pull my shirt over my head. I'm not looking forward to this next bit.

I screw up my face as I step into the pool. The water is freezing, and my whole body comes over gooseflesh. I force myself to crouch down, the water up to my waist, and I wash myself, still thinking of how lucky I am that the other two aren't here.

That would be all I need.

It's hard enough being around two people in love. Their smiles, the softness in their eyes when they think you can't see, the way they touch each other in passing, all the time. I was relieved when they suggested they go on ahead of me to Vellsberg. It's enough to make you scream, all that tenderness.

Of course, it doesn't help if you're in love too.

If Ebba had been here, she'd have worked it out. Then she might have thought it was her I was thinking of, while I was getting blood on my hands.

Just thinking it makes me want to die of embarrassment.

I splash my face with water, trying to cool it.

"Bit early for that, isn't it?"

My head shoots up.

Someone's coming down the path between the bushes. Silently, I curse myself. I'm naked in the pool, my teeth chattering, and my weapons are inside the barn. I stand to drag my shirt on over my head, and that's when the person steps out onto the grass beside the pool.

For a moment, we just stare at each other.

I've never seen anyone like her.

She looks a little older than me. Her black hair is tightly braided and looped up around her head, she is wearing a quilted wrap-around jacket in what was once a bright blue, bound around her waist with a faded yellow sash. Her skin is a warm brown, her cheeks reddened from the spring breeze, and her winged eyebrows arch as she looks me over in turn.

I can't look like much. A tall, boney girl with white skin, nearly-white hair, cut short, a jagged burn-scar across one shoulder, and no common sense. Plenty of people mistake me for a boy when they see me clothed, but I suppose that won't happen this time.

The woman's hand rests on a knife hilt tucked into her sash, but she seems more amused than anything.

"My people have laws against dirtying clean water," she says.

I blink. She's speaking the tongue of Arngard, but—

"Are you going to stand there all fucking day? Get some clothes on."

I stare at her. She stares back, her calm stance completely at odds with her words.

"Move."

Bewildered, I step out of the pool and pull my shirt on over my head. It sticks to my skin.

❧ 3 ❧

"Who are you?" I ask, trying to stop my teeth from chattering.

"Aisulu, Carrier of the Blue Wolf Clan, so watch yourself," she says. "And you're one of the crazy Rus, that's plain enough, though I didn't expect to meet your kind here. What trouble are you stirring up?"

"No trouble," I say. "I'm going to get dressed." I point to the barn.

"I'll come with you," she says.

I don't have much choice. She follows me into the barn, going straight up to Hero while I pick through the packs for a loincloth. Once I've padded it and pulled on my britches, I see she's nose-to-nose with my horse, blowing air through her nostrils as Hero snuffles back. If I weren't so cold I might laugh, but I'm shivering, and it's making my ribs hurt.

She catches me watching. "What are you looking at, Rus?"

"My name's Torny. Why do you keep calling me that?"

She reaches into the pocket of her riding britches and pulls out some dried apple rings. Hero lips them neatly out of her palm.

"I don't know what you're doing here," she says, "but I'm a guest of the Lord of Vellsberg, so my advice is keep your fucking nose clean. Go back to whatever hovel you came from and tell your people there are no pickings for you here, understand? We have our misunderstandings, the Empire and the Confederacy, but on one thing we are both clear."

She covers the distance between us in two strides, and grabs a fistful of my shirt.

"I only need to know your name if I kill you," she says, her face still unnervingly calm. "To add to my accounts for the Unlit King. Until then, I don't care."

She lets me go, gives Hero one last pat, and walks out of the barn.

I groom Hero. I rubbed her down last night, but after seeing her so friendly with my unexpected visitor, I want to be close to her. Maybe I want to remind her who I am, or maybe I want to remind myself.

When we left Frithberg all those weeks ago, Berengar carried letters, with both Captain Erland and Prester Grimulf's seals. They gave us free passage down the War Road, but here in the Empire's lands they won't mean much. The Lord of Vellsberg is Berengar's kin: he'll see to something for Berengar and Ebba. But me?

They've been not-saying it for weeks.

There's no place for me here.

Ebba has her healing, her herbs. She's learned some of their tongue, and she's learning to write. And, of course, she has Berengar. She'll be fine.

Me, I have nothing. I have weapons I can barely touch, ever since Ebba saved me from the Harrower. I have aching ribs and nights full of horror. I have muscles that have stiffened and shrunk, and even if I build them back up, who will let me use them? Here, women are expected to wear skirts and cover their hair. I will never wear skirts again.

And now I'm bleeding. Another part of womanhood I would happily foreswear, along with skirts and long hair. I've no need for it.

I have knowledge that I am now the sole possessor of. I have blood that inherits a bloody throne. I have two dead friends, and so many dead enemies.

It's selfish, but I miss Galen. I miss the way he cared for me. If I could raise him from the death he begged for, I would. Without a thought. Without mercy.

Sometimes I wish Ebba had believed everyone when they told her I was lost.

It was easier, sometimes, to be lost.

It's evening when I hear a rider approaching. I'm ready this time. I have my knife and my sling at my belt, and I wait under cover of the trees to see who it is.

It's Ebba, on Berengar's mount. She's much better at riding these days. I remember when even leading a horse made her nervous.

I should go straight out and greet her, but I stand under the trees a little longer, watching as she checks the clearing by the pool, the burned-out remains of the old mill, then swings down and leads her mount into the small barn. I walk to the door and lean on it, watching as she tethers the bay gelding next to Hero, making sure he has food to eat before she unbuckles the saddle.

Her dark hair wisps loose from under the kerchief she covers it with, and in the evening light it gleams reddish, like the bay's coat next to her. The ochre dress she wears is better fitted than the smocks we wore in Frithberg, and it skims her waist and flares out over her hips, twirling out as she turns to lay the saddle and the blanket over the post, and turns back, the brush in her hand.

She sees me, and smiles.

"How was your day?" she says, as the bay whickers.

I shrug, and hold up two rabbits.

"Oh, good," she says. "Dinner."

I settle myself outside the barn by the fire pit, skinning and cleaning the two carcasses. After a while, Ebba comes and joins me.

"I thought you'd stay there tonight," I say. "I thought—" I stop, but Ebba raises her eyebrows. "I thought Berengar wouldn't want you to ride by yourself."

I mean *let you*, not *want*, but I don't say that.

"He en't seen his ma since last year," Ebba says. "They've a lot to talk about."

"Including why he brought a Northerner home with him?"

She shoots me a look, half-amused, half-exasperated. "At least I din't have to meet the lord. Berengar has to report to him tonight. There's a banquet tomorrow. Some kind of feast day."

Something about the way Ebba says this makes it sound like she's not looking forward to it, and that surprises me. When Berengar talked about his return, he always talked about presenting her. Not me, of course, but he was all for her being introduced to his family.

"What's the matter?" I ask. Some stupid little piece of my heart is jumping, and I know why, and I try to shut it up, try not to even think what it wants me to.

"Who am I goin to be to em?" she says, her eyes down, her hands busy with the meat. "I knew who I was back in Birchold. I had a place an a purpose. Here . . ."

The sky is darkening over the new green edges of the spring growth. Our fire lights up her face, the smoke mixes with the first stars and the rill of the mill stream tumbling from the pool to the ruined wheel is sweeter than music.

"I thought I knew my place," I say quietly. "Turns out—"

"What?" Ebba asks, the fire lighting the depths of her brown eyes.

But the words catch in my throat.

I do know my place, I think, looking into her eyes. *It's beside you. It's you.*

Ebba jumps up.

"The herbs," she says, and I'm left knowing I showed too much of myself again.

The awkwardness between us needles me. I hate it. I hate that I used to be able to put my arm around her shoulders, or sleep with her curled against me, and now those things feel forbidden. It's not just her who jumps. I've shrunk from her touch as well, and she's seen me do it. So has Berengar, though he never says anything. He doesn't have to. Everything he does for Ebba says: *Mine*. There have been times when I wished him gone, and for Ebba and me to be back at Sorleyson's wayhouse in Frithberg, warm together in the dark, ignorant of who we really were.

And then I remember why I never deserve to feel those things ever again, with anyone, and something inside me folds up tight and hides itself away.

We eat our rabbit stew by the fire, wrapped in the horse blankets. We're further south than either of us ever imagined we'd travel, but the nights are still cold here.

Berengar told us this mill was destroyed in a border raid, back before King Arn united Arngard, when the borderlands were wild territory, and instead of rebuilding it to be burnt again, a new one was built within the walls of Vellsberg. The barn is newer, used for storing hay from the far fields.

I'd like to know what that strange woman was doing out here

when by her dress she's no Southerner, but Ebba just shakes her head when I ask her. She seems distracted, but I don't want to ask why in case the answer is me. In the end she brings it up herself.

"This is where Prester Grimulf came from."

At the mention of the prester, we're both quiet. I never knew him, though it was my hand that slit his throat at the end, but Ebba . . . She doesn't speak much about him, but I can feel her hatred. I know he kept her close when they first travelled east, and she's told me, briefly, how he killed her uncle and took his holdings, but more than that seems locked away between her and Berengar, one more thing I can't ask about.

She doesn't say anything for a while. Then:

"She cried to hear he was dead."

"Who?" I ask.

"Berengar's ma." Ebba sighs. "I've a bad feelin about this, Torny. That woman weren't pleased to see me, not one bit. She near enough glared a curse on me. An Grimulf . . . no one pretends he an Lord Vellsberg got on, but . . ."

"But if they knew what we did," I finish for her, "they wouldn't be any happier to see us."

She pulls the blanket tighter around her.

"More'n more," she says, "I see the only way we'll fit here is if we keep our mouths shut an our selves secret."

We both stare up into the star-scarred sky.

"I en't sure I can do that," she says at last.

Two

ILLUMINATION

EBBA'S TALE

Vellsberg

 've seen Vellsberg once already, but I rein in Beyard an let Torny look it over as we crest the hills to the west. We thought Frithberg was a marvel when we first arrived, but seein Vellsberg I feel again how deep the chasm is between what we knew an what the world is.

The fort inside its double ring of walls sits on a hill on the southern bank of the Vell. The river is wide here, snakin between the steep hillsides, an the town is ringed on three sides by water. A stone bridge spans the Vell, an within the walls rise tiled roofs an square towers. The waters of the Vell throw off lances of light, so that we squint against it as you squint against the sun. Above us, the lord's hall stands out against the sky. Beyond it, the river flows east, down to the coast, where it joins the Iron Sea.

I've only ever heard tell of Sunacre, Arngard's royal palace. It's a holy place, set around a lake full of islands that were once sacred to the gods, but I've heard nothin like this. Vellsberg has a keep, a garrison, a holy house across the river, an yet this is the least of the Empire's outposts, on the edges of its northern reaches. The *Regna*, Berengar says these outer lands are called. The *Corda*, or heartlands, are where the Emperor's court journeys, the *Regna* are cared for by local lords like the Lord of Vellsberg, an at the very edges are the *Limina*, the distant lands that pledge obedience to the Emperor. Like Arngard.

It makes me dizzy to think what may be beyond those outer limits. Once, my world had a centre, an that centre was my ma's arms, followed by my uncle's fists. Then there was Frithberg, with its carved wooden kirkhouse on its rocky outcrop, juttin up from the plains like the broken bone of some ancient giant. Now all of those are gone, an I'm caught between these whirlin rings, circlin like a hawk, unable to settle.

Berengar is at the gates already, waitin to vouch for us to the guard. He shows em the papers that gave the three of us passage all the way from Frithberg, stamped wi the Prester's seal, but the guards barely look before bowin to him. His face is alight wi pleasure. I have not seen him look like this before, an it hurts a little to know that I en't responsible for it.

One street rises straight an steep from the gate to the inner walls, but Berengar leads us through the zig-zag streets to either side, greetin those we meet. Many of em know him, I realise. The men an women bob their heads respectfully, an look at us out of the corners of their eyes.

I glance at Torny. She's bin silent this whole time, since we saw

Vellsberg from the hills. In her breeches an cloak she looks like a tall skinny boy on a short sturdy horse. I catch a few smirks on the faces of the people lookin at her.

"This is my mother's house," Berengar says at last, as we reach a stone house built right up against the inner walls. We pass through double gates into a yard. A small stable faces the gates, there's a neat kitchen garden to the left, an to the right lies an orchard, the fruit trees frothy white with early blossom.

Bilhildis, Berengar's ma, stands on the kitchen step, a basket of herbs over her arm. She looks just as she did yesterday when first we met. Her head is covered with a long, fine white veil, an her plain grey dress is high-necked, wi narrow sleeves to the wrist an a full skirt. Her bare face an hands stand out strangely against the grey. Her eyes are hazel, like her son's.

"My son," she says. "You're back."

Berengar beams. He don't seem to notice her coldness, the way she stands between us an the kitchen like she's defendin her home from invaders.

"Will you come to afternoon prayer before the Feast of Embers?" she asks.

"Not today," Berengar says. "I want Ebba to see the abbey. We'll be back in time for the feast."

Bilhildis allows Berengar to kiss her cheek before he mounts up again. Neither Torny nor I have stirred, nor said a word, an Bilhildis has not looked at us once. Without lookin I know Torny's temper will be flashin in her eyes, but Berengar don't seem to notice any of it. Instead he jerks his head an we follow him out into the street, an straight down this time to the gate.

"I want to show you the scriptorium," he says. "You've never seen anything like it Ebba, I promise."

I can't help but smile back. This is Berengar, after all. He's bin by my side through winter an war. Of course he's happy to be home, an I of all people shouldn't resent him for it. There's a lightness in him I en't seen before – maybe ever.

I want to ask him what he tole his ma when they talked last night. About me. We agreed when we left Frithberg that the name I'd bin given, Salvebearer, was too dangerous to use. I would just be Ebba, a girl with an outlander's accent an some herb lore. So now how can I be upset if that's all he tole her?

So I don't say it, an instead I ask, "Did the prester study here?"

"No," he says, an he reaches over an touches my sleeve. It's the first time in days. Ever since we came close to Vellsberg, the easy touches between us have stopped. "The abbey wasn't built until after King Arn brought peace to the borderlands. There's no part of him in those halls."

I relax a little. For all its charm, I'm dreadin the banquet tonight in the hall where Grimulf grew up. For now, I'm free of him.

At least, that's what I think. The moment we're inside the abbey walls, I feel him all around me. The monks in their robes, the smell of incense an beeswax, the kirktongue on Berengar's lips an the lips of the men who greet him - all are splinters of him, workin under my skin, needlin me. I wish I had my wolfhound, Fetch, beside me for comfort, but I left him back in Frithberg wi Captain Erland so's I wouldn't be followed by tales of the Salvebearer an her tame wolf.

Torny has not said a word. It's startin to worry me, but then Berengar beckons me into a long room, an as we walk behind the tilted desks where the monks bow over their pages, my eyes grow wide, an my mouth opens.

I know my letters, for Berengar has bin teachin me, but here on these pages I cannot tell em apart. They are graceful, rounded marks, an around em curve tight, complicated knots, the heads of beasts, men in robes, their faces unnaturally smooth. These are painted in colours like jewels, colours richer than I ever saw.

They paint *gold* onto these pages.

Berengar en't lookin at the pages. He's lookin at me, his eyes crinkled up wi pleasure, his smile quick an wide. I'm giddy wi the beauty laid out before me, an he can tell. It pleases him, my giddiness. I feel the air between us spark. I wish that I could take his hand, lace my fingers through his, but I remember how Grimulf watched for any sign of sin, an how this is the kind of place he learned in. Berengar too, for that matter.

I keep my hands to myself.

The monks work on as we pace the length of the long, well-lit room, an it's like we're ghosts, unheard an unnoticed. I try to peer over their shoulders, watchin words an knots appear from their brushes. Berengar stops to speak softly wi one, an I continue up the line of sunlit desks.

I'm nearly at the far end when a bell starts tollin overhead. The nearness of it startles me, an I look up to see the great doors at the other end of the scriptorium openin. Wood grinds on stone as the monks arise amid the bells. I look round, but Torny is nowhere to be seen, an Berengar is all the way at the other end of the room, talkin to a tall, thin man in robes.

A young monk who will not look at me stands at my shoulder.

"Berengar of Vellsberg has asked that you wait in the library while he is at prayers," he says. "This way."

"Can't I pray too?" I ask.

The monk still won't look up, but I see the disapproval in his face.

"He is with the Bishop of Corvennes," he says, as if that answers me, an ushers me into a room wi shelves an books on every wall.

I stand among em, blinkin, half angered at my treatment, an half bedazzled by the room. Until a few moons ago, I din't even know what a book was. Here there must be hundreds.

"It's unnerving, isn't it?"

A figure stands at a desk where the light falls through the window. She speaks the Southern tongue, an I stumble to reply well.

"Your pardon?"

"The monks," she says, nodding me over. "They'd rather not have women here at all."

Her eyes are bright blue in a face dusted wi freckles, an her pink lips tip upwards in a smile. She's a few fingers taller than me, an her hands where they rest on the desk are delicate. Her light brown hair is pinned up under her sheer veil, an the pins have tiny jewels on em. Her dress is light pink, an shows the graceful slope of her shoulders.

"I'm Rosamund of Merzen," she says.

"Ebba," I say, still tryin to make my tongue work properly. "Ebba of—" I hesitate. Eldinghope an Birchhold en't known here, but who can tell? In the town Prester Grimulf came from, maybe word of his deeds will spread. I don't want people to remember me when they hear of his last conquests.

Rosamund cocks her head. "You're from the *Limina*, aren't

you?" she says. "You speak very well,"—she's lyin—"but your accent betrays you. Arngard?"

I make a face. "You're polite, mistress."

She smiles. "It wouldn't make any difference if you were a princess from the *Corda*," she says. "If the monks could ask their visitors to leave their women outside the gates, like they do their horses, they'd be so much happier."

I giggle. "I'm lucky to be allowed here wi the books, then."

"They are beautiful," she sighs. "I suppose monks are good for something."

I join her by the desk. A small book open before her shows a picture of a woman, wrapped in red ribbons, bathed in gold. Her face is turned up, full of peace. Then I see that the ribbons are blood and the gold is fire.

"Who's this?" I ask.

"The Blessed Hekatera." Rosamund's mouth twitches in a not-quite smile.

"What happened to her?"

"She was scourged," Rosamund says. "That means whipped. But she felt no pain. And then the king tried to burn her, but she walked through the flames. Finally she ordered him to cut off her head, because she was ready to meet God. Everyone who saw it was converted. Are you well?"

I snatch my hand from the desk, my eyes fixed on the page.

"It . . . sounds familiar," I manage.

"It's a hagiography," Rosamund says, like I should know what that means. She frowns. "You look pale."

I stare at her blankly. "Forgive me," I say. "I have to go."

I all but run out of the library an through the empty scriptorium.

❧ 16 ❧

The monks must be at afternoon prayers, so there's no one to see as I burst through the doors into the covered walkway.

Torny is sittin on the wall next to an ancient man in robes. They both look up at me, but the man's eyes are blind under a heavy scar.

"Ebba!" she says. "What's the matter?"

"We need to go," I say.

"You look like you've seen a spirit," Torny says.

The old monk wheezes a laugh.

"Devils, girls," he says in Arngard's tongue. "They're all devils down here."

"Please," I say.

She nods. "The horses are through there," she says. "I'm coming." I hear her sayin her goodbyes to the ancient monk as I pass under an archway. Beyard, Hero, an the mount Berengar rode are tethered by the gate. I'm already on Beyard's back when Torny joins me.

I don't breathe easy till we're outside of the walls an on the way back down to the river.

"What happened?" Torny asks. "Did you and Berengar fight?"

"No!" It comes out sharper than I mean it to.

We ride on in silence. I'm annoyed now, feelin like I have to defend Berengar to Torny, like she always assumes the worst of him. It don't help that it almost do feel like I fought with him. Can't he see how everyone here treats us? An tellin me there was nothin of Grimulf in that place, when the whole place reeked of him . . .

"What's the matter, Ebba?"

My head is too full: of Berengar's happiness, that seems to make him blind; the way Bilhildis an the monks acted like I weren't even there; Rosamund's kindness, an the beautiful picture of the girl in torment. Not a girl. A saint. A saint like the prester wanted to make of me. An most of all, emptiness, where before there was light. Not that I understood it, but I felt it, an I thought I'd found somethin that would be part of me forever.

Seems I was wrong.

"Nothin," I say.

We return, for we've nowhere else to go, to Bilhildis' house. She don't even receive us, only sends a servant to show us to a room wi one big bed. The servant seems well enough; she explains that we must wash an dress for the banquet, an to that end she brings us warm water an soap. I fumble for the words in my embarrassment, but finally I manage to explain we en't got no good clothes to wear. She gives me a small smile an says the master tole her already, by which she must mean Berengar.

Torny's all a fidget next to me. "Ask her where the latrines are," she says in Northern. I do, an the servant points the way to an outhouse by the stables. Torny shoots out the door like a cat lit on fire an I don't see her again until after the servant brings our clothes.

The clothes are all laid out on the bed as she comes back in. I'm wrapped in a length of dryin cloth, cleaned an waitin to ask her help wi my hair. She stands by the door like she might dash back out again, an looks from me to the bed to the dresses an back.

"I'm not wearing that," she says flatly.

I know how she feels. Goodness knows where Bilhildis got these dresses from, but they're for someone shorter'n Torny an slimmer'n me, an each comes with a long white veil. They're both in shades of nasty green, like ditch water.

"Come an do my hair first," I say. "Maybe they'll look better afterwards."

But Torny's scowlin. There are high pink spots in her cheeks.

"I'm not wearing that," she says again, an leaves the room.

In the end I get the servant to braid my hair. I'm embarrassed askin, an as I sit wi the woman pullin at my scalp, I get more an more annoyed. Torny's run off, never mind she don't speak a word of Southern, never mind that I might not want to wear these clothes any more'n her.

There's a clatterin on the stairs, an Berengar bursts into the room. He's smilin, his curly black hair pushed off his face, his eyes alight. "Ebba? I'm sorry, did you get bored? I forgot how long the monks are at their prayers. Did you like the library? Did you like the books?"

I look up into those hazel eyes an I am helpless in em. I remember how it was when he first taught me to write, back in Birchold, wi birch bark an a steel stylus an Grimulf lookin over our shoulders. Us makin sure he treated me wi contempt while the prester was listenin, so's he wouldn't think we cared for each other. An then the nights I lay bundled against the cold all this last long winter, thinkin of him down in Eldinghope while I was up in Birchold, strung between my weary bones an my worrisome heart. The first night after Frithberg when we lay curled in each other's arms, an never slept a wink, so hard our hearts were hammerin.

"Yes," I say. "The books were beautiful. I en't never seen anythin like em."

The servant has moved aside, an she stands with her eyes down. Berengar looks me over critically, then turns an bellows down the stairs. "Mother! This is no good! We must have something better than this for Ebba!"

I feel my cheeks burnin. The dress is bad, it's true, but it would of bin nice not to hear it said like that.

Is he an idiot? An unkind part of me thinks, the part of me that sometimes sounds very like Torny. *His ma gave me this dress for a reason. Don't he know even that?*

Bilhildis climbs the stairs, hackles up an on her dignity.

"I have nothing from before my widowhood," she says. "I did what I could, but without warning or knowing the kind of people they are . . ." She gives me a cold look.

That's when Torny comes out of what must be Berengar's room.

Wearing what must be Berengar's clothes.

There's a silence that grows an grows.

Bilhildis turns an descends the stairs wi disgust plain on her face. Berengar shoots Torny a glare, which she don't even acknowledge, an goes after his ma.

I'm watchin Torny.

"What?" she says.

"You look—" I start, but then I stop cos I don't know how to finish. Instead of an oversize shirt tucked into britches stained wi mud an horse spit, she's wearin narrow hose in dark blue, an a short tunic in the same colour over an ochre undershirt. The tunic's front is decorated wi silver thread an small amber beads. Her short white curls are damp an tousled, an her pale grey eyes make her face look like bone against the rich colours of the borrowed clothes.

"You look perfect," I say.

"I only did it to annoy him," she says, but I see the smile on her lips as she turns, an I'm glad I managed that at least.

Three
BELLS

TORNY'S TALE

Vellsberg

Vellsberg feels heavy. All this stone piled together, and above the town, the lord's hall, with its thick walls and blind stone face. We ride our horses round those walls and up the steep road to the hall's gates, because here in the south a horse means you are worth seeing, and so we couldn't possibly walk. I grit my teeth and follow Berengar. His mother sits side-saddle behind him on a ridiculous little carved wooden chair, her long widow's dress hiding her feet.

Ebba's seated behind me the same way, for the dresses these Southern ladies wear aren't suitable for riding, but she doesn't have the silly chair to contend with, just a padded seat. She's hooked her arms around my waist, and the warmth of her is comforting and unsettling all at once.

"Remember to be nice, Torny," she murmurs as we pass through the castle gates, torches lighting the courtyard.

"I'm not the one who needs telling," I say, and she prods me in my sore ribs, but gently.

I'm glad she can't see round me, because Bilhildis is giving us a look that would turn milk. I ignore her, letting Ebba slide down first as a servant takes Hero's head, holding her steady for us to dismount before leading her away.

I grimace. My lower back aches, and there's a twisting in my guts that I could really do without. The padding between my legs makes me feel awkward.

"Are you all right?" Ebba says. Her hand twitches, as if she were about to place it on my arm, but thought better of it.

I nod. Berengar couldn't convince his precious mother to find a decent dress for Ebba, but finally she did consent to lending her an embroidered russet over-robe and a pair of gold-washed clasps. Bilhildis also managed to find, with great annoyance, a sheer bronze veil instead of the long white shroud-like thing she wears. Now it's held in place over Ebba's thick braids with a golden circlet, and the veil picks out the auburn lights in her hair. The servant did a better job of her braids than I could have, which is just as well since I couldn't face sitting with her like I used to. I even find myself thinking that the green of the dress isn't so bad, now that I see her done up properly in it.

I'm fairly sure I've stolen Berengar's clothes for the evening, but to my surprise he didn't say a word after that first look, just found himself another set. Maybe he's not so bad.

Bilhildis doesn't move from her silly seat until Berengar comes to lift her down in his arms.

I bite my lip. One night, I tell myself. One night in her house, one night of flouncing and scraping and – if banquets here are like feasts back home – a lot of drinking, and then . . .

I push the panic out of my mind. Berengar turns to look at Ebba, but his mother says something to him and firmly takes him by the arm. He mouths an apology over her shoulder.

I roll my eyes.

"Come on," I say, offering my arm in the same way he did. "Let's get this over with."

Ebba looks up at me and half-smiles. "An I thought we Northerners were meant to be the cold ones."

She tucks her hand into the crook of my elbow, and we follow Berengar and Bilhildis up the stairs and into the hall of the Lord of Vellsberg.

A huge fire warms one end of the hall, set into the wall instead of laid in the centre of the room as it would be back home. The high table where the lord and his guests sit is raised on a dais, and the low tables are laid in rows beneath it. In the thick walls are window slits filled with horn, and raised niches with carved stone seats where people sit talking or playing games. Heads turn as we enter, but their attention is on Berengar.

The lord's chair is empty, but Bilhildis steers Berengar towards a knot of well-dressed people. One or two wear holy man's robes, and others look like merchants, but I'm already looking past them. There in a niche, in a much cleaner blue jacket bound by a fresh yellow sash, is the woman from yesterday. She's looking straight at me.

She raises one winged brow and smiles in a way that couldn't be called friendly.

"Ebba," I say, but then there's a flurry of movement as a group enters through one of the doors near the fire.

Theogault, Lord of Vellsberg, is a gaunt man in long black robes. His face is lined and haughty where Berengar's is still youthful and warm, and his shoulders are narrow and pointed where his nephew's have the breadth and strength of a young man, but the resemblance is there. The lord and his kinswoman Bilhildis both have deep lines framing their mouths, and the same hardness in their eyes.

As the lord takes his seat, the hall swirls with movement as his guests and retainers follow. A prettily-dressed boy comes up to Ebba and bows her to the right-hand table, but as I move after her, a servant approaches and points me to the left.

"Sir," he says, and I laugh, unable to respond.

Ebba says something in Southern, and the man looks up at me, eyes going wide and then narrowing. He steps back, but he scowls as I follow Ebba to the women's table.

I wonder whether Ebba is thinking what I'm thinking, that it's rude to place your guests down among the low tables. I look up, and sure enough, Berengar is sitting at the lord's right hand, in the place of honour.

"That's the girl I met in the library," Ebba says to me.

Between a woman on Theogault's left, who must be his wife, and Bilhildis, sits a pretty girl with blue eyes and dark blonde hair. She's well-born, that's obvious from her creamy dress and the gold thread embroidery at her neck. She's tucked between the two older women just like Berengar is tucked between the lord and a tall man in kirk robes.

Berengar's looking for Ebba. When he finds her he frowns, and turns to speak to Theogault, but the lord cuts him off.

I have a bad feeling about this.

"Oh look," says Ebba, "is that the woman you tole me about? What was her name? Aisulu?"

Towards the head of the women's table, the woman in the blue jacket has already had her beaker filled, and is drinking from it. She toasts us when she sees us looking.

"Ebba," I start, but the lord rises, and the hall falls quiet.

Theogault, standing outlined against the fire, begins to speak, and Ebba whispers his words to me.

"The Ember Days remind us that life is not unmixed," she translates. "It holds both sorrow an celebration. Yesterday we repented, today we feast. But today, too, we have sad news. Grimulf, Prester of Arngard, protector of the faith, my foster-brother, is dead. He died a martyr's death at the hands of the people he sought to save."

The listeners murmur, and make the White God's sign, but there's no shock. It's clear word has already spread.

"We mourn him an pray that he shall take his rightful place, an for the eternal damnation of those who in their pride destroyed him." Ebba's voice shakes a little. "But we also have joyous news. My nephew Berengar has been returned to us, by the grace of God, an therefore a celebration we have long anticipated may— oh no."

Ebba is staring at the lord, horrified.

"What?" I say. The lord's words have provoked smiles and nods from his audience, but Berengar is struggling to rise, and Ebba's skin is ashy. In the distance, a bell begins to toll.

"The girl," she says. "Rosamund. She's his *betrothed*."

Berengar's eyes are fixed on Ebba, but she's thunderstruck. Up at the table the pretty blonde girl is smiling and blushing, unaware of the effect the announcement has had.

The lord is still talking.

"Ebba," I say, giving her a shake, not caring that people nearby are staring at us. "What's he saying?"

She turns to me, her eyes dull.

"His nephew's companions, who he rescued from the northmen, will be given safe haven in a convent," she says.

I stare at her. *Rescued?* I think. *Convent?*

"Over my dead body," I grate, choking on my anger.

"That's the idea, girly," says a voice from the door.

A Northern voice.

Out of the corner of my eye I see the woman in the blue jacket jump up, hand at her belt.

And then the screaming starts.

"Raiders!" shouts Ebba, scrabbling backwards. The man at the door has already run through the guard posted there, and his sword is lodged in the back of one of the servants. The women around us are screaming, and the men are fighting to get free of the tables.

Ebba's pulling the women nearest us away, pushing them towards the end of the hall where there are doorways. "Get out!" she's shouting. "Go!"

I watch, frozen, as the Raider at the door kills a third man, and starts up between the tables. Behind him come more, all of them big, all of them scarred, their faces stained black with soot and their eyes alight with pleasure.

A blue-and-yellow blur moves past me. The woman, Aisulu, has drawn a long, curved sword, and she leaps from the tabletop right in front of the first Raider. One foot uncurls in a perfect kick, and the Raider's heavy swipe is too late to cut her. He sails backwards into the attackers behind him, and then the woman chops down as another comes after her.

Outside I can hear more bells, loud and terrible.

Ebba is beside me again.

"We have to run," she says, but we both know there's nowhere. This is the lord's hall. It should be the safest place there is. If they're here, they're everywhere.

I need to move, but I can't.

I need to fight, but I'm helpless.

A few steps away, a man runs at the Raiders, only to have a sword thrust through his unprotected neck.

Blood arcs through the air and hits my skin like rain.

Ebba slaps me hard across the face.

"Run," she screams, and at last I do. I, who once commanded an army, who once stood before a dead man and demanded his Luck, turn on my heels and flee.

The women are cringing in a room behind the hall, near a thick iron-bound door. Bilhildis stands before them, her arms akimbo, as if she'll shame the Raiders into dropping their swords. Behind her stands Rosamund, her pretty face blotchy, her cheeks streaked with tears. Bilhildis says something to Ebba.

"There's a way into the keep," Ebba says, "but the lord has the key."

I look between Ebba and Bilhildis, and despite everything I almost laugh. Their faces show the same stony determination.

Rosamund pushes forward, a scabbard in her hands. She says something I think means, "Take this."

She thinks I'm a boy too.

Bilhildis snaps something at her, and I know what she's telling her.

She's a girl.

She can't save us.

My heart thuds. As Rosamund hesitates, I reach out and take the sword from her.

"I'll get him," I say.

The sword is heavy in my hands, and I'm already starting to slip out of my body into the mist in my head. I grip the hilt hard, forcing myself to feel the blade's weight. These days there's no Harrower to slide inside my skin and take over. I have to do this myself.

In the main hall, Theogault is trapped on the other side of the huge fireplace, the high table overturned before him. With him are some of the men, while others help Berengar and Aisulu hold off the Raiders. As I watch, one of the attackers circles towards me, his eyes on the central fight. He hasn't seen me yet.

My insides are water, and my muscles feel like jellied eels, but I slip from the side door and up behind him, swinging the sword round and up into his side. The tearing of the sword through his flesh is horrible, and it bites into his lower ribs. I yank at it to free it as he stumbles and goes down, panic making me almost lose my grip. Another Raider has seen me and is trying to find a way past the melee. I try to keep my eye on him as I fight to free my sword.

He gets past the fight as I brace my foot on the still spasming body of his companion. My sword comes free at last, and I stagger back towards the fire, off balance as he lunges.

Someone bobs up between us, jabbing up and under the attackers ribs with a long dagger. The man sways back, parrying, and Berengar darts back beside me, his hand finding my arm and pulling me to my feet.

"Take him," he says. "I have your side."

It's the nicest thing he's said to me since Frithberg.

"Look to the lord," I say.

Steadier now, I watch the Raider as he tries to keep us both in sight. Raiders tend not to wear armour. Mail slows you down, and Raiders like to move quick. This one is protected about his sides, and his neck is covered by a chain cowl, but his legs are uncovered.

I dart forward, forcing him to block, and then fall back. He follows, forgetting there's a body at his feet, and trips forward onto my waiting blade, which slices up into the inside of his thigh. He almost comes down on top of me, but Berengar steps forward again and his dagger finds the man's throat before he can skewer me.

"Not bad," Berengar says, yanking the sword out of the dying man's loose grasp. He looks me up and down. "You've ruined my best hose already, I see."

I can feel a cramp starting in my side.

"The lord," I gasp. "The key."

We thread our way through the wreckage of the dais to where Theogault cowers behind his fallen table. A few well-dressed bergers are trapped with him, their faces grey with terror. Through the haze of smoke it occurs to me that despite their fear, his womenfolk acted very efficiently under attack.

Berengar speaks calmly to the lord, pulling him from behind the table and guiding him towards the side door. The bergers scrabble to follow.

"Eyes front," someone cries out, and I look to see a Raider leaping the remains of the table. I catch his downswing on my borrowed blade, and at once I know my mistake. He is bigger and heavier than me, and his weight bears me down. I stumble back, my arms shaking, and my foot slips in some spilled gravy. I fall, and the single-edged sword bites into the wood of the dais beside my head. The Raider yanks it free and raises it over my breathless body.

I am ashamed to say it, but I close my eyes.

There's a thud and a choking sound – a horrible, wet crunch.

I look up to see a slim blade protruding from the Raider's throat. I scramble aside as he sinks to the floor.

The blue-clad Aisulu looks down on me for a moment. She raises an eyebrow at me, then turns back to the fight in one fluid movement.

Theogault and the others are out of the hall, so I place myself before the doorway with my borrowed sword. My muscles are tiring now, but the Raiders are tired too. Another Raider breaks towards me, but he's cut down by Berengar as guards fight their way into the hall from the other end. We share a look, different to our usual battle of wills, wondering which of us will go to Ebba.

I turn away first. I reckon he has some explaining to do, and anyway, I'm hardly proud of myself. He slips past me, and I watch as the guards and the male guests led by Aisulu close on the last of the Raiders.

The leader, the man who spoke as they first entered, is the last to be beaten to the floor. Raiders don't surrender, so no one stops to see if he will plead mercy, but as they draw back, he sways on his knees. His arms hang bloody and useless by his sides.

"You made a mistake coming here," Aisulu says, and he struggles to focus on her.

"Without you, Qesar bitch, I would have my revenge," he wheezes, blood speckling his lips. "I wanted the poacher's family on my blade." She spits on him, but he laughs. "This is the price for taking our northern hunting grounds from us," he says. "Tell them. We'll murder them all, and whelp our sons on their bitch-women."

He falls with a crash, his helmet smashing onto the stone floor.

Aisulu mutters something in a language I don't understand, and turns to me.

"We should leave now," she says.

I stare at her. "We?"

"The lord will order the town closed until he finds out who let them in," she says, wiping her blade on a body. Her yellow sash is stained beyond all repair, and her dark hair escapes its braids. She wipes sweat from her face with her sleeve. Blood smears across her cheek. "If you want to escape, do it now. I heard what he has planned for you and your lover."

My cheeks burn. "She's not—"

"She's right." Ebba is beside me, wearing that stubborn look I know all too well. I cringe, knowing she heard the woman's words, but Ebba doesn't shrink from me. "We have to go, Torny. I en't come this far to be shut up in some stone prison."

"But what about Berengar?" I say. Seems she avoided him.

Ebba's face closes. "He should of known," she says.

"Then we should go," says Aisulu. "Now."

Four
REPENTANCE

❧

EBBA'S TALE

Vellsberg and Merzen

he main street is on fire. The wooden shopfronts, the timbers under the tiled roofs, the stables an haylofts. The Raiders came straight up to the castle gates, torchin everythin before em. Ash an sparks fly on the night air. It reminds me of . . . other nights.

Is it bad that I feel happy?

Torny an I make for Bilhildis' house. We're losin precious time, but our belongins are there. There's no sign of the servants. I hope they're hidin somewhere safe. The house is far enough back that the Raiders din't come here.

Up in the room I grab anythin I can make out in the dark, stuffin it into our bags. Torny's in the stables, gettin our sleepin rolls an feed for the horses. I run down the stairs into the kitchen an look for food we can take with us.

"What are you doing?"

I look up.

Berengar stands in the door, sword in one hand, his tunic ripped. The banked fire gives faint light, but I can see his mussed black curls pushed back from his face, his high cheekbones. His hazel eyes are full of hurt.

That flyin happiness I felt as we rode away from the castle dips an falls. He looks so lost. I remember our first kiss, deep in the canvas maze, under the burnin stars. How he came wi me, even to the edge of death.

"You're all right," I say, takin a step towards him.

He sags against the doorpost. "You're safe," he says. "I know you're scared, Ebba, but you're safe. You don't have to run."

He stumbles, an I catch him, leadin him to a seat.

"You're cut!"

"It's nothing," he says, but I'm already reachin for my curebag, wi the vials an balms packed by Ma back in Birchhold. Wi my other hand I tug his torn tunic open across his back.

There is a cut, but that en't what stops me. He's right, it's shallow, more of a scratch. But even by the dim light of the banked fire I can see his back is a mass of bruises. Dark stripes cover him from his shoulders to his waist, older than the brief time between the attack an now.

"Berengar?"

"What's wrong?"

"Who did this to you?"

"One of the Raiders," he says.

"No," I say, comin round to face him. Somethin's quickened in my lungs, my heart, an anger that leaves me almost breathless. "Who beat you?"

He stares at me, then smiles.

"Oh *that*," he says. "That's just penitence. Yesterday was the first of the Ember Days. I fasted and repented with my family. It was such a relief, Ebba."

"A relief?" I say. "You've bin beaten black an blue!"

"I'm free from sin," he says.

"Sin?" I whisper.

But I don't need him to answer me. I know very well what sin this young man needed cleansin of. It's the same that made our welcome so cold, our presence a problem to be solved. The sin of association wi me.

Everythin my worry cleared away comes crashin back down.

"I'm leavin," I say.

For a moment we look into one another's eyes, an I think he's goin to tell me he'll come wi me, away from his family, away from the fire an the beatins, an the people who would tear us apart.

Then he ruins it.

"How can you do this to me?" he says.

An just like that, all my fondness dies, an in its place is rage.

"Me?" I say. "How can *I*?"

I sling the bags over my shoulder, my curebag at my hip. The veil got torn off back at the castle, an the russet over-robe is upstairs wi the gold circlet. I'm still in the nasty green dress cos I din't have time to fight my way out of it, but I tore the skirt to the waist before ridin down here so's I could sit astride the horse, not sideways an helpless like these southerners prefer their women.

"Berengar of Vellsberg," I say, "I en't your dog. You din't rescue me, an you sure as hell don't get to order me about. These last two days I've bin good. I smiled while your mother scorned me, while your holy men ignored me, an now your kinsman plans to shut me away. I'm leavin."

"How dare you speak about my family that way?!" he says, "when they've taken you in—"

"They en't done a thing for me," I say. "They'd wish me dead if only it din't dirty their consciences to do so. No wonder they loved the prester so much, they're just like him. The only decent one among em is your betrothed, though she en't much use in a fight."

"Rosamund of Merzen is a lady," hisses Berengar. "Something you'll never be, thrall."

I think he knows we're done the moment the words are out his mouth, cos he kind of shrinks.

"Then have her," I say. My heart's gone numb.

I shoulder my way past him an out to the stables. Torny's just strappin our bed rolls behind our saddles.

"Ready?" she says, then, "Ebba, what's the matter?"

I just shake my head, my face screwed up against the tears. I push one bag into her arms an buckle mine over my bed roll. Torny's lookin at me worried, but we en't got time.

"Let's go," I say.

There's no sign of Berengar in the courtyard. We leave his mother's house an the orchard he loved behind us. My eyes sting. We ride down through the back streets, where there's no noise, no fire, an reach the town gate. It's standin open, barely scratched, witness that someone let the Raiders in. Bodies are piled around it, most of em in the colours of the Vellsberg guard. Beyond, by the bridge, are two longships, scuppered an burned in the turf. Drag marks show a third escaped downriver.

On the hill across the Vell, smoke an flames rise from the abbey.

The bells have stopped.

Aisulu waits under the walls, in the shadows.

"I nearly left," she says as she joins us on the road. "What kept you?"

Torny looks at me, but I shake my head.

"Suit yourself," Aisulu says.

She leads us down the southern fork of the road, away from the borderlands. The moon gives us enough light to make out the road, but there's no depth to it, an my mind is wanderin. I'm thinkin of those marks on Berengar's back, how they echoed the ones that Uncle Ulf once put on me, an my ma, an my brother . . .

"Keep your damn eyes open," Aisulu says from alongside me. "We've got to put a lot of road between us and Vellsberg before moondown."

"Why?" I ask. "An why did you invite us along? You could of moved quicker without us."

Aisulu grunts. "I could," she says. "Don't make me change my mind. Here."

She pushes something wrinkled into my hand. It's some kind of dry fruit. I put it in my mouth, expectin sweetness, an chew on it.

I nearly spit it out.

"What?" I manage to croak.

Aisulu laughs at me. "Sour plum," she says, grinnin. "It'll wake you up."

I wince as I swallow down a mouthful of sour juice, but it has shaken me out of my dreamin.

"It's a fair question," Torny says from behind us. "Why did you invite us? When we met, you made your feelings quite clear."

Aisulu shrugs. "I thought you were Rus," she says. "You speak like the Rus."

"Who are the Rus?" I ask.

Aisulu laughs again. "Who are the Rus?" she asks, like I'm jokin, but from our silence I guess she understands we mean it. "You just met them."

It takes a moment.

"You mean the *Raiders*?" I say.

"Yes. The Rus."

Torny an I look at each other, although the dark makes it hard to see anythin more'n the pale blur of her face.

"You thought I was a Raider?" says Torny.

"Until I saw you fight," Aisulu says, an she spits. "You're in bad shape."

Neither Torny nor I say anythin, an maybe that's a mistake.

"What happened?" she says. "The lord spoke of the north . . . Word is there's been a war in the *Limina*. You two see any of it?"

We don't answer, but maybe that's an answer in itself.

"I heard a few crazy stories," she says. "Seems some prester was killed dispatching a devil. They say the Northern kingdom's in chaos, and the young king struggles to hold his land. Seems he's overstretched himself after losing his holy man."

"You seem to know an awful lot," Torny says.

Aisulu shrugs. "I'm Qesar Carrier" she says. "We cover a lot of ground, and people tell us things."

"Who are the Qesar?" I ask. "Are you from the *Limina*?"

"What does that word mean?" Torny says.

"The edge-lands," Aisulu explains, "Tributary lands, like Arngard, where your little king pays the Emperor a yearly tithe to keep him happy. No, the Qesar Confederacy is a free state. We have our two kings, the Kagan and the Noyan, and more land than this Emperor could dream of. Currently we're at peace with the Southerners, although it isn't always so."

"*Two* kings?" I say.

"Makes it easier," says Aisulu, "if one has an accident."

I can't tell if she's jokin.

The moon goes down a little later, an we find a place off the road to sleep. I lay down near Torny. She's in her bed roll, but I can hear her teeth chatterin.

I want to curl up against her like we used to, an keep her warm, but I don't. I can't. I've spent the last moon curled up against Berengar, his arm across my waist. What if I forget who Torny is? I know how she feels about me, she tole me herself. What if I forget an turn in my sleep an kiss her, the way I kissed Berengar, up until two nights ago?

She might kiss you back, some treacherous part of me thinks. *She wouldn't push you away for fear some god is watchin what you do together.*

I'd tried to explain to Berengar that en't what the White God cares about, but he got angry an tole me I din't know what I was talkin about. That must of bin part of the sin he was so eager to have beaten out of him. Maybe he's right. I en't felt the White God's light in me since we left Frithberg.

I fall into dreams that are fears runnin loose, watchin the Raiders chop their way through the bodies of the ones I love. I want to wake up but I stop myself. I'm half-hopin to see amidst the gore a face that don't fit right, wi teeth like arrows, cos I could do wi some help right now. But my Follower is gone, an the blood flows like ribbons over the golden books piled at my loved ones' feet.

Aisulu wakes us before dawn. We walk the horses through the grey light as the mist lifts.

"Where are we going?" Torny asks, through a mouthful of bread an ham. She's changed out of Berengar's ruined clothes, an she's back in her dirty britches an shirt. It's a relief, one less reminder. There's still splatters of blood along her hairline, an shadows under her eyes.

Aisulu don't answer straight away. She looks us over an shrugs.

"I'm headed to the *Corda*," she says. "I've an arrangement to keep. That's why I couldn't get stuck in Vellsberg. What about you?"

Me an Torny look at each other an shrug right back.

"Our plans have changed," Torny says.

"Will you go back north?" says Aisulu, an I'm sure she's testin us cos I see a faint smile on her lips when Torny snaps, "No!"

"You can come along with me," Aisulu says. "Without passes, you won't get far alone."

It's true. Without em, we'll be turned back from any town.

"Last night you said we'd slow you down," Torny points out, narrowin her eyes.

Aisulu smiles, an dimples show in her brown cheeks. "I could do with someone good-looking to liven the scenery," she says to Torny.

Torny chokes on her bread.

She's flirtin, I think, an I realise I en't ever seen Torny flirted wi before, nor a girl flirt with another girl for that matter.

I'd bang Torny on the back, but Beyard's between us, an anyway she's already coughed up the offendin piece.

"Pity you're more of an ornament than anything," Aisulu

continues, as if nothin happened. "You barely managed one of them by yourself last night. You'd think you'd never killed before."

I know this kind of talk. It's the kind you usually hear men do, pushin one another to see what they'll brag about, in bed or in battle, an laughin if they take it sore, or tell tales too tall to be believed.

Problem is, Torny has killed, en't she?

I see her face close up.

"I'm the ornamental one," I say, but Aisulu don't even glance at me.

I'm uneasy. This woman is readin us like Rosamund of Merzen would read a book.

"Tell me, Rus," she says, her voice sweet. "Who did you kill?"

Torny looks away.

"Let me guess," Aisulu drawls. "The poor bastard they married you to."

"Stop it," I say.

"The poor bastard they married *her* to," Aisulu says, noddin at me. "No, I saw him last night, didn't I? He escaped. All right, last guess. Theogault's holy half-brother."

I can't stop my shock from showin on my face.

In one movement, Torny swings herself onto Hero an kicks her into a canter, leavin me standin in the middle of the dirt road.

Aisulu raises her winged brows.

"Lucky guess," she says, smilin.

"Who are you?" I ask.

"I told you," she says. "I'm a Carrier."

"An what's that mean?"

"I negotiate," she says, mountin up herself.

"What?"

"Trade." She nudges her dark bay into a trot. "Come on, we'd better catch up."

I mount Beyard, but I follow at a walk. Ahead of me, Aisulu's long black braids toss across her well-worn blue jacket like whips. I'm tryin to think.

So there's a whole other power, nearly as big as the Southern Empire, that knows of the Raiders an is sometimes at war wi the Empire itself. An this power, the Qesar Confederacy she called it, sends lone women riding through its neighbour's countryside to negotiate trade. An one of em just so happens to be at Vellsberg when somethin Berengar tole me en't happened for generations happens: Raiders come up the Vell an attack. An it's not just the attack. They're let inside. Looking for payback for the loss of their huntin grounds. All by chance.

I think not.

If Grimulf taught me anythin, it's that someone always has an interest. When he murdered my uncle an took his land, it looked like punishment for my uncle rejectin the White God, but really it had bin planned since the beginnin. Grimulf promised to make the east of Arngard safe for merchants, like the slimy Dagomar he housed me with in Frithberg. That meant bringin it under his control an protectin it from the Raiders, but also snatchin some of their trade in thralls.

I don't like to think about that. I don't like to think how I'm responsible for helpin to open that trade route, so that people like my Ma can be bought an sold.

I push the guilt away before it can turn my stomach, an I turn my thoughts back to our new companion.

There's always an interest. So what's hers?

Five

BLOOD

TORNY'S TALE

Merzen and Vindhaff

I ride until my cheeks stop burning with shame and anger, but it takes longer for my eyes to stop stinging. I remember the look Aisulu gave me as I lay on my back in the hall. Now I know what it was.

It was scorn.

For the first time in a long time, I remember how it feels to be Torny of Gullcroft, a nobody from the furthest edge of nowhere. What was it Galen called me once? Egg-hunter? Even that jibe seems comforting now, because for it to be an insult you have to know something about the north, you have to care enough to joke about it. Here no one knows where I'm from, and nobody cares.

Funny how I thought that would feel good.

Under me, Hero relaxes after our gallop. She's pulling a little, wanting to drink from the river tucked beneath the cliffs on our right. The bank stretching between the road and the river is lush with bright spring grass and dotted with yellow flowers. Birds sing in the trees around us.

I give in. My guts are still unsettled by my bleeding, and the spring sun is warm in this protected valley. Ebba and Aisulu will catch me up soon enough.

Hero's so eager to drink she near enough drags me to the water's edge. Across the river, under the grey stone, a heron stalks delicately through the shallows. I kneel by Hero, and splash cold water over my face and slick back my hair. I can feel the knees of my britches soaking through with damp from the boggy ground, and the noise of the water fills my ears. Hero delicately dips her nose into the river and snorts softly. The sun is warm on my back.

It's nothing like the north, a part of me thinks treacherously. Warm, sheltered, green. Where I kneel, golden flowers turn up tangles of open faces to me.

The pressure comes from nowhere, so sudden I can barely breathe, squeezing my chest like a vice, splitting my skull in two. The clear water turns red.

I stumble to my feet, pushing myself back from the water's edge. Hero raises her head, but she's not responding to me. She's facing the way we were headed, her ears pricked forwards to where the valley curves out of sight.

Then I hear it too.

Hoofbeats.

The sword Rosamund of Merzen gave me last night is strapped across my pack. Murmuring to Hero, I have time to unsheathe it, but nothing more.

Round the bend in the road come four horses. Their riders are in green uniforms, their heads uncovered. For a moment I think they'll pass me, but then the lead rider signals the others, and they wheel across the grass, their horses' hooves digging into the soft turf.

I stand with the sword naked in my hand, trying to breathe, but the weight on my chest is growing, the pain jagged behind my eyes.

The leader stops a short way from me. I have to screw up my eyes to look up at him against the sun.

I suppose he'd be described as handsome. Dark blond hair to his shoulders, a neatly trimmed beard, and blue eyes in a tanned face. He sits easily on a horse that stands a good two hands higher than Hero, and looks me over. There's something unpleasant in it.

He asks something in Southern, but his eyes are already flicking from my face to the sword in my hand, and his own hand is on the hilt of his blade before he's finished speaking. When I don't answer, his fingers close on the hilt.

He says something to his men. One of them drops from his saddle and walks towards me, his hand also on his hilt.

"Stop," I say, my voice steadier than I feel.

The soldier glances at the leader, who nods. The soldier comes on, slower this time.

I need to learn their tongue.

"I'm not worth this," I say. "I'm just a girl."

The leader doesn't react. His man is only a spear's length from me now, and I back along the river bank, the ground boggy under my feet. The weight on my chest is like a stone. I raise my sword between us, and his is up before I'm done, quicker than thought. My whole body feels weak.

The birds are still singing, the grass is green, the flowers gold.

I'm going to die, I think. I'm going to die, and the sun will be shining, and nothing will be the way I thought it would be. And I don't even understand why.

And then come the hoofbeats from behind us, and the leader's turning to see who's coming, and a voice rings out over the meadow.

Aisulu addresses the leader like a queen. Her back is ramrod straight as she guides her horse with one hand, her coiled braids gleaming in the sunlight. The leader hesitates, but she's already thrusting out a hand with her pass held in it.

Somehow, Ebba is beside me.

"What happened?" she murmurs. "Torny, what did you do?"

"Nothing," I manage. The pain in my chest and head is making it hard to speak.

She lets out a long breath. "You've still got blood on you," she says quietly. "An the sword too. He's sayin they're on their way to Vellsberg."

The leader rides up to take Aisulu's pass. He gives her the same invasive look he gave me, then unrolls what looks like a decorated page. Unlike the simple page and seal I saw Berengar use, this is written in coloured inks, bearing several wax seals. The leader asks something, and Aisulu answers with so much disdain I feel myself shrink. Not the leader, though. He narrows his eyes, says something, and spits.

"What are they saying?" I ask.

Ebba has a small frown on her brow as she watches them.

I wonder what she sees when she looks at him, and something inside me sickens.

"His name's . . . Neklaus, I think," she says, and I can't help but see the way her eyes run over his face and body. She drags her attention back to the conversation.

"Aisulu's sayin we en't come from Vellsberg," she says. "She's asking why he wants to know." She looks up at me, her eyes troubled. "Torny, I don't trust her."

I feel a spike of irritation.

"Sometimes you have to lie, Ebba," I tell her. "Haven't you learned that yet?"

I turn away and gather Hero's reins without meeting her eyes.

The leader of the soldiers casts one last look at me. I try to meet it, but look away before I want to.

Only a short time since, no one could meet my eye.

This is better, isn't it?

It ought to be.

The leader raises his hand, and his men fall in behind him, leaving the flower-studded meadow and taking the road towards Vellsberg.

"Stop dawdling," says Aisulu as their hoofbeats die away. "We have to move. Fast."

"Why?" I say, and cringe when I hear how much like a sulky child I sound.

Ebba's watching Aisulu carefully. "Cos you tole em we din't know about Vellsberg," she says. "Who were they?"

"Advance guard," Aisulu says over her shoulder as she sets the pace. Her mount doesn't seem tired. "There's more. Let's get off the road before they reach us."

Turns out that's easier said than done. The road winds through the valley, following the lazy curves of the river as it loops its way north to the Vell. The river runs against cliffs, and on the side where the road lies, the land rises steeply. There are no paths a horse could take, and anyway, there's no cover. Three riders would be visible to anyone on the road.

I lose count of the number of bends we round. Aisulu's ahead of us, so I can't see her face, but her strong shoulders are tense. Ebba doesn't speak either, just rides along beside me, her jaw clenched. She still isn't as comfortable in the saddle as I am, and a more wayward mount than Beyard would take advantage of that.

Just as I feel I'm about to scream with frustration, the valley divides. The cliffs across the river open up, and a bridge leads to the far bank, where a path disappears up a ravine. Aisulu doesn't slow, just leads us over the bridge, and into the cool shadow of the ravine.

For a long time we ride in silence, the sound of the horses' hooves bouncing off the stone to either side of us. The tops of the ravine are wooded, and the path itself is russet with beech leaves. The new green leaves are still just tight-wrapped buds on the trees above us. The path climbs slowly but steadily, until we come out among the trees, well above the level of the river.

Ebba rides up beside me and takes hold of my reins, slowing us both, allowing Aisulu to draw ahead.

"There was a signpost back before the bridge," she says softly. "It said Merzen."

"And?"

She gives me an impatient look. "Merzen's where Rosamund's from," she says.

"I don't see why it matters," I say, itching to take my reins back. She actually rolls her eyes.

"If the soldiers come from Merzen, they'll speak to Rosamund," she says. "She'll tell em about us. About how we left before Theogault closed the gates."

"So what? Maybe she'll tell them how we saved the lord's life too."

Ebba sighs. "Maybe. I don't like any of this."

"You're the one who wanted to leave," I say.

I'm not being fair, and I know it, but somehow I can't help myself. Ebba drops my reins in disgust, and rides on ahead of me. I bring up the rear, still smarting.

At least the pressure has lifted. For a moment I try to feel what my body is feeling, but it's too much. As soon as I'm sure there are no choking fingers round my throat, no hooks buried in my heart, I shut it out again.

This was something else, I tell myself. Something simple. And it's over now. It's gone.

The day clouds quickly, and by late afternoon the sky is low and grey. Apart from brief stops to let the horses drink, we've been moving all day, and the skin of my thighs is starting to chafe against the rough weave of my britches. I'm sore and stiff all over, and not looking forward to the soaking the sky promises.

A wind picks up, the way it does before rain sets in. I hunch my shoulders against it, and see Ebba and Aisulu do the same. The budding trees have no shelter to offer us.

Then, through the black trunks, I glimpse a haze of white. For a moment I think it's mist, and I shiver, but then I see it's rippling back and forth in the wind.

It's a bank of white blossom.

The beech trees end in a neat boundary line, and the road runs between stretches of cultivated land. The green of the new shoots glows like treasure against the rich dark soil, and beyond that, a bank of fruit trees tosses in the wind, white petals swirling down from the branches.

The rain hits us when we're halfway between the woods and the orchard.

It pelts down. I don't even have time to pull my cloak up over my head before the cold drops form rivulets and stream down my neck. My exposed cheeks and hands sting, and Hero puts her head down and breaks into a brisk trot. The rain bounces off the packed surface of the road, and I realise there are tiny hailstones among the drops.

We reach the orchard. The road rises to crest the bank, and between the swaying trees and the wind-whipped blossom rises a round stone tower with a tiled roof.

It's a kirkhouse in the Southern style. That means a village, which means people, which means questions and answers. Ebba, Berengar and I have spent the weeks since we fled Frithberg avoiding any settlement, even solitary homesteads, but that's easier in the border lands, where all there is to live among is scrubland and violent memories. We're well inside the Southern Empire's borders now, and this village doesn't even have a proper wall to keep anyone out.

"Maybe there's a barn we can shelter in?" Ebba says over the wind. The blossom scuds like snow, sticking to us.

"No," says Aisulu. "I'm a Qesar Carrier. I have documents sealed by the Emperor himself that say I must be granted free passage. I don't hide in outhouses like a vagrant."

"But they'll want to know where we've come from," I say.

"We keep going," Aisulu replies.

Ebba and I exchange looks. We've come to a halt, the horses

miserable and starting to tire. They stand with their heads down against the bitter wind, resigned.

"The horses need rest," I say. "Does your pass say anything about housing us?"

"Or not askin questions?" Ebba adds.

Aisulu mutters something in her own tongue. I don't understand, but cursing is similar the world over.

"Fine," she says at last. "But let me do the talking. You," she points at me. "Keep your mouth shut."

I'm too weary to complain.

We ride into Vindhaff to very little interest from the villagers, who are too busy securing shutters and doors against the wind. A few children gape at Aisulu, but adults nudge them on their way. A man speaks briefly with Aisulu, and then we're ushered through a gate into a close little yard. That's when we learn this place's name. There's no stables, but there is a three-sided stall against the side of the house where a donkey is tethered. Fitting our three mounts under the low roof is awkward. I stay with the horses, while Aisulu and Ebba go inside. Aisulu doesn't have to say anything – I can tell from the look she gives me that she thinks I should stay out here where there's no one to notice me.

I'm unloading Ebba's pack from Beyard's back when I hear the door bang. I look up expecting to see Ebba, but it's a small angry old man who untethers his donkey and yanks it after him, out into the cold. He pauses to spit on the ground at my feet. The result of Aisulu pulling out her pretty bit of painted paper again, I bet. At least we have more space.

Hero and Beyard are dried and brushed by the time I hear the door bang for a second time.

Aisulu, wrapped in her cloak, ducks under the cover of the stall, and shakes back her hood.

"Here."

She hands me two dry blankets. With relief, I strap one over Beyard and the other over Hero. Both horses tear mouthfuls of hay from the manger by their heads. The smell of warm horse and hay soothes me. Aisulu has turned to her own mount.

"I didn't unload your pack," I say, patting Hero's neck.

"Good." Aisulu has her back to me. "Don't touch my stuff, or my mare will hurt you."

Her voice is hard, but her hands move over her horse's sides with tenderness, rubbing her down carefully.

"What's her name?"

Aisulu snorts. "We don't name our horses."

"Why?"

"They're not people, and they're not things."

"How do you speak to them?"

Aisulu turns to face me across Hero's back.

"Why don't you go see to your friend?" she says.

Her dismissal is like a slap.

I could ignore her, I think, looking at the coiled braids on the back of her head as she goes back to her work. I could try to speak to her, to find out what's happening. Try to explain to her.

But I'd just end up saying something I shouldn't. I'm not a warrior, I never was. I just played host to the Harrower. As if I could ever explain that.

I shoulder the packs and dash through the rain to the main hall – except it's not a hall, because we're not in Arngard, and here things are different. The walls are stone, even in this tiny place, and the fire is set into the inner wall.

By the big fireplace is Ebba, with her hair down across her shoulders, her attention on a bubbling pot, and the warm light turning her brown skin golden. She looks up as I dump the packs.

"You must be freezin," she says. "Here."

She passes me a bowl and pours steaming liquid from a kettle. I have to pad my palms against the heat of it. It smells familiar, a mix of dried flowerheads and leaves. I recognise the calming scent of mayweed, but that's all. I never was much good at remembering herbs.

I look around. A big table stands behind Ebba, and drying herbs and bulbs hang from the rafters overhead. There's another room on the other side of the wall that holds the fireplace, but everything's quiet.

"Where is everyone?" I ask.

Ebba makes a face. "Aisulu kicked em out."

I take a sip and burn my tongue. "She makes friends easily, doesn't she?"

Ebba giggles. It starts as nothing much, but then it grows, and soon she has to put the kettle down she's laughing so hard. I start to laugh at her laughter, and immediately spill the scalding drink over my hands. Swearing, I put the bowl down on the table, while Ebba hands me a rag to wipe my hands.

It comes away grimy, covered in horse hair.

"You need to wash," Ebba says, smiling.

"I just want to be dry."

"Hang your clothes up wi the blankets," she says. "I'll warm some water."

The blankets are over a wooden frame by the fire. I move it sideways so that they shield me, and strip off my wet clothes. Ebba hands me a pot of tepid water, and I start to wipe myself down. It's been a while since the millpool outside Vellsberg. When I reach my loincloth I'm suddenly aware of my discomfort.

"Um," I say.

"Yes?"

I haven't told Ebba yet.

"I'm ... bleeding," I say through the shield of blankets.

"Where?" She sounds alarmed. "Can I see?"

"No!" My cheeks burn. "Not like that. You know, woman-bleeding."

"Oh," she says. "En't you had it before?"

"No."

"Did you just start?"

"Two days ago."

"All right. I can make you what you need if we can get some cloth."

"What's that you need?" says Aisulu, the door slamming closed behind her.

Instinctively, I cross my arms across my bare chest, even though Aisulu's on the other side of the drying frame. A gust of cold air makes me shudder.

"Have you got any plain cloth?" Ebba asks.

"Why?"

I squeeze my eyes shut. For some reason I really don't want Aisulu knowing this.

"Never you mind," says Ebba. "I can ask the mistress here if you've got none."

"So you *do* bite," Aisulu says.

My hands itch to slap the condescending tone out of her.

Ebba doesn't deign to reply. I hear the clink of the ladle in the cauldron, and the drag and creak as Aisulu pulls out a bench by the table. I finish my washing as quickly as I can. With her in the room I feel vulnerable.

Ebba sticks an arm around the side of the drying frame, holding the dirty green dress Bilhildis chose for her.

The skirt's ripped, but it's dry and fairly clean, apart from some soot patches and a faint smell of burning. I try to tell myself it's just for now, just until my clothes dry. But it's no good.

"Ebba?"

"Yes?"

"I can't wear this."

"I know it's ripped—" Ebba starts.

"No," I say, bracing myself. "I can't wear skirts. Give me a blanket, I'll be fine."

There's a silence. I grimace, hating that I sound so stupid, like a child. I imagine Ebba's confusion, Aisulu's contempt.

Then an arm in a faded blue sleeve hands me another bundle.

The clothes are old, hard-worn like her quilt jacket, but both the riding britches and the grey tunic are clean. They are cut wide, but I wrap the spare material around myself and secure them with the ties, the way Aisulu wears hers.

The material is good quality, but thinning where it's been washed over and over. I find that comforting.

I step out from behind the blankets.

Aisulu doesn't even look up. She's digging through her saddle bags, and as I come and sit by the table, she pulls out a neatly folded length of undyed cloth.

"There you are," she says to Ebba, who's pouring me another bowl of hot liquid.

Ebba passes me the bowl. "It'll help wi the cramps," she says. Then she looks over the cloth. "Thank you, Aisulu."

Aisulu shrugs, and looks at me.

"Fucking hell," she says. "Come here."

I don't move, but she scoots closer to me along the bench anyway. "Have you got any more hot water?" she asks.

Ebba passes her some.

Aisulu dips the edge of her sleeve in the water, and takes my jaw in her other hand. The shock of her strong fingers touching me makes me tense up. Her dark eyes are very close, her expression unreadable.

She turns my face towards the fire, and dabs at my hairline with her sleeve.

Ebba is very still. She's watching us, and again I feel the now-familiar pricking of my cheeks growing hot. I hope the firelight disguises it.

I should say thank you too, but my tongue is stuck to the roof of my mouth.

Aisulu doesn't seem to notice anything. She turns my face the other way, and Ebba turns back to the fire. Swearing softly under her breath, Aisulu cleans the last spots of blood from my skin.

Six

TRANSFORMATION

EBBA'S TALE

Vindhaff

I can't lie. The way the headman of Vindhaff simply *gives* Aisulu his house worries me. I come from a place where any stranger, let alone an outlander, was treated as a threat or a nuisance. If she'd of shown her imperial writ to my uncle, I can tell you exactly how far it'd get her. Yet here the man sees it – I en't even sure he can read it, mind – an clears out. There's somethin goin on, an until I understand it, I en't goin to be able to rest.

The rain eases just before sundown, just as I'm finishin sewin the cloth pads for Torny. I lay em aside an stand.

"I'm goin to the kirk," I say, pullin my cloak around my shoulders.

Torny looks up in surprise. Aisulu keeps her eyes on the meat she's choppin.

"I'll come too," says Torny quickly, an I can't stop my eyebrows from risin. I thought she was done wi gods.

I'm tryin to think of a way to nicely ask her not to when Aisulu says, "You're staying right here."

"Why?" snaps Torny.

"Because it's easier for us if everyone thinks you're a boy," says Aisulu, her eyes still on her work. "Plus," she adds, "I don't trust you not to get into trouble."

Torny opens her mouth.

"I'd like to be alone," I say.

Torny closes her mouth.

I leave before I can see the hurt in her face.

The kirk is at the east end of the village, standin in its yard among the blossom trees. The wind still tosses the sodden branches, an the path to the kirk door is white wi petals. I try to step lighter. It's daft, I know, but even like this they're so pretty I don't want to bruise em.

The kirk is made of stone, its tiled roof dull greens an yellows. It's smaller than the ones I glimpsed in Vellsberg, nothin like the monastery Berengar showed us, but when I open the door an step into the dark inside, I see the stone walls are a foot an a half thick. The only daylight comes through narrow slits set high in the walls. There are three larger windows wi rounded tops set way above the altar in the east, but these are shuttered up against the wind an wet.

The altar itself is stone, covered with an embroidered cloth that may be red, or some other dark colour. There are no beeswax candles, an no golden offerins. The wooden box pews are like the ones in the kirk in Frithberg, but that's all.

Instead of walkin down between the pews, I walk along the south side, lookin around me. I can see there's figures painted on the walls, up between the slits, but the light comin through em dazzles me, poor as it is, an I can't make em out.

Someone coughs an I jump half out of my skin.

Sitting in the box pew I just passed is an old woman, her head covered, glarin at me. I sit quickly in the closest box pew an hold my hands before my face.

I wanted time to look at the quiet, private thoughts about Berengar I'm carryin, but it's impossible wi this stranger sat so close beside me. I can tell she's still glaring. Sittin wi my eyes closed, I can feel every ache in my back and legs from our ride an the damp hours spent restless on the ground.

I'm about to give up when someone beside me says, "Who's this?"

I jump for the second time.

The speaker is a man in black robes with a smooth voice. I dislike him.

"One of the guests, Father," the old woman says. "She came wi the Qesar."

The man looks at me. "I have heard the Lord's word has reached eastward," he says, "but that the heathen tribes worship him as only one among their many devils."

I want to leave, now, but he's blockin the door of the pew. I can feel em both waitin for my answer.

Breathe, I tell myself. *You survived the Prester. You can handle this.*

I fold my hands demurely in my lap an straighten my skirts.

"The Lord's word travels slowly," I say, "but its spread cannot be stopped."

I hear a little shiver in my own voice. Is that good? Will he take it for maidenly fear, or guilt?

"You see, Father," says the woman, pleased. "It's as you say. All will come to the table, one way or another."

The man is still watchin me, I can feel it. Of course I don't look at him. I remember how the Prester would watch me for it, to see if I looked at the men we travelled with. Another sign of guilt.

"What a wonder," he says. "Tell me, among your people, are you punished for worshipping the one true God?"

I duck my head, afraid to speak in case I'm trapped by a wrong answer. I wonder whether under his robes, the old woman's worn dress, their bodies carry marks like the ones on Berengar's back. My whole body itches wi the desire to leave.

Behind me, the door opens.

"You must stay for the Evening Prayer," says the priest.

The small stone kirk fills up quickly. The scrape of wooden overshoes on the stone flags echoes above the rustle of skirts an cloaks. People come in quietly, shakin off the droplets. Our side of the kirk fills up wi women, while the men sit in the box pews across from us.

The kirk-father stands with his back to us. He raises his arms, an the rustlin dies.

A voice rises into the new quiet, high an brave. I look up in astonishment, an see a young woman standin in the front pew. Then another voice joins it, a warm, mellow note, an I see a man stand on the other side of the kirk.

More an more villagers stand, their voices raised in – is it song? Can you call somethin that seems wordless song? The notes go on an on, carried onwards by different voices. They soar an dip, an I feel my skin prickle as my hairs stand up.

The stone walls ring with it, sharper'n bells.

The kirk-father drops his arms, an the voices meet on a single note, almost a shout, that echoes in my head.

In the silence that follows, I feel my heart poundin.

I take a breath.

The kirk-father turns an speaks in kirk-tongue. I scrabble to understand the words, but only one or two sound familiar. He speaks what must be a greetin, for the villagers around me answer him in kind. Then there seems to be an exchange, questions an answers, the single voice leadin, the many followin. I'm the only one tongueless among the crowd.

I shift uncomfortably. Memories that en't welcome are pressin me, seekin entry.

Then the voices around me join as one, an with a shock I find I know these words.

They're the words Berengar an Erland took such pains to teach me, on the cold journey to Birchhold. The tenets of faith that made Berengar lose his temper wi me, the oath I tole Erland I was old enough to take.

I feel again the heat on my skin. My lips are already formin the words. My eyes sting.

There's beauty in this, in all of it. The voices, the echoes, the tongue I never learnt. It swirls around me like fragrant smoke, heady as beeswax, blindin as gold. It reminds me of fire, an light, an there, at the centre of it all, somethin terrible, somethin that will overwhelm me if I let it.

I hear sobbin, an for a moment I think it's me.

Then the sobbin turns to a howl.

The unity of voices stutters, dies. A single, jarring voice remains.

I look about me, dazed, as the people around me start to speak, in fear this time.

It's the young woman who first stood an sang. She's clawin at her dress.

"I'm burning!" she screams. "Get it off, get it off! Ohhhhh . . ."

An that noise is the worst of all, a kind of hopeless croon, as her fingers snarl in her sleeves an her eyes roll back.

We are massed too closely for her to fall to the floor. Her pew-mates catch her, gabblin at one another.

My pulse is steadyin, my head no longer spinnin.

"Let me see her," I say. "I know a little healin."

The old woman turns bright, wide eyes on me. Her face is strangely lit.

"This isn't healing-work, girl," she says. "This is punishment."

I was brought up to do as my elders tole me, but I broke myself of that habit. I push past my neighbours, out of the pew an down the aisle, until I can see the young woman.

She's shudderin an dancin in the arms of the women beside her, her eyes white under half-closed lids. It looks like she's havin a seizure.

"Help me lay her down," I say to the kirk-father, but he's useless, his arms half-raised in forgotten praise.

Women's hands help me lift the young woman out of the pew, an we lay her down, her head in someone's lap. She's still twitchin, but it's softer now. Her kerchief has come loose. Her friend strokes her hair an speaks to her softly, though from what I've seen anyone in a fit can't hear nor sense such things.

I try to untangle her clenched fists from the ripped cloth of her dress, but she's locked em so tight I'm scared I'll break her fingers if I force em. She's torn her neckline down the central seam, an her white undergown is ripped too. I smooth the material back to feel for her heartbeat, but as the gown falls open I snatch my hand back.

Her body is covered wi livid red marks, like burns.

At last I listen to the words her friend is murmurin.

"There is a fire in the north. . . like an axe he falls. . . like an axe he has two heads . . . the fire shall mark the sinners, the fire shall spare the meek. . . let the meek walk before you, let them be as a stone among flames . . . he is coming . . ."

She en't alone. Others are speakin em too.

One by one, the hairs stand up on the back of my neck.

Finally the kirk-father stirs himself. He pushes me aside, an starts prayin loudly over the young woman. Others have started cryin, a wailin I know as the sound of mournin, even though the young woman en't dead.

I get to my feet, my heart hammerin.

There's a voice in the heart of all the other voices, where their noise makes a space for it.

I have always favoured fire.

Seven

WASTE

TORNY'S TALE

Vindhaff

It's only when I go to put on the pad Ebba's sewed me that I see where we're supposed to sleep tonight. On the other side of the wall that houses the kitchen fireplace, there's a room with a couple of heavy, undecorated chests, its own small fireplace, and a large bed.

I stand looking at it, my heart jumping.

At home we sleep wrapped in cloaks or sleeping rolls laid on the floor. Some people might have their own beds, like the guests in the wayhouse where Ebba and I used to work, but here in the south, beds are shared.

Whatever happens tonight, I'm going to end up lying next to either Ebba or Aisulu.

My guts churn and clamp, and I grunt with pain.

"Rus! Come and help me!" Aisulu shouts from the kitchen.

I change as quickly as I can, tying the pad in place under my loin cloth. I try not to look at the bed.

"Rus!"

"Coming!"

Aisulu is sat the table, putting chunks of roasted meat into bowls of Ebba's thick barley stew.

"I didn't realise your girl was a church-louse," she says. "Will I have to go prise her away from her prayers?"

I pull a bowl towards me and take up a spoon.

"She's not my girl," I say.

"Could have fooled me," says Aisulu, digging into her own bowl.

"We're friends."

"All right," she says. We eat in silence. The meat is good, red and tender. *Rich food*, I can almost hear Ebba say in my head. *Why's an outlander worth this kind of welcome?*

"So if you two are just friends," Aisulu says, "you won't mind if I try?"

"What?"

"With Ebba." Aisulu picks something out from between her teeth thoughtfully. "She's pretty, and that boy she was following about has hurt her. I bet if I asked her what's wrong, let her cry on my shoulder—"

I slam my empty bowl down harder than I mean, makin the table jump. "Leave Ebba alone. She's not like that."

She's laughing at me.

"Like what?" she says, and it's a challenge.

I don't have an answer. All I have is an ache in my gut, and the kick of my heart in my chest.

"What are you going to do?" she says. "Lie between us in bed to make sure I don't touch her?"

My cheeks are flaming. I can't even hope the firelight hides it. Sure enough, Aisulu smirks at me.

"Do you always hurt people?" I snap.

Her smirk disappears. "What did you say?"

I don't think. All I know is suddenly she's the one off balance.

"Why do you do it?" I say, searching for something to needle her with. "Is this why you were sent away from your people?" Something like panic flashes across her face. "They were going to force you to marry?"

But I see I've lost it, whatever it was. Her shoulders relax, and she sits back, confident and disdainful again.

"You Rus," she says. "You're like children. All you understand is force. My people don't require us to give up our loves, man or woman. You can't understand that maybe being sent away is a mark of honour, can you?"

She leans forward.

"Being a Carrier is something only the best of us can do. We have to ride, fight, hunt, learn languages as we need, carry gifts and messages, and secure the best terms for our folk. What's the highest honour *you* could dream of?"

Being tied to a rock by my mother and used as a vessel for a blood-thirsty god.

I feel frozen in place. Despite the fire I'm cold.

Her mouth twists in contempt.

"They wouldn't even let you fight, would they?" she says, watching me.

And I can't disagree.

The only times I was allowed to fight, it was because there was something in me. Something the people around me feared but thought they needed.

Be honest, I tell myself. *You thought you needed it too. That's why you invited the spirits in. You didn't believe you could be a warrior by yourself any more than anyone else did.*

As a girl, my chances were bad to begin with.

I look up, meeting Aisulu's eyes. I'm waiting for her to take her advantage, run with it, really hurt me.

But something's changed in her face.

"Come on," she says suddenly. She stands up, and jerks her head towards the door.

"What?"

"Come with me."

She leads me outside. The air is cold and damp, but there's still light in the spring sky.

"Stance," she says.

"What?"

She pulls me beside her, her hand hard on my forearm.

"Show me your stance," she says.

I hesitate. She scowls.

"Do you want it or not?"

I settle my feet into the stance I used to use for staff practice.

"Wait there," Aisulu says. "I'm going to get your sword."

I expect her to fence with me, the way Jarle used to when we practised staffs back in Frithberg, but she doesn't. She corrects my stance, then has me hold the sword in the guard position. I hold it there until my arms tremble, and a stitch starts in my side over my still-tender ribs.

Aisulu frowns.

"You've let your muscles waste," she says.

I think about those endless misty days and nights, the way Galen would beg me to eat, and I would laugh at him, because I felt no hunger. I thought then that the Harrower was giving me strength, but in the days after the battle of Frithberg, as we rode south, I learned the truth of it: my body had eaten itself to lend me my unnatural strength.

"You were injured?" Aisulu asks. I nod. "Where?"

I lower the sword's point into the mud of the yard, and put my hand to my ribs. I'm too tired to speak.

She comes round to my left side and makes me raise my arm while she runs her hands over my side. I don't know what she can tell by it, but she grunts. Then she prods me, hard.

"Ow!"

She gives me an evil grin. "Mostly healed," she says. "Stop whining. You need to build up your strength. Maybe it *is* a good thing we're sleeping here tonight—"

The yard gate slams against the wall, and we turn.

Ebba strides towards us, her face pale.

"We have to go," she says.

So in the end I don't have to worry about the bed. I make Ebba eat her portion of the meat and barley while I pack our things, and Aisulu readies the horses.

None of us say, "It's probably nothing," although for a moment after Ebba tells us about the girl in the kirk, I do think about arguing in favour of staying the night. The girl may have the falling sickness, and as for the marks . . . But I've not seen Ebba like this before. She is calm and grim, like whatever happened at the kirk is inevitable.

I don't have time to ask her about it. Aisulu comes in and tells us the horses are ready. She lights a torch from the fire, then banks it. We follow her out into the damp night air, and lead the horses in single file out of the yard.

We try to be quiet, but it's not late enough for everyone to be asleep, and anyway, who would sleep after excitement like that? There are shadows in doorways, faces behind shutters. Still, no one challenges us. Maybe they're glad to see us go.

"They'll tell others about us," Ebba says to Aisulu.

I expect Aisulu to complain that she never wanted to stop in the first place, or that Ebba should have minded her business and stayed away from the kirk. But she just says, "People who live rooted to one spot never trust those who move freely."

I wonder how many times Aisulu has left a soft bed and a warm hearth in the middle of the night.

We follow the road out of Vindhaff, the light from the torch just enough to see by. The wind soughs through the branches of the woods around us, and shakes droplets down on us. At least the cold keeps us awake and moving.

I can't tell how much later it is when the torch gutters and dies. By then I am stiff and cold through, so weary I can barely lift my feet. My hand jerks on Hero's reins, but she doesn't even respond. I stumble, and Ebba reaches out and grabs a fistful of my cloak.

"Stop," she says. "We en't goin further without light, Aisulu. We got to stop now."

Wordlessly, Aisulu turns her mount off the path. I stumble after her, Ebba's hand still on my back. If she didn't have us, maybe Aisulu would have just kept going all the way through till dawn.

We stop under some trees where the ground is relatively clear. Ebba pushes me down with my back against the trunk of a tree. I don't complain. I close my eyes as she leads the horses to where Aisulu is hitching hers. I can feel the damp of the loam begin to seep through the seat of my borrowed britches.

Sail cloth rustles to my right as Ebba struggles to unstrap the packs in the dark.

Aisulu's feet crunch in the mast as she comes closer. "Here."

Ebba grunts as she takes the weight of the pack in her arms.

"How far away are we?" she asks as she sets the pack down.

"Not far enough."

"Those soldiers will follow us, won't they?"

Aisulu says nothing.

"May as well say it," Ebba says. "They saw Torny covered in blood. Them in Vellsberg will tell em we ran. So what I want to know is why are you still with us? An no flirtin this time. It don't work on me."

"Is it working on her?" Aisulu quips, but Ebba ignores her. At last Aisulu says, "I heard what the lord said." Her voice is quiet. "Do you know what a convent is?"

"It's a holy house for women," Ebba says. "We wouldn't of gone."

"I don't think you understand," Aisulu says. "You would not have had a choice."

"What d'you mean?"

"Vellsberg is not the *Corda*," Aisulu says, "but for its size, it is important. Trade and defence, you see? And the new scriptorium, of course. Some of the most valuable illuminations in the Empire are made there. The House of Vellsberg may not be part of the *Corda*, but they have ambition. They seek to build power through the church. If it makes you feel better, the boy's family wouldn't have accepted you even if you'd been a nicely born homegrown maiden. The Merzen girl must have been his betrothed since birth."

"It don't," Ebba says shortly. "An that don't tell me why you reckon we'd of bin trapped."

"That pretty little Merzen girl has powerful family in the church. An abbess who oversees convents and an uncle who's a bishop, to start with. The House of Merzen have members in holy houses throughout the Empire. And now it looks like the House of Vellsberg have a martyr in the family, even if only an adopted one."

"A martyr?" Ebba's voice is tight.

"The holy man who died converting the Northern heathens," Aisulu says. "The one you two know nothing about."

Ebba lets out a long breath.

"From what I know, he was at daggers drawn with the Lord of Vellsberg," Aisulu continues. "But dead family are so much easier to get along with, aren't they?"

Are they? I suppose I should know. My body is cold and heavy, and it's getting harder to follow the thread of their voices in the dark. I think of Vigdis among the black rocks.

"Believe me," Aisulu says. "Theogault of Vellsberg knows you were with his nephew, and his nephew was with the holy man. And a saint in the family means money and influence. I don't think he'd be pleased at the thought of witnesses."

A hand is on my shoulder, shaking me. "Come on," Ebba whispers, and her voice shakes, just a little. I let her tug me into the bed roll she's laid out for me. The cold makes my new-healed ribs ache and groan, but I don't care. I just want to sleep. I can feel Ebba settling beside me as my ears ring with sleep like waves. Her voice comes from far away.

She says, "Will they make him a saint?"

And Aisulu says, "Not yet. First, they need a body. And miracles."

With the sound of gulls in my ears, with the mist rolling in, I sleep.

Eight

CONVOCATION

EBBA'S TALE

The Charcoal Forest

orny's dreamin, if you can call it that. She's stiff an cold, her eyes wide open.

I don't bother shakin her. I know it don't work.

I take her clenched fists in my hands, tryin to warm em. Aisulu's off scoutin the road, an I'm meant to be makin breakfast. Torny should be up by now.

"C'mon Torny," I mutter to her, chafin one hand, then the other. "I need you awake."

The sword she took from Vellsberg is lyin sheathed besides her. I know I should be glad we have it, but it makes me uneasy seein it there.

Torny's still starin into space, her jaw workin as she grinds her teeth.

I sit back on my haunches, tryin to think.

I could ask Aisulu for help, but I don't like lettin her see Torny like this. I even kept it from Berengar when we were travellin south. I had hoped she'd stop dreamin when we left the north behind, but if anythin, she's worse since we crossed the Vell.

We en't had a proper night's sleep since Vellsberg, I tell myself. *Anyone'd be worse after the last two days.*

But I know Torny. An I know how much worse she might get.

Think.

I've still got my leather cure bag, packed by Ma for me what feels like a lifetime ago. I en't touched anythin but the salve since we left Frithberg, but maybe . . .

I sort through the neatly stored bone vials, their wax seals coloured accordin to use an danger. They're all unbroken except for one with a black seal that I quickly pass over. The labels are in Berengar's fussy hand, written the night before I left Birchold for good. No wonder I en't looked through this bag properly in weeks. It's full of memories.

I pick out a vial and go back to Torny. I break the brown wax seal an wave it under her nose.

Torny gasps, drawin air into her lungs with a sound like a death rattle. Her body bucks away from the vial.

Blinkin an coughin, her eyes waterin, she looks up at me.

"C'mon," I say. "I know you're tired, but we need to go."

"What was that?" she asks.

"Hartshorn," I say, stopperin the vial an puttin it away.

Torny looks down at her white hands, scuffed wi leaf loam. The tips of her fingers are so white they're almost blue, an there are crescent-moon marks where her nails dug into her palm.

"Not again," she says. She looks up, twistin her neck round. "Leave me alone!" she shouts into the empty forest around us.

I put my hands on her cheeks, makin her look at me.

"There's no one," I say. "You were dreamin."

She's shakin her head. "You don't understand," she says. "It's happened before."

"What's happened before?" demands Aisulu, stridin up to us. I was so focussed on Torny I din't hear her comin. "You shouting down the forest so every bastard in it knows where we are?"

Torny ducks her head.

"No breakfast?" Aisulu snaps at me. "Well, it's too fucking late now. Let's go."

I settle my pack an mount up. I en't got the strength to deal with Aisulu right now.

We ride on mostly silent for that day. Torny comes back to herself, though she's still tired, an she don't speak, which shows more sense than I expected. Aisulu's wound so tight you can practically hear her twangin like a bowstring. We all feel it, the silence at our backs. We're waitin for it to break.

But the woods get deeper, an the quiet stays unbroken.

The path we follow is little more than a track in some places, an I get the feelin Aisulu must have come this way before to know it, though it en't how I'd imagine an outlander trader to travel. But then she en't a trader, is she? She's a Carrier, whatever that really means.

Maybe it means sometimes you have to move without bein seen.

We eat more of the dried jerky as we ride, though I politely refuse the wrinkled sour plums.

Aisulu keeps goin as long as we have light, but no longer. For that I'm thankful. We find shelter between two rocky crags just above the path. The land here is all wooded hillsides, sheer valleys wi small streams tanglin their way around boulders an fallen trees. Rocks break through the dead leaves of last winter.

We eat meagrely, an I'm so worn out I don't care. The crags hide our fire, meanin Aisulu lets us build it up to burn through the night. The earth under the overhang is dry an sandy. I'm already dreamin of sleep, of warmth.

I lay out our bedrolls side by side, mine an Torny's. I try to put her on the inside, between me an the fire, but she won't let me. Maybe it's best. I don't want Aisulu knowin too much about Torny's dreams.

All those things I thought the night we left Vellsberg are still there, but I quiet em. I don't know where we're goin, an sure as spring thaw I don't trust the person we're goin wi, but she is who we have, an if it will keep me an Torny safe, I'll follow her for now.

I don't think about the girl wi flames on her flesh, or Berengar back in his uncle's hall wi pretty Rosamond. I feel Torny's warmth at my back. I don't let myself think about that either.

Just before I fall asleep, I look across the fire, through the warm dancin air bendin the cold night. Aisulu sits watchin us, her dark eyes unreadable.

The next mornin, I wake to a cold back. Torny is up already, an there are flatbreads on a stone by the remains of the fire. I get up, shakin out my crumpled skirts, a warm, bland flatbread stuffed in my mouth. I come round the edge of the rocks guardin our camp from view, an see Torny an Aisulu down on the path. Torny's holdin her sword, an Aisulu's speakin to her, adjustin her stance, showin her how to move with her blade.

I remember how we used to sit up on the kirkrock, watchin the warriors train. I knew she wanted it, but I guess I thought she wanted it the way I used to want Jarle the stablehand – like somethin you know you'll never have, not really.

I go back to the fire to pack away our bedrolls.

Our second day in the forest goes much as the first, an the third.

The forest is vast, I realise now, for we see barely any sign of others, except for the path itself. Sometimes we catch the scent of woodsmoke, but Aisulu seems unbothered. "Charcoal burners," she says, as if that's all anyone needs to know. She even lets us halt while she an Torny go off huntin. They come back wi woodpigeons.

They also keep up their practice, every mornin an every night. It's somethin I have no part in, so I make myself busy elsewhere. In the evenins Torny waves away the salve for her ribs, an I stop offerin. At least Aisulu en't snappin at us anymore, an Torny sleeps without dreamin. But when I think about what comes next, there's nothin, just shapelessness, wind in the trees.

At least for now it is a soft wind.

We come to the boundary stone on the fourth day. We left the narrow paths this mornin, an travelled a wider road, which explains the marker. I know from Berengar that it marks the meetin of two noble houses' lands, same as the stones back in Eldinghope bearin the names of my Da's kin. Here the marker en't just a stone, but a carved column.

In some ways it en't so different to the carvins I used to admire in the kirk in Frithberg, animals an men entwined in battle or fellowship. Four heads at the top, lookin in all four directions. It's hard to tell if they're men or beasts. Below em, an armoured figure, bigger'n the rest, stands lookin out at us.

I look away.

"Whose land are we crossin into?" I ask.

"The House of Lughambar," Aisulu says, ridin by without a glance.

"That's a good thing, is it?"

She shrugs. "They're friendly with the Qesar, and they're rivals of the House of Merzen."

"How's that?"

She grins. "The river-ways deliver goods through the lands south of the charcoal forests. The Qesar make sure the goods reach this far west."

Trade again, I see.

"They din't seem exactly happy in Vindhaff," I say.

Aisulu looks round at me. "Did that boy of yours mention *Imperium Infractum*?" she asks.

I shake my head. "That's kirkspeak," I say.

"It means the Unbroken Empire," Aisulu says. "The Emperor and his court started using it a few years back. They say the Southern Empire stretches back to the earliest empire in these lands, founded a thousand years ago."

"Does it?"

Aisulu shrugs. "Who knows? But what Merzen and Vellsberg know is that the idea of *Imperium Infractum* puts all the power in the south, in the Emperor's court. The lords of the *Regna* stand to lose certain rights if the Emperor has his way."

"What does that have to do wi Vindhaff?"

"My pass comes from the Emperor himself," Aisulu says. "All rights afforded to the Qesar do. So to Vellsberg and Merzen, who oppose the Emperor's plans—"

"You're an outlander, but you're also under the protection of the Emperor," I say. "That must make you popular."

Aisulu actually laughs.

"I know where we'll be welcome tonight," she says, stretchin in the saddle. "And the night after that we'll reach the Qesar Concession at Lughambar. Things will be easier now."

She en't wound so tight anymore. I've bin thinkin of her all this time as someone sure in herself, but I see now that maybe all that hardness was hidin somethin else.

The sun shines golden on us as we ride down the road. I see marks of wagons, hooves, but not many. That's as much as I can tell, but I see Aisulu castin her eyes over the road too. Her shoulders stay relaxed, so I guess she don't see anythin to warn her of what's comin.

It's late afternoon when we reach the village. This place has a stockade, an a gate, an what we see as we come to an untidy halt is that the gate is shut, even though it's still daylight, an there's men on the stockade above, watchin us.

But it's what's in front of the gate that makes me freeze.

Someone has hacked down an oak. It must of bin a big one, cos the stump is as wide across as my arm, an the earth around it is churned up an pale wi wood chips where they cut the trunk to pieces an dragged it away.

In the middle of the jagged heartwood stands an axe, its blade lodged downwards, its handle stickin up, like a single person did this, then paused in his toil for rest.

The blade is sticky an dark, an red droplets spray across the white heartwood.

The people over the gates don't move. Their helms shadow their eyes, cover their cheeks an noses, makin their faces look not like flesh, but carved stone.

They watch us.

Without a word, we ride on.

"What was that?" Torny asks, when we're back under cover of the woods.

Aisulu's led us off the road again. Neither of us ask Torny what she means: the bloody axe, or the silent agreement we all came to, the feelin that we needed to get as far away from that place as possible. In the sudden shade, my teeth are chatterin. I grind my jaws to keep em still.

Like an axe he falls . . .

Aisulu's lips are pressed into a line.

"I don't know," she says, an I hear a tremor in her voice. "If there's sickness, sometimes . . ."

"The kind of sickness you mean comes in summer," I say, tryin to keep my own voice even. "It scares people. They din't look scared. They looked . . ."

"Certain," says Torny. The days in the forest have mended her. Her cheeks hold colour an she's lost the dark circles under her eyes.

"The axe is a sign," she says.

"But what does it mean?" says Aisulu.

My mouth is dry. *Like an axe he has two heads . . .*

"We have signs like this in the north," Torny says. "They tell everyone that a place or a person is cursed. People know to leave when a curse-pole is raised."

Her voice is steady but her knuckles grippin the reins are white.

"The Qesar have signs like this too," Aisulu says. "They . . . call things to them."

We're quiet. Around us the woods are movin, breathin. A breeze blows chill at my neck, where my braided hair is pinned up off my nape.

"So who are they cursing?" Aisulu asks.

"Or," says Torny, "what are they calling?"

"Where are we stayin tonight?" I ask, tryin to block out the words I heard back in Vindhaff.

Aisulu an Torny exchange glances. Somethin about that small gesture hits me, hard. It's maybe the first time I've seen em act in tandem, checkin wi one another like they're on the same footin.

"Somewhere a long way from here," Aisulu says. "Come on."

Dark comes before we can find shelter. The trees have thinned, an the land has opened up. No gulleys or overhangs to hide us here or to mask our light. In the end Aisulu finds a hollow between some trees. The ground under the loam is damp, but the dip gives us some little relief from the wind. We tether the horses over the lip an settle in. The ground's too damp to lie down at the bottom of the hollow, so in the end we prop ourselves up between tree roots in our bedrolls.

Wi no fire we're cold an hungry. The bread Aisulu passes round is hard an gritty, an we finish the jerky in three bites each. As night falls Torny shifts restlessly beside me. Wordlessly, I offer the salve, an she take some an reaches under her shirt to rub it over her ribs.

"Here." Aisulu prods my shoulder, leanin across the gap between us.

She offers me a skin. I take it, drink from it, an start to cough.

"What is it?" I say when I can breathe again. It en't mead, nor nothin like anythin I've tasted before. I push it into Torny's hand in return for the salve box.

Aisulu laughs an says a word I can't begin to pronounce. "It means . . . fire-sap," she says, tryin to put it in our tongue. "Liquid that gives you life. Except we use it for the world, not people."

"Quickenin," I say, still feeling the warmth in my mouth an heart. "Like when flowers come out in the spring."

"Yes," she says. "We say there are three fires that must be lit before the world awakens. The fire in the Upper Airs, the fire in the Living Waters, and the fire in the Dark Earth. The first is lit by Taghr, the Daylit King, and that warms heaven, but the second two fires are lit by his wife Sarik, the Sunlit Queen, and those are the two that save humans from winter and death, so our thanks is due to her. Fire-sap is made from the first of the thorns to bloom, so we say it is the fourth fire, and we offer it to Sarik to thank her for her yearly kindness."

"So this is sacred wine?" Torny asks, a little breathless from her own mouthful.

"The Sunlit Queen is generous," Aisulu says. "She won't begrudge us some borrowed warmth."

I hear Torny take another swig as I tuck the salve into my cure bag.

"What does a Qesar Carrier do wi sacred wine when you en't borrowin it?" I ask.

"Ooh," Aisulu drawls, so I know she's laughin at me. "Heathen rites. Speaking with devils. That kind of thing."

There's an edge to her mockery, an she en't answered my question, but we all feel a change between us. In the thickenin dark, her words have called to mind the bloodied stump.

"What are the signs you said your people have?" Torny asks abruptly, passin the skin back to me. I hand it wordlessly to Aisulu. "These rites. Are they to call this queen of yours?"

Aisulu drinks as well.

"No," she says. "They're not something anyone should do."

"But they do them anyway," Torny says, her voice ragged.

Aisulu passes me the skin again. I consider refusin it, but Torny takes it out of my hand.

"Yes," Aisulu says. "It's forbidden, but they do."

Her voice is quieter now.

"What do they call?" Torny says. I hear the gurgle of the skin.

Aisulu don't answer straight away. She waits for the skin to come back to her.

"Do your people believe in . . ." she searches for the words "the dead who don't lie down?"

A cold hand reaches inside of me an wraps around my heart. She hands me the skin an this time I keep hold of it. Torny's drunk enough as it is.

"Oh yes," Torny slurs in the dark. "We know them."

"We call them needlemouths," Aisulu says. "They consume anyone in their path. I've seen it."

Under the sliver of the dying moon, wi the wind whippin the branches over our heads, I hear a sound from Torny like a sigh.

"Does anyone escape them?" she asks. "Once they've been called?"

Aisulu's quiet for a long time.

"No," she says at last. "They don't."

It's a bad night. I can't rest. The night noises an the chill keep me company under the skin of sleep.

Torny wakes me, her body rigid, her breath comin in laboured gasps. At first I think she's chokin, but then I see her eyes are open, an her hands balled into fists.

The hartshorn is in my cure bag, under my head.

In the dimness I can't see Aisulu, but I see her bed roll has bin packed away. Gone to scout ahead, I hope. Torny's gaspin breath seems to echo between the trees as I sit up. My fingers shake as I work my way through my pack as much by touch as sight.

When I hold the hartshorn under her nose, she jerks away from me, but it takes her longer to come round. Her eyes flicker back an forth under half-closed lids, like she's watchin things dartin through the misty air above us.

I stay with her as she wakes. The dawn breaks, grey but bright, catchin in her white curls, makin the dirt on her skin stand out. Her body softens, an her fists uncurl, twitchin. There's flecks of blood around the nails. The skin has been bitten raw.

At last she blinks at me, shiverin.

"Time to get up," I say.

Even though it's daylight now, the cold seems worse than before. It's hunger, I know, an lack of sleep. We need food an warmth an rest.

Torny's coverin her eyes an groanin. That fire-sap stuff of Aisulu's en't done her any good.

Which reminds me. Much as I'm glad she din't see Torny in one of her states, Aisulu should of bin back by now.

"You sit up," I say. "I'll get some water."

I climb over the lip of the hollow. It's light now, so I see everythin clear.

Aisulu an the horses are gone, an around the hollow, their spears held ready, wait the carven-faced warriors from yesterday.

Nine
MIST

TORNY'S TALE

Durkno

hat am I afraid of?

A tree cut down, an axe with some blood on it? I've seen better curse-poles and holy signs than that. I've seen whole villages standing before me, knives in their hands, shuddering like one beast as they make a single *cut—*

Ebba grabs me as I trip, keeps me upright as the world swims around me.

"This is why you shouldn't get drunk," she hisses at me. Our escort look at her, but this far from the Vell none of them speak our tongue.

They're leading us back down the road, towards the village we passed yesterday. Wisps of mist wrap around the trees on the lower side of the road. This isn't the country of ravines we passed through with Aisulu, but the valleys are deep enough to still lie in shadow. Mist on cold mornings is normal. I should ignore it, like everyone else is doing.

I shouldn't be afraid of these men either. Apart from the metal helms and the spears they bear, they're dressed in plain wear. No metal armour, no uniforms, only leather jerkins, and some of those are so old they look like heirlooms. Up close I can see some of them hold the spears like a stick or a burden, unused to them. They're farmers, muscles hard from harvest, not war.

Aisulu would say at least they have muscles.

Where is she?

My own limbs feel loose-jointed, and my head hurts. My chest is full of dread. Is this how Galen felt every morning after emptying his skinful of spirits?

I squeeze my eyes shut and almost trip again.

Ebba hauls on my arm.

"Hey," she says, prodding me in the ribs. "Wake up!"

"I'm awake," I grunt.

The mist is getting thicker, I'm sure of it. The path weaves in front of my eyes.

"This is about Vellsberg," she mutters. "Theogault knows we ran, the Merzen soldiers saw us on the road, an that girl in the kirk in Vindhaff—"

"Ebba," I whisper, or think I whisper. The helmed guards shoot looks at me, so maybe I was louder than I thought. "Ebba," I try again.

"What?"

"There are people following us in the woods. I can see them in the mist."

Ebba looks at me distractedly. "What mist?"

I understand. The mist is for us. For me. The mist is to keep me safe from the soldiers who are not soldiers. They mustn't know about the mist.

I wink at Ebba to show her I know all this, and nearly fall over my own feet.

Ebba steadies me, and says something to the man walking beside her. I hear the Southern word for 'water' but that's all. The man shakes his head.

"Just keep walkin," she says. "This en't good."

The path flows beneath me. The mist is thicker, and now there's a smell, a heady, familiar smell that I should be able to place but can't. It comes in at my nostrils and makes my head swim.

"I'm scared," I say. "I know they can't touch me, but I'm scared."

"They *can* touch you," Ebba hisses back. "Torny, I need you to sober up. These men can hurt us if they want to. I need you to be sensible."

"Nobody can touch me," I say, and then a pain jabs at my arm.

"Shut up," Ebba says, her nails still dug into my flesh. "Shut up and stop being stupid."

I look at her in surprise.

"You're scared," I say. It hadn't occurred to me at all. "You mustn't be scared Ebba. It's me they're here for."

The forest thins. We're back in the clearing, the stockade before us, topped by those unmoving figures. The axe is still there, driven into the new-cut stump. The blood has darkened overnight. Before the gates stand a row of people.

The smell is thick and the clearing is full of mist.

"No," Ebba says, standing very still. "It's me."

An older, thick-set man steps forward, flanked by two helmed guards. He sends ripples through the mist, and although I'm standing still I feel seasick.

He walks straight up to us and addresses me in Southern.

I am going to have to learn this damn tongue.

Ebba turns a little to me, keeping her eyes on the headman.

"He says this place is called Durkno," Ebba says, frowning. "He says—" she stops. "He says you can go now. He says they have no quarrel with you. Only . . . only with the False Disciple."

"What?"

The headman scowls, and says something to me. He refuses to look at Ebba.

"He says leave now," Ebba says. "He thinks you're a man. Torny, maybe you should go. See if you can find help."

I've recognised the smell now. It's woodsmoke, mixed with something acrid.

"No," I say. I can feel the world swaying, but I try to stand straight. "Tell him I'm yours."

Ebba closes her eyes for a moment, then speaks.

Finally the headman looks down at her. Even through the mist, I can see the hatred in his eyes, the fear.

"He says his daughter's sick," Ebba translates. "But I don't understand – he thinks *I* made her sick. He wants me to heal her."

I look around at the helmed villagers.

"This is a funny way to ask a favour," I say.

"I don't think he's askin," Ebba says.

Durkno isn't much bigger than Vindhaff. As we stumble along, pushed by the guards, we see the stone kirk at the centre of the village, and the remains of a large bonfire are scattered blackly before it. The ground around it is churned, as if people danced around it. The people themselves are nowhere to be seen.

Ebba stares at the ash as we pass, her fingers wrapped tight around the leather strap of her cure bag.

"The axe was his weapon," she murmurs to herself. "He cut down the Harm Trees. He favoured fire."

Padded by the mist, her words sound like an incantation.

We're led to a stone house near the kirk. The headman takes us up to the door, then one of the helmed men blocks our view while the headman goes inside. We can hear his voice raised in argument.

"He's tellin em to leave," Ebba says.

Two women stride through the door, one dragging the other. The first turns from us, but the second, the one resisting, twists back, her face anguished. She catches sight of us and cries something.

Ebba looks shaken.

The headman comes back out and gestures us in. No one touches us. It's clear they'd rather use their spears than their hands if it came to it.

The door slams behind us.

We stand for a moment in the dark of the room. The fire is out cold, and now I realise I didn't see any new smoke from the village chimneys, just mist and ash. The whole village is unlit.

A wail comes from the next room.

"Come on." Ebba takes my hand and tugs at it. "That must be her."

We walk through the dimness.

"What did that woman say?"

Ebba's fingers tighten in mine.

"She said, 'Why did you choose her?'"

And then we come to the doorway, and look into the bedroom.

And we see why all the fires in Durkno have been put out.

The girl is younger than us. In the gloom it's hard to see how much younger, and she's rasping as she breathes, her face crumpled.

Ebba's pack bumps to the ground. Both hands are clamped across her mouth, as though to stop herself from screaming.

"What happened to her?" I ask.

The girl's bare feet are propped up, the soles blackened and blistered. I edge closer, and see blisters and raw skin on her legs as well. Her skin is caked with soot, and now I can smell burned hair too, the same acrid scent that wreathed the village outside. The smell jolts through me, and for a moment I feel the lap of water, the moon crazily splashed across the surface, and arms holding me tight while my left shoulder burns—

I touch my shoulder where the scar tissue is still white and shiny under my shirt, and see that Ebba's shaking.

"Hey," I say, reaching out to her, but she flinches back, and that starts off another memory, of the way she was when we first met, when she had just come off her uncle's farm. All our overlapping selves like reflections, like wraiths, jostling shoulder to shoulder—

We are nothing but our pasts.

The thought is almost like a voice in my head, but I've heard voices before, and this is just a thought, I tell myself. *Just a thought.*

I can feel my head clearing. There's no mist in here, and now I think to myself *it was only smoke, not mist. Just smoke.*

"What happened?" I ask, and I don't know if I mean us or the girl.

Ebba's shaking her head, as if she's trying to deny the sight in front of her.

"It's all right," I say, although it isn't.

Ebba lowers her hands and moves towards the girl, though I can still feel the tremors running through her as if they were my own.

She steps past me and looks at the girl's feet.

"They made her walk the fire," she says.

Ten

PURIFICATION

EBBA'S TALE

Durkno

ll of it swirls in front of my eyes. Sparks flyin through the winter night, a black tide surgin across my uncle's land, golden flames on the pages of holy books. Everyone in need of miracles.

But here I am in this dim room, an this girl must of bin lyin here most of the night an all this mornin, cos a fire don't look like much durin the day, an more than anythin, miracles need to be seen. Whatever happened to her will of happened last night.

As if I don't know what happened.

"I need to see her," I say, steadyin my voice. Behind me Torny moves to the shutters, fumblin wi the bolt. So she can do that much.

As the light spills in, I see someone's mopped the poor girl's face clean. There's a jug of water by the bed, an a beaker, an on the floor a wider bowl, some soot-stained rags soakin in it.

I fill the beaker, an sit as carefully as I can beside the girl. Her breath is catchin in her chest from breathin smoke, an when I first put the water to her lips she splutters, but she drinks a little.

"Mama," she says, an coughs, shiverin.

She looks to be about twelve.

The room is chill, but if she grows fevered from her burns, she'll need warmth.

"Set the fire in the kitchen," I say. That should warm the room some.

I can hear Torny movin clumsily in the other room, an bite down my impatience with her. I've never seen her drunk like this, an just when we least need it.

I gently pull back the covers an look the girl over properly. Her feet are the worst, the skin blackened, cracked, blistered, weepin, raw. At least I've seen plenty of burns before. No one who's lived wi yearly visits from the Raiders can grow up without knowin how to treat smoke in the lungs or burned flesh. The smell of it is familiar, an not so bad as it could be.

If the wounds don't rot, if fever don't take her, she'll live.

The sickness I felt when I first saw her has gone. My hands are busy, my mind workin. Now I'm *angry*. I seen folk burned alive in battle, cut open, crushed, whipped, drugged. I en't seen a girl sent wide awake into flames before.

Well. That en't entirely true, now is it?

What can of possessed em?

I think it before I can stop myself. Cos that's the heart of it.

Not what. Who.

On instinct, or maybe memory, I take the girl's hands an turn em palm up.

On the palm of her right hand is a blister, where someone held it over a flame.

I sit back, flame an ash surgin inside me, chokin me. *How?*

I look down at my own right palm, but there's no trace of that first test the Prester put me to. Of course there en't. It was months ago, an we were all alone.

How could they know?

The kitchen door slams open, an I hear the headman shoutin at Torny to put out the fire. The idiot thinks it'll burn his daughter. As if he en't the one who did that.

Later I'll remember how grief an fear make people forget what sense they have, how guilt becomes anger, how anger turns outwards, not in. But right now I want someone to whip.

I storm into the kitchen, stride up to him, an smack him across the face.

His mouth goes slack. I wonder if a woman's ever hit him before.

"Don't you *dare*," I hiss in Southern. "*You* did this. This girl could die, cos you an all the people who ought to keep her safe put her in the fire. What did you *do* to her?"

His mouth works, but it en't him who answers me. A woman's voice comes from behind him.

"We were sent a sign." The woman we saw draggin the girl's mother from the house steps into the kitchen. Her hair is covered, an unlike the headman an his wife, she en't panicked.

I don't want to know, but I ask anyway.

"What sign?"

"We heard what you did in Vellsberg and the Merzen lands."

"I din't do anythin," I say, but I hear as I say it how it sounds like a lie.

Torny is standin by the fire, frownin between us. I really have to start teachin her their tongue.

"We didn't want to stop you, False Disciple," the woman says. "We tried to protect against you. We raised his sign. But the flames came anyway."

She comes towards me, raisin her hands.

"I did nothin," I say, steppin back. "We rode straight past this place."

"And we rejoiced, to think his sign had turned you from our gates," says the woman. Her fingers are at her throat, pullin back the fabric of her undershift. "But still—"

I want to close my eyes, but I force myself to look as the woman peels back the undyed shift.

The print of imagined flames run red across the woman's livid skin.

The fire shall mark the sinners, the fire shall spare the meek . . .

"You only left the girl," the woman says. "All the rest of us were marked."

"Ebba?" Torny whines behind me. "What's happening?"

"We know what you did at the Feast of Embers. We know who comes after you," the woman says. "We only want to be ready."

Let the meek walk before you, let them be as a stone among flames . . .

My stomach falls away, an I feel queasy an dizzy, tryin to block out what's comin.

"I did nothin," I say again, shakin my head.

"What's she saying?" Torny asks.

"We thought that meant she was pure," the woman says. "That she could carry us through the fire. But we were wrong."

Torny's nails are diggin into the flesh of my shoulder. "Ebba?"

The woman is starin *through* me.

"The sin in her burned," she says. "Now you must undo it."

"You're mad," I say, my tongue cleavin to my mouth. "Fire can't be undone. A child can't carry your sin."

The woman smiles. "It's been done before. Undo what you did, while you still have time. He's hunting you. Soon he will catch up."

"Get out," I say. "All of you. If you want me to help the child, *get out.*"

At last they leave, the headman's eyes still viperous, his cheek still red from my slap. The woman leads the way, her shoulders still bare, the red traces on her skin proudly visible.

I lock the door after em.

"We've got to get away," I say.

Torny's lookin at me in confusion, her mouth open. I feel like slappin her too. What idiot drinks themselves stupid when they're bein hunted?

"What was that, Ebba?" she says. "Those marks? What was she saying?"

I shake my head again. "This place en't right."

I want to tell her, *I'm scared.* I want to curse her for bein just another sicklin who needs my care.

Instead I go next door, an I care for the girl.

I do it badly, I think. I feel like I'm reachin across a distance to her, the noises she makes deadened, my fingers clumsy. I pack poultices on the girl's feet an bind em as well as I can against her cries. It's like I move through a mist of memories of the many times I've done this work before, in the stale after-smoke of raids, or the dread after the Prester killed my uncle an took my homeland under his power, when I feared for the people who had betrayed me. The dimness of the room reminds me of the cold dark days of my midwinter service in Birchold, movin from bed to bed by torchlight, an the empty peace that came wi lyin down too tired to think at night, everythin in me as quiet as the frozen ground.

That was only a few months ago. Now it's spring. I should be alive again, like everythin else in the world.

But here I am, trapped in the dark, treatin the wounds of a girl who could of bin me.

For one dizzy moment, there seem to be three of us. The girl who walked unscathed through flames, the girl who burned, an the girl whose life I took away.

A dog howls, the girl under my hands turns grey, an I see Lana Sebsdota's face from the tent in King Kolrand's camp, the night before I saved Torny. Her dead face is grey an slack.

I wait for it to stretch, for her eyes to open, for the arrowhead teeth to flash as my follower comes to me. I want so badly to be tole what to do.

The Prester must have loved that about me.

"Ebba?"

I look up. Torny's a black shape against the white bars of light.

"What?"

Her face slides into focus, the worry in it. Her skin has a grey tinge.

"You disappeared," she says, doubt in her voice.

"I was thinkin," I say.

I look down. The girl's face is her own again, an she's lookin at us both muzzily.

"Let's get you somethin to help the pain," I tell her in Southern.

I brush past Torny to the kitchen, an set a half-filled kettle on the hearth. All the while I'm brewin, I'm thinkin.

Aisulu sold us out. She took the horses to hobble us, an left.

But how did these folk find us?

Did she ride back here in the middle of the night after gettin Torny drunk an helpless? Or did she only mean to leave us, an the men from Durkno caught her on the road? Did she sell us out to get her own freedom? Did she hold up that piece of paper an wax an tell em the cost of stoppin a Carrier wi the Emperor's leave to pass freely throughout his reign? Or was it somethin baser'n that?

It en't like she ever tried to hide who or what she was. I know more'n anyone what it feels like to wear your difference on your skin, to feel eyes on you wherever you go. *Outlander.*

I know how you shake that, too.

Give em somethin even rarer to look at.

An what could be rarer than whatever rumours have made it this far?

False Disciple. We heard what you did. We know who comes after you.

What if the dead never lie down? What if every single one of em is still there, jostlin shoulder to shoulder, waitin for their chance?

I feel the grip on my wrist, the kiss of the flame on my palm.

Before you do the work of God, the body must be made ready for God to enter into it.

"Ebba? The mist wants to come in."

Torny's face is sickly-lookin in the flickerin firelight.

In the bowl, the herbs are overbrewed, the liquid dark an filmy, its steam bitter.

"I've ruined it," I say. "Get me my cures, will you? I'll make some for you too. You en't lookin too well."

As I let the drops fall from the black-stoppered vial into the last measure of fire-sap, I look one last time for the light I used to think was part of me.

But it's gone. I can't feel it, can't even remember what it felt like.

"Drink this," I say, handin the mix to Torny. She drinks it down quickly, like I tell her to. Her face contorts, she bends over, an for a moment I'm worried she'll throw it all back up. Instead she curls up on the dirt floor, an whimpers like a hound. She don't even look at me.

Come, I think. *Enter into her. Make her what I need.*

They come after dusk.

The headman's daughter is sleepin, an I'm sittin weary on the floor by the dyin fire, Torny's head in my lap.

Whatever I was hopin for, it en't happened. Torny's bin dreamin since I gave her the draught, but this en't the open-eyed sleep I've seen before. She's got her eyes screwed shut an her face pressed into my skirts, curled up with her arms tight around her. She's moanin an mutterin to herself, but too quick an broken for me to understand. It sounds like the same thing, over an over.

I try to move her, but she's deaf to me, her muscles locked. So I put a blanket around her an I sit still, my legs growin numb, waitin for em.

Maybe I ought to of spoken to em. Maybe I could of tole em I en't who they think I am. But I tried that an they won't listen.

I'm both too weak an too powerful to be heard, unless I say what they're waitin to hear.

I hear footsteps an trampin as they come an array themselves outside, an then a poundin rattles the door, makes Torny moan. That's good. That means she can hear.

I awkwardly pull myself up, my skirts tanglin. One leg's numb. I feel for my cure bag an hoick the leather strap over my head.

"C'mon Torny," I say, half-crouchin by her, my numb leg full of needles. "Time to get up."

She's cold an dazed, but she seems to be able to hear me an I help her up. She's blinkin, strugglin to focus, an I curse myself for playin wi things that should be left alone. Ma taught me not to meddle wi cures, but after so long worryin about her, part of me just wanted her to be strong again.

But I've made her worse. She staggers as she stands, her eyes blank, her whole body hunched around herself.

The door shudders under more blows.

"They're trying to get in," she slurs.

"Stay behind me," I say, glad she en't completely gone. "I'll get us through, I promise."

She weaves, but keeps her balance, still mutterin under her breath.

I open the door.

The headman is standin there, backed by helmed men, one of em holdin up a single torch to light us. A man in black robes who must be the kirk-father flanks the headman. This one really is young, an he grips a spear same as the others, his eyes wide. Even I can see he don't know what he's doin. Our eyes meet, an for a moment I feel sorry for him.

"Watch out, Father!" The headman pushes forward, puttin himself between me an him, like I'm a dangerous beast.

"I've done what you asked," I say. "My friend's sick. Let us go."

"What's wrong with her?" the kirk-father asks, peerin round the headman.

"She's fevered," I say, puttin out a hand to steady Torny as she sways by my side. "If you don't want sickness here, let us go."

"Oh no," the headman says. "We've got orders. You stay. He's coming for you."

I sense somethin pass between the men around us. Uncertainty, maybe, or fear.

"Who?" I ask.

"The one who told us about you," the headman says. "The one who told us of the Holy Martyr's return. Father, you have your words?" The young kirk-father nods uncertainly. "Well then, men. Bind them."

I step back as the helmed men advance. The kirk-father looks as alarmed as I feel, but he starts intonin kirk tongue, holdin his spear close to his chest. I wonder if they know what he's sayin, or if it's just a sound that tells em what they want to hear, not words nor meanin.

"You don't want to do this," I say.

"No," Torny croons behind me. "It wasn't me. I didn't do it."

As the helmed men close around us, the headman smiles in satisfaction.

"He'll be well-pleased," he says. "Well-pl—"

A grunt from one of the men interrupts him, an the light tumbles, shadows jumpin across our faces. A spear jabs past me, under my outspread arm. It buries itself in the headman's unprotected stomach, right under his ribs. I watch it twist an jerk free, see the tip waver black in the torchlight, glintin red. It snakes back an jabs right, then left. Two more grunts from either side of me, an the headman standin, his mouth openin an closin.

A thin bubble of blood forms between his lips as he stares at me, then pops.

The two men to either side of us hit the ground, one winded, one punctured. I turn to see Torny jam the spear down with all her strength into a man tryin to drag himself upright.

It's horrible.

The others freeze, fumble wi the spears. They handle em clumsily, like new toys they en't bin taught how to play with, but the moment they realise they're just pointy staffs we're done for. I bend an scoop up the torch an hold it overhead.

"You did this," I say, barely knowin it as I speak it. "You called this on yourselves. May the White God see what you did. May the White God know you and judge you."

I grab Torny, whose knuckles are white about the spear haft, an I thrust the torch in the remainin men's faces, forcin em to stumble back. The kirk-father stands an stares, his mouth open an noiseless.

"You're goin to let us go," I say. "You know what we did. You know who comes after us."

An I raise the torch, an drive it into the thatch of the headman's home.

"Don't follow us," I say. "Rescue the girl. She's the only one pure enough to save you."

The fire catches quickly, quicker'n I hoped. I see the panic of it in their faces as I back away, an then I pull Torny wi me an I start to run. I'm expectin to see the gates closed, but they're open, an torches stand in brackets beside em. Helmed men are runnin towards the headman's house, an I pull Torny into the shadows as they pass us. A horse stands ready by the gate, a boy holdin its head. Before I can stop her, Torny darts towards it, an slashes her spear at the boy's face. He shrieks, stumbles back, an the horse rears an kicks, catchin him in the side. He thuds against the stockade, an lies still.

Torny hangs onto the horse's reins an brings it back to all fours, the spear at her feet, forgotten. Then she swings onto its back, an holds her hand out to me.

I take her hand an scramble up behind her. She kicks the creature hard, sendin it through the gate in a frantic rush, an as we pass the torches she leans over an grabs one out of the bracket an passes it to me.

The horse hates havin the fire so close to it, an I hold the torch as high an as far back as I can, illuminatin the eery flicker of trees around us, closin us in a tiny movin realm of light. An all I can think is: *What have I done?*

People do a lot of things to girls. Things they think no one will see, or won't complain about if they do. Maybe they dress it up in words – the good daughter, the bad child, the chosen one. Maybe they don't bother to justify it at all.

Do they think there's a hole in us that swallows everythin they give, always forgettin, never learnin?

I hang onto Torny for dear life, jolted an sick an terrified, an Torny is mutterin somethin I can't hear, but it sounds like '*they're here they're here they're here*' an in all of this there is nothin, nothin else I could have done but everythin as it came to be. I move within a small, poor-lit circle through the dark of the world, an any light I once thought I had I know now is nothin but hope in the face of horror.

We end the night on foot, the torch burned out, the horse too spooked an blind to carry us further. We let it loose an continue up the road. We've nothin at the end of it, no clothes, no packs, no mounts, no pass. We walk side by side, the grey cold growin, an Torny is fadin again, her feet stumblin beneath her, when we hear hooves.

I can't get her off the path quick enough. I can barely keep myself upright, let alone hide us both.

Riders appear through the pre-dawn, splashes of red an blue visible against the grey. Bare headed, dark-haired, on strong, graceful animals.

They pull up short when they see us. The mist, real this time, snakes between the trees an across the path.

"Torny? Ebba?"

One of the riders swings out of the saddle an walks towards us.

"Aisulu?" Torny slurs. "What're y'doing here?"

"Coming for you," Aisulu says.

I stare at her, an she stares back.

"What the hell happened?" she says.

Seems she expects an answer, but I'm too hollowed out.

"You left us," I say.

"And now I'm back," she says. "Here, wear these. We're taking you back to the Concession."

Torny an I are hustled into Qesar trousers an wrapped in quilted cloaks. Aisulu reaches up to tuck Torny's dirty white curls under a round felt cap, an her fingers brush some dried blood on Torny's cheek.

"What happened?" she says again. "Torny?"

But Torny's eyes have fluttered shut, an Aisulu barely catches her before she slumps to the ground, already asleep.

Eleven
REFUGE

❧

Qesar Concession, Lughambar

 wake up in a room of pillars. One wall is shuttered closed, and sunlight falls in broken bars across the pillars, dust floating in the golden air. There's a breeze, cool but pleasant, and I'm swinging gently, like a baby being rocked. I can hear rushing water, what sounds like a smithy, and people calling to one another in a tongue I don't recognise.

I swing for a long time, half-awake, safe and hazy. I don't know where I am, and I find I don't care.

After a time I can't count, one of the bars of light falls across my face, and the smell of cooking meat drifts through, mingling with the breeze. My stomach growls.

I try to swing myself upright, but my muscles protest, and my legs get caught in fabric. I find myself rocking violently, and it's only then as I turn over onto my face that I realise I'm in a sling of fabric, hung between two of the wooden pillars. All around me hang similar slings, all limp and empty.

I fight my way out of it, landing with a bump. My whole body aches, and the soreness in my ribs is back, along with an aching in my thighs that tells me I rode hard. But why, and how, or when and where from, I don't remember.

I'm wearing rust-coloured trousers in the same style that Aisulu wore, and my own shirt. I pull on the boots left neatly under the sling where I was sleeping, and pad between the pillars to a bright-lit door.

Outside lies a sunny, busy courtyard. As I blink away the sun-blindness, I see the river runs along the right-hand side, bordered by a wooden quay. A boat is docked there, riding high and empty on the water. Somehow I'm not surprised to see the carved horse-head on the raised stern, looking over a small deck and two banks of oars, although the ship looks nothing like the craft I know.

At the other end of the quay is what looks like storehouse, with a small open smithy next to it. Along the side opposite the river are the stables, and there I see a familiar white muzzle and star, head stretching to reach over the slightly-too-high for her bar.

I walk across the yard to Hero, because I'm too sore to move any faster. She whickers to see me, and lips my hands and lets me put my arms around her neck. Under the roof, the stable smells of sweet hay and fresh horse droppings, a strangely comforting mix.

"You must be the Rus," someone says.

I turn to see the tallest woman I've ever met. She overtops me by a full handspan, and where I'm wiry at best, she has shoulders that most men I know would envy. Her arms and thighs look like they're carved from stone under her trousers and shirt. Her skin is a warm brown, lined around her eyes and mouth, and her greying hair is chopped so short it's almost shaved over her ears. At her wide leather belt hangs a sheathed knife and a blue sash of some sort, glinting with beads.

She smiles at me, showing her teeth.

"I'm Kizmid," she says, in accented Northern. "We met this morning, but we didn't have a chance to be introduced."

"This morning?" I get the feeling she's laughing at me.

"You were tired," she says. "Did you sleep?"

I nod. Things are coming back to me, not this woman, but memories of dark trees and white mist, and men with their faces hidden. But there's something else that I don't want to see, and I rush back to the sun dancing on the river, the sound of the smithy, Hero placidly snuffling my sides in case I have something worth finding.

"Do you know Aisulu?" I ask.

Kizmid nods and jerks her head towards the wooden building I came from. Now I see that the end away from the river has the slatted sides propped open before an outdoor cooking pit, and people are gathering on the long tables just inside.

"Let's eat," Kizmid says. "She'll join us. Your friend's with her, and I reckon Varkha will want to meet you."

The tables are set with trenchers of meat, and each person has their own bowl, spoon and knife. Kizmid goes to find a spare for me, and I try to brush horsehair from my shirt and hands as I look about me. Men and women mix and talk on the benches with no division. Many share features with Aisulu and Kizmid – thick black hair, warm brown skin, dark eyes set over broad cheekbones – but here too there's a mixture. Some have blue or green eyes, or darker skin, and a red-head sits at another table, just as you'd find in the north, pale skin weather-beaten and freckled, speaking in the same tongue as the others and treated no differently, as far as I can see.

Kizmid sits down next to me, the bench bending a little under her as she triumphantly drops a bowl and spoon in front of me. For the first time, I notice that the blue at her belt is not a sash, but an intricate braid made up of smaller braids, strung with silver and brass beads in different shapes. Kizmid sees me looking. "That means I'm a captain of the Water Qesar, Rus." She starts carving meat from the trencher in front of us, and serves me first. "Try it."

I take a bite, and my mouth lights up, first with spices I've never tasted before, a complexity of flavours I could never have imagined, and then—

"Kizmid! Did you feed her the chilli lamb?"

My mouth is on fire. Through streaming eyes I see a familiar figure, and then a jug is dumped unceremoniously in front of me.

"Drink this," orders Aisulu, and I grab it, expecting water, only to find it full of what seems like milk, except when I take a mouthful it's salty and sour.

"What?" I gasp, putting it down, but Aisulu pushes it back into my hands.

"Keep drinking," she says.

Kizmid isn't even pretending not to laugh.

"And that," she says, "is how you kill a Rus."

After my mouth cools to just uncomfortably warm, the three of us sit and eat. Aisulu explains each dish and where the spices in it come from. I sit quietly and eat what I'm told to. Aisulu and Kizmid joke that it's because it's my first time eating good food in my whole life, but really, it's humiliation. Not at the joke, but at the size of the world summed up in these dishes. A world so vast that the spices travel for months by land and sea to reach this corner of it.

"These aren't even the good ones," Aisulu says. "We just get the low grade spices and spoiled stock. The good stuff is all for sale, of course. But Varkha knows we all work harder and travel faster to reach the Concession if we know we'll get a decent meal."

"Who's Varkha?" I ask. "Ebba's with her?"

Aisulu nods.

"Varkha's the Negotiator," Kizmid says. "She runs the Lughambar Concession, and she's the link to the outside world. She oversees every deal, or her close confidants do."

"Is that what you are?" I ask Aisulu.

Aisulu and Kizmid burst out laughing. It strikes me I've never seen Aisulu this easy and happy before.

"No," she says. "Definitely not."

"You'd better go to her," Kizmid says, mopping up her gravy with the squashy, tasteless flatbreads the Qesar favour. "I have to get the *uareh* sanctioned. My ship," she says to me.

Aisulu stands and waves me up. She calls out something in Qesar, a thank you or a goodbye, and around us men and women call it back to her.

She leads me back through the pillared room where I woke up, then down a corridor with rooms to either side. Instead of doors, these have shutters that can be slid aside, and I see desks where scribes and accountants must work. Beyond these rooms is a garden, partly bare, with new-planted rows. Across the garden is a building completely unlike the workaday wooden structure behind us. White-washed stone walls topped with a wooden second floor and roof, beams and panels intricately carved.

We enter and walk along a flagged corridor panelled with carved wood. To either side lie more rooms, but these have doors, not sliding shutters. The style of the carvings match the carved horse-head on the ship in the river – Kizmid's ship, I suppose – but these are much finer. Ahead, the corridor is bisected by a thick counter topped with polished metal. Aisulu steps up to it and taps it.

"This is the—" she frowns as she tries to translate the word. "We call it *dzarnyn*, the skin. It's the line between what's inside and what's outside. Outsiders stay on that side, we stay this side, do you understand?"

I nod.

"Good. When you meet Varkha, be respectful. I had to argue hard for her to let you in. Do what she says, and you'll be safe here."

She leads me back to another door, and knocks.

The first thing I notice about Varkha is her voice. Firm but soft, with a warmth to it that I can feel even though I don't understand her words, and strong enough to pass clearly through the closed door.

The second thing is her size. I've never seen a woman so fat. I don't pay much attention to clothes, but I can see this woman is dressed in more riches than most people see in their life. The cut of the dress is similar to the ones we saw in the hall at Vellsberg, but the embroideries are entirely Qesar, glinting with gold thread. Her thick dark hair is braided and pinned up on her head like a crown, and glittering gold pins skewer it, edged with gemstones. There must be yards of it. Her eyes are lined with black paint, but her face is friendly.

"Torny Vafrisdota," she says, using a name I haven't heard in months.

I glance at Ebba, seated off to the side. She's staring at me with an odd look on her face, worried but also relieved.

"Thank you for your hospitality," I say, coming forward to clasp forearms as friends in Arngard would. Varkha seems surprised, but accepts. Out of the corner of my eye I catch Aisulu shaking her head in resignation, and I remember too late I should have bowed.

"You're welcome," Varkha says in perfect Northern. "The Qesar take hospitality seriously, Torny. While you're here, you and Ebba will be fed, housed, and cared for as one of our own."

I can't help it, my eyebrows shoot up at this generosity.

Varkha smiles. "Yes," she says. "As I said. We take this sacred duty seriously. We are not like the Rus, offering friendship only when it suits them."

My pride stings, but I can hardly argue with her. Who among my own people have offered me as much?

"Ebba has told me of your journeys, and your need for asylum," Varkha continues. "Aisulu has already argued your case. She says she owes you both for saving her. I believe the Qesar can help you."

If she notices my surprise at the news that Ebba and I apparently saved Aisulu's life, she doesn't say anything.

"However, we have rules that you must follow if you are going to find shelter here. First, obey our customs. Aisulu will teach them to you. Second, find work. No Qesar stays idle while there is work to do. And most importantly, do not cross the line. The *dzarnyn* is there to protect us, you included. This place is called the Concession for a reason. This is not our land. It belongs to our hosts. It is their generosity and our hard work that allow us to live here. That balance is maintained by knowing where things belong. We keep what's inside in, and what's outside out. You do not cross the line without my say so. Do you understand?"

Ebba and I both nod, and Varkha smiles. It's a welcoming smile, the smile of someone who is delighted to have us.

"Welcome to the Concession," Varkha says. "Aisulu, why don't you teach them about bathing first?"

Aisulu leads us back through the gardens and corridors to the pillared room, which she explains is the sleeping quarters. This time I notice that beside each woven sling bed, hung on a nail stuck in the pillars, is a small bone marker.

"Find one that's free," Aisulu says. "Here." She gives us a marker each. Mine has a boat scratched into it.

"Water Qesar," she says when she sees me looking. "Like Kizmid."

She hangs her own marker on an empty nail. I see a wolf head scratched on hers.

I find another empty nail nearby. Ebba chooses one near mine and props her cure bag against the pillar below.

"Will it be safe?" she asks.

"Stealing is a defilement," Aisulu says. "Anyone who tried it would lose their place in the Concession. Come on, I'll show you where we wash."

She leads us back out into the bright spring sun.

Between the doorway and quay stands a large hide tent that I didn't notice when I first woke up.

Aisulu pulls aside a flap, and warm, humid air hits my face.

The front of the tent forms a small ante-chamber between the outer flaps and the inner walls of the tent. I stick my hands out in front of me to feel where I'm going. My fingers tell me that while the outer hides still bear the hair of the horses they come from, the inner ones have been scraped smooth.

In the dim light coming through the entrance, I see Aisulu undoing the ties holding her top. She grins at me, her teeth flashing white in the shadows.

"Everything off," she says.

"Everything?" The word comes out of my mouth like a yelp.

"This is a Qesar steambath," Aisulu says cheerily, shucking her top and bending slightly to untie her wide breeches. "Everything."

I look away.

"Are there men in there?" Ebba asks.

"Normally we bathe mixed," Aisulu says. "But I know you don't. Only women will join us this afternoon."

Ebba starts pulling off her own tunic with what I think is unnecessary enthusiasm. "I feel like I en't bin clean since Vellsberg," she says.

I close my eyes.

"Need help, Rus?"

I open my eyes to glare at Aisulu.

Which is a mistake.

She smiles back, completely naked.

"What's the problem?" she says. "I've already seen it, remember?"

I nearly turn and walk out of the tent, but Ebba puts her hand on my arm.

"I need to speak wi Torny," she says to Aisulu. "Go an get this steam bath ready for us, will you?"

The Aisulu we travelled with would not have taken orders, but here in the Concession she just shrugs, with no consideration for the effect this might have on decent people, and ducks between the hides that form the inner doorway.

Ebba stands in front of me, still in her white undershirt.

"Shall I go?" she says.

I stare at her. "What?"

She looks down.

"It's me, en't it?" she says. "I'm makin you uncomfortable."

It takes me so long to work out how to say what I'm thinking that she looks up, worried.

Our eyes meet.

"It's not you," I say. That sounds bad. "Not *just* you," I correct myself, although thinking about it, that's probably worse.

"Oh," she says, taken aback. Then her eyebrows shoot up. "*Oh*. You mean?" She jerks her head towards the inner chamber.

"Not just her," I say. I feel my cheeks start to get hot.

"Ohhh." Ebba's eyes are large. "You mean *all* the . . ."

"Other women too, yes," I say, quickly, trying to get past the horror of this talk.

"There might not be that many," Ebba says, "or you might not like em. No need to look disappointed!" she adds, watching my expression change.

I cover my face with my hands. "I can't do this," I mumble. Inside of me, so many different feelings are boiling up, I don't know which one to feel first.

Ebba puts one hand on my shoulder.

"You don't have to," she says. "You can leave. But . . ."

I look at her over my hands. "But?"

"It might be . . . fun?" she suggests. "I'm thinkin if we'd washed together wi Jarle back in Frithberg . . . I mean, remember that time we swam in the river in summer?"

I raise my eyebrows at her.

"I was nervous then too . . . but it was nice," she says. "This en't the same, I know that. An I en't sayin you should do anythin you en't happy with."

"But?"

"But maybe it can just be nice," she says. "That's all."

She gives me a pat on the shoulder, then turns away and pulls the white undershirt over her head, and ducks after Aisulu. A cloud of steam warms my cheeks.

The idea that these things I feel could be anything other than painful or embarrassing has never occurred to me.

I start to undress, hanging my shirt and breeches over a wooden frame alongside Aisulu and Ebba's clothes.

It would be nice to be warm again, I think.

Naked, I step between the inner hides.

In the north, we take washing seriously. We don't do it unless it's absolutely necessary. When we do, we prefer it to be cold and very quick, unless we're sick. We use fine-toothed combs to get rid of the lice. The men oil their beards, the women braid their hair, and we definitely don't make large tents from dead horses, and then fill a metal tub with hot rocks and fling water all over them to create great clouds of steam.

After a short while in the heat and the dark, I begin to think that maybe we should.

"You know," Ebba says thoughtfully, "I en't ever bin *really* warm, not really."

I close my eyes an lean forward, my elbows on my knees. I know what she means.

The warmth penetrates my muscles, easing the aches and strains after our days on the road. It's like a weight pressing on my chest, and every breath I draw into my lungs warms me from the inside too. I'm sweating, and my whole body feels flushed, but I also feel so relaxed I don't want to move.

The only light comes from the hearth under the metal tub of stones, and the steam thickens the air.

The flap opens, and another figure joins us. I panic for a moment, thinking it's a man, but then I recognise Kizmid's build. She's briefly outlined against the hearth as she stops to ladle water from a smaller bucket over the stones, which hiss and crackle. This water is scented, and as I breathe in I feel it travelling into my lungs and clearing my head.

"Some kind of oil?" Ebba murmurs to herself.

On her other side, Aisulu says, "Remind me to introduce you to Serke. You'll have a lot to talk about."

Kizmid nods a greeting and takes a seat beside Aisulu. I try not to stare, but there is so much to stare at. Kizmid's body is different to the bodies I'm used to, her waist thicker, her muscled legs bowed. When she sits, I see a puckered scar in her side, where an old wound has healed.

Aisulu and Kizmid speak softly in the Qesar tongue, leaning towards each other without embarrassment.

I glance at Ebba, then look away again. I'm not ready to be quite so easy with her, not yet.

I close my eyes and sweat.

"Rus," Aisulu says.

"What?"

"Kizmid's going to show you how we get clean," she says, grinning. "Kizmid, she's still healing, so be nice to her." She pokes me in my side, and I make a face.

"Ribs, huh?" says Kizmid. "If I had a gold ring for every time I've broken mine . . ." she shakes her head. "Sit here," she says.

I straddle the bench in front of her. "What are you going to do?"

"We have a saying," Kizmid tells me, reaching up to a shelf and pulling something off it. "The Rus don't wash, they only dirty the water."

"That en't fair," says Ebba. "If we knew what Qesar were back home, we'd probably have somethin to say about you too."

"What Stahranid doesn't know the Qesar?" Kizmid laughs again.

"What's a Stahranid?"

Kizmid looks at Aisulu, eyebrows raised.

"Ebba's from the north too," Aisulu explains. "She's never met her folk."

Ebba and I are both staring at her.

"You *really* need to meet Serke," she says, taking the large pot that Kizmid hands her and scooping something dark out with her hand. "Ready?"

"For what?" I ask, or try to. Kizmid puts both hands on my back and starts to scrub. For a moment I think I'm being attacked, and I rock forward, before I realise that her hands are rough with something that feels like sand.

Looking up, I see Ebba hunched over under a similar onslaught from Aisulu.

Aisulu catches my eye over Ebba's dark hair.

"What's the matter, Rus?" she says, grinning. "Scared of a bit of salt? And I thought you people liked the sea."

I give up on talking back. Instead I brace myself against the bench and try not to wince when Kizmid's strong hands travel over my tender ribs. The rough rasp of the scrub is warming, and coupled with the heat and the dark, my head is soon swimming. Kizmid seems tireless. By the time another person joins us, splashing new water on the hot stones, the steam envelopes me and I lose my way.

Among the steam I see figures, many of them. I think blearily that I never heard them come in, and they mustn't have known we were still here, because some of them are definitely men.

Aisulu will have something to say about that, I think.

Then I realise they're clothed.

I try to look straight at them, but my sight grows dark. All I glimpse is the folds of a cloak, the bulk of furs, the glint of silver in braided, unwashed hair. Some wear the helms of the men of Durkno, spears with bloodied heads standing like saplings in the mist.

And gold.

One figure is small and slim, a gold torque around its neck. The metal glows like the embers under the hot stones.

It reaches one hand out to me. I see the tattoos, lines and dots.

It mustn't touch me. If it does, something awful will happen.

The darkness chimes with the voice of glaciers. My whole body spasms, my back arching out of my control.

"Easy!" growls a voice in my ear, but it seems a long way off. Strong muscled arms are wrapped around me, trapping my arms to my sides. My muscles loosen, and I feel myself lifted.

At first I think my sight really has gone, everything is so dark, but then sunlight hits me full in the face. I feel stone flags under me, and then someone throws cold water in my face. I cough, and roll over, blinking.

"Torny, are you all right?"

"Ebba," I croak. I can see her next to me now.

She puts a loose, undyed cloth around me. She's already wrapped in one.

As my eyes focus I see Kizmid and Aisulu standing back, watching me. Aisulu's holding a bucket. Of course she's the one who drenched me.

"The heat got to you," Kizmid says. "It can do that if you're not used to it. I thought you were having a seizure."

I wipe my face on the cloth. There's still salt scrub itching my skin, and my head feels muddy. My stomach is doing slow flips.

"I think I'm going to be sick," I say.

Kizmid tries to look sympathetic.

"Could you do it somewhere else?" she says.

In the end, I don't throw up. Ebba sits me on the stone wharf, my feet dangling over the river, and I sip from a beaker of water.

Aisulu pads around the steam tent, still barefoot. She hands the wrap-dress to Ebba, who stands to slip it on over the plain cloth towel she still wears, while Aisulu bends to drape the quilted jacket around me. For a moment I feel her fingertips on my shoulders.

She sits next to me. Her bare feet are golden over the dark water.

"All right," she says. "I know that wasn't just the heat. I'm not an idiot, Torny. And don't you go sneaking off, Ebba. I know you've been hiding something from me."

Ebba stops mid-sneak and sits back down beside me.

"You freeze when you fight," Aisulu says, "I've seen you. You have trouble sleeping, and trouble waking up. Ebba acts like a mother hen. And then this morning in the woods you were covered in blood, and somehow, I don't think Durkno just let you go."

I glance at Ebba in confusion. "Covered in blood?"

She won't meet my eye, just stares down into the river. I realise she's shaking.

Aisulu is watching us both in something like alarm.

"Don't you remember?" she asks me.

"No, I—"

I remember the axe in the tree stump, and drinking in the dark, the way the fire-sap burned my throat. As if in a dream, I recall helmed men, people shouting at Ebba in Southern. "There was a girl. She was sick. And Ebba had to help her. She gave her something to drink. I drank it too. But I thought that was a bad dream..."

I trail off. The blackness the bar of sunlight woke me from this morning is back, pierced. There are helmed men, and spears, and torches. There's a woman with flames printed on her skin, and fear, and mist. Mist where it shouldn't be, seeping through walls, out of people's mouths.

I feel dizzy again.

"Don't laugh," I say. I don't know why that's the first thing I say. "Back home, I killed a lot of people."

Aisulu looks at me, then at Ebba.

"It's true," Ebba says, still looking down. "She did."

"Don't take this the wrong way," says Aisulu. "But... how?"

How do I explain something like the Harrower? How do I explain the mist, that swallowed everything, that masked the faces of the living and the dead?

"You remember in the woods?" Ebba asks. "When you two were drinkin? You called em needlemouths. The dead that don't lie down."

Aisulu nods.

"One of em got inside her," Ebba says. "A powerful one."

"She's not here anymore," I say quickly. "Ebba got her out."

I reach for Ebba's hand to reassure her, to remind her that whatever's scared her now, it's all right, she's faced worse. But she won't let me touch her.

Aisulu looks between us.

"Are you sure?" she says.

Ebba draws her knees up to her face and wraps her arms around her legs. Something about the way she's locking herself away from me strikes me cold. Ebba never was good at lying.

"I was so scared," she says. "You were sick, an I was so scared of who was comin, of what he'd do to me."

"Who?" I say. "What do you mean? Who's coming?"

"They knew me," she says, her face pressed into her knees. "They called me False Disciple. I couldn't fight em, an I can't fight him. But you could. When you were strong. So I tried to put the Harrower back inside you."

Twelve
TRANSGRESSION

EBBA'S TALE

Qesar Concession, Lughambar

ow could you?" Torny asks.

I hide my face in my shift. "I'm sorry," I say.

Torny gets up. I wait for Aisulu to follow her, but she lets Torny go off alone.

We sit wi the rushin river an the sun leapin off it in needles.

"Are you telling me," she says, once Torny's lost behind the steam tent, "that she used to be a killer?"

"It wasn't her," I say.

"How can you be sure?"

"She en't killed anyone since the Harrower left," I say. "Except Vellsberg an Durkno."

Aisulu raises her eyebrows.

"I mean she en't killed anyone the way the Harrower would of."

"Well?" Aisulu suggests, cattily.

"You weren't there," I say.

I remember bodies impaled on spears. Curse poles made of men.

"But you were," Aisulu says. "You both were. I was right, wasn't I? You were their devil, the one that killed Vellsberg's holy man. That's why Durkno folk calling you False Disciple scared you so much."

I can feel the tension in me, the way I felt standin before my uncle when he had reason to beat me, an he knew I knew it. Wi this, Aisulu can destroy us.

"Fuck," she says. "Varkha'd better not find out. She'll have me skinned. I had to argue hard to have her take you in as it was, but this . . ." She shakes her head. "That's why I went on ahead of you. I wanted to know you'd have a safe place to stay before I brought you here."

I'm so ashamed all I can do is press my face into my hands.

"I'm sorry," I say. "I din't trust you. I thought you'd sold us out."

Aisulu pats my shoulder awkwardly.

"I left you in danger," she says, "I'm sorry for that. Whatever you did, you're both alive and free."

I know she's tryin to make me feel better, but I'm rememberin Ma. How I felt when I realised she'd drugged my brother Stig in the days before my uncle tried to murder him. How I could barely bring myself to look at her. An now here I am, no better than her. Betrayin someone who loved an trusted me all cos of my own fear.

Varkha's true to her word: the Concession is kind to us. We're given clothes from their store, worn an patched, but clean. Every mealtime, all work comes to a halt, as men an women come to the long tables an sit an eat together off the long shared trenchers. The food is unfamiliar but good, an I wonder what Ma or Aud, who worked us hard in the wayhouse kitchen, would say if they tasted it. Thoughts of Ma remind me of the mysterious Serke, but Aisulu tells me she's away from the Concession on some errand, an my curiosity goes unmet.

Torny keeps to herself. The first evenin she barely says a word, an when Kizmid an Aisulu join a large group of the other workers in the yard before supper, she follows em. I knew she weren't goin to be happy wi me, but it still hurts. I can see Kizmid showin Torny the stretches they do to warm up, Torny's white curls standin out in the golden light before sunset. Some of the Qesar around her lean over to speak to her, then look to Kizmid when Torny shakes her head. I see Kizmid makin introductions. Then a cry brings em back to their places, an the practice starts. Torny may look out of place, but thanks to Aisulu she already knows the openin moves. I watch em as their bodies move together, wipin out the sense of difference.

Then I go to the kitchens to help cook. No one bothers wi me, no one asks me who I am or where I'm from. They hand me a knife, see I can handle it, an that's it.

I go to bed long before the others, my body heavy in the sling, an listen to the river eatin away the earth beneath me.

The next mornin I go back to the kitchens. No one talks to me, but I know what to do. I grew up wi this work. Doin it makes you useful an unseen. Right now that's all I want. Maybe that's also why by the time Aisulu finds me that afternoon, she's flushed, like she ran all over lookin for me.

"Varkha's asking for you," she says. "She has guests."

"Guests?"

Aisulu shrugs.

"Varkha wouldn't ask for you if she thought there was any danger," she says. "You remember the way?"

I wipe my hands an nod. I make my way through the livin quarters an past the rooms where Qesar scribes are bent over work tables wi paper an countin boards before em. In my chest I feel a knot of sorrow for Berengar, an the way he'd lose himself as he wrote.

I cross the garden to the stone buildin where I first met Varkha. The carved panels glow an I remember the kirk in Frithberg before it burned. I walk up the corridor towards the polished wood an metal of the *dzarnyn*.

"Ebba," Varkha calls from an open door.

She smiles at me as I enter. I'm surprised to see that the *dzarnyn* continues through the wall, cuttin the room in two, its metal inlay elegant in the light of the lamp suspended above it. A tray stands at Varkha's elbow, a jug, beakers, an other implements laid out. On the other side of the counter sits a tall, pale-skinned woman. She an her companion are both dressed in the Southern style, but in greys, wi their hair strictly covered, only their faces an hands bare.

The younger one's cheeks are sprinkled wi freckles, an her eyes are cornflower-blue.

"Rosamund?" I say in Southern. "What are *you* doin here?"

"That's her," Rosamund says. "That's the girl Berengar brought back from the north."

The grey-clad woman next to her draws herself up.

"Varkha," she says. "Why are you sheltering a traitor?"

I think about turnin on my heel an leavin, but two things stop me. First, there's nowhere to go, an second, Varkha is still smilin.

It's a nice smile. It's a smile that says, *things aren't as bad as they seem, we can work this out.*

"Gisla," Varkha says. "Remind me of the rules of your brother's great shrine at Corvennes."

Gisla is still glarin at me. "Don't patronise me, Varkha. The Lord offers shelter in His mercy even to the most miserable wretch. This heathen woodpile of yours is not a place of holy sanctuary."

"No, of course not," Varkha says, busyin herself wi the burnished bronze jug an the ornamental brasier set beside her. "Here, taste this." She pours a stream of clear gold liquid through a polished strainer into an engraved beaker, an hands it to Gisla.

Gisla takes it an sips the steamin liquid, her attention switchin to her cup.

"Hmm," she says, frownin. "Are you trying to buy me, Varkha?"

"With *mulsum*?" Varkha laughs, pourin another beaker an offerin it to Rosamund. "I would never try to buy you so cheaply, Gisla."

"*Mulsum* spiced with cardamom," Gisla says. "So you have new stock? I thought the Stahranids were making difficulties."

"Oh, you know me," Varkha says. "I don't like to disappoint my customers."

Gisla narrows her eyes. "Very well," she says. "You've made your point. Sit, girl."

Varkha pats a carved wooden chair next to her. The *dzarnyn* forms a barrier between us an the two southerners, a reminder of the thick walls that surround the Concession. Even here the Qesar are separated from their customers.

Rosamund holds her beaker in both hands, not drinkin. The

scent of spiced wine drifts across the counter. I'd forgotten how pretty she is.

"Ebba," Varkha says, handin me a beaker too. "Gisla of Merzen is the abbess of the Hekateran convent here in Lughambar. I believe you've already met her niece Rosamund?"

Me an Rosamund both look away.

"Ebba came to us as a guest," Varkha continues.

"As a fugitive!" Gisla snaps.

"And we offered her hospitality," Varkha says, like she en't heard Gisla.

"Varkha," Gisla says, "this is very good *mulsum*, and frankly, I don't care if you rob the Stahranids blind so long as it means we have cardamom and pepper again. But do you know what happened to the last people to offer this girl hospitality? Our neighbours were massacred and the scriptorium at Vellsberg was plundered by her people!"

"The Raiders are *not* my people!" I say, thumpin down my beaker. "Every summer since I could stand, I've helped bandage the ones who survived, an I've laid out the ones that died. So don't sit there in your stupid Southern skirts an tell me you know the first thing about my people, cos you don't."

Varkha leans over an silently tops up Gisla's cup.

"I'm sorry for what happened to Vellsberg," I say, my voice shakin. "But it weren't us. We were meant to be safe there. We were meant to—"

But all I can think of is hair like crows' wings, fire reflected in hazel eyes. My throat closes up.

"You thought you were going to marry Berengar of Vellsberg," Rosamund says quietly.

There's a shocked silence, an then Gisla barks wi laughter.

"You're joking," she says, but she's already lookin between Rosamund an me, her smile fadin.

"He was meant to marry me," Rosamund says.

"You should be thankin me," I say. "I left him for you, din't I?"

But even as I'm sayin it, my thoughts are catchin up wi my mouth. Rosamund's here with her aunt, the abbess, an these grey skirts are a long way from the jewelled pins an colourful dress she wore when we first met.

There's no excuse for it. The first thing that leaps in my heart is hope.

"He din't want you," I say.

Rosamund's hands tighten on her beaker, an tears roll down her cheeks.

"How *dare* you?" Gisla says, drawin herself up, one hand on Rosamund's shoulder. "Do you *know* who my niece is?"

"No," I say. "I don't. But I bet I know who you are. You're the one whose convent we were meant to be held in, en't you?"

Gisla snaps, "An oblate's place in my convent costs *gold*, you barbarian."

"An how much would Theogault pay to make Berengar's past go away?" I ask. "Must be quite a lot if he'll do it for his noble cast-offs too."

"That's *enough*." Varkha's voice rings through the room. "Ebba, the laws of hospitality that give you shelter here also bind you. Apologise."

I look at Gisla's haughty, furious face, an the protective hand she's put on Rosamund's shoulder. I look at Rosamund's flushed face, the way she can't lift her eyes to mine.

"I'm sorry," I say, still, angry, "but you have everythin, an I have nothin."

"Ebba," Varkha says, warnin me.

"That's not true," Rosamund says quietly. She hiccups through her tears. "You don't need him. I do."

In the silence, Varkha looks up at Gisla. "You're an abbess," she says. "You've settled hundreds of such things between girls. What should we do?"

I could tell Varkha there's no point saying such things to someone like Gisla. From the look she's givin me, her plans include dungheaps an wild dogs an probably cuttin out my tongue.

"I want to talk with her," Rosamund says. "Alone."

"Absolutely not," Gisla snaps.

"Please." Rosamund wipes her face with her hand. "Auntie, you and Varkha have real business to discuss. I didn't come here to spoil that."

Varkha gestures to a set of doors set in the wall to her left. "The stock room is just here. We'll only be a few steps away."

"This Rus has killed people," Gisla snaps. "If you think I'm leaving her with—"

"That was the other one, auntie," Rosamund says, sniffin. "Go on. You haven't had fresh spices since last autumn. I'll be all right."

"Ebba," Varkha says, "there are rules and limits to my generosity. Don't make me regret it."

Gisla just glares at me as she leaves.

Rosamund settles her skirts an sips her spiced wine.

"I'm sorry about my aunt," she says. "She's upset. All my family are."

I look down.

"I didn't come here so my aunt could call you names," she says.

"So why did you?" I ask.

"You have to leave," Rosamund says. "You have to go away, and never come back."

My mouth drops open. How I ever felt sorry for her, I don't know.

"That's what we've bin tryin to do," I say. "But here you are. Why did you follow us, Rosamund?"

"I'm not *following* you," she hisses, leanin forward. "My aunt *brought* me here, because there's nowhere else where I'll—" she cuts herself off. "We don't have much time. I don't like this any more than you do, all right? Berengar of Vellsberg would have been a good husband. He's young, and kind. You don't know how happy I was when—" she screws her eyes closed, an takes a breath. "Everyone thinks you did it," she says. "They won't rest until they have you."

"But Berengar knows we din't have anything to do wi the attack," I say. "We were with him—"

"All the way from Frithberg," says Rosamund. "Yes. I know."

Her bright blue eyes meet mine.

"They know about Grimulf," Rosamund says. "Lord Theogault... and my uncle, the bishop. Berengar told them."

My heart tightens in my chest. *If I ever see that boy again*, I think to myself, *he is goin to be sorry.*

Some of what I'm thinkin must show on my face.

"He was trying to help," Rosamund says. "He thought they would be—"

"What? Pleased?" I snort.

"Convinced," Rosamund says, her face troubled. "During the

attack, part of my bride price was stolen. Now my uncle's taken over. Ebba, you're in great danger."

"You'll be shocked," I say, "but this en't the first time."

Rosamund buries her face in her hands, her elbows propped on the counter. "Listen to me, will you?" she pleads. "My uncle's furious. He's sent someone to track you down, and bring you back. And this time they won't be putting you in a convent, believe me. I only just managed to get away with Gisla."

None of this makes any sense.

"What d'you mean, you got away?" I ask.

For the first time, I look at her. Really look at her. Her blue eyes are rimmed wi red, her skin's blotchy, an her hands are shakin.

"You're afraid," I say.

"You don't know him," she says. "You don't know what he'll do."

I shake my head. "Who, Rosamund?"

"My cousin," she says. "Neklaus. He's been asking for my hand since I was twelve. My uncle was so angry. When Berengar said he wouldn't have me, my uncle said Neklaus could."

I know that name.

"The guard?" I say. "The pretty one?" I remember dark blond hair and blue eyes, and the way he spat at Aisulu as she showed him her pass.

Rosamund's eyes are wide. "You've seen him?"

I nod.

"Does he know you're here?"

"No," I say. "We met him on the road from Merzen to Vellsberg. He din't know who we were."

"He knows now," Rosamund says, her face white. "If he finds out I helped you . . ."

Everythin I felt before has fallen away. I look into her eyes, an I see somethin familiar.

I reach across the table, an take her hand.

"He's hurt you," I say. "Over an over, am I right?"

She draws back from me. "How?"

Is this what I was like? I wonder. *I thought no one could possibly know. Cos it's meant to be unthinkable. An all the while we're marked clear as branded livestock to those who look for it.*

"My uncle," I say, "was not a good man."

We hold each other's gaze, her hand lyin in mine.

"My uncle's . . . hard," she says. "But my cousin is a monster. He'll walk over corpses to get to you. You must run as far and as fast as you can."

We sit together silently in that beautiful room. Next door we hear the murmur of voices.

"Thank you," I say. "You warned me, even though I caused you pain." I squeeze her hand. "I really am sorry."

"Me too," she says.

"Gisla can protect you?"

She nods. "Even Neklaus won't risk offending the noble houses whose daughters are under her rule by trying to take me from there. I'll take my first vows as soon as possible. I'll pass beyond his reach."

"But doesn't that mean you'll never marry?"

She pulls back her hand an fusses wi the cloth coverin her hair, tuckin gold-brown strands under it.

"I know you hated the idea so much you staged a massacre and ran," she says, half-smilin. "But women in my family have always considered the church at least as good as a husband. Believe me,

I'd rather this than what my own mother has."

I can't fault her on that. "Somethin else we have in common," I say. "If I see Berengar again, I'll be givin him a piece of my mind for all he put you through."

Rosamund gives me that small smile again. "I feel sorry for him already," she says. "And Ebba, the betrothal . . . Theogault and my uncle arranged it while he was away. Berengar didn't know. When he realised what he'd done by telling them about you, he was frantic."

The doors open. Gisla an Varkha return, Gisla's arms loaded wi small, expensive-lookin packages. Gisla gives me a haughty glare, an sweeps Rosamund away before I can make my mouth work again.

Varkha glances across at me. "Aren't you going to drink the *mulsum*?" she asks. "It's not cheap, you know. You only got some because they did."

Berengar din't know.

"The cardamom alone costs more gold than you've ever seen in your life," Varkha's sayin. "What do you want?"

A young Qesar boy has stuck his head through the door. "The young lord from Vellsberg called for the ladies," he says, "but I see they're gone."

"What?" I say. "Vellsberg?"

"Ebba!"

But I'm already swingin myself over the counter. I'm over and out the door before she can catch me.

Berengar din't know. He was stupid to tell Lord Theogault an Rosamund's family about Grimulf, but of course he'd know that at once. He'd try to find a way to make it right.

The thought spurs me through a high-ceilinged hall an across a garden with a white stone path an a sunken pool in the centre. A pointless garden, nothin for eatin or healin, just like the hall would never keep the heat in durin the winter – these things are the face the Qesar show to their Southern customers, their own ideas of riches mirrored back to em.

The thick stone walls of the Concession stand ahead of me, an a curtained carryin chair is just disappearin through the heavily guarded gateway.

"Wait!" I shout. "Berengar!"

A blond head looks up, and bright blue eyes set in an unusually handsome face fix on me. I stumble to a halt. My heart squeezes.

Neklaus of Merzen smiles at me as the Concession gates swing closed.

Thirteen
EXILE

Qesar Concession, Lughambar

t first I'm scared of what might happen if I sleep, but the practice-form in the yard warms and works my body, until by the time we've eaten and I've visited Hero in the stable, I feel so sleepy I don't care anymore. Aisulu helps me into the sling of cloth, and I sway and slip off into a dreamless sleep.

I wake late again, the slings around me empty. I feel rested. *Whole.*

I hear the river, and noise from the yard, and then the shout that marks the start of practice. I climb out of the sling, splash my face with water from the bowl near the door, and hurry to join in at the back. The Qesar around me smirk, but I get the feeling it's just the welcome any latecomer would get. I try to follow the practice, even though my body is still stiff, and I only know some of the moves.

I find Aisulu for breakfast, and we eat in companionable

silence, both of us tired. Kizmid commandeers us to help her in the warehouse. She keeps us busy until noon. As we eat, another ship docks. The captain, sporting the same thick blue braid at his hip that Kizmid wears, greets the men and women seated at the long tables, but I can see this is a supply stop, not the end of the voyage.

After we finish, we help unload. Bales come off, barrels and food go on. The small crew show no curiosity towards me. In the quilted jacket and comfortable britches, maybe I'm just another Qesar, unusual but not unexpected. Kizmid swings a bale onto her shoulder, and laughs when I try to do the same and stagger.

"Keep it low," she says. "You're built like a tentpole, not a packhorse."

I watch Aisulu's muscles tense as she takes the weight of the load on her back. The spring sun warms me through like the steam bath.

We're almost done when there's a movement by the doorway to the sleeping quarters. Varkha comes out, her richly embroidered clothes standing brightly out of place among the faded workclothes of the Qesar in the yard. Her left hand is wrapped around Ebba's forearm. She's not quite dragging her, but Ebba stumbles as she pulls her into the light and across the yard.

Varkha snaps something in Qesar to the people nearest her, and they turn back to work.

"Uh-oh," breathes Aisulu next to me.

Varkha stops in front of us.

"You two must go," she says. "I made it clear what I expected of you when you arrived, and your friend has chosen to ignore me. She's put us all at risk. The Lughambar Concession can't shelter you."

"What happened?" I ask, looking between her and Ebba.

Ebba meets my eyes, but she looks dazed.

"She crossed the *dzarnyn*," Varkha snaps, "and she was seen by the very person who's hunting you." She glares at Aisulu. "He'll go straight to the House of Lughambar, and now I will have to beg and scrape and lower our fees to put right the damage she's done to us. The *dzarnyn* is there for a reason."

"To keep what's outside out, and what's inside in," murmurs Aisulu, "but Varkha—"

"Don't," Varkha says. "Aisulu, you brought them here. You promised me they'd obey. I can't believe you were so reckless on account of two strays. But that's Carriers all over. Off on your own, never thinking about those of us who rely on the good will of our hosts."

Aisulu takes it, to my surprise. She bows her head and lets Varkha's anger stream over her.

"I'm sorry," she says when Varkha quiets. "I made a mistake."

I look at her, mouth open. Kizmid stifles what I think might be a snort.

Varkha says something to the captain of the ship we've been loading. He barely glances at us as he answers. Aisulu's face is still lowered, so I can't see her reaction.

"That's settled," Varkha says. "The ship leaves before dawn. I can stall for a day. They'll take you back north, where you belong."

Varkha strides out of the yard, as angrily as she swept in. The whole thing has taken less than two minutes.

"What does she mean, north?" I ask.

Kizmid hoicks a bale up to her shoulder. "They're headed to the coast," she says.

"Near the mouth of the Vell?"

"No," she says, "the Samara runs north west. You'll end up on the western coast."

Aisulu shakes her head. "And here I thought you were the difficult one," she says to me. "For a short girl you get in a lot of trouble, Ebba."

Ebba's eyes are bright, but she sniffs the tears back. "Sorry," she mutters. "I was stupid."

"Well," Aisulu says, "we haven't got as much time as I thought. You'd better meet Serke."

We fall in behind her, more out of shock than anything.

"Why'd you do it?" I ask Ebba. It's the first time I've spoken to her since yesterday.

"I thought it was Berengar," she says. "But it was that soldier we met on the road."

"Him? What's he doing here?"

In an undertone, Ebba tells me what the Merzen girl told her. I remember the way the blond guard looked at me, but mostly I'm thinking, *you risked all of this for a boy who nearly had you locked away?*

"So when you were rushing out to see the Vellsberg boy, was it to black his eye?" Aisulu asks over her shoulder. Ebba and I jump.

"No," Ebba mumbles.

I can almost feel Aisulu's eye-roll, even though she has her back to us. It needles me how quickly Ebba threw everything away at the thought of Berengar, but I bite back my own anger.

Aisulu leads us through the living quarters and out into the kitchen garden. There she turns left down a stepping-stone path to the corner of the building. The evening is coming on, but even in the fading light I can see that the herbs aren't the familiar kinds. Ebba turns her head as she walks, taking note despite everything.

Light spills out of a door at the end of the stone path.

"I brought you visitors," Aisulu says as she steps through the open door ahead of us.

The answer comes in another tongue, light and lilting.

I step under the stone lintel and stop so abruptly that Ebba walks into me.

Serke stands her workroom, an ochre dress wrapped across her flat chest, black curls tumbling over straight shoulders. Her brown eyes are rimmed with black, her plum-coloured lips widen in a smile, and she stretches out open arms to us. Her hands are long and narrow, and the tip of each finger is dyed a dark honey red.

"Welcome," she says in Southern, and I should be pleased that I understood it, except I'm too busy realising that this woman has a man's body.

She looks me in the eye and her smile deepens, like she knows me. The air around her smells of summer forests and shady flowers.

Then her eyes fall on Ebba, and she exclaims something in Southern that I definitely don't understand.

"The tall one only speaks Rus," Aisulu says, jerking her thumb at me.

"Oh dear," Serke smiles. "I will try. These are your guests Varkha is upset about? You are far from home," she says to Ebba.

Ebba is staring at her.

"You're like me," she says.

"Ebba's from the north," Aisulu says.

Serke tilts her head at an angle, a question in her eyes. "Is Ebba a Rus name?" she says.

"Abda," Ebba whispers. "Ma called me Abda."

It's the first I've heard of it.

"And your mother?"

"Roshna."

Serke's smile breaks wide open. "Abda *haca* Roshna," she says. "*Sta hada siyati.*"

"I don't know what that means," Ebba says.

Serke steps forward and takes both Ebba's hands in hers.

"Welcome," she says.

She gestures us to seats on benches along one side of a wooden table. She stands on the other, moving from hearth to shelf, reaching up for the herbs hanging drying from hooks in the ceiling.

"Your garden's special," Ebba says. "I en't recognised half the plants we passed. There are ones I'd bet en't from the Empire either."

Serke's face is wreathed in smiles. "You have some plants up north that would surprise me," she says. "This is the most north I've been. I've heard of lichens that grow in the cold lands that stop bleeding."

"Oh," Ebba says, "I've some in my pack. Only dried, mind, fresh is best, but I din't know I'd be gone this long. I've mainly balms an tinctures, not the herbs themselves."

Serke's eyes are alight. "You're a healer?"

"My Ma is," Ebba says. "I learnt some from her . . ."

"Could I see? I could show you some things of mine too."

Ebba's cheeks are flushed with excitement. "I'll need to get my cure bag."

"We'll get it," Aisulu says, rising from the bench, her hand on my shoulder. "That tea will take a few minutes, right?"

Two pairs of bright brown eyes turn to us.

"Yes!" they say together, and laugh.

I rise to follow Aisulu. By the time I'm through the door the two of them are already examining a bunch of dried leaves, their heads close over the table.

"I didn't know Ebba had another name," Aisulu remarks as we walk back through the garden.

Neither did I, I think, but I don't want to tell her that.

The last light softens stone, wood, and leaves to a blue-grey.

"I thought Serke would be Qesar," I say.

"She is," Aisulu says. "And she's Stahranid. Can't people be two things at once in the North?"

Her tone tells me she's joking, but thinking about it, I realise the answer's no. Not really. Look at Ebba. She was always an outlander.

"We don't travel much," I say.

"We'll have to start calling you the Homebody Rus, so that people don't confuse you with the sea-going bastards that get everywhere," Aisulu says. "Being Qesar means being lots of things at the same time. Serke fits in well."

"She's a man," I say.

"Is she?" Aisulu says.

"There's no one like Serke back home," I say.

"Isn't there?"

I don't answer her. Truth is, Serke shakes me in ways I could never have expected. There's something familiar about her, though I'm sure I've never seen anyone like her in my life.

We pass rooms where scribes have left their accounts for the day.

"Serke is Qesar because we took her lands from the Stahranids," Aisulu says, "but before that, the Stahranids conquered them and added them to their empire. Who knows, if the Sister-Queens can repair the damage done by their mad brother, maybe they'll take them back. What?"

I've stopped dead.

"There's *another* empire?" I ask.

Aisulu smiles crookedly. "Oh, Torny," she says. "The world is much bigger than you imagine."

A shiver runs through me, the cold breath of memory on my nape.

But of what? There's nothing but dread and rising mist.

We pass silently into the dimness of the sleeping quarters. It's empty, and through the outer door I can hear the workers in the yard, the thud of their feet as they move through the practice-form, the cries of the leader marking the moves. I find the poles where our markers hang, and sling Ebba's small leather pack across my shoulder. Aisulu waits for me, outlined against the inner door. The shadows hide her face.

The gurgle of the river beside the wooden wall drags my thoughts to the boat, to the current tugging me downriver, back to everything I ruined.

"I can't go back," I say. "Don't make me."

I hate how childish I sound, how frightened.

Aisulu comes to me, puts her hand on my arm.

"Can't you tell?" she asks. "I'm giving you every reason I can think of to come with me."

And then, in the dark, she kisses me.

It's so quick, I don't have time to react. She steps forward, presses her lips on mine, a little to the side in the gloom. But already I see dark figures in the doorway behind her, glints of gold at their throats, and something is wrong, all of it is wrong.

There should only be one key.

I freeze, and she feels it. Then she's stepping away from me, and I know I've ruined this too.

"Aisulu," I say, but she turns and strides through the doorway where now I see no one, no dark figures, no glint of gold. Only her retreating shoulders, her dancing braid.

I lean against the pole, Ebba's pack still clasped in one hand, and touch the left-hand corner of my lips with the other. My lips feel cracked against my fingertips, rough, and I wish suddenly that I knew whatever secrets Serke does, with her plum-coloured mouth and her sparkling eyes. I want to be like her, to have that grace, that confidence. There must be a way to learn what would turn a single kiss from a lost thing that died the instant it was born into a long-lived certainty.

I catch Aisulu in the garden, on the stepping stones leading to Serke's well-lit door. The night is cold, and my skin's all risen in goosebumps.

She keeps her face turned from me, so I catch her wrist in my free hand.

"I'll come," I say. "There's nothing for me there. Let me come."

Her face is half-lit by light falling through the unshuttered window, and I see something in it, something that's washed away like tracks in the sand under a wave. I think it was fear.

"All right," she says. "I'll talk to Kizmid. You'd better give Ebba her things."

She leaves without looking at me.

I stand in the doorway for a moment, shaken. Serke and Ebba stand side by side now, plants spread across the worktop under two hanging lamps, faces turned down, brown forearms warm in the golden light as they reach across one another, pointing and examining each withered treasure. Despite Serke's lean height and Ebba's short, rounded figure, I feel as though I'm seeing double. Ebba's not by herself anymore, and that makes me jealous, as jealous as I ever was of Berengar. She and I shared something he couldn't, even when they touched or kissed. Now, watching Ebba smile as she repeats the names of herbs in an unknown tongue, I feel more alone that I did when she and Berengar were together. I wonder if that tongue is the same one her secret name comes from, and what else we never said to one another.

I thought she was my world.

But the world is bigger than I knew. I cling to that, to whoever told me that first, though at the time I didn't listen.

It has to be. Otherwise I will never be free.

Ebba looks up, laughing.

"Torny," she says, "come here. I want to show you something."

Serke straightens and smiles. A gold filament rests in the hollow at the base of her throat, and I remember who else used to smile at me, when there was no call for smiling, because he knew the world was wide and large, whatever darkness called.

There is mist in the room now, coiling around me, eating up the edges, coming for my heart.

I fall to my knees, Ebba's bag clutched to me.

"Fenn," I say. There are waves crashing through everyone's faces. And I see the knife go in.

And I see the light go out.
It never ends, no matter what I do.

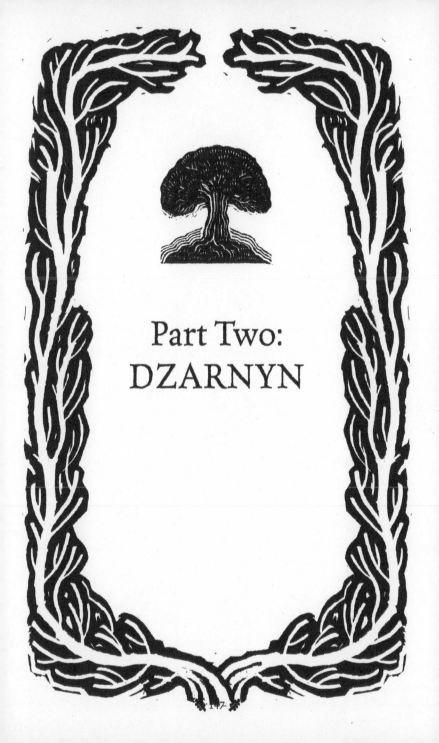

Part Two:
DZARNYN

"War against the Qesar was waged for seven years. Had it not been for the faithlessness of the Qesar, it could doubtless have been concluded sooner. Yearly they made humble submission to the Emperor, who yearly granted clemency. Yet soon enough some new affront to God was uncovered, some treason or murder, or devil worship among the springs and stones, so that the Emperor had to send his lords to take the field against them. These campaigns were known as the Westlands War, and thereafter the Emperor sternly reduced the freedoms of the Qesar within the Empire, requiring oaths of faithfulness and obedience, and remanding them to enclosed life within the Concessions."

From the *Annals of the Southern Empire*,
in the Vellsberg scriptorium

"All people of all nations are to be honoured
for their virtues, regardless of birth.
This is the first precept.

All people are at liberty to worship their gods,
so long as they obey the laws, honour the
Soul and the Breath, and pay their taxes.
This is the second precept."

From the *Iassax Law* of the Qesar Confederacy

Fourteen

DIVISION

❦

EBBA'S TALE

The Samara River

he thought of headin north again hadn't really sunk in, so when Aisulu stands grim-faced over Torny, lyin pale an cold in Serke's bed, an tells me she'd agreed to fly south wi Kizmid that night, I never think to refuse.

We hold conference there, in the curtained alcove that serves as Serke's sleeping quarters.

"My crew are used to leaving quickly," Kizmid says. "They'll do what I tell them."

"So long as we can get away without Varkha noticing, we'll be all right," Aisulu says. "She's too busy here to waste time chasing us, and however angry she is, she won't endanger an *uareh*. I'm more worried about her."

We look down at Torny. Serke sits beside her, one hand on Torny's wrist, countin her heartbeat. She looks up.

"You said she's done this before?" she asks. Kizmid and Aisulu nod.

"She's bin havin bad dreams since we left," I say. "I thought they'd get better, but they got worse. The last few days I sometimes couldn't wake her without hartshorn, an she had fits yesterday an the day before." I don't add that I'm the reason, but my face is burnin, an Serke looks at me keenly.

"Can you cure her?" Aisulu asks.

"Not easily," Serke says. "I'd need to know more about what started this. Even then, these things take time and preparation."

"You could come with us," Aisulu says, but Serke, glancin at Kizmid, shakes her head.

"*That* Varkha won't overlook," she says. "I'm beginning to see where your reputation for recklessness comes from, Aisulu of the Blue Wolf Clan."

Aisulu frowns, but lets it go. "I'll get more clothes for you," she says to me. "You'll pass easier in Qesar-wear. I'll come for you when it's time."

Kizmid and Aisulu leave us. Serke draws me over to her kitchen table. "We only have a few hours, Abda," she says. "Let's share what we can with each other. Show me your balms."

Unpackin the vials an boxes prepared wi Ma over the winter, I feel my resolve weakenin. I think of Ma back north, of everythin I din't ask her. I tole her I'd be back in the spring. But me an Torny have no silver, no passes, nothin that would take us beyond whatever port Varkha's boat left us at. An then what?

"Aisulu tells me Torny was some kind of warrior," Serke says.

"She had—I don't know the word," I say. "We call em Spirit Riders. Spirits that cling to a person, take em over. Make em do things. A powerful one took Torny."

"This Fenn?" Serke asks.

I shake my head. "He was a boy she knew. I know he died, but we never talked about it. The spirit that took her was ancient. More like a god."

Serke watches me, her head on one side.

"How did she free herself of this spirit?" she asks.

"I helped her," I say. "Me an her friend."

"That's a heavy healing," Serke says, her eyes narrow.

"It en't what you think," I say. "I had help."

"What did the spirit make her do?" Serke asks.

I've reached the bottom of my pack. I pull out a bone vial, stoppered wi black wax.

"She made people kill each other," I tell Serke, my eyes on the vial. "She killed as well, but I think that was the evil in it. The way she turned people. It was war. But she made it slaughter."

I hear the anger in my own voice.

Serke wraps her long, graceful fingers around mine.

"Slaughter is not inhuman," she says. "We wish it was, but we know it isn't. Do you wonder whether the slaughterer was your friend, not the spirit?"

I don't need to nod. She already knows my answer.

"I'm sure she wonders too," Serke says.

If I was expectin some kind of ruckus as we left, I was wrong. In the deepest part of the night, Kizmid comes for me. I hug Serke goodbye, an Kizmid hoists Torny in her arms. Serke kisses Kizmid's cheek an whispers to me, "Look after your friend, Abda. You both have burdens. Maybe now is a good time to ask for some help."

She don't know that freein the Harrower cost me every kind of help I had.

The lamps are all out, but I keep a hand on Kizmid's belt, an follow her through the dark. We take a route through the kitchen to avoid the sleeping quarters, an it's only as I climb into the boat that I remember Beyard an Hero. The Qesar prize horses, so I comfort myself they'll be well cared for, an that is how we leave the Qesar Concession in Lughambar.

Torny sleeps for three days, an by the time she wakes, we're well on our way south.

I en't at Torny's bedside when she wakes. Maybe I should of bin, but no, I'm on deck, watchin the hills pull slowly by. Travellin against the flow is long an hard, not what I had in mind when Aisulu first suggested flight. I soon worked out why Varkha wanted us sent north – the river flows down to the sea, an we'd of bin long gone from her doorstep in a day or two.

I hope Varkha had the sense to tell anyone who came lookin that was where we headed.

The Samara en't like the Vell, markin the boundary between Arngard an the south. Above Vellsberg, the Vell can't be used by boats, there's too many waterfalls an rocks. But the Samara is an old river, throwin its coils between the wooded hills. She's swollen wi the spring rains off the hills, though Kizmid says it's several spans lower'n it was when she an her crew made the journey down. Most people en't daft enough to try to travel upstream more'n a short way at this time of year, Kizmid says. Only the Qesar ships, the *uareh*, risk travel while the waters are still high.

I'm sittin by the tiller when I see Torny's white head rise above the low slanting roof of the space below deck. I've bin put on the tiller after two days of bein taught it, since everyone has to work on a Qesar ship. I call her, an she turns. She's holdin herself up on the lintel, but her cheeks are pink, an the darkness is gone from under her eyes. She walks up the steps to me.

"How're you feelin?" I ask.

She yawns, rollin her shoulders. "Better," she says, an hesitates. "What happened?"

"You had a fit," I say. "But Serke said you'd be all right. She tole us not to wake you."

Torny looks worried.

"You remember Serke, don't you?" I ask.

She nods, but she don't seem certain.

"Where's Aisulu?" she says, her eyes already movin over the dark heads below us as they lower like a wave over the oars.

That's it. Not a word about me, not how I am, nothin.

"Down there," I say, noddin to a bench towards the prow. "An Kizmid—"

"Rus!"

Kizmid's lookin back from the foredeck, her hand raised. Torny raises her hand in return. Down in the benches Aisulu's head bobs up, her eyes fixed on Torny, an it nettles me. She din't care one way or another about Torny before Durkno, but now . . .

"You well?" Kizmid calls.

"I'm fine," Torny calls back.

"Then get down in the benches," Kizmid says. "Be nice to her, children. It's not her fault she's broken!" She adds somethin in Qesar an her crew cackle.

Torny rolls her eyes and gets to her feet. "This is going to hurt, isn't it?" she mutters.

She don't even look back as she climbs down to where Aisulu sits.

That evenin we stop when the sky behind the hills turns red. Kizmid is on watch before we moor, her fingers playin over the blue braid of her rank at her hip. I'm sure she's lookin for landmarks; these moorins are known to her. They're sheltered, tucked up in smaller tributary streams or under riverside trees, away from other settlements. There are signs of firepits, an strewn in the grass or dirt I sometimes see cracked bones, leftovers of meals long past.

Mainly we eat fish. The river is large enough, an part of my job as tillerman is to check the trailin lines off the back of the *uareh*. When we dock I sit wi some of the crew an help gut what we caught, or knead dough for flatbreads to be cooked in the embers. Everyone takes turns cookin, an their hands flash silver wi their small sharp knives an scales from the fish while they talk. Qesar tongue is different again from Southern or the Kirk-speak I had to learn for the prester, an I give up much hope of followin. It seems speakin the Northern tongue is something the Carriers an Negotiators learn, but not the river crews or the Concession workers.

"So why d'you speak it?" I ask Kizmid, an she gives me one of her wolfish grins.

"Rivers run north where I'm from, girl," she says. "You think the Rus stick to the Iron Sea when they go raidin? They come up the rivers too, if the towns upstream are rich enough."

"Do they raid the Samara?" Torny asks. She's across from me, dabbin a cleanin oil I got from Serke on her open blisters. When they dry a little we'll put salve on em an bind em over so's she can go back on the oar tomorrow.

Kizmid an Aisulu share a look.

"Not for a long time," Kizmid says. "But Aisulu told me their northern hunting grounds have been taken and ships under the Emperor's banner now protect cargos in the Iron Sea. I don't think these folk realise what this will do."

"What d'you mean?" I say.

"The Rus have been pushed out," Kizmid says. "But without their raiding, their people starve. They won't stop. They'll just move. I don't think Lughambar is ready for what might come up the Samara this summer."

I feel sick. *I* know. I've spent my life seein it, year after year.

An I'm the reason they're comin.

"Will the Concession be all right?" Torny asks.

Again, that look between Aisulu an Kizmid.

"The Concession will be fine," Kizmid says, gettin up, an it's clear that's the end of that.

Torny gets quiet, an Aisulu nudges her.

"I told you," she says. "Hero will be treated well. You think horse-breeders would waste the chance to add her strength to their foals?"

"I know," Torny says, bent over her blisters.

So they've bin talkin about leavin the horses. I meant to say somethin myself when Torny woke, but I din't get the chance.

"I know it's hard," I say. "I miss Fetch, too. I missed him so much on our way to Vellsberg."

"Who's Fetch?" Aisulu asks.

"A hound," I say. "I had to leave him when we rode south."

Aisulu gives me a look full of disapproval. "You left your hound? How could you?"

"You left your horse," I say, stung.

"Horses are different," Aisulu says. "Horses belong to each other. Hounds belong to us."

Torny mutters somethin about needin cloth for her hands, an me an Aisulu are left glarin at each other.

"I'll help," Aisulu says, gettin up an followin her into the dark.

I throw the fish guts into the fire, pass the cleaned fish along to be cooked, an go to the river's edge to wash my hands in the basin of water taken for that purpose. The Qesar believe dirtyin water is a defilement, so they take water from the river wi prayers, an wash what they must over the earth. I avoid the moored *uareh*, where Aisulu is right now probably "helpin" Torny, an take myself back to the fire where the talk is in a tongue I can't understand, an even busy hands can't make me feel part of somethin I en't.

The next day it rains.

We're all too wet, cold an bad-tempered to speak. The rowers don't sing, the oars get out of rhythm, an I catch the tiller on a submerged mess of branches, an nearly break it tryin to wriggle it free. I know Torny must be sore all over from her first day at the oar, but we barely look at each other. I give her the oils to clean her open blisters an toughen her hands. The fire takes too long to light an the smoke chokes us when it does.

When Kizmid orders me to come check cargo below deck with her, I'm just glad to get out of the rain.

The space below deck is low an cramped. Hooks on the wall allow hammocks to be strung up, an thin panels can be slotted into place to cut the space into rooms. Kizmid slides away one of the panels, an shows me a neatly stashed wall of barrels. She shows me how to check the knots on the cords bindin em in place.

"What's inside?" I ask.

"Never you mind," she says, her back to me as she crouches in the low space. She opens a chest an starts checkin the contents. "I didn't bring you down here so you could nose about. We've got more important things to talk about."

She's speakin Northern, maybe so's the crew can't eavesdrop.

"Serke trusted you, Ebba, and that's good enough for me. And Aisulu wants your friend with her, that's clear, and if she keeps her head down and rows with the others, I won't complain. But this running, it won't do you any good without a plan. Do you know where you're going?"

The future opens up ahead of me, blank an bleak.

"No," I say.

Kizmid growls to herself, a gruff *Hmmfff.*

"I thought you'd be headed back into Qesar lands," I say. "That's where you came from, en't it?"

"And what would you do there, girl?" she says, not unkindly. "You don't speak the tongue, you don't know our ways. You've got no family to sponsor you, no clan ties. Don't get me wrong, the Confederacy will have you. We take anyone who'll swear to the law. But I tell you now, if you're not descended from the Three Clans like Aisulu, you need ties. You're nothing without them."

"Serke welcomed me," I say. "Maybe—"

"Maybe you'll go to the Stahranids?" she says, finishin my thought for me. "The Sister-Queens are still rebuilding after plague and war. You may look like you belong, but what have you got of them beyond your name?"

I focus on the knots under my fingers, tryin not to cry.

"You've got ties back north, haven't you?" Kizmid asks.

I think of Ma an cousin Rafe, Fetch, even Captain Erland, who promised to take care of my people while he oversees Eldinghope.

I do. I might be an outlander, but I'm outlander here, too.

"We can't go back," I say. "There's a hunt between us an home."

"There's more than that, Aisulu tells me," Kizmid says. When I don't answer, she says, "Torny told her why the Rus are headed south this year. Your home—"

"It en't my home anymore," I say, before she can talk about why Arngard wanted the Rus barred from Eldinghope. My fingers tug on knot after knot, seekin out weakness.

"Normally, you'd be right," she says, as if the talk between never happened. "Normally, I'd head east. But Aisulu's asked me to take her south. To Ban Granis."

The name's familiar. Berengar tole me about this.

"That's where the Emperor goes in summer, en't?"

Kizmid nods. "The summer court is where the important pleas are heard, so long as the Empire isn't at war," she says. "The ruling families of the *Regna* and the *Limina* come to lay tributes and pleas before the Emperor. Delegations from neighbouring kingdoms come too."

"So there'll be Qesar delegates?" I ask, wonderin what Aisulu's interest is.

Kizmid looks at me oddly, like I'm missin the point.

"Oh," I say. "The *Limina*. Arngard'll send delegates." I remember the similarity I noticed between King Kolrand, the one time I saw him, an Torny, an my hand flies to my mouth. "Not the king?"

"No," Kizmid says. "Rulers don't like leaving their thrones empty, but they send trusted people to negotiate on their behalf. And delegates have safe passage to and from the summer court. No one is allowed to waylay them."

One of the knots under my fingers is loose, an I point it out to her. She reties the knot so deftly I can't follow her movements.

"You mean we could travel with em," I say. "I tole you, we wouldn't be welcome. Din't you listen?"

"If there's anyone who can bargain with merchants, it's us," Kizmid says. "They'll take you gladly once the Qesar have worked on them, I'd bet. Once you're with them, no one could touch you, especially not some jumped up guard from the *Regna*."

I flinch when she says touch, I en't sure why. This whole talk is rubbin me up the wrong way. It's not like Torny an I have a choice – we threw our lot in with Aisulu an now we're with her, like it or not. Torny clearly does like it, an I can't part ways wi Torny, so why is Kizmid talkin to me like this, like I might just step off the ship an continue on my way alone?

Unless she thinks I might.

Unless that would be a problem for em.

I think about it as I gut fish an knead dough, as the smoke gets in my eyes an the white flesh under the blackened skin burns my tongue as I eat. The wet makes the fire smoke more, an I move away from it. Standin under a tree, hearin the rain comin down an splutter against the flames, I watch Torny's white curls gleam beside Aisulu's dark head.

I en't stupid. I know what this is.

Torny don't need me anymore.

I feel it when we go to sleep, our bedrolls under a canvas stretched across the oar pits, the benches moved, Torny an Aisulu's squeezed together in the place where their bench usually stands. I feel it when I wake stiff, the damp seepin up from the hard deck. I feel it watchin em in the mornins, Torny takin her place wi the others as Kizmid or another member of the crew leads em through the practice-form to warm em up for rowin.

I overhear Aisulu explainin that there are different forms for different skills – stance-forms for empty-handed blocks an blows, blade-forms for swords an daggers, staff-form, bow-form – an different clans have different forms, so the crew take turns teachin each other the ones they know. Torny's lost at first, stiff from the oar, but she learns. I see it. Every evenin she practises with Aisulu, an every mornin she's a little more sure of herself. I see her muscles build in her shoulders an back. They stand out against the bone when she heaves back on her oar, her bound hands callused now, no longer bleedin, no longer needin my salve.

Of course we talk. You can't live on a *uareh* an not cross each other a dozen times a day, even if that day is mostly spent in the benches or by the tiller. We just don't say anythin important. An it's not like we're fightin. Torny passes me food, tries to tell me the rowing songs Aisulu translates for her as they sit in the benches. But other things are gone. I don't catch her lookin at me. When we sit side by side there's no taut thread between us anymore. If our fingers brush against each other, she barely notices. We're normal together, which is what I wanted.

An every evenin, she an Aisulu stand in the dusk, an Torny watches her like a hawk, like a hound, tryin to learn to move like her, to be her.

One night, the first dry night in a long time, I'm lyin in the prow. The crew are on the shore, sittin round the fire, but there's warmth in the air, even though it's dark. Sweet air is flowin out of the south, an I want to taste it. I'm lookin up, a blanket round me, watchin stars appear.

The steps creak as Torny joins me.

"Ebba?"

I turn my head a little, lettin her know I hear her.

"What do you do?" she says in laboured Southern, layin herself down beside me.

"That's not bad," I say.

"Aisulu's making me learn," she says. "So?"

"Countin stars," I say, "but I lost count."

She looks up. "I can never remember them," she says.

The Stag an the Hart twist their necks above us, the Squirrel sits waitin. I know em easily, just as I know the plants in Ma's garden, from years of her showin me. The Shepherd slipped away below the horizon as we left Arngard, an wi the new warm nights I know the Dancer will be risin soon, though it's early yet.

"Did no one teach you?" I ask.

I feel Torny's shrug. "Brenna didn't care about stars," she says, namin her foster-mother for the first time in so long it shakes me. She din't name her much back when we were in Frithberg together, before any of this began, when she still thought she was Brenna's daughter. After we fled south, she tole me she'd found out her aunt, Vigdis, was her true mother when she was back in Gullcroft, but that was all.

Now I try again: "What about Vigdis?"

Torny falls still beside me.

"She tried to teach me a lot of things," she says finally. "But it seems I was only ever good at one of them."

She's talkin about the Harrower. My face flushes in the dark as I remember Durkno. But I also remember Serke askin about Fenn, an how I had no answer. An now it strikes me the same thing is true of Vigdis. I know she's dead, but I don't know how.

"Torny," I say, an I can feel her pull away even at that. "We never really talked about what happened last winter. Maybe we should."

She lies silent a long time before she answers.

"I don't want to," she says.

"But so *much* happened," I say. "I've tole you my part of it."

"Have you?" she says.

"Of course," I say, surprised by her tone.

"You've told me about your family," Torny says. "You've told me about your uncle dying, and taking your mother and brother away from Eldinghope, and your cousin Rafe following you to Frithberg for the fight. And you wouldn't shut up about Berengar, and how he was teaching you to read and write." Her words sting like a slap. "But you never told me about the Prester."

I feel myself recoil.

"I did," I say. More'n anythin I want to leave him behind me, lyin cold and harmless in the blackened embers of the kirk at Frithberg, but it's no use. I feel his pursuit of me, still. I feel him stridin through the blood-splattered hall at Vellsberg, echoin in the voices of Vindhaff, his hand heavy on me, holdin me in the fire at Durkno.

"No," Torny says, "you didn't."

We're still lyin shoulder to shoulder, but there's a distance between us now. Lookin up I see the stars are covered wi raggedy clouds come up from the hills.

"Are you still angry about Berengar?" I say.

"Of course I am!" Torny snaps. "How could you be so stupid? We were safe at the Concession, and you threw that away!"

"No," I say, "I mean—are you angry I loved him?"

"Oh," Torny says, the wind goin out of her. "No. It's just—"

"What?"

She rolls onto her side to face me, though in the dark there en't much to see.

"I wanted to be with you so much," she says, an I can tell what it costs her to say it. "But in the end, it's been nothing like how I thought it would be. I thought all I needed to be happy was you. But that's just what I told myself when I was so lonely I thought just seeing you again would make me better."

It hurts my heart that it din't work. But I also know what she's feelin. I felt it too.

"You know that pin you left me?" I say. "The whalebone one."

Torny's quiet, but she nods. I roll over to face her.

"It was all I had of you," I tell her. "When I felt weak, it reminded me what you're like. Strong. Unafraid."

But my words en't workin. As I speak, Torny curls herself up, covers her face with her hands.

"I'm none of those things," she whispers.

"Yes," I say, an I put my hand on her shoulder. "You're all of em."

She's quiet for a long time.

"Ebba?" she says finally. Her voice is breathy, like she's bin winded.

"Yes?"

"Can I kiss you?"

I gulp. I don't mean to, but suddenly swallowin seems hard. I think about how I felt wi Berengar, or how I used to imagine it might be wi Jarle, back in Frithberg. This en't anything like that. But I also think about the warmth of her as we slept back to back, an more, further back, to Frithberg, an the way she fought for me. The way I held that carved piece of whalebone in my fist an knew what strength was, all cos of her.

"Yes," I say.

Her cold fingertips find the curve of my cheek, running down past my ear an slidin under my hair to stroke my neck. She breathes out, an I smell the woodsmoke on our clothes, the sweat of her skin mixed wi the scent of river water. Her hand cups the nape of my neck an she moves towards me carefully, like she's takin aim, tryin not to miss.

When her lips touch mine, I'm waitin for it – for light, for dark, for an answer. I want this to be the moment I understand. The thing that will fill me up, give me back what I've lost.

But that don't happen. Our lips are strangely still, both of us waitin for somethin else. I feel her falter, an I panic. I press my lips against hers, trying to be sure, but she pulls back, her hand movin to my shoulder, where it lies awkwardly.

"Are you all right?" I ask.

She nods.

"D'you want to try again?" I hear myself ask, and part of me curls up inside myself with embarrassment.

"No," she says. "I—I just wanted to be sure. I needed to know."

"Oh," I say. "Sure?"

"Sure that it's gone," she says, takin her hand from my shoulder.

"Oh. Is it?"

"Yes," she says. "I know what to do now." She's getting up, the deck creakin under her. "I'll see you later," she says, and the *uareh* sways beneath her as she jumps down to the oar pits an across the walkway to the bank.

I sit up in the prow an gingerly touch my fingers to my lips, the same way you check a scratch or a sting. But there's no pain, just a kind of numbness.

Out around the fire, voices rise in a song as hands beat time. Ragged at first, then comin together, they soar an drop, an lookin over I see Torny's white head, tucked in close to Aisulu's through the dancin flames.

It's only then I realise she avoided my most important question.

After that night, the weather gets better. The skies stay clear, the air warms, an the green edgin on the trees grows into itself, clothin the slopes an the fields as we slide through em day after day. The moon is nearly new again too, like it was in Durkno.

Torny barely looks at me again after that night. I steer around her like I might a barrage of dead wood, slow an careful, no sudden moves. I don't want her to know that I can feel myself fadin from her eyes.

One warm spring evening, Aisulu comes up to me as I'm repackin my cure bag.

"We'll be leaving the Samara tomorrow," she says. "The town of Gallucia is less than a day upstream from here. The *uareh* will be transported overland to the Arauris river by the Gallucian tollsmen. You, Torny and I will be leaving tonight."

"Why?" I say, foldin bandage cloth between the stoppered bone vials.

"We have to assume you're being hunted," she says. "The river will be watched, and any Qesar will be under suspicion. We'll hike overland and meet Kizmid downstream. It's going to be a fast march, so prepare yourself. Don't leave anything you don't want searched."

I put my hand on my cure bag, thinkin of the vials sealed up wi black wax.

"Where does the Ara—"

"Arauris."

"—take us?"

Aisulu smiles. "All the way to Ban Granis," she says. "Downstream, too. No more fucking rowing. We'll be there before the full moon."

Fifteen
PEAK

TORNY'S TALE

Between the Samara and the Arauris rivers

hen I think back I can't recall the days. They melt together, bound by effort, the full-body ache of rowing, the tightness when I pull a muscle in my shoulder or back, the bite of healing blisters on my palms. And always, shoulder to shoulder, thigh to thigh, Aisulu on the bench beside me, between the world and me. I get to know the unwashed scalp of the rower in front of me, the sting of drizzle and rain, the hoarse words of a song to keep us in time. I'm surprised when Aisulu tells me the meanings of the songs.

"They're all love songs," she says one night, handing a bowl of soup to me by the fire. "Abandoned lovers riding off with their hawk or hound to find their beloved, mostly."

"Do they find them?" I ask.

"Always," she says. "Sometimes too late. But some have happy endings."

"So the song ends when they find each other?"

Aisulu smiles. "There's no song if they're together," she says.

When I think back, it's as if I'm in a long tunnel. Behind me is a black room, and before me a point of light, and as I climb up through the dark earth, my body grows warm, until the chill is only in the deepest parts of me. I sometimes feel it in the middle of night, when a voice whispers to me all my faults, but I press my back against Aisulu's, and she warms me.

Then comes the new moon. We're rowing between the wooded foothills of a much more mountainous range than any we've seen before, when one afternoon Kizmid orders us over to the bank. Aisulu gets up, pulling me with her, and beckons Ebba from the stern.

When we're ashore, she hands Ebba and me our old clothes, the ones that we wore on the ride to Lughambar. Aisulu and I change quickly in front of the *uareh*, although Ebba goes a bit further away, out of sight of the crew, leaving her cure bag by a sail-cloth pack at Aisulu's feet. She needn't have bothered. The crew are busy anyway, Kizmid resetting them to fill the gap Aisulu and I have left. Aisulu bends over the packs, stowing food and her weapons. I see her placing a small parcel in Ebba's cure bag.

"More bandages," she says.

Once we're done, we toss our Qesar clothes back aboard. Kizmid salutes us with one hand, the other resting easily on her captain's braid, and the *uareh* pulls away.

Now that Aisulu's dressed like me, in britches, shirt and cloak, we look like three locals, so long as no one gets close enough to look at us. The breeze is cool, and already I miss the comfort of my quilted Qesar jacket. Aisulu shoulders her pack.

"Ready?" she says. "We've got to get to the top before nightfall."

After weeks of rowing, my legs are unhappy to be climbing the steep wooded slopes. The going is slow. We follow game tracks, but sometimes these pass places that human feet can't go, and we have to double back and find another path. The woods are a mix of trees coming into bloom. Red-furred squirrels slither down trunks or bound across branches, and everywhere birds are trilling and crying, a cacophony I hadn't noticed except at dawn from the river. Instead of water, I smell loam and moss. The richness seems completely new; I must have breathed them in before, but, if so, I can't remember how or when. The air is so clean I can't help gulping it like fresh snowmelt.

Slowly, the forest starts to thin. The light is slanting through the branches now, which means we're heading towards evening with no sign of the summit. But Aisulu doesn't seem bothered. We don't talk, but she walks easily, her thumbs hooked in the straps of her pack, as though we have all the time in the world.

The sun slants lower, the old leaves rustle beneath our feet, and then we reach the edge of the treeline.

We stop, and beside me Ebba gasps.

The mountains in Arngard are bald above the treeline. The earth is blasted, the rock bare. I briefly remember scree and silver tarns, before a door in my mind snaps shut.

For a moment I wonder if I'm seeing things.

Before us the mountainside dips, cupping a lake. The grass around it is greener than the summer sea, and the banks are studded with hundreds of flowers: blue, white, yellow and red. The lake reflects the blue sky and the white-topped peak that flows towards it up into the air, like an inverted waterfall. I get dizzy, tipping my head back to stare at it.

I shake myself, looking back down to the lake. Ebba's already half-running towards it, shouting something I can't hear.

Aisulu smirks at me.

"You knew this was here!" I say.

"Your face," she says, shaking her head. "I knew you were barbarians, but come on."

I punch her on the shoulder.

"This is the most beautiful place I've ever seen," I say.

She just smiles and steps out onto the grass.

That was the tipping point. Although the lake looked north, back towards the vanished lands of winter, that was the step that took me into the south.

One day at the oar, Aisulu taught me the word "watershed," although I already knew its meaning. The line that divides the flow of rivers, where standing water must go one way or another. Just like us.

The land by the lake is marshy, so we sleep on a ledge above it, close to one of the streams that tumbles down the sides of the peak into the soft green basin below. We eat our cold ashbreads and jerky early, watching the sun slip west. We don't light a fire, just wrap ourselves up and lie back looking at the sky, our hoods over our hair. The stars bloom like flowers.

I wake in the middle of the moonless night as if called. At my side, Aisulu's roll is empty.

I feel groggy, but I struggle upright.

I look upwards. The slope above is black and featureless against the night sky, but I think I hear a voice. I shake off my sleep and start to climb, using my hands to keep my balance in the dark.

There's a goat trail running up beside the stream and as my eyes adjust I can make out the rocks and grass to either side. The voice is above me, waning as the night air steals it, but it's Aisulu, I know.

I reach a place where the ground is flat underfoot, and there, on the grass below the white-capped peak, Aisulu is kneeling, facing away from me. The stars blaze overhead as she raises her hands with something in them, then lowers whatever it is to her face and tips her head back. Her voice is not quite a chant, but there is a rhythm to what she's saying, well-worn, like she knows it by heart.

There is a name nestled in her words.

It's my name.

"*Tyr embal* Torny," she says. "*Bareg kanyn, Ai Nakota, Kaeueg, aed Gamligi uhsev. Bardzyr rettyn aja symyn k'uhy: aeza oud, anay'ha iblis mulk aezyn, aeza tyr embal* Torny."

She lowers her head all the way to the earth, presses herself down, then sits back on her haunches, reciting. She raises her hands again, and this time I see what she holds.

She lowers the knife, presses the flat of it to her forehead, and then pulls back her sleeve and makes a quick cut. I can't see the blood, only the flash of the blade. Then she raises the other object – a small water skin, I see now, and tips it over her wrist, washing the wound.

I'm close enough to catch a whiff. It hits the back of my throat and makes me flinch. It's the raw spirit, fire-sap. My memories are jumbled, but I remember Aisulu saying it was sacred wine. And I remember something else. The Qesar have signs, she said, to call things to them.

I can't help it. A shudder goes through me, chased by a cold fear

I need to kill as quickly as possible.

"Aisulu!"

She turns, twisting from the waist. "Torny?"

I take a step, and my legs are so stiff they nearly topple me.

"What are you doing?" I ask.

She rises. Her eyes are black pools in her strong face.

"Praying," she says, reaching for me. The sharp sting of the fire-sap is still on her breath.

I take a step back.

"In secret? In the dead of night? With a *knife*?"

Even in the gloom I see her lips twitch in a smile.

"Torny," she says. "How do you pray?"

"I don't!" I snap.

"But you did."

It isn't a question. Without wanting to, I see the tree rising, the animals strung up, the club coming down, feel the blood like warm summer rain on my face.

I have nothing to say. When she reaches for my hand, I let her take it. She pulls me down beside her.

"I'm praying to Ai Nakota," she says. "We call them the Wanderer. They're a very powerful god, particularly for protection. I was asking them to protect you."

My hand is still in her hand.

"I've never seen you pray before," I say.

"The treaty with the Emperor allows us to maintain Concessions and travel through his lands," she says. "But it does not give us freedom to worship. All of us here must recognise the White God in our oaths, and foreswear our own."

"I wondered why I never saw anything at the Concession," I say.

The night is cool, and I find myself sitting closer to her, shoulder to shoulder, thigh to thigh, like we're back at the oar.

I see the pale flash of her teeth. "Oh, it was there," she says. "We hide our secrets in plain sight, Torny. It's the safest way. Any hidden thing leaves a gap in the world that others are drawn to. Place something before their eyes and they forget to see it."

I look down at the knife and the small water skin where they lie on the grass.

"You mentioned a king and queen," I say.

"Taghr and Sarik," she says, as though speaking the names of friends. "The Daylit King and the Sunlit Queen. They rule the Celestial Realms, and the Realm of Living Waters where humans live. Gamlig is the Unlit King of the Dark Earth, the realm of the dead."

"You said his name," I interrupt. "*Gamligi*."

"Yes. Tonight is Gamlig's night, the night when the moon resides in the Dark Earth, and Ai Nakota leads the souls of the dead there."

Suddenly I feel very lonely.

"Aisulu . . ."

"Yes?"

"What were you saying?"

Her hand squeezes mine.

"I call you," she says, looking into my face, her voice soft but steady, "Ai Nakota, Wanderer, on Gamlig's night, when you are neither man nor woman, when the sky is the sea, when you have other tasks."

As she talks, she picks up the skin, takes a sip from it, and hands it to me. I'm scared, scared of the hidden things the smell conjures up, the pain and the loss, loss of myself, of my senses, but her voice reassures me. I take a sip from it, feel it slice me open as she speaks.

"I call you, Ai Nakota," Aisulu says, and her voice is powerful now, "on Gamlig's night, from your duties beneath the Dark Earth, and I commend these into your care: my soul, the homeless ghosts of my people, and my sworn friend, *tyr embal*, Torny."

My burning lips and throat are like a line of pure white leading to my heart. The space between us feels like the hush before a storm that will whip the waves higher than the cliffs.

"Sworn friend?" I manage. "I don't remember swearing."

Aisulu sighs – not with relief, but with something subtler, hungrier. "Do you want to?" she asks.

She holds up the knife.

"It'll hurt," she says. "But not a bad hurt."

If you told me that the world had shrunk to this, I would believe you. Her warm breath on my face, laced with fire-sap, the starved air between us, the stars I cannot name above, and all around this mountain, water flowing down, in pools and streams, to a great encircling sea, into grass and flowers like jewels and death, into trees like frozen ghosts, all of life quickening upwards, higher, into the snows, into the starlight.

"I don't care," I say.

She takes my left hand in hers, holds the tip of the blade over the white blur of my palm.

"Do it," I say.

She cuts me, light and quick, a line down the centre of my hand that slowly turns black with blood. She hands me the knife.

"Now me," she says. "Just the skin."

A thin mist is rising from the pool below us. I remember Galen whispering through bloody lips as he taught me to butcher men like pigs among the hovels of the Slipskins. There was blood then too, not just Galen's, nor mine nor my enemy's, but innocent blood, marking me, binding me.

I look up into Aisulu's face. It's like looking into a mirror, burnished and hazy. The cut on my palm is starting to ache.

"I can't," I say, dropping her hand. "I don't want to hurt you."

She reaches up and cups my face. Everything disappears with her touch, her eyes.

"Don't be scared," she says. Her voice is unlike I've ever heard it, breathless and unguarded. "We were always going to hurt each other. This is the good way."

I take her hand from my face, hold the knife steady, and make that same black mark on her. It's done almost before I know it, as if her skin parted willingly before my blade. She picks up the fire-sap and quickly bathes her cut and mine.

"Now," she says, holding her left hand upright between us. Her open palm is an invitation. I place my hand on hers so our marks align. Her fingers tangle with mine, strong, rough from the oar, unhesitating.

"Can you feel it?" she murmurs. "It's the same for both of us. Not just the pain. Our strength. Our fear. I know it cost you something."

My fingers tighten on hers. "And you?"

Her lips tweak in a half-smile. "It always costs," she says.

My head is whirling, full of mist, full of loss.

She leans across and kisses me.

This time I don't falter. I meet her halfway. I open my lips, taste the spirit on her breath, feel how her desire meets mine.

The mist is still inside me, but it can't pass through me anymore, can't overwhelm me. We are bound, I see that now, by the tug and surge of the blood inside us, and her wanting for me breaks over me like a wave, until I surface, gasping, not for air, but to see where on earth I am.

The mist is gone, if it was ever there. Greyness in the east lets me see her clearer than before, her winged eyebrows, her golden-brown skin, the flush on her wide cheeks. Her hair escapes her braid in tendrils around her forehead, and her chapped lips are warm red in the new light.

"What does it mean?" I ask.

And she tells me.

Sworn friends drink from a single cup.
They never relinquish one another.
Each protects the other like their own flesh.
They travel together until the Wanderer takes them.

We try to finish dressing our hands before Ebba wakes up. I feel a little bad going through her cure bag, but Aisulu points out we already know which ones to use from all the times Ebba's treated our blisters and grazes. Instead of using the bandages she packed yesterday, Aisulu reaches down and tears a strip off the hem of the Southern-style shirt she's wearing. It looks strange on her, hanging shapeless where I'm used to the clean, close lines of her Qesar jacket hugging her broad shoulders, her strong waist.

She makes a small pad of material to hold against my cut, even though it's all but stopped bleeding, and then ties it in place. I can't help leaning forward to kiss her as she does, and she has to rewind the bandage where she lost concentration and left it loose.

When I think of the south, I think of this. Warmth, happiness, and that buried laughter, making our shoulders shake as we shush one another.

"What's goin on?"

We turn together, our movements shackled like prisoners. Ebba's rolled over in her bedroll, her hair tousled, muzzily rubbing sleep from her eyes.

"Nothing," Aisulu says, still grinning. "We just scratched our hands."

Ebba frowns. "Hey, that's mine."

"Sorry, Ebba," I say, trying to make my voice meek. A giggle ruins it. Behind me, Aisulu's free hand grabs the back of my shirt, and tugs, telling me off. "We didn't want to wake you."

Ebba looks at me, a mixture of surprise and hurt that I don't understand.

"We're done," Aisulu says, pushing the leather bag between us, and draping the flap shut. "Here."

Ebba takes the bag and hesitates. I realise she wants to go through it, see what we've touched.

"We didn't take anything," I snap.

She turns away. The morning seems cooler.

"There's dangerous things in here," is all she says, her back still to me.

Like the things you gave me, I nearly say, but Aisulu tugs at my shirt again to shut me up.

"We didn't mean anything," she says.

Ebba doesn't say anything.

Aisulu looks at me and shrugs. I grin and lean towards her, but she ducks past me with a smile, and gets up to make breakfast.

From the pass of the mountain, we can see the surrounding peaks. Aisulu points out a smudge of smoke in the east: Gallucia, the town where the Samara and the Arauris meet, and where the Qesar pay tolls on their cargo, and for river-travel.

"Don't that harm your profit?" Ebba says as we head downhill.

"Everything we ship comes from lands to the east of the Confederacy," Aisulu says. "What d'you think we do to the traders bringing the goods into our territory?"

Ebba frowns. "So you tax em first, then you get taxed?"

"The Qesar don't strike me as tax collectors," I say.

Aisulu laughs. "Don't let me and Kizmid fool you," she says. "The Confederacy runs on tolls, import tax, wealth tax, inheritance tax . . ."

My mouth is hanging open. "What about riding off with your hawk and hound?" I ask. "I thought you were all nomad warriors?"

"That's ancient lore," Aisulu says, "from the time of the Three Clans: the Blue Wolf, the Red Hawk, and the Yellow Ox. The Three Clans are the pure Qesar, the noble families. Our genealogies stretch back long before the Confederacy, when the eastern steppe was our territory. Then the clans came west, claimed tribute from the lands we settled, and found we could make a good living the way people in that part of the world have always done – trade and tax."

"So is Kizmid from the Blue Wolf Clan too?" Ebba says. "Is that how you know each other?"

"Not really," Aisulu says. "Kizmid's what we call Fourth Clan –

no history, no family. Only Qesar descended from the Three Clans can fill certain ranks, although sometimes someone from the Fourth Clan can be adopted. My clan adopted Kizmid, for her skill as a navigator."

Sunlight falls through the leaves as we make our way down the mountain. The cut on my hand has faded to a dull throb, but I find I can barely feel it through the excitement bubbling in my chest. I can feel Aisulu beside me, even though we aren't touching; every footfall, every breath.

"So . . ." Ebba says behind us. "What clan is Serke?"

Aisulu looks over her shoulder. "Fourth Clan, of course," she says.

"Serke has a history," Ebba says. She's quiet, but I know Ebba's moods, and I know what kind of quiet this is. She's angry.

"She didn't mean it like that," I say.

"I know what she meant, Torny," Ebba says. "She meant Serke's history don't matter. Serke may be Qesar, but she en't *pure*."

Aisulu raises her eyebrows. "I don't think Serke cares much about purity," she says.

"But you do," Ebba says, "don't you? You said bein one of the Three Clan means bein pure Qesar. What does that mean?"

We've stopped walking. Aisulu draws an exasperated breath.

"It means we can recite our histories all the way back to the Three Clans in the east," she says. "It means I know who my ancestors are and what they expect of me, and it's not my fault if you don't."

She turns on her heel. Ebba looks at me and opens her mouth. Irritation fills me.

"Why do you have to be so difficult?" I cut in, before she can say anything.

Ebba pulls back as if she's been slapped.

"Aisulu's helped us more than she ever needed to," I go on. "She's kept us safe, even when *you* put us in danger. Because of you, Varkha and the Concession may be in trouble. Everything the Qesar do is for survival, but they still helped us. She's being nice to you. And you say *she's* the one we shouldn't trust?"

Ebba narrows her eyes. "You're so eager for her to like you, you overlook anythin that don't fit what you want to see," she says.

"I don't!"

"D'you think I'm blind? I've seen the way you look at her."

"You're right," I say. The cut on my left palm throbs. "I do look at her. I do want her to like me. You know why? She's the only person I've ever known who's showed me who I could be. Who didn't laugh, or think I was stupid, or who wanted me to be different. I never had anyone understand who I am before."

"That en't true," Ebba whispers, dropping her gaze.

"It feels true," I say.

For a moment I'm standing over her, and I realise how much smaller than me she is. Her head's bowed, her face hidden. She knows she's wrong. I turn and stride off after Aisulu, my skin tight with anger and satisfaction.

I catch up with her quite a long way further down. Rocks jut out of the loamy earth, forming turrets and ravines. Aisulu has climbed up along a stone ridge that rises between the trees below, giving us a view over the river. It's a lot closer than it was. She's scanning the lengths back east towards Gallucia.

"What do you see?" I ask, but then I see it too, even before she points.

The *uareh* is upriver from us, the oars working, fording a white

'V' through the brown spring waters. I hear a tempo rising from the valley, much faster than the hauling rhythm of the oar songs I've sung alongside Aisulu before now.

"What's the matter?" I ask.

There's a scuffing of dead leaves as Ebba comes up the slope behind us.

"The Gallucians love their declarations and seals," Aisulu says. "Especially if they inconvenience Qesar. Maybe Kizmid's just making up time."

I don't think she believes it any more than we do.

"They're rowin downstream," Ebba says, her eyes following the *uareh* as it disappears between wooded banks. "An that's no oar-song."

Aisulu turns to us.

"Listen," she says. "We need to get down there now. We stay hidden, we stay close, and we board fast." She looks at Ebba. "Do you understand?"

Ebba frowns. "Trouble?"

"Maybe nothing," Aisulu says. "Or maybe word that Qesar sheltered someone they shouldn't has reached Gallucia. If it has . . ."

Ebba's frown fades.

"I'm sorry," she says. "Aisulu, I never meant—"

"Now's not the time," Aisulu says. "Let's go."

Sixteen

SEVERANCE

❧

EBBA'S TALE

The Arauris River

 hug my cure bag to my chest as we race down the hillside to the river, tryin not to turn my ankle on a loose stone or the slough of dead leaves underfoot. I can feel more'n hear the horn vials rattle against one another.

Aisulu an Torny are ahead of me, sure-footed as deer, an I curse my skirts, hitched up in the same clumsy clutch wi my cure bag. My stumblin fall seems to echo between rocks an trees as I half-run, half-slither downhill.

The track steepens, an I glimpse green ahead an down, the edge of the forest. An there's another noise too, over my poundin heart and the thuddin of feet. A fast, high-pitched drum, distant but unmistakeable, that keeps pace wi my shakin legs, that suddenly cuts dead an the shout that follows, one voice made of many.

Below me I see Aisulu stick out her arm, right across Torny's chest, holdin her back. They're just within the treeline. I slow myself too. Aisulu's already got her pack off her back, an she digs in it, drawin out a small, double-curved bow an a capped quiver. She hands somethin that looks like a small purse to Torny, who fastens it quickly at her belt, then unwinds a dark length from it.

I hear hoofbeats.

A toy bow an a hand sling, like children guardin sheep. A dry sob convulses my chest, an I fight the urge to hide. I force myself to take a step down, an another, half-climbin as I reach a steep bend in the track, an then scurry down to the next bend. Here I can see what the others can.

The *uareh* floats off shore, Kizmid tall in the prow, her arm bent back. In the oar pits each outer rower sits, oar lowered against the current's drag, their oar-mate standin, the same small bows in their hands.

On the green spring grass between the river an the trees dance four horses, one rearing on its back legs, their tack gleamin wi metal, the riders in dark green uniforms. Their swords are in their hands, an the soldier on the rearin horse is shoutin, tryin to turn em around, back the way they came.

Everything moves slowly. I see the arrow in his horse's flank, the way he clutches at the reins an curls forward, tryin to bring his mount down. I see the confusion on the other soldiers' faces, as beyond em Kizmid's arm cuts round an down, an a volley of arrows find their marks. The arrows' flight sounds like rippin linen, followed by thuds an cries. Two men go down with arrows in their throats, an the remainin two fall as the rearin horse founders, an the other beasts bolt.

Aisulu steps forward, out from under the trees, an shoots. Her arrow finds the soldier trapped beneath his injured mount an he collapses. Torny strides out beside her, the sling already haloin her body, an looses as the other fallen soldier tries to rise. He tumbles back like wood.

The rowers are already back on their benches, haulin against the current to bring the *uareh* round to the bank. Aisulu an Torny linger beneath the trees as I scramble down to join em, my skirts tanglin round my calves as I half-slide down the slope.

The *uareh* touches grass, an Aisulu an Torny lope towards it.

I stumble out into the sunlight, screwin up my eyes. Still huggin my bag to my chest, I run towards the glint of sun on water. I can hear Kizmid's deep voice callin me, an Aisulu an Torny are wavin to me from the oar pits, when my foot catches an I sprawl forward.

A moan makes my heart freeze.

I look down the length of my body.

A hand is holdin my foot, an beyond that a face, horribly bloody beneath a dented skull.

The soldier gargles at me. Torny's shot caught him in the temple, broke his skull, but he en't dead. He's holdin me an fixin me with his eyes beneath blood an black hair, hazel eyes, his left brow stove in, the eye weirdly exposed, round an white, like it might pop out—

"*Ebba!*"

My heart is galloping, but so is the earth, shudderin an breakin open beneath me, the vials in my bag splintered an leakin through my hands, like water, like blood, like potions for dreamless sleep an death. There's a dyin boy before me, an for a moment I think it's him, his hazel eyes an sweet lips, his anger emptied now, nothin left but fear: Berengar. Berengar, who was so good a match that Rosamund cried to lose him. Berengar, who kissed me in the canvas maze. Berengar, who after everythin I miss, and who I'd choose again, however disappointin that makes me.

The earth is poundin like the dead are knockin to be let out, an I look back to the *uareh*, but not to measure the distance, only to reach across it once, silently, to see my friend waitin for me an to tell her I en't comin.

Torny's eyes meet mine. The earth is really shakin now.

Southern soldiers scout in squads of four. Here comes the second squad, catchin up to the first.

I en't sure what I expected. Shoutin, or cryin, or somethin. Maybe I thought Torny would try to leap ashore, come drag me with her no matter what. But as I meet her grey eyes, Torny looks away.

It's Aisulu who rushes to the edge of the *uareh*, shoutin my name, but Kizmid grabs her shirt an pulls her back. The gap between the bank an the *uareh* is already too large to jump, an now Kizmid is shoutin orders while Aisulu watches me with eyes wide. The high, tight beat of the rowin-drum sets a counterpoint to the thunder of hooves comin ever closer.

Torny en't looked back once.

I look away from the river, an back to the soldier.

"It's all right," I say, crawlin to him. His face after all is a stranger's face, broken an scared. He whimpers, an I take his hand. "I'm with you. Your comrades are comin. I'm here."

I can't hear anythin but his uneven breath and the drummin earth. Everythin else is carried away by the river, muffled in water. I open my cure bag, see the damage to the vials en't so bad. I take some ruined cloth an gently wipe the soldier's face. The blood's too thick to clean, but I keep it from runnin into his eyes. I don't think about the stone just yet. I take his fear an I calm it, like a hound. I had forgotten I could do that.

The horses circle me, but I don't look up.

"This man needs water," I say in Southern.

Two worn boots hit the bloody grass beside me, crushin a host of white daisies beneath em. I look up into forget-me-not blue eyes.

"Hello, Salvebearer," says Neklaus of Merzen. "I've been looking forward to meeting you."

Seventeen
SMOKE

TORNY'S TALE

The Arauris River

y left hand heals slower without Ebba's oils and balms, but it feels right, somehow, that this hurt should take its time. Aisulu says my problem is I haven't let my past hurts heal, so I hide it under layers of cloth and try not to look at it. Maybe that way, next time I look, it will be a scar.

When I saw Ebba stumble, I thought she'd just get up. It was a hard fall, but the grass was soft and new, the earth like a pillow beneath her. But then she looked back at the wounded man, and I knew. I think I still called to her, but I knew. She'd made her choice, just like I'd made mine on the mountaintop the night before. Aisulu's words filled me: *Sworn friends drink from a single cup.*

Well, now I knew. Ebba was never going to share mine.

I expected to feel more, but the truth sunk inside me like a stone.

If anything, Aisulu seemed to feel it more than me. It was her who tried to go after Ebba. Kizmid pushed her back to her place beside me and forced her down. As we sat side by side at the oar, pulling until our backs felt like they'd break, Aisulu seemed dazed.

Kizmid scowled and shook her head, but I've learned by now that the Qesar are practical. You do your best to help fate fall out in your favour, but, in the end, what happens, happens. One of the rowers took Ebba's place at the tiller. That first day I kept expecting to see her dark head when I looked up, and each time I remembered, the stone sunk deeper.

Later, when we rested, Aisulu and Kizmid stood heads together, speaking in Qesar. Aisulu was agitated, Kizmid putting her hand on her shoulder to steady her. When she came back, Aisulu seemed calmer.

"She'll be all right," Aisulu whispers when we sit side by side at the oar again. "Ebba's clever. She's a survivor. Remember Durkno."

A needle in my side digs in and *turns*. I've tried hard not to think of Durkno, ever since I lay by Ebba on the boards of the *uareh* and felt my lodestar die.

Let's keep it that way, a voice inside of me says.

After that, no one talks about Ebba's departure. Instead they answer me patiently in Southern, as I try out this new tongue like a baby bird tumbling from the nest. When they say "your friend", they mean Aisulu. They never mention Ebba at all.

Underneath the laughter and the oar-songs, there's some mood I can't catch. We're still rowing, even though the river carries us now, and it's no longer the slog it was coming up the Samara. When we stop at night, Kizmid chooses only the most inaccessible and hidden of moorings, and we stay aboard the *uareh* except for cooking and relieving ourselves. The Qesar prohibition against dirtying water still stands, even when we eat cold jerky and dried fruits rather than light a fire.

"What happened?" I ask Kizmid that first night. We're checking the ropes holding the barrels in place.

"The Gallucians held us," she says. "They impounded our goods and tried to stall us. They must have had an eye out for us and sent for those soldiers as soon as we arrived."

"How did you get away?"

Kizmid smiles. "Same way trade works everywhere, Rus. Bribery."

She passes me a rope to tighten it, and I wince as my bandaged hand twinges. Kizmid sees and rolls her eyes.

"Rowers hurting their hands," she says. "Honestly. The Qesar don't carry dead wood, Rus. If you row slow, I'll dump you overboard."

"I'd dirty the river," I say. "Can't have that."

"Ha!"

But I can tell she's smiling.

And that's all it takes. From then on Aisulu and I sleep curled together, my arm across her waist or hers across mine. Sometimes I remember the fear I felt back in Vindhaff, when I thought I'd have to share a bed with her. Now in the dark she raises her face to mine and kisses me silently, unseen, while all her fellows sleep, and by day we sit shoulder to shoulder, and when the oar opens the cuts and makes the blood bloom again on tightly-bound bandages we wince together, and laugh. I like our togetherness, our sleeplessness. It means I never dream.

One day when we're resting, padding and retying each other's dressings, Aisulu leans over and whispers in my ear: "Every stroke makes me think of you."

And my whole body burns.

I'm not used to this fire.

"Where are we going?" I ask her at night.

"To Ban Granis," she says, "and then . . . anywhere you want."

And she kisses me, her breath mingled with mine.

The moon waxes. On the seventh night after the mountain, Kizmid allows us ashore.

The land around us has changed with the rushing current. The mountains have drifted east, and for a day we pass through stony-bedded wastes, hills covered by scrub rather than forest. Now the river tightens, forced between ravines, and we can't row, only drag the oars against the current, and brace padded poles to fend off the walls of rock.

We reach the end of the ravine before sunset on the seventh day, and Kizmid orders us to moor as soon as we're out. I go to stretch my stiff legs. My whole body aches from tensing over the oar. Around me the crew are doing the same, shaking out and stretching.

The chill of the ravine wears off in the warm sun. My drenched leggings and tie-front jacket might actually dry out before the sun sets.

Aisulu climbs up from below deck with a pack on her back. She nods to Kizmid and the crew comment in Qesar as she passes them. She smiles and responds to each one. For a moment I feel on the outside, watching them through fog, unable to understand. Dread coils in my stomach.

Then Aisulu reaches me, takes me by the hand, and tugs me gently towards the rocky heights behind us.

"I hope your legs still work," she says, smiling.

We follow a narrow sheep-trail up the side of the cliff. Loose pebbles scatter through the low scrub beside the trail as we climb, and my thighs protest. The plants look dry up here, nothing like the lush green we walked through only a few days before. The trail meanders in hair-pin bends, but despite my aching muscles we reach the top fairly quickly.

The plateau stretches around us. I go at once to the edge overlooking the ravine, feeling the cool air rush upwards from the swift water. The river has a strange blue-green tint I've never seen before; I didn't notice when we were riding it. I walk the lip of the ravine, admiring the noise and colour, the white froth on the variegated water. When it spills out into the wide pool where the *uareh* is moored, I see the bright colours mixing back into the muddy browns and greys of the earth. Finally I raise my eyes to the horizon.

"What do you think?" Aisulu says next to me. She slips her hand in mine.

I shake my head. "I've never seen anything like it."

Downriver, for miles upon miles, orchards full of blossom turn the landscape pink and white. Here and there a field splashes green across a few acres, but the rest shimmers and shifts like a ghostly mist across the land.

"It looks like an enchantment," I say. "The fruit from these trees must be magical."

I can feel Aisulu smile without needing to look at her.

"They certainly turn to gold in the Ban Granis coffers," she says. "They're nut trees. *Ametlas*, yoke-nuts, and *pistaki*."

"And that's Ban Granis?"

"Yes."

Golden-grey towers and domes, encased in stone walls, rise among the orchards. Even this far away I can tell this town is bigger than any I've seen before. It could swallow Frithberg, where Ebba and I used to live, several times over. The centre of the town rises above the walls, built on a gentle hill. The hill seems crowned with another circle of walls, four square watchtowers rising out of the haze and into the evening.

"When it's clear you can see the bay beyond the towers," Aisulu says. "It's a perfect circle. They say once there was a town—"

"—that sunk beneath the waters?" I say. I try to keep my voice light, but Aisulu hears the shiver in it, and gives me a curious look.

"Yes," she says. "Do you have one of those too, in the north?"

I nod, not trusting my tongue.

"Funny," Aisulu says, lookin south again. "I've travelled a long way through many lands, and everywhere I hear that story. It seems there are drowned cities all over the world."

I shudder, and Aisulu frowns and squeezes my hand.

"What are we doing up here?" I ask, wanting to change the subject. "We're missing practice." Below us on the sandy shore, the crew are forming lines, getting ready to move through the forms without us.

Aisulu smiles. She's shrugged off her tie-front jacket, and the short tunic underneath tightens over her muscles as she crosses her arms, watching me.

"It's a good view," she says, looking me up and down.

I feel my cheeks heat up. Kissing in the dark when no one can see is different to this. This is how she treated me when we were new to each other, those first few days out of Vellsberg. I didn't know what I wanted then. I know now.

She tilts her face up to mine, and kisses me. Her hands hold my shoulders, her nose bumps mine. I feel the late sun on my face, see it gilding the curve of her cheek before I close my eyes. My mind turns as white and ghostly as the orchards below us.

She steps back again, still smiling, but not the smirk she wore before, a smile that tells me she's as giddy with it as I am. It's the first time she's kissed me in full daylight.

"You didn't bring me up here just to do that," I say, though my voice is a little unsteady.

"No." She walks back to her pack, where she set it down on a flat rock jutting roughly westwards, looking over the lowlands. She kneels down and starts unpacking it.

"We need a fire," she says over her shoulder. "Find me some fuel."

The plants up here are already parched: straggly grasses, and some tough, woody scrub a bit like heather. Here and there across the plateau are small groups of gnarled, silver-barked trees, their leaves dark as storm clouds.

When I return to the rock, the sun is setting into a bank of cloud in the west, their tops lined with red.

Aisulu has made a circle of stones for the fire, and is already coaxing some sparks into a tangled bed of grass. The faint red glow lights her lips as she purses them to blow. I wordlessly hand her more grass as the sparks take, then the scrub, watching her build the tiny points of heat into flames. It's never occurred to me how magical fire is until I see her make one. Necessary, yes. I've always known that. But this is almost mystical, creating something from nothing, watching it feed on what we give it.

Aisulu sits back on her heels, and places the things from her pack before the fire. A bowl and a knife, the ones she always carries, and three small pouches, as well as the wineskin.

The first pouch holds grains. She pours them slowly from her hand into the bowl. Then she raises the wineskin, pours some into her hand, and sprinkles the clear drops around the bowl and fire. She raises the bowl as if offering it to someone, and then takes another drink of the fire-sap. She offers it to me, but the smell hits me and I wave it away, feeling dizzy.

Aisulu takes another mouthful and bows before the fire. I get to my feet and leave her to it. Over by the ravine the cold air coming up from the river clears my head, and I sit there until I'm chilled through. The sun is down now, the sky dark except in the west, and I watch Aisulu from a distance, her outline against the fire, as she raises and lowers her arms, chanting prayers I can't understand.

When I rejoin her, Aisulu is kneeling quietly, head bent before the fire, her hands raised palm up before her chest.

"Torny," she says. "Get me the clothes from the pack."

I search through the pack. There's a Qesar-style jacket, wide divided skirts, and an undershirt, neatly rolled up. As I pull it out I catch another scent, an unmistakeable one.

It's Ebba's. These are the clothes she changed out of before we left the *uareh*.

Without meaning to, I hold the shirt up to my face and bury my nose in it.

When I look up, Aisulu's watching me. The shadows make her face beautiful and strange. She holds out her hand.

I hesitate. All of a sudden I want more than anything to keep this shirt, to have it close to me for when I need it. I think of Ebba telling me she kept the bone pin I left her, that it reminded her to be strong.

"What are you going to do with them?" I ask, but I already know. She's going to burn them.

"You could just wash them," I say.

Aisulu gives me sad smile.

"What's the difference?" she asks. Like she knows that without her scent, it's just a piece of cloth.

She beckons with her fingers, gesturing for me to hand it over, and I realise this is a kind of test. *Who will I choose?*

Defeated, I pass her the shirt. She takes up the knife from the rock beside her, and starts to rip the cloth to pieces, feeding each one into the fire.

"Why?" I ask her. "It seems a waste. Qesar hate waste."

She doesn't look up. "A person's clothes carry their essence," she says, "and we're being hunted. We need to purify ourselves of the link with her so that we can't be followed, in this world or any other."

She puts her hand on mine, and nods at the jacket. "Help me."

So I unsheathe my knife.

Night falls, and for a while, the ripping of cloth and the crackling of the fire are the only sounds.

When the last thread has turned to ash, Aisulu bows before the fire and says a prayer. I catch the name *Ai Nakota* again, and *Sarik*.

Then the ritual seems to be over. Aisulu sits back, stretching her legs in front of her and shaking them out.

"You asked me why I brought you here," she says. Her voice is easier now. "You know I said we're not free to worship our own gods here in the Empire?" I nod. "Well, to honour that law, one of our number takes it upon ourselves to pray for the rest. And that person here is me."

"Why you? Why not Kizmid, since she's the Captain?"

Aisulu beckons me closer, and despite myself I scoot next to her, into the warmth of the fire.

"I'm a Carrier," she says. "I go abroad alone, unseen, I speak many tongues, and I may use disguise or deception in the dispatching of my duties. This makes me kin to Ai Nakota, the Wanderer. They too move as they like through all the realms, carrying prayers to the gods, and souls to their rest. So one of my duties is also to carry the burden of unlawful worship, that my kin may find safe and lawful haven here."

I shiver. "You speak of this duty the way my aun— my mother used to speak," I say. "As if this is something holy."

"It is."

"Aisulu?"

"Yes?"

"I was wondering about your name. Aisulu. And the name of this god, Ai Nakota."

She puts an arms around me. I don't have to turn my head to hear her smile.

"Clever girl," she says, pressing her face into my neck and nuzzling me just below my earlobe.

All the stiffness in me from burning the shirt melts.

"So it's the same?" I ask.

"I was born during the new moon," Aisulu says. "Among Three Clan families, children born then are given names that start with the Wanderer's title, to mark them."

"Is that why you became a Carrier?"

She lays her head on my shoulder, staring into the fire.

"No," she says.

"It seems odd," I say, when she doesn't offer anything else. "Who are your parents? Your family are powerful, aren't they?"

"My father is head of the Blue Wolf Clan," she says. "My mother led her people in the war with the Empire over the Westlands before I was born. My clan was honoured to provide the last Kagan."

"Who?"

"Our king," Aisulu says, and the way she says it, with a shiver, calls to mind the blur beyond the four towers of Ban Granis, and the dark waters of the Floodlands. Something tells me there's a drowned city here too, under her words.

My mind catches on a memory.

"The night we met," I say, "you told us the Qesar have two kings. In case of accidents."

"The Kagan, and the Noyan," Aisulu says. It's strange. It's like there's something she wants me to know, but she can't bring herself to just tell me.

"Who are they?"

"The Kagan is the Soul of the Clans," Aisulu says, "and the Noyan is the Breath. The Noyan commands the armies, and the Kagan commands the gods."

"And the Kagan is . . . chosen?"

Aisulu nods.

"Who was he?"

"My kin," she says. "The Kagan is divined by certain signs from among the sons of the Three Clans. He was chosen. Just like I was chosen to be a Carrier."

"Why were you chosen?"

She takes a long breath in. "Because I'm clever," she says.

"Because I learned all the languages I was taught. I'm brave, I'm quick. I fight well and I don't give up."

"And?"

She turns to look me in the eyes.

"And I made a mistake," she says. "Now I'm going to make it right. I need your help, Torny."

I search her dark eyes. "Anything," I say, and mean it. "What do you need?"

She doesn't answer at once. Instead she opens one of the pouches, and scatters something that looks like prickly burs on the fire. The air fills with a sticky scent, like damp hay drying in the sun.

She sits back, her eyes fixed on me.

"You look different," she murmurs, putting her hand to the side of my face.

I lean forwards until my face hovers close to hers.

"Different how?" I whisper.

She smiles with parted lips, her eyes moving from my eyes to my mouth and back again. I can barely breathe.

"There's something the songs say," she says. "The first time you meet them, the heroes and heroines are all described the same way. 'Light in their face and fire in their eyes.' It's the light of Taghr's favour. It's how you know them when they appear in the story." She tilts her chin up until our lips are barely a hairsbreadth apart. "You're one of them, Torny. I knew it the first time I met you."

"No, you didn't," I say. "You thought I was a crazy girl defiling a river."

She laughs and leans forward, her kiss grazing my lips.

"No," she says, "You're wrong. I saw a warrior, strong and unafraid."

Ebba. Ebba under the stars, Ebba on the green grass, Ebba under hooves and swords—

Jarred by the images that flood my mind, I pull back.

"No," I say, "I'm not."

The smell of the burning burs is starting to bother me. There's a depth to it I don't like, an undertone like rot, a sickly sweetness that hits the back of my throat and makes me feel nauseous.

Aisulu crawls closer, following me.

"I didn't know the Rus went in for false modesty," she says.

I shake my head. The smoke has thickened, seems to crowd my lungs.

"Torny," she says, "who are your parents?"

My heart falters. I stare at her.

"Go on," she says, and her voice has changed. "Tell me whatever lie you like."

I start to get to my feet, but she grabs my wrist. The night has surrounded us, and she sits in the circle of hazy firelight, chaining me to it. Her eyes are blazing now.

"Tell me, Torny," she says. "Tell me who you are."

I try to pull my arm away, but she's holding it hard, nails digging in. The tendons in her wrist stand out under her golden-brown skin.

"I can't," I gasp, trying to twist out of her grasp. I half stand, struggling against her, but my head is swimming. Aisulu's face is set, her eyes not leaving mine, and her grip reminds me of a dog, jaws locked in a tug of war.

A mist is creeping up behind me, up from the weird green waters, over the lip of the ravine.

"Shall I tell you?" Aisulu says.

"No!"

I rip my arm out of her grasp and turn to run, but she's up and on me so fast I barely stumble two steps towards the edge of the cliff. She pushes me to the ground and pins me with her body, her eyes seeking mine. My head bounces on the stony ground, bringing tears to my eyes, and the mist creeps closer.

"Let me tell you," she says. "Your mother was a witch, isn't that right?"

"Stop!"

"And your father . . . your father was a king."

"No!"

"What does that make you, Torny?"

I'm sobbing now, and the mist is slipping in around me, weaving between our bodies, and I fight it, feeling the cold, the undertow.

Aisulu takes my head between her hands, forcing me to look at her. "Stop fighting, Torny," she says. "I'm here. I'm with you."

I focus on her face, panting with fear. If I stop fighting, the mist will take me.

"Why are you doing this?" I sob.

"Because I know who you are, Torny," she says. "You're the Rus-king's sister. You're the last of the Northern witches. You're *special*, do you understand? Even if you don't want to be. And I'm going to help you."

"It's coming for me,' I whisper. The mist is thick around me now.

"Let it come," Aisulu says, her eyes still burning into mine. "You have nothing to be afraid of. It should be afraid of *you*."

There are shapes in the mist, and glints of gold like fish scales on

stone. I'm cold. The shapes are indistinct, but I glimpse details –
a braid decorated with silver beads, a mouth of rotting teeth, an
empty eye socket.

A shadow moves towards me. It's wearing a band of bright gold
about its neck.

It stops in front of me, and waits.

The other shapes fall back. I breathe in, letting the mist into
my lungs.

"Fenn?" I say.

The shadow shivers. I get the feeling, in this muffled place, that
it's laughing. It starts to move away.

"Fenn," I whisper. "Come back."

The shadow keeps going. I take a step after it, and my feet
crunch on wet sand.

"Fenn," I say. "Don't leave me. Please. I'm so sorry. Come back."

The shadow hesitates. I can feel its expectation as it waits for
me. It wants me to follow it.

I take another step, then another. The other shapes are still
there, ringing me like columns, and the details are flickering on
the edge of my vision. A broad chest covered in black blood, a
shaved head, a tattoo blurred with age. I try to blot them out, hope
they'll disappear. I *know* them.

I feel the shadow turn from me, and in a panic I run after it.

"Fenn!"

Icy water splashes over my feet and up my shins.

"I can't follow you," I call.

The shapes are drawing closer around me.

"I can't," I say. "I have to go back."

The shadow wavers, just out of reach.

The shapes are all around me.

"Who are you?" I ask.

You know who we are, the shapes say, one voice of many voices. *We are the Slaughtered, and you are the Butcher.*

You buried us, but we dug our way out.

Eighteen
CAPTIVE

eklaus has come prepared. An iron collar, with a long metal bar attached, an two manacles, one above the other.

"You should be thanking me," he says in Southern as he locks my arms in front of me. "There's a mouth-guard that can be locked on here." He taps the back of my neck. "But that seems a bit brutal for a first meeting, don't you think?"

He steps back an smiles, lookin me over. The iron chafes against my collarbones, an my hands are trapped one over the other where my ribs meet my belly.

"I hope you have good balance," he says. "You'll have to ride. We don't have time to parade you through the towns, however pretty you look."

An he reaches down an tugs at my braid.

My skin crawls.

The soldiers are movin the boy Torny hit. With horror, I see they're goin to strap him over the back of a horse.

"If you do that, he'll die," I say in Southern. "His skull's cracked."

Neklaus smiles wider. "The last people who listened to you ended up very dead, Salvebearer. Remember Durkno? I see you do. Now, quiet, or I'll put the mouthguard on you."

I force myself to look away from the young man lashed across the back of his friend's horse.

He's gone, I tell myself. *Would of bin hard to save him anyhow. Don't think about it.*

Neklaus has one of those sideways seats across the back of his saddle, though not padded an decorated like the one I rode in at Vellsberg. He picks me up an heaves me into it. His hands dig painfully into my sides, an for a moment I tense, wonderin whether to squirm an protest. But more'n his hard hands, I remember his smile, an I feel myself fall limp as he arranges me.

"Good," he murmurs. "No fighting. We're going to get along very well, you and I."

There are leather straps an buckles for my thighs. He tuts over my skirts, then hitches em up.

I look into the distance as I feel his hands touch my thighs. From the horse's back I can see the torn turf of the bank, an the river, heavy wi spring melt an silt. I let myself tumble downstream, after Torny. I want her to come for me, harder'n I've ever wanted anythin ever before.

The buckles bite into my skin, an now Neklaus is fussin wi my skirts, drawin em back down over my legs.

"There," he says, "that's better. Just this one now."

The seat has a low wooden back that juts into my tailbone. Neklaus reaches around me wi both arms, feelin for somethin.

He looks up at me, that handsome blonde face full of laughter.

"I feel like I'm taking my betrothed hunting," he says. "Wouldn't that be pretty? Maybe I'll take Rosamund like this, when we're married."

But I'm gone far away from him now, outside of any flesh he can hurt. I barely feel the heavy leather strap around my waist, or the way he tightens it a notch too far. I'll feel all that later, when we're joltin between hills, when my whole body aches from bein held in this unnatural position for hours, when the iron an leather has chafed me bloody.

For now, I feel nothin. I close a door on the world, an I find myself somewhere quiet an familiar.

It feels like home.

The only interruption comes when we're out of the valley of the Arauris. The soldier wi the head wound starts to fit. He's level wi me, an I can see the bruisin behind his ears. I know what it means, but I can't help myself.

"Stop!" I cry in Southern, turnin my head against the collar towards Neklaus in front of me. "He's fittin. He'll die if you don't stop."

Neklaus waves to the men, slowin his horse, an they follow.

"Clear his mouth," I say to the soldier wi the fittin man lashed behind him. "He'll choke."

But the soldier don't move, just sits starin straight ahead. None of the soldiers will look at me. I en't noticed before, but now I'm alert an lookin for their reaction to their dyin comrade, I see they all look straight ahead, like deaf men.

Neklaus dismounts an comes round to the other side of the

horse, at my back, diggin through a saddlebag. For a moment I think he's lookin for my cure bag, but then he comes to me, a piece of metal in his hands.

"I warned you," he says. "Now, lean forward."

I stare at him.

"Lean forward," he says again, "Or do I have to make you?"

Behind him, the dyin soldier is chokin. No one moves as the noise fills the air.

Slowly, I bend at the waist. The tight leather strap digs into my stomach, forcin the breath out of me, an my wrists are trapped painfully between my body an my legs.

Neklaus places the metal over my mouth, then passes two leather straps over my face and up over the middle of my head, before they buckle onto another passed round my neck at my nape. Even braided, my hair gets in the way, an my eyes water as strands are yanked from my scalp. I'm strugglin for breath by the time Neklaus lets me sit up.

The metal encases my jaw, coverin my mouth but leavin my nose free. Two leather straps lie either side of my nose, obscurin some of my sight, an join at my forehead. The strap lyin across the middle of my skull takes most of the weight, an already I can feel a headache startin.

Neklaus reaches up an taps the front of the mouthpiece.

"Put your tongue out," he says.

It takes me a moment to understand what he means, but I do as I'm tole. The tip of my tongue meets hard metal spikes.

"This hole is for your tongue," Neklaus says, "if you can't control it. Not another word, do you understand?"

The injured soldier lies slumped, gluggin an twitchin. I look down at Neklaus rather'n see the boy's last moments.

I nod, my movement cut off when the mask hits the collar with a clank.

Neklaus smiles. The spring sun comes dappled through the leaves, pullin glints of gold an amber from his hair an beard. His blue eyes dance.

"I was worried you'd disappoint me," he says. "But I can tell you won't."

By the time we come to a halt, we've joined a road an night has fallen. That's all I know. By torchlight, Neklaus removes the mouthguard, then unbuckles the straps holdin me onto the seat, an sets me on the ground. I fold up at once, my legs numb, an I don't feel the ground when I hit it. I hover somewhere in the space between the night an the torches.

Far off, I feel Neklaus pick me up, an carry me inside. I'm wrapped in a cloak, the collar an manacles hidden beneath it.

Neklaus takes me to a room. It's familiar. Wooden bed frame, mattress stuffed wi straw, an ewer of water beside it on a chest. A fireplace built into the wall, Southern style.

Neklaus lays me on the bed an I stare into the fire. Whatever happens next, I won't feel it. Not for now.

But Neklaus pulls the cloak off me an unlocks the manacles, freein my hands. He removes the pin holdin the strip of metal to the collar, leavin just the collar around my neck. He turns my head this way an that.

"Look at me," he's sayin. I think he's said it a few times before I hear it.

My eyes come to rest on his face.

"There's a window," he says, nodding at the far wall. "It's barred against bandits, so don't waste your time unshuttering it. You'll have water, and food. There's a chamber pot. If you try to talk to anyone, or do anything but obey me, I will take these things away. If you are mute and good, you may sleep here alone. If you are not, I will manacle you again, and put you in the cell these places have for captives. There are already two men in there. Do you understand?"

I nod. I don't dare speak. I can tell that pleases him.

"Excellent," he says. "I'll be back soon."

I hear him lock the door behind him. I'm thinkin again, slowly comin back to myself. Bars on the windows, doors that lock wi keys, not just bolts, an a cell for captives. This en't an ordinary wayhouse.

The pain I've bin holdin back is startin to be felt. Seems there's a price for bein able to think joined-up thoughts.

I curl up on my side an let it wash over me.

After a while, it separates. I can feel the chafin of my collar distinct from the pins an needles in my legs, an the bruisin on my tailbone en't the same as the sting where the leather rubbed my thighs raw. I stare into the fire an watch the flames as my body puts itself back together.

The lock scrapes an the door opens. Neklaus comes in, a tray in his hands. He puts it on the chest beside the ewer, then shrugs somethin off his shoulder an puts it beside me. It's my cure bag.

"I saved your poisons," he says, smilin. "Healer, heal thyself. Don't bother looking for the prize. I took it." He winks. "I'll be back for the tray."

When the door locks again I force myself to sit up. My head throbs, my jaw stiff from being held closed by the mouthguard for hours. The tray holds soup an hot spiced wine. I drink the wine first. As I do, I wonder if Neklaus might have laced it, but I dismiss it. If he wanted me dead, he had plenty of chances, an if he wants me asleep, I'll take it. But I doubt it. Neklaus is the kind of man that prefers his prey awake.

The wine en't as bad as I thought it'd be. The spices en't much, not after tastin Varkha's *mulsum* back in the Concession, but it warms me, an clears my head a little.

Next I tear up the bread an put it in the soup, then force the slush down. It's tasteless but it's warm, an I en't eaten since this mornin.

I put the tray near the door, so Neklaus en't got cause to come close to the bed, an then I dip my hand into the water in the ewer. I'm surprised to find it warm. I wipe some over my face to get the dirt off me. When I look at my hands I realise there's dried blood on em from the soldier. I dip em both into the water, an rub em clean on my skirt.

Then I open my cure bag. Some of the vials have cracked from when I fell by the river, an the cloth I keep for bandages is stained. I find the vial wi the black wax, an feel a moment of triumph. I don't know what Neklaus means by my prize, but he en't taken what I feared.

I hold the vial in my hand, huggin it close to my chest, an for the first time in a long time, I say a prayer of thanks.

My captor has left me a way out.

Then I stow it back where it belongs. I'll need to find a way to keep it on me, but for now I put it back in the cure bag. I don't want Neklaus noticing it.

When he comes to take the tray, he finds me kneelin in prayer by the fire.

"Your games won't work with me, thief," he says, smilin. "I know what you're hiding. I know what you are."

I meet his gaze. Mute an obedient, that's what he asked for. Let him have what he wants until he's sick of it.

Despite the ache in my jaw, I smile back.

I sleep ill that night. Several times I hear the lock scrape, the door creak, an see a strip of torchlight on the stone wall. I know Neklaus is tellin me he could do much more'n watch me while I try to sleep. Still, the room is warmer'n the *uareh*, an the smell of the fire instead of river-damp lulls me. In the end I slip deep enough to dream.

I'm back on the horse. Lashed behind another horse, head lollin, is Torny.

I open my mouth to speak, and feel metal wedged between my teeth. Leather straps snake up over my head like livin things.

An very faintly, like an old echo, I hear a voice.

Eyes . . . up . . .

I wake up to see Neklaus lookin down on me. The shutters are thrown open, an his hair shines in the mornin sun. He's wearin a fresh uniform, clean an pressed.

"Time to get up, Salvebearer," he says.

I feel like there's no breath in my body, I've frozen so still. But that echo is still wi me. I meet his eyes.

"Now," he says.

I'm thankful I din't undress the night before. I pull back the covers an sit up.

"You'll need your shoes," he says.

No part of me wants to turn my back on him. I stay sittin, waitin for him to leave. Instead he gets down on his knees in front of me an reaches for my leather shoes.

Then he takes my left foot an puts it in his lap.

The feel of his hand on my ankle makes my insides curl up. I feel myself startin to leave again, like I did when he tied me to the seat, but this time I'm ready for it. I want to be gone, I really do. I want to be as far away from him as I can be. But I need to be here. No one else can protect me now.

He ties one shoe on, then the other. I even move my right foot into his lap for him, and that small compliance makes me feel unclean. But then I see his brow furrow. He seems vexed.

He don't want me present. He wants me the way I was yesterday, mind an body strangers from themselves. He likes my flesh empty.

I know all this in an instant. The thoughts en't even words in my head, I just feel it, like shapes in a dark room I've lived in all my life.

Outside, I see that the building stands by a milestone on a wide paved road. The servers here wear a sort of uniform as well, a bit like the soldiers but in blue. On their chests is the symbol of the cross, made up of six-sided shapes, like honeycomb. They're readyin fresh horses, not the same beasts as yesterday. Their saddles are stamped wi the same emblem. I remember what Neklaus said about the holdin cell. This must be some kind of military stable.

None of the servers or the four soldiers from yesterday look at me as I follow Neklaus into the sunlit yard. I pay more attention to em today. I remember their green tunics from our flight from Vellsberg. These are Merzen troops, from Rosamund's family.

Their hair is cut short to their napes, Southern style, an unlike the servers, their green uniforms are stained an mended.

It occurs to me that Neklaus an his men have bin trackin us ever since Vellsberg, well over a moon ago. An now four of em are dead.

Who do they think they've bin trackin?

Or what?

When Neklaus turns to me wi the metal strip an manacles, I don't leave my body like I did yesterday. I'm ready for it, for one thing, an now I'm curious. As he pins the strip in place an moves on to my wrists, I look past the shine of his hair, the blue of his eyes, his long lashes against the angles of his cheekbones.

There's dirt in the creases of his skin, an circles under his eyes. His lips are cracked, an his hair an beard are growin out. He's lost the polished air I remember from that first sight of him in the flowered valley.

He looks up at me, an for a moment I see somethin like rage in his face to find me lookin at him.

Then he gives me a nasty smile an produces the mouthguard.

"I don't trust you," he says, loud enough for others to hear, as he buckles the metal in place. As the straps settle across my cheeks an over my crown, I remember my dream, an my spirits rise. My Follower's gone, I know that, but the echo gives me hope.

This time when Neklaus lifts me into the seat behind his saddle, I don't flinch when he pushes back my skirts to fasten the leather straps around my thighs. I can't stop the flush in my cheeks above the metal mouthguard, cos it is humiliatin, an it's meant to be. But I cling to the voice from my dream, an I keep my eyes open, my soul behind em.

✤ 214 ✤

When he sees my thighs bandaged against the chafin of the leather straps, Neklaus tuts like a mother chastens an infant. I wonder in a sudden panic if he's goin to rip the bandages off an place the leather over the raw skin to make me bleed worse. Somethin about it is so awful that in that moment I almost do leave, no matter my dream nor my resolve.

But as he tuts, I see the men around us – for they're all men – hesitate. I see em still, even those wi backs turned to us, as their leader does this thing that offends all decency.

An I know somethin then, too. Whoever these strangers think me to be, they en't happy wi what Neklaus is doin.

I think of the men layin dead an untended by the river wi Qesar arrows in em.

I think of the soldier chokin unaided across his comrade's mount in the forest, the others denied help for him.

An the part of me that I en't proud of, but that knows how to survive, tells me: *Here is an opening. Here is how you can live.*

The horses follow the road at a brisk pace. This en't the backways an tracks Aisulu took us down, nor even the roads marked by the four-headed columns we used on the way to Lughambar. The road is easily wide enough for two wagons to pass side by side, an it's paved in old stones, rut marks worn deep in their faces. The land around the road is cleared of brush an trees. I guess it to be near enough as far as an arrow flies, to deny shelter to bandits.

Bound as I am, unable to control how the movement of the horse jolts me, it takes me a while to notice the milestones. Some are broken, some seem to be missin, but I start to wait for em, countin. It keeps my mind off the pain an numbness divvyin up my limbs.

The road is busy. We pass carriages, riders, people on foot. All of em stare at me as we pass. I see some of em makin the White God's sign.

By mid-mornin I'm achin an dizzy with hunger an heat. We've passed at least a dozen milestones, an guessin at the gaps I'd say it's nearer fifteen. Neklaus has ridden us hard, an I'm beginnin to think he's lost his mind. The horses are sweatin, strings of foam flyin from their mouths, an if he keeps this pace they'll be done for the day before we hit noon, unless he intends em to drop under us.

But just as we near what I know must be the next milestone, we wheel off the paved road an into a wide yard. As the horses slow, blue-uniformed servers surround us, takin reins, unbucklin packs, holdin up beakers of water to the sweatin soldiers. Neklaus swings off the saddle beside me an strides towards another man, already holdin out a pass.

"Special envoy," he's sayin. "All necessary help ordered by the Bishop of Corvennes."

A server comes round to me, arms already raised to help me down, but freezes in shock when he sees me bound.

"Don't touch her," orders Neklaus. "Dangerous prisoner."

"She looks like a child," the man says, not lookin up from the pass. He seems to be readin it more carefully than Neklaus likes, cos he snatches it back.

"This isn't a child," he says. "She's responsible for the deaths of more men than you can imagine."

Some of the servers cross themselves.

The man gives me a dubious look, but waves Neklaus on. "Fresh mounts will be ready soon," he says. "Refresh yourselves at the kitchen, latrines over there." He points around the side of the stables, where five horses are being led out by grooms.

Neklaus comes over to unbuckle my legs, and lifts me down. My legs are sore and full of needles, but this time I keep my balance.

The server starts removing the seat an packs, not lookin at me.

"Fancy a visit to the latrine, Salvebearer?" Neklaus says, smilin at me.

My stomach drops, an I fight the urge to be sick. I can't even shake my head wi the mouthguard in place.

One of the soldiers appears at Neklaus' side.

"Captain," he says. His tone tells me this is a new title, an not one he likes. "We should send word to the Bishop that our quarry is caught." He's an older man, face sun-weathered an lined, wi grey stubble on his cheeks. "He will expect it now we've joined the Golden Way."

Neklaus scowls. "This is sensitive news, Sergeant Hadric. We should bear it ourselves."

Hadric gives the smallest of nods, but says, "These are imperial messengers, Captain, trusted by the Emperor himself."

"And they owe their highest loyalty to the Emperor," Neklaus says. "We don't want it reaching other ears first."

Again, Hadric's chin dips in acknowledgement.

"My lord Bishop," he says, "will expect to see eight men returning. Four less may put him out of temper."

Neklaus' blue eyes narrow, but Hadric stands quietly, like he can't feel the weight of his captain's displeasure.

"You may inform the Bishop to expect our arrival in Ban Granis as quickly as the Golden Way allows," Neklaus says at last.

"Yes, Captain," Hadric says. "I'll tell the men to expect three changes a day. Lotho," he says, beckoning another soldier wi two fingers, "help the Captain with the prisoner."

I recognise the man whose horse bore the dyin soldier. He must be around the same age as Neklaus, late twenties or so. He salutes Neklaus, his eyes carefully not restin on any part of me. I get the feelin he's under orders, maybe from the sergeant.

Together, Neklaus an the soldier lead me to the latrine. No mysterious newness there. Latrines are latrines the world over: a pit, a seat if you're lucky, an stench.

"She'll need her hands free, Sir," the soldier says, an I feel my legs go weak wi relief.

"I'll do it," Neklaus says. "Wait outside."

He stands close to me, hands hoverin over the pins to free my hands. He smiles at me, an it's the smile of a gallant man, not a soldier towerin over a bound girl.

"I don't know how you've bewitched them," he says in a low voice, "but don't think you've won. You aren't safe anywhere, Salvebearer. I hunted you once like a prize. Next time I'll hunt you with hounds, like vermin. Remember that."

My nerveless hands fall from the open manacles.

"Be quick," Neklaus says. "We've a long road today."

He leaves me blessedly alone to my needs.

That day I learn what Sergeant Hadric means by "three changes." We ride the new horses hard until just past noon, when we reach another wayhouse like the one we stayed at last night. There we eat, change horses again, an ride on. Mid-afternoon we make our third change of mounts at another stable, an by evenin we reach another wayhouse, though Hadric calls it a *mansio*. At each one the uniformed servers stare at me an cross themselves. I guess we must of covered sixty miles or more this day alone. Neklaus has worn out twenty horses on me in a single day. It sets my head spinnin.

At the *mansio* Neklaus escorts me again to a room wi bars on the window an a door that locks, still accompanied by Lotho. I'm sure now that Hadric has tole Lotho to "help" Neklaus on purpose. Lotho never looks at me directly, but he rode all day wi me in sight, an whenever we dismount he's by Neklaus' side.

This time when Neklaus frees my hands an unclasps the manacles from my collar, Lotho is there to see the bloody broken skin at my neck an wrists. His hands are full wi my cure bag, an he don't say anythin, but I know he's seen it.

I can feel Neklaus' fury at bein dogged, but I'm too dead to care. My whole body feels broken, my skin rubbed raw, my muscles bruised from being trussed an jolted. I've worn the mouthguard since mornin, save for a few minutes when Neklaus fed me soup an water. My jaw feels locked closed, an my neck an temples are one unending blot of agony.

"You may get her food," Neklaus says to Lotho, as he reaches up to unbuckle the mouthguard. He's takin no chances anyone may speak to me. "Stupid dog," he mutters as the other man leaves, an he smiles at me. "This would be so much easier if you didn't have a tongue. But then, I guess we couldn't make you talk, eh?"

He removes the mouthguard an rests one finger against my cracked lips.

"No tricks," he says, "or I'll have to guard you myself."

I wish I had the strength to bite.

Instead, once he's gone, I gather myself, stagger to the fireplace, an hope I've guessed right about the kind of prize I am.

When Neklaus returns wi Lotho his shadow, they find me kneelin before the plaster wall, my hands raised in prayer. In charcoal on the plaster I've drawn the White God's cross an a double headed battle axe, one upon the other.

I have the satisfaction of seein, as Neklaus' drags me from my knees an throws me on the bed, Lotho in the doorway, the tray fallen from his hands.

The smash of pottery fills my ears as Neklaus' fist falls like a hammer.

In that jagged dark I feel the metal bit between my teeth, the straps of the bridle across my face. There's a poundin in my head, an before me I see the stump of a tree, blood spattered across the white an splintered core.

The axe stands blade down, the handle towards me.

Before you do the work of God, the body must be made ready for God.

I put out my hands. Blood flows softly, like ribbons from my manacled wrists.

She was scourged, but she felt no pain.

My palms are black wi soot.

They tried to burn her, but she walked through the flames.

I grasp the axe, my spine bendin like a willow to its weight. I feel the collar around my neck.

Finally she ordered them to cut off her head.

When I pull the axe free, it comes easily, cleanly, lighter'n wood. I hold it before me, an look down at the gory stump.

The Prester's dead eyes look back from his severed head.

Everyone who saw it was converted.

I awake in mornin light. My head is throbbin, an as I lie there I feel the pain radiating from my left eye socket. I can't open my eye, an my skin feels tight an tender.

Gradually I blink my right eye open an focus on a figure across the room from me.

Lotho is standin against the wall, his face bruised.

He's lookin straight at me.

"Good morning, Salvebearer," he says. That an the fact that he's alone wi me tells me somethin's changed.

I open my mouth, but all that comes out is a croak.

He comes to me an offers me water. I sit myself up an drink, then try again.

"I need to pray."

"There's a shrine in the yard," Lotho says, "but—"

"Then you will help me there," I say.

There are new clothes for me, the wrong size, but clean. While I change, stiffly, an rebandage my thighs an wrists, Lotho stands outside the door.

He follows beside me as I walk through the hallway unaided, rememberin the layout of the last *mansio*. They are the same. The light of the yard blinds me, but Lotho leads me to the shrine set in the wall.

Cut into the white stone of the shrine is a man enthroned in power, his arms upraised. Rays surround his head, an he sits in a circle atop the cross. Soldiers sleep at its foot, an to my surprise, two crows sit on either arm of the cross. I pretend not to see the uniformed servers watchin me.

Lotho helps me kneel before it, an then many things happen at once.

I hear Neklaus' heavy footfalls as he strides towards us, shoutin for Lotho to get away from me.

I hear hooves clatter into the yard, followed by shouts of surprise.

An I hear Hadric say: "Imperial messenger for you, Captain, direct from Ban Granis. The Salvebearer must be delivered as soon as possible, unmarked. She's to be questioned by the Emperor himself."

I look into the carved god's serene face wi my one good eye, ignorin the clamour of men at my back, the clamour of my heart in my chest.

Let's try again, I say to that part of me that's bin dark for so long. *White God, I have a bargain to make with you.*

Nineteen
KNOCK

TORNY'S TALE

The Arauris River to Ban Granis

I wake up in a dark, damp, narrow space. I'm back underground, in the Harrower's tomb, trapped by spiralling lines of rock. Panic rises in my chest. I strike out and hit wood.

For a moment I think it's one of the barriers I broke through to reach the heart of Sleeper's Howe, but then I feel boards pushing into my back, and when I reach to the sides my arms are constricted. I'm in a wooden box.

My panic ebbs and swells. *Am I buried?*

But I can hear water. Water rushing and slapping, not just wood but oars. The air is stale, but it smells of pitch, not dirt. I can hear the creak and haul that's become so familiar to me. I'm not underground, I'm in the *uareh*.

But where? This isn't the below-deck, with its sliding partitions.

Then come heavy footfalls on the wood, directly overhead.

I'm between the oar pits, under the walkway.

What the hell are they doing?

I bang on the boards, shouting Kizmid and Aisulu's names.

On the right, beside my shoulder, someone bangs back.

"Aisulu?" I shout. "Aisulu? Get me out!"

But the same knock comes, a steady two beats. I hammer back, but there's no voices, nothing but that steady one-two beat.

They're not letting me out.

I try to cover my face with my hands, and graze my knuckles on the wood. I can raise my arms, but my elbows crack against the sides of the space. My head aches.

Slowly, I run my hands over myself. I'm wearing my Qesar clothes with another, looser jacket over the top. I can feel something soft under my head, like folded cloth.

What happened?

Aisulu did something to me. She drove me into the mist, and I don't know why. And now I'm here, hidden in the bowels of the *uareh. How did I get here? And why won't she let me out?*

By my waist, my hands feel something. Flatbreads and jerky on my right, where I can reach them, and a waterskin on my left. Relief fills me, and a breath that's almost a sob shakes my body.

Warm clothes, food, and water. She's looking after me, so it must be all right.

Suddenly I understand. Aisulu is protecting me. Just like when she burned Ebba's clothes. We're being hunted, and here, this close to Ban Granis and the heart of the Empire, I need special protection.

Maybe whatever happened last night was a mistake. Maybe she wasn't trying to send me into the mist. Maybe—

But my thoughts cut out at the onslaught of images, and I have to clench my hands until my nails bite into my palms to block them out.

Food and water. Focus on that.

The jerky is tough. I let it sit in my mouth, sucking at it as it softens in my spit. Its salty, smoky taste has become so familiar I barely remember what other food tastes like. Between bites I tear off small portions of flatbread and hope they'll stop my stomach griping.

My mouth dry from the jerky, I drink from the waterskin in gulps. I screw up my face against the aftertaste, a brackish, stagnant flavour that coats my tongue. I drink again to clear it, but it's no use.

My stomach knots, and I wrap my hands around myself as cramps drive through my pelvis.

Too late I recognise the taste.

The water's laced with something that tastes like the smoke from the fire.

Bewildered, I squirm in the darkness. I want to curl up, but the straightness of the space won't allow it.

I beat against the wood to my right again, but all that comes are those steady double knocks, measured and unhurried, and a kind of keening clamour, a chorus of voices below the earth.

"Aisulu!" I shout. "Aisulu, what have you done to me?"

The pain in my stomach grows, and I have to gulp down bile. My thoughts are harder to keep hold of. I know from Ebba what happens when drunk men pass out and vomit on themselves.

It takes all my strength to turn in my wooden prison. I wedge myself on my side, my shoulders squashed against the wood, my left arm curled under my head, my right hand around my stomach. I hope that's enough to save me from choking if I do vomit. The blackness is spangled with lights, and my whole body feels like it's spinning and sliding downwards, into some endless void.

The double-knock comes again, at my back now, but I'm too wracked to knock back. I feel it through my chest, the keening in my ears, someone beating to come in.

I'm in many places at once. Lying stiff inside a hen-coop, sweating and dreaming on the bed of a flat-bottomed boat above ancient dead waters. Lost in a labyrinth, asleep on the hard wooden planks of the wayhouse attic. Among the sea-mists and black columns of Far Isle, searching for someone. Deep in the dark earth of the cliffs, listening to the gulls shriek and the waves suck at my bones.

A stone fortress at the crest of a hill in a sea of grass, a plain criss-crossed by glittering rivers . . .

As unfamiliar visions overwhelm me, I try to shove them down. I think of the sunset over the orchards, the pool among wildflowers at the top of a mountain, the spring sun on my face.

But they claw upwards, like old friends desperate to reach me, and I can't cut them down.

In the mist, among tattooed arms, among silver pendants on blue, I see new sights: the gaily coloured bridles and tack of horses dressed for ceremony, gold ornaments dancing in the sun, long black hair piled high, strands whipped loose by the wind – and a voice that is both a child and a man. It cuts through the babble of the mist.

We're here, says the mist. *You have given us more power than we ever knew in life.*

We are coming for you.
And that double-knock beats again at my back.
Let us in. Let us in.

Twenty

NECROPOLIS

EBBA'S TALE

The Golden Way to Ban Granis

A messenger from the Emperor himself can't be gainsaid, no matter how furious Neklaus is. Sergeant Hadric has won, at least for now.

The sergeant finds a light, two-wheeled cart, an hitches it to one of the horses. He stolidly ignores Neklaus' curses as he gives orders to the uniformed servers. The servers keep their eyes down, stayin as far from Neklaus as they can.

"I'm your captain!" Neklaus screams in the sergeant's face, makin the horses dance.

"Yes, sir. And the Emperor orders the girl brought to him quickly and quietly," Sergeant Hadric says, his hands not pausin once as he checks the horse's tack. "Lotho, hold the horse please."

Hadric returns to me where I'm waitin by the shrine.

"Come with me," he says, an leads me by the shoulder to the cart. He hands me up, an lets me settle myself, my cure bag on my lap.

"I have to hobble you," he says. "But I'll leave your hands free if you swear in God's name not to run."

Neklaus snorts.

"I swear before God," I say.

So Hadric manacles my ankles but leaves my hands free. Neklaus paces around the gig like a cat denied cream, but Hadric sits beside me, reins in his hands, ignorin him.

Lotho hands me my cloak. I wrap it around myself, coverin my hair an my bruised face, an Hadric gives an approvin nod.

Neklaus kicks his horse viciously, propellin it into a canter right out the *mansio*'s gates. As the gig an the three mounted soldiers turn south onto the Golden Way, Hadric nods to Lotho, an the young soldier kicks his own horse into a canter, speedin after their captain.

We've passed three milestones before the sergeant speaks.

"I'm sorry," he says. "You should not have been treated that way."

"I'm a fugitive," I say, "An outlander. A woman. I know what happens to us when we're caught."

"You come from a heathen land," Hadric says. "We're different."

His complacency annoys me. I can't stop the spark that lands on my tongue.

"What was his name?" I ask. "Your comrade. The one who died while you did nothin."

Hadric is quiet long enough that I've time to regret my words.

"Coel would have died anyway," he says. The way he says it makes me think he knew him well. I know now why I feel safe wi the sergeant. It en't just that he's defied Neklaus. He reminds me of someone else who loved the men he led.

"You know that en't what matters," I say, rememberin what Captain Erland tole me all those months ago as we rode to war. "He could of met his God wi courage."

Hadric says nothin. He don't need to. The difference between him an Erland is Hadric en't got the rank to protect the men he loves.

Another milestone passes, broken almost at the ground, grasses growin up around it.

I think of Rosamund, drawn an pinched in the Qesar parlour in Lughambar. *My cousin is a monster.*

"He hates women most, don't he?" I ask.

Hadric nods, once. "You're lucky," he says.

I laugh. I can't help it.

"Laugh all you want," Hadric says. "Powerful people want you alive and whole. If they didn't, a black eye would be the least of it."

An Hadric risked his standin wi this man to remind him of that, I think.

"Thank you, Sergeant" I say. "For sendin that messenger."

Hadric shifts on the bouncin seat of the gig.

"I knew what was comin," he says. "It's a dance he does. A *courtship*. I've seen it before."

Despite the warm spring sun on my face, I feel cold.

"Listen to me, girl," Hadric says. "They say you were with the martyr Grimulf in his last moments, so you must have seen murder and devilry. I was posted to the borderlands as a lad, so I know what Northerners are capable of. But believe me, you will need all the protection you can get, from the most powerful sources there are, heavenly or profane. So pray for Coel, and pray for yourself. I've done what I can, and I will pay for it, I know. All who cross the Captain do."

The road stretches smooth an empty ahead an behind us, the clatter of the wheels an of the other two horses ahead an behind the only noise apart from the warm breeze.

"Tell me," I say. "Is Rosamund of Merzen safe?"

Hadric frowns over the reins. "How do you know Lady Rosamund?"

"She was in Lughambar," I say. "She visited me in the Concession."

Hadric curses. "Filthy Qesar," he spits. "Spies and thieves, meddling in our business. No wonder you have two houses of the *Regna* after you, running with them."

"The Qesar have bin nothin but kind to me," I protest, surprised by this change.

"Kindness!" Hadric scoffs. "The Qesar work for the downfall of the Empire. Everyone knows it, even those fat Lughambar merchants who house them. Well, they got what's comin to them."

"What d'you mean?" I ask, my heart tight.

I sense a satisfaction in Hadric that I don't like at all.

"Raiders," he says. "Came up the Samara on the spring tide after the Feast of Embers. They looted Lughambar and burned that Qesar hole to the ground."

It's easier not to speak after that. I don't want to, anyway. Hadric has saved me for now, but the news of Lughambar shakes me. I know the Qesar will have fought. What of Varkha, with her sweet spiced *mulsum* an her beautiful clothes an hair? She forced us out, but now more'n ever I understand why. I mistook their generosity for safety, an I should of known better'n anyone that outlanders are never truly safe.

An what of Serke, with her knowledge an her welcome? The

only person I ever met who spoke the language I might have spoken, had my mother never bin taken north.

I turn my face up into the sun, eyes closed, an try to warm myself.

We keep the same pace as the day before, three changes of mounts an a *mansio* at dusk. The gig en't comfy, but it's heaven compared to the seat an the straps. At the *mansio* that night, Lotho an Hadric bring me food an more bandages, an Hadric tells me gruffly he'll keep the key to the room as he unlocks the manacles on my wrists. The iron collar is still around my neck. Neklaus has the key, an no one dares ask him for it. I clean an dress the sores under it as best I can.

In the night I'm woken by banging on my shutters.

"It's me, Salvebearer," Neklaus croons outside my window. "I know what you are. You can't fool me. You're the same as all the rest."

I lie awake in the dark room, watchin the remains of the fire. I don't try to sleep. I pray.

In the mornin Hadric an Lotho let me pray before the shrine. Neklaus leaves at a gallop like he did before. I sit next to Hadric, my ankles hobbled, an today we don't speak. It seems safer.

Every day is like this, the three changes, the blue servers at each stoppin place, Hadric's stolid presence, Lotho's shadowin of Neklaus. At each shrine I kneel an every night I hear that bangin on my shutters.

I know what you are.

My dreams are filled with echoes. Often I feel the bit between my teeth, the straps across my face. On the seventh night after my capture, the prester visits me.

False disciple, he says, *I've been meaning to thank you. You've given me powers you could never imagine. There is more to death than I knew. We will be together soon.*

I wake in a cold sweat, the shutters shaking.

Salvebearer, it's me.

At every shrine I feel eyes on me, eyes that know they shouldn't look, but do anyway.

An that is power, of a kind. I feel tongues twitchin in their mouths as they turn from me, hurry away behind doors an shutters, eager to tell—what?

That a girl with a bruised face is prayin on her knees while four soldiers wait to hobble her? That a captain is ridin twenty horses to sweat every day to deliver her to the Emperor? That she comes from the north, where martyrs are made an they kill their own kings?

That mornin Hadric tells me we should reach Ban Granis by nightfall. Instead of stoppin at the last *mansio* we'll push on.

"In the dark?" I ask.

But the days are longer now as the world turns towards summer, and anyway, the way to Ban Granis is well lit, the servers tell Hadric, slippin glances at me as I sit beside him.

We come among the orchards by evenin, as we leave the last *mansio* before the city. Neklaus has raced ahead as usual, tailed by Lotho, an the other two soldiers ride ahead an behind the gig.

From a distance, the orchards look ghostly, dappled pink an white, but as we come among em I see they're almost done. The blossoms that are left are brown, dyin, an the sweet smell has an edge of decay. Many trees are already bare of blossom, their fruit green an swollen. Along the strict line of the Golden Way, I see the bulk of Ban Granis risin above the trees, crowned wi four towers.

Hadric is even more silent than usual.

"Have you bin here before?"

He shakes his head. "I've served the Empire all my life," he says. "I've kept the borders. But this . . ."

I know what he means.

This is the heart. This is the cause. When I look at it, I see the fires before Frithberg, the sacred groves levelled, the war that dogged Arngard for ten years.

"They say there are enough relics in Ban Granis to build a host of saints," Hadric says. "They say here the holy dead outnumber the living."

I think of the Prester, with his lamb-white curls an his red, red blood.

That's when I see the first of the buildings along the roadside.

"What's this?" I ask.

Small stone buildings, like booths or huts, lined wi carved blocks, or topped wi broken statues an urns. These first are broken an scattered, but as we ride towards the city they multiply, some standin open an empty, some kept in repair.

"This is the necropolis," Hadric says. "They're tombs."

The tombs grow more numerous. Some of em seem so ancient they're crumblin to dust. Others look newer. The styles tumble amongst one another, domed, square, in grey an golden stone, an the orchards retreat to either side. There's no order. Tombs are built facin different directions, abuttin one upon the other.

Dusk is fallin, an above the city ahead I see the constellation of the Dancer risin, the first time I've seen it this year.

I fix my eyes on the towers. The streets below em seem lit up, an as we near the city, lit torches are set on tall, sturdy poles every few dozen yards. They light the road a little, leadin us in a trickle of light towards the city.

I can almost see the gates when we come to a puddle of darkness. The soldier ahead of us shouts suddenly, his horse rearin. Hadric shouts back, an tightens the reins, tryin to guide the gig around the soldier. I see the man's face, an then on the ground what brought him up.

It's Lotho, lyin in a pool of blood.

I turn back to Hadric.

"Neklaus," I say. "Go!"

Hadric smacks the reins over the horse's flanks, yellin. I twist, an see the first soldier's down, the second ridin after us, then topplin sideways as an arrow pierces him an flings him sideways from the saddle.

There's a whistle an a thunk next to me, an Hadric slumps, an arrow growin from his back. He falls from the gig, draggin the reins with him, an the horse wheels in panic, drivin the gig off the road an among the tombs.

I try to hang on, but the gig flips, throwin me from it, an I'm flung to the ground where I gasp for breath.

I try to get up, but my legs are hobbled.

I prop myself up on my elbows. Hadric's body is a few yards from me, by the side of the road.

Grimly, I pull myself towards him, an turn him on his back.

He en't dead.

"Hadric," I say. "I need the key. Where's the key?"

He burbles a reply, blood runnin from the corner of his lips.

I wish I din't know what was happenin, but I do. His lungs are fillin wi blood, an he's drownin.

"I'm sorry, Hadric," I say. "I'm sorry."

An I start to search his belt. There's a knife an a purse strung on it, an I force my shakin hands to untie it, to tip it up an empty it.

I can hear people comin.

The key falls among the folds of Hadric's shirt an I feel after it in the dark, among the tombs, tryin not to feel or hear Hadric's death.

I find the key an fumble for the lock on the hobbles.

One manacle opens, an I start on the others.

I hear voices now, several of em.

The second manacle falls open, an I snatch up the knife from Hadric's belt.

Hadric's hand falls on my wrist, an tugs.

I do what I've bin tryin hard not to. I look into his face. I know what he wants.

"I can't," I say, and I'm beggin. "Please. I'm sorry, I can't."

This en't Lana driftin into the White God's light. This en't some drops in the dark.

This is slaughter.

This is mercy.

But it's a mercy I can't give.

So I stay. I drop the knife an I hold his hand, an as he dies I listen to him, look into his face, an grip his hand.

And behind me Neklaus of Merzen says, "What did I tell you, lads? Everyone who listens to her ends up dead."

Part Three:
HEARTLANDS

"The Kagan, the Soul of the Clans, Celestial Father, is to be chosen from among the sons of the Three Clans. He shall abide in sacred Izoloh, where the throne of Taghr touches the earth. He himself shall divine the length of his reign, and his person shall be sacrosanct. His blood must not be shed, even in death. This is the third precept.

The Noyan, the Breath of the Clans, Commander of the Horde, shall be chosen by the representatives of the Three Clans and the officers of the horde, in a general council. It is his duty to see that the laws are obeyed on the battlefield, and to punish those who flout them. This is the fourth precept."

From the *Iassax Law* of the Qesar Confederacy

Twenty One
KAGAN'S PRAYER

AISULU'S TALE

This is the hymn upon rising
To the Celestial Father, Soul of the Clans.

I hear Kizmid coming up the path, small stones springing away down the slope with her every step. She grunts when she reaches the top.

"Too much rowing, Captain," I say. "Your legs have forgotten how to work."

She snorts. "Poor Carrier," she says. "All leg, no brain. How is she?"

I haven't looked away from Torny since she went under.

"No fits," I say. "No vomiting. She's breathing normally."

"We have to go," Kizmid says. "The *uareh* from the Ban Granis Concession is here. Our orders are to get you both there as soon as possible. She'll have to go in the hideaway."

"This isn't how it should be," I say. "I should be with her. I should be there when she surfaces, and it should be me who sends her under again, until it's done."

Kizmid puts a hand on my shoulder.

"Come," she says. "I'll carry her."

As Kizmid gathers up the limp form, I take up the pack and kick out the smoking remains of the fire. Around us, the night is growing grey with age. I follow Kizmid down the narrow path. Torny's pale head lolls across the crook of her arm.

The scar on the palm of my left hand itches.

> *You watch over us from Taghr's throne,*
> *In sacred Izoloh, heart of the Clans.*

The first night I stumbled into the Concession in Lughambar, and saw Kizmid, I thought I might die. Not because of her, but because with her came everything I'd fled. You were there, behind her shoulder, waiting to greet me. I thought I'd left you behind, but this was your third visitation. I saw you first in the fires of Vellsberg, the blackness under your golden skin as they ate you from the inside out. The second sent me out through the dark alone, blinded by that bloodied stump before my eyes, by things even Sarik's goodness couldn't cleanse me of.

I came through the inner gates in a frenzy, riding like all the needlemouths of the north were behind me, but it was you. Trailing behind me like a horse on a long rein, unseen, unfeeling, dragging me backwards, lashing me on, until I saw Kizmid's face. And there you were, in her shadow, wet and cold from the river where they buried you, your eyes burning into mine with that unnatural fire, and I remembered what I'd done.

Tsomak, my brother. My charge, my king. My failure. I tried to outrun you.

Now you're with me all the time.

You are the first among us.

You were old enough to know me when I was born, Tsomak. Still young enough to be allowed in the tent when my mother, Third Wife, was giving birth, with your own mother, First Wife, in attendance. Old enough to remember how quick it happened – my mother's waters breaking at moonrise on Gamlig's night, my first cry heard as the Wanderer reached their zenith in the sky. Old enough to lay the arrowshafts in my grasping fists when my mother named me before the clan, and to have blunted the tips beforehand, so that I wouldn't cut myself when I tried to put them in my mouth.

You loved me, Tsomak, as older brothers do not always love little sisters. When my mother weaned me, you fed me, and when I got my first cuts and grazes, you were there, pulling me up by the shoulders, showing me how to bite my lip against the pain so that I learned not to cry, like a warrior.

Your breath warms the world.

You were not alone in caring for me, because a Qesar child is never alone. There are always hands reaching out, offering food, a warning smack, a steadying grasp, pointing out mistakes or lending help. We grow surrounded by our family, and our families are broad. It was only after leaving them that I understood what that means.

The first time I left, it was for you, Tsomak. The second time it was because of you.

You visit us, Celestial Father, in Gamlig's realm,
Where our shadows rest beyond flesh.

Tsomak was not my father's heir.

He was the youngest of First Wife's children, and maybe he loved being my older brother because among his full siblings he was the baby. They were all in service, or already out in the world, when I was born.

It was he who taught me to be still. Thanks to him, my hair got braided for festivals or visitors, and I learned to hunt with a hawk, even though I hated the heavy leather glove, the weight of it on my arm, and most of all I hated that blind head turning to and fro, petty death hooded and seeking.

Born under Ai Nakota's sign, marked theirs by name, I was always a candidate for Carrier. When I was a child, that meant nothing but a little extra pride and mystery. We honoured Ai Nakota differently. The Daylit King and Sunlit Queen had shrines within the walls of our compounds, but the outer gods did not. Gamlig's offerings were left by grave markers in the burying fields, while I had never seen a shrine to Ai Nakota. They were a secretive god, and their holy places were kept secret.

But this wasn't something I thought much of, not even when Tsomak grew old enough to enter service, and my training began. Tsomak was away, and I had to learn to keep myself still without his hand on my back. After all, I had learned enough about the world beyond my small sphere – our grasslands home, our hillside vineyards over the Great Lake, the Blue Wolf Clan's compound in the port town of Bacaeydon on the Agate Sea – to be eager to see more of it.

My mother had ridden with the Noyan, the commander of the horde, for five years after her service. She taught me to weave, and at the same time she taught me geography, other tongues, and tactics. Second Wife had been a Negotiator, so she taught me about trade routes, goods, and the art of negotiation while I helped her cook. With First Wife I learned ceremony and the history of the clans. She was dedicated to Sarik, and it was she who distilled the fire-sap each year for the Sunlit Queen's offerings. My father, when he was home, taught me the Iassax law, and such family rites to the ancestors as a minor daughter needed to know.

Woven into all these lessons were stories of Izoloh. My mother spoke of the Noyan receiving the Kagan's blessing at the Ceremony of the Breath when she rode with him. Second Wife made me memorise the sales patter about the mysteries of goldwork known only to the sacred smithies. First Wife had me name all the Kagans past, their clans, the length and exceptional events of their reigns, the manner of their deaths. These were strange and poetic: *Flown with the Geese, Sunk with the Moon, Embraced by Silver*.

"And when will the current Kagan, Soul of the Clans, Celestial Father, leave this realm?" First Wife would ask.

And my answer, steadily diminishing.

"In the Moon of Milk, Enclosed in Jade, eight years from now. Seven years from now. Six."

It was a sign of Taghr's favour that the Kagan should know the year and manner of his own death, for what hurts us more than the uncertainty of life?

And always the reminders that with the Kaganate came riches and influence.

> *You intercede for us, when Taghr longs for war.*
> *You advocate for us, when Sarik forgets her children.*

It should have been obvious to me even then, as my childhood dropped away, that my clan were positioning themselves in the hope of a new spring.

Most Qesar never aspire to see Izoloh. It's a kind of heaven-on-earth, a mythical place. The Kagans of centuries past are buried there under the streams that criss-cross the plain, their spiritual power flowing like a horde over the flower-studded grass and out into the world. Wild horses roam free around the stronghold, where the rocks jut upwards towards heaven, and ancient markers map out the edges of this holy earth, carved with names and tongues so old only the priests of Izoloh can read them.

Maps of the Qesar Confederacy show it square in the centre of our lands, but that is a symbol and a lie. Izoloh is the heart of the Confederacy, but since when was the heart in the centre of the body?

Because it was always around me, some part of me expected that one day I would see those markers, cross its borders, feel the weight of its meaning on my shoulders as I climbed its flanks.

But as a Carrier, my future lay outside our lands, not within them. Izoloh might be glimpsed once, on a ceremonial voyage, known like a dream, not a home. My imagination turned outward. The stories I'd heard of the Stahranids made me hope I'd be sent there, but during Tsomak's service violence broke out again between the Qesar and the Stahranids. Tsomak was among the ranks when the Noyan freed mad Prince Shuru, and the horrors that prince wrought on his own people in his efforts to depose his father is the stuff of legend.

The news was told to me by my father, who used it as an example of unparalleled strategy: by freeing Prince Shuru, the Noyan ended the war between the Qesar and the Stahranids. By encouraging the prince's ambitions, the Noyan ensured the Stahranids would be too busy fighting among themselves to worry about taking back the cities and trade routes now under Qesar rule.

And how did the Noyan know where Prince Shuru was under guard, or why his father the King had placed him there? How did he know just what to say and do?

That, my father taught me, is the role of the Carrier. Let the Negotiators handle trade. You deal in knowledge and power. Not for yourself, but for the good of the Qesar.

One Carrier can bring peace or war. It's not the glory of the Kaganate, but it's honour nonetheless.

Izoloh remained a fairyland, only half-real. Outside, beyond the borders – the *dzarnyn*, the same word we use in the Concessions – that was where my future lay.

And then, three years later, Tsomak came home.

You comfort the Homeless ghosts until they find peace.
You bar the Hungry Ones from our tents.

Tsomak's time with us was brief. He was to return to the horde, to ride again with the Noyan after his service as a soldier, just as my mother had.

The longest day of summer was my birthday. We count age from the new year, but since the day I came into the world was easy to remember, my mother made me my favourite food, spicy meat dumplings, and my father came to eat with us.

He brought Tsomak.

When he came up to the fire pit near my mother's tent where we were cooking, there was a moment where I didn't know what to do. He'd been my whole world, and then he was gone. Now he was a hero of the Stahranid wars, and I was a child of thirteen.

He looked me over, a strange expression on his face.

"Aisulu," he said.

Most people apart from my mother called me Seventh Daughter.

"Tsomak," I said. I wanted to say *I missed you*, but I didn't know how.

He held out a small pouch.

"For you," he said. "For all the New Years I missed."

I took it and tipped the contents into my palm.

There were seven figures, individually wrapped in scraps of silk. Through the thin material I could see they were gold, no taller than my little finger, but beautifully detailed.

It was my family. Not all of them, of course. My father, wearing the symbol of the Blue Wolf Clan. My mother, with her spear. First Wife with her bottle of firesap, and Second Wife with her counting board. And then there was Tsomak, a hawk on his wrist, and me, reaching back for an arrow from my quiver.

I knew what they were. They were for my family shrine, when I left home.

The seventh was the stylised figure that topped every shrine. Crowned, enthroned, arms spread in blessing, the Kagan oversaw every home, blessed every family.

"They're beautiful," I said.

"Izoloh gold," my father said, his eyes wrinkling in pleasure.

"I thought it sounded like you," Tsomak said. "Aisulu, Izoloh. I believe you're meant to go there."

There was a strange intensity in the air. My father and mother glanced at one another, and Tsomak kept staring at me. My parents were proud, excited, but when I looked into Tsomak's face, I saw sadness.

"Thank you," I said. It wasn't just the figurines. Talk like that is considered an omen. I wondered whether my name had been chosen for exactly that reason, its closeness to a powerful word. Either way, Tsomak had spoken in a way my parents interpreted as prophecy.

We ate the dumplings. Tsomak returned to Bacaeydon. Summer died, my training continued, and my brother stayed away.

> *Soul of the Clans, you who climb the spine of the world,*
> *May your shadow always find its way home.*

Twenty Two
IMMERSION

EBBA'S TALE

The Bishop's Palace, Ban Granis

he holyman is at prayers when Neklaus drags me before him. My legs are numb, barely able to hold me up, an my feet are still hobbled, but Neklaus holds my shoulders hard enough to bruise, keepin me upright.

In the candlelight an the gloom before dawn, I see a thin man hunched over his clasped hands. He's kneelin in a small personal chapel, apart from the rest of the palace. On the altar is a white bone box, carved wi robed figures an edged wi gold. Before it lies an open book, gold splashed across a page. Next to it stands a goblet set wi precious stones, full of deep red wine. In its stem is a crystal, an buried in the crystal is a nail.

Not an iron nail.

A fingernail.

When I realise what it is, I don't seem to be able to stop lookin. It still has what looks like skin an flesh attached to the reddened base, like someone just tore it free.

I force myself to look at the man in front of me instead. He's turned away from me, an over his shoulder I can just see the pale angle of his cheekbone, his colourless lashes lowered over half-closed eyes. His shape is familiar. I focus on that. The memory of my journey into the city in the back of a cart, wrapped in sailcloth beneath the dead weight of Captain Hadric an Lotho, hovers at the edges, but I push it away.

Better to think about the sharp shoulders, the glint of candlelight on gold pages.

The scriptorium, I realise. The tall man leading Berengar to prayers, the book Rosamund showed me. *The bishop . . . my uncle . . . my bride price.*

The Bishop of Corvennes takes his time. At my back I can feel Neklaus gettin wound tighter an tighter. It's all he can do not to speak, but somethin's holdin him back.

Even in shock – because that's what this numbness is, I know that well enough – I have the sense to know that anyone who can restrain Neklaus is worth being scared of.

Finally, the Bishop rises, unfoldin upwards.

"My son," he says, holdin out his hand to be kissed.

"Father," says Neklaus, but he holds me in place between us, not movin to take the Bishop's hand. "I have her."

The Bishop lowers his hand, an looks me over.

"Ashes and blood," he says. "Really, Merzen. You could have had her washed."

"She's too dangerous for that," Neklaus says.

The Bishop laughs. It surprises me, the rich timbre of the voice escapin that tall, gaunt frame. It has genuine warmth, an for a moment I want to hurl myself at the feet of this man who seems, just now, almost fatherly.

"Merzen, I'm surprised at you," the Bishop says, turnin an gesturin for us to follow. "You know we have the baths at our disposal. She'll be quite safe from escape. Have your men guard her."

"Father," Neklaus says.

The Bishop stops abruptly an looks into Neklaus' face. "Oh dear," he says. "I suppose you managed to bring some of them back? Captain Hadric has served the family for decades."

"They betrayed us, Father," Neklaus says. "They informed the Emperor."

The Bishop of Corvennes holds Neklaus' gaze, an Neklaus, amazingly, squirms. It occurs to me that maybe Neklaus en't usin the word Father as a title, but as a fact. My face must show somethin, cos the Bishop's eyes flicker to me, an he smirks.

"I send you after two girls, and you return with one, and all your soldiers dead," he says. "Oh Neklaus. This isn't good, is it?"

I can feel Neklaus shakin through his whole body.

Whatever this is, I do not want to be between em.

The Bishop turns on his heel, an Neklaus stumbles after him, draggin me out of the chapel an over the black an white tiled floor of an open-roofed hall. We follow him down another corridor, out into a garden, an then turn sharply to follow a long wall, before descendin a stair to a lower level.

The change in temperature hits me at once. The air here is cold, an the light from a single horn-filled window very faint. Under a marble dome is a pool, flush wi the tiled floor, an before it is a strange wooden contraption, a long wooden arm balanced on a central pivot. One end rests on the floor, an the other holds a kind of seat wi the same wide leather buckle as the one Neklaus used to secure me to his saddle.

I tense up as Neklaus pushes me towards the seat. His strange fear before the Bishop needs somewhere to go, an here I am. He holds me by the scruff of the neck, an takes out his knife.

My body is so far from my own by now that I barely flinch.

I look up an meet the Bishop's impartial gaze. It's like he's watchin a butcher choose cuts in the market, his only real interest that he en't bein cheated.

"Leave her shift on," the Bishop says. "We don't have time for extra contritions today."

My ears are still strugglin over this new word when Neklaus slides his knife under my chin an cuts *down*.

As the ruined dress is cut off me, my eyes drift beyond the Bishop to the darkened recesses of the cold room. There's two raised stone slabs piled wi long shadowy bundles in sailcloth. But just then Neklaus pushes me into the seat an buckles me, usin the leather strap to secure my wrists. He steps back, an I'm balanced on the seat. He bends an releases a bar on the pivot, twistin me until I'm over the pool.

The Bishop steps forward.

"You were baptised by Saint Grimulf at the holy pool in Birchhold," he says, givin the name a clipped Southern sound.

I just stare at him. The words are reachin me, but it takes me too long to understand or respond. I've only just realised what the bundles on the slabs are: the bodies of the men who tried to protect me.

"Think of this as a second welcome," the Bishop says.

He raises his hand an makes the mark of the White God in the air, murmurin in kirk tongue.

His bone-pale hand is the last thing as I see as the seat drops beneath me, an I'm plunged into the freezin water of the pool. I gasp, water floodin my mouth an nose. I feel my spirit bein forced back inside me, an that's what scares me most.

He was tellin the truth. This time there's no escape.

The first time I surface I throw up water, the second whatever was left in my stomach from the day before. The third time I go under I'm ready for it an hold my breath as long as possible, but he seems to want me drowned, an by the time I'm raised I'm vomiting water again.

I hang there, wracked by coughs as my lungs try to clear themselves. When I finally sit back the Bishop smiles at me.

"That's better," he says. "You're awake now, aren't you?"

Too late I see the flick of his hand towards Neklaus, an feel the seat plunge downwards again.

I tire quickly. I can't hold my breath as long nor catch it, still coughin as I'm dunked, an my chest starts to ache horribly.

"Stop," I manage to beg after the seventh or eighth time. "What d'you want?"

I can taste blood in my throat.

The Bishop gestures for Neklaus to pivot the seat back to land.

"See?" he says. "Most amenable."

I hunch over on the seat, the sodden shift tangled around me, shiverin in the cold air. The Bishop gives Neklaus orders I can't hear, then turns back to me as Neklaus leaves.

"You've caused me a great deal of difficulty, Ebba," the Bishop says. The shock of my name in his mouth is a strange one, almost like being stripped. "This could all have been achieved so much less fuss if you had simply allowed yourself to be sent to my sister's convent."

I search his face. "Gisla?" I say, seein again the tall grey-clad woman who came wi Rosamund to the Lughambar Concession.

The Bishop of Corvennes narrows his eyes, studyin me.

"Instead," he says, "you've cost me weeks of pointless searching, and more men than I care to count. Not only did you arouse Neklaus to such a state that he appears to have singlehandedly eradicated a squad of men *after* your capture, on top of those lost in skirmishes, but the squad we sent down the Samara to the coast fell victim to the Raiders on their way upriver to Lughambar. As you can imagine, it has taken some patience not to order your immediate disposal."

"Why din't you?" I ask.

The Bishop smiles.

"Because as soon as the first riders came out of Arngard with news of my old friend's death," he says, "I knew two things. I had to bring him home, and I had to find the Salvebearer. And then what should I hear but that my niece's betrothed, Grimulf's own clerk, was riding south in the company of a girl out of the North? So I sent word to Vellsberg that any female companions should be placed in Gisla's care. It should have been so simple. I didn't even bother to stay for the feast, so confident was I in my allies. Of course, by the time I was informed of my mistake, you had already fled. And here we are."

Footsteps ring on the tiles outside.

"Now that you've been purified," the Bishop says, "I have something to show you."

Neklaus enters, a folded linen sheet over his arm. The wild force of him has sunk back beneath the handsome face, the energetic body. The Bishop catches me lookin him over, an his smile widens, almost conspiratorial.

"Let her down, Merzen," he says.

Neklaus comes to me, his sunny face open as a child's. The leather strap has swollen, so he has to yank it hard to loosen it enough to get the metal tongue out, forcin the breath out of me. He does this wi the same breezy air that I know he would use to saddle a horse, or punch someone in the gut. Once I'm free, he lifts me down, and drapes the linen sheet around me. I wrap myself tightly, glad to be better covered. I'm shiverin badly now, but neither man seems to notice.

"This is the *frigidarium*," the Bishop says, waving one hand as if interrupted in the middle of showin me his home. "An early cold bath is meant to enliven the spirit, but I leave that to the young." He smiles at me. "However, it has other useful qualities. Do you know, Ebba, that cold inhibits decay?" My teeth are chatterin too much to answer. "But of course you do. You helped in the hospital at Birchhold. The Vellsberg boy has been most informative. I believe you froze the dead to preserve them for burial in the spring."

Neklaus makes me follow the Bishop as he moves into the darker recesses of the room. My ankles are still hobbled, an I stumble on the slippery tiles. The Bishop pauses wi one hand on the canvas-covered bodies piled on the first slab, still smilin.

He walks on to the next slab, topped with a covered box. I don't let myself look at the pile as I pass. They're dead cos of me.

"Do you know," he says, "how hard it is to get anything done right in the North? It has been an unspeakable trial from start to finish, even with competent men in the right places. Grimulf proved to be incorruptible before death, which should in itself be a sign of beatitude, but getting him to remain incorrupt afterwards took finesse, and that is not something the North has much notion of. Can you believe my agent had to intervene to stop them *burning* the remains? Luckily, the merchant Dagomar has some skill in the transportation of flesh," the Bishop continues, reaching for the edge of the white sheet covering the box on the slab. "His work has bought us time. What do you think?"

He pulls back the cloth. Even deadened by the cold, the smell hits me first: sickly sweet, like rotted lilies, an underneath it, the richness of incense, the rasp of smoke.

The Prester lies before me, his flesh still whole, three moons after his death.

I jerk myself back from the box, into Neklaus' waitin arms, as the Bishop bursts out laughin.

"I can see why he chose you," he says, as the echoes bounce away between the tiles. "You're delightful. It's like watching a peasant try to understand silverware. Put her in the guest chambers, Merzen. The ladies can see to her, at least until Dagomar arrives with our guests. I have several delicate interviews to conduct before the coming Feast of Embers, but this has confirmed everything. We'll deal with the rest later." He claps his hands in satisfaction, then gives Neklaus a stern look. "Don't linger."

I am relieved to be taken from the man's presence. His jollity is almost worse than Neklaus' rages. This time Neklaus directs me with his hand on the back of my neck. Sodden, frozen, shackled, I do my best not to slip as he presses me before him. He seems strangely elated.

We climb above ground again, along the corridor, through the same tiled hall, then turn into a courtyard. It's after sunrise, an the pale gold of the southern sun is already warm. We cross a sunken garden between planted beds, circle a marble pool, an head towards vine-wreathed trellises. Wooden stairs rise along the far wall to a wooden gallery. Neklaus pushes me up the stairs an along the gallery, stoppin before a heavy wooden door. This he opens, shovin me before him into the dim room an lockin the door behind me.

I stagger forward, only to be caught by two figures.

I look up into the worried faces of Rosamund an her aunt Gisla.

"Ebba!" Rosamund cries.

I take one look at her pretty freckled face, an burst into tears.

Rosamund's aunt may be shut away in a set of rooms without proper light or freedom, but she en't lost her briskness. She strips me down, wraps me in linen from the bed, then bundles me in blankets. I cry through most of it, my teeth still chatterin, but the first fury of tears has passed, an by the time I'm settled in a chair, the sobs have given way to a blocked nose.

"How did you get here, Ebba?" Gisla asks, handin me a beaker of hot wine. Her oval face has the same strictness I remember from Varkha's parlour, though more haggard.

So I tell em about the fight between the Qesar an the guards, an how I was captured an taken by Neklaus, an all the sorry story of Hadric an Lotho an the others. Rosamund perches beside me, workin a comb through my hair. When I reach the end, an tell em about enterin the city in the cart under the bodies of the guards, her hands tremble, tuggin my hair.

Gisla's face grows more severe as she listens.

"The Lord forgive them," she says. "Sergeant Hadric was a good man."

Rosamund rests a hand on my shoulder.

"We never returned to the convent," she says. "Neklaus was waiting for us outside the Concession."

"But that was weeks ago," I say.

"Yes. Neklaus 'accompanied' us to my uncle's palace at Corvennes, and then we were conveyed here."

Kidnappin women seems to be a family tradition.

"Your uncle showed me the Prester," I say. "He ought to be rottin, but he en't."

Gisla glances at Rosamund. "Then it is as we thought. Ormund has secured the body. His designs advance."

"What designs?" I ask. "What is all this? An why does he need me?"

"We weren't sure," Rosamund says, lookin sideways at her aunt, like she's waitin for approval. "At first we thought this was just about the hagiography, and my betrothal. But it's bigger than that."

"The book?" I ask.

"It was a gift," Rosamund says. "A collection of the lives of the Northern saints, created in the Vellsberg scriptorium as part of the price to be paid to my family. It was stolen."

"I don't understand," I say. "You thought we'd taken it, but now the bishop has it."

Again, that look between Rosamund an her aunt.

"Neklaus told us you had it on you when you were captured," Gisla says. "Just before he brought you up here. He came to gloat.

He said he had proof that the raid was a ploy."

"He must be lyin," I say, but my thoughts are slowly catchin up wi me.

Aisulu, who took such pains to avoid the roads, then left us to get captured at Durkno. Aisulu makin us cross the mountains rather than risk Gallicia. The way she looked through my curebag that mornin on the mountain when she thought I was asleep, an the way she tried to reach me when she realised I wasn't comin with em.

How did the Raiders enter Vellsberg?

Someone let em in.

I lean back, almost spillin the wine over myself.

"It was Aisulu," I say. Rosamund's eyesbrows shoot up. "That's what she was carryin. It was the Qesar all along. But why?"

"The book has an unusual story in it," Rosamund says. "I read a little of it. It includes the story of Saint Grimulf, martyred in Arngard, and his disciple, the Salvebearer."

"But," I say, "that's impossible. Berengar only tole em about Grimulf the day before we met."

Rosamund gnaws her lip. "There's something else," she says. "The martyrdom was wrong. The book showed both Grimulf and the Salvebearer martyred by fire."

I carefully put the beaker down, my hand shakin.

"When we were fleein Vellsberg," I say, "the villages we passed through *knew*. They'd already heard of Grimulf's death. In Durkno they called me—"

"False Disciple," Gisla says. "Yes. We heard."

"Neklaus came from Durkno," Rosamund says. "After he caught us at the Concession he told us what he'd seen."

"In great detail," Gisla says, shudderin.

I look between em. Rosamund warned me about her cousin, but I'm not sure Gisla knows. "He's—"

"Mad," says Gisla. "Yes. He always has been. He used to kill things as a child."

Rosamund gives me a look that says he did much more than that.

"I don't understand," I say. "What does it matter what the book says? Why burn a town to steal it?"

"If the Qesar took it," Gisla says, "they'll have had some dark use for it. You can't trust them."

"An your bishop? What use can he have?"

"The story showed Grimulf as a hero standing against the loss of freedom," Rosamund says. "We think it may be meant to inspire resistance."

"We may be from the *Regna*," Gisla says abruptly, "but the House of Merzen has always been a great believer in the Church. It is a source of influence and riches."

Rosamund looks surprised.

"Oh, don't be naive, girl," Gisla tells her. "Why do you think our family has such good standing? It's because half the court's wives were schooled by me, and the other half have sisters and daughters in our convent halls. Some of the greatest houses of the *Corda* pay tithes to the Bishop of Corvennes. I'm a true believer," she says to me, "and believe me, I have had my faith tested. But the world is profane. Faith is not enough. The divine must be separated, displayed, so that it is not mistaken or misused."

"Like a bloody nail in crystal?" I say.

Rosamund screws up her face an nods.

"Relics," she says. "Though they're not all so gory as uncle's chalice."

Gisla glares at her. "Relics are objects of power," she says to me. "They remind us of those whose faith withstood the ultimate test. They bring our souls closer to God."

"An they're part of the influence an riches?" I guess.

Gisla opens an closes her mouth.

"Yes," says Rosamund. "People travel to see them. Pilgrims mean money."

"So your uncle is . . . makin his own?"

"We think he may have planned Grimulf's death," Rosamund says. "If we're right, you're in terrible danger, Ebba. You're part of the set."

My ears ring. I take a gulp of the wine again in case it helps.

"Berengar was sent to Arngard with a message for Grimulf from the Emperor himself," Rosamund's sayin, "and my uncle has the Emperor's ear. Grimulf was given a mission to suppress heresy at all costs. We believe he was never meant to survive the war in Arngard."

"Burnin don't leave much for relics," I point out. "But of course, how stupid of me. The holy don't burn, do they? That's why the villagers put a little girl into the flames."

To be fair to her, Gisla looks sick.

"How did he even know about me?" I ask, but even as I say it, somethin that's bin naggin me finally comes clear. "The bishop said he had the Prester's body thanks to Dagomar," I say. "There was a Dagomar in Frithberg. He hosted the Prester. I met him. He's a merchant."

"Dagomar the slaver," Gisla says, "He's worked for my brother for years."

I see my home, Eldinghope, an the ships of soldiers landin to secure it in Grimulf's name.

"He said he wanted a route across the Iron Sea," I say. "Why?"

Gisla shrugs. "The Qesar and the Raiders control the northern routes," she says. "With a base in the Iron Sea, Dagomar could rival them. Or do business."

"The Qesar run slave routes?" I say.

Both of em look at me like I'm crazy.

"Their wars produce more slaves than all the banditry and want in the Empire," Gisla says. "Why, Rosamund tells me your own mother was a victim of the northern routes." The shock of hearing her say it is like a slap to the face. "Judging by your looks, I'd say your mother was likely captured during border disputes between the Qesar and the Stahranids. She was probably transported by the Water Qesar to the Amber Coast, where she was captured by Raiders. The northern routes are productive, but there is a certain amount of . . . wastage."

Wastage. Lost goods. My mother, taken as spoils by my father, cos no one thought she was owed freedom. Given another name, cos her own din't fit. Birthin two children who were good only for bondage an sacrifice.

"So your uncle has himself a martyr an his relics," I say. "An now he has his hagiography back, an me too. He said Dagomar was bringin guests, an he had work to do before the Feast of Embers, but I thought that was when the attack on Vellsberg happened."

Both women look worried.

"The Ember Days are saints' days of special penitence," Rosamund says. "There are six."

"The Day of the Blessed Hekatera is almost upon us," Gisla says.

"It marks the beginning of summer."

"And the opening of the summer court," Rosamund says. "The day when the Emperor declares all changes in the Empire. Auntie, tell her. She deserves to know."

Gisla purses her lips.

"You've heard," she asks, "of *Imperium Infractum*?"

I frown. Aisulu tole us about it. "The Unbroken Empire," I say. "They say the Empire's existed for thousands of years. Has it?"

Gisla's mouth twists.

"They raise houses on ruins they could never rebuild," she says, with a venom I en't expectin. "It's a story, that's all. Stolen glory, dug out of crypts and old scrolls, about the *Corda*'s right to rule. The story isn't important. It's there to distract from what they're really doing."

"The Emperor claims that since the Empire has existed for so long, all the lands within it belong to him," Rosamund says.

"The House of Merzen has existed since the time when the *Regna* were free," Gisla snaps, "when the south cowered from our attack."

She don't say it, but I hear it, under her words. Maybe I hear it cos I've lived through the same thing.

When the Regna were free, an pagan.

I look at Gisla in her long grey dress an veil, a woman who has found power through the kirk. It must of bin generations back, that pagan freedom. After the *Corda*'s success, my guess is the House of Merzen grasped where the power lay an sought it out, like water flowin downhill.

"Everyone expects him to declare the rule of *Imperium Infractum* law at the opening of this summer court," Rosamund says.

"What's he offerin?" I ask. "Lords don't just hand over their lands, from what I've seen."

Rosamund gives me a thoughtful look.

"Everyone who lives and works on our lands would be subject to the nobility," she says. "No freeborn representatives, no bargaining, no say in how the lord chooses to dispose of the land. No inheritance of land within freeborn families. No right to leave the land without permission."

She sees my eyebrows rise.

"The freeborn and the half-free have rights in the *Regna*," she explains, "but not in the *Corda*. The Emperor seeks . . . alignment."

"An Merzen en't happy wi that?" I ask. "Seems to me you'd jump at the chance."

Gisla has regained her composure. "We are the free nobility," she says, "just as the freeborn on our lands are free. If Merovec has his way, our lands would be his, leased to us so long as we were loyal."

"Merovec?"

"His Imperial Majesty," Gisla says. "Holy Patriarch and Emperor."

I'm silent a long time, thinkin this through. Rosamund finds me a dress of hers to wear, although it's too tight an I have to leave it unlaced. The underside of my hair still lies damp against the nape of my neck.

"There's somethin I don't understand," I say to Rosamund when we're alone. "How does Dagomar fit? Why does your uncle work with a slaver? For gold?"

"Money must be part of it," Rosamund says. "Auntie won't say it, but I think it's because if we don't submit to the Emperor's plans, and the freeborn of Merzen stay free and fight for us, we need labour. You must have field-thralls in the North?"

I nod. Yes, there were thralls workin the fields of my uncle's land in Eldinghope, an in the fields around Frithberg. If my uncle had failed to pay his debt to the man I worked for, I would of been sold as a thrall. When the Prester paid it off, by law he bought me an my uncle's debt.

There's a rappin at the shuttered windows.

"Cousin," calls a sing-song voice out on the gallery. "Salvebearer. I've come with your foo-ood."

Beside me I feel Rosamund stiffen.

"Or you can starve," Neklaus goes on. "Like nuns immured in holy contemplation. Then the Bishop will have some nice new relics, Salvebearer, and your sweetheart noble boy can write your Acts and Lives. I wonder what he'll put in yours, cousin?"

Rosamund's hands have balled into fists. I put my hand on her wrist.

"Maybe I should tell him to get started," Neklaus says. "He's here in Ban Granis, paying court to the Northern delegates in Dagomar's care. Can you believe, Salvebearer, that little king you have in Arngard is coming all the way here to see the Emperor. I wonder what for?"

Me an Rosamund look at each other. We don't speak until Neklaus gets tired of tauntin us an goes away, leavin the food scattered across the planks outside the door in pique.

"Rosamund," I say. "If I can speak wi King Kolrand, I think I can get us out of here. We have to get to Dagomar."

Twenty Three
WANDERER'S PRAYER

*I call you, Ai Nakota, on Sarik's Night, when all
mothers remember their children.*

 was in my sixteenth year when by himself, on a
horse I didn't know, Tsomak returned.

Everyone changes during service. My mother
had warned me that Tsomak would be a man
now, and might not have time for a young girl. He'd stayed on
three more years than the minimum term, and I hadn't seen him
since I was a child, since he had given me the figurines.

He came straight from the Noyan. The man who had
commanded my mother and father during their long romance.
The man who had won a victory so paralysing over one of our
rival powers that for years we'd dominated the trade routes from
the east as all the Stahranid routes fell to banditry. Those were
good years – silks, spices, precious stones, ivory, furs, lacquer,
porcelain – all of these and more passed through our warehouses

in Bacaeydon, and the Noyan was the reason for it.

So when Tsomak rode through our gates, my family wanted a hero, not a ghost.

I was on lookout. I'd volunteered for more shifts, knowing Tsomak would be coming home, and I'd been given them, even though I should have been studying. So I was up on the high rocks that formed a natural lookout point just outside the stockade of our summer grounds. It was among those rocks where on warm nights I would sneak out with the other young people of the camp. There I told secrets, sang songs I wasn't supposed to know, drank stolen wine, and kissed boys and girls among the shadows, learning my liking was open to either.

But that day I was working under the early autumn sun. When I saw the horse, I thought we had a dead messenger.

That happened sometimes. Messengers bearing important news would strap themselves to their mounts, so that even if they were hit, their horse might reach safety with the written message intact.

The rider was bowed over the horse's shoulders, lolling to and fro. I'd whistled to the guards on the stockade and had my bow ready before I realised who it was.

As soon as I recognised him, I scrambled down from the lookout point. By the time I reached the gates, Tsomak had already been taken to his mother's tent. I didn't see him for days. Instead, I asked every single person who'd been there, who'd helped him off his horse, who'd held him as he collapsed, who'd helped carry him.

Tsomak had come back missing one of his souls.

No one knew what had happened. His horse was tired, but not hard used. His body was unmarked. His pack held personal items and letters from the Noyan and Tsomak's immediate commander, commending his service. He had been brave, he had distinguished himself, and now he was as helpless as a babe.

There was no sign that anything had been wrong when he left for home.

After two days, I was desperate. My father had been sent for from the warehouses in Bacaeydon, but I couldn't wait.

When I was small, sneaking in and out of tents was a game we'd play. We'd crawl under the edge, slip between the inner and outer walls, find the fastenings and untie them just enough to slip through and surprise someone or steal food.

We never sneaked into First Wife's tent. We were all far too scared of her for that. Stories of the beatings she'd given her own sons were legendary, and no one wanted to test her arm. But now, when I was really too big to be sneaking in anywhere, I found myself on my knees in the dark, running my hands around the edge of the outer skins of First Wife's tent, trying to find a loose peg where the gap was big enough for me to wriggle under.

Between the two layers of skin, all sounds were muted and odd. The comforting smoke of a dried-dung fire was overlaid with another, sicklier scent, and the wind against my back seemed to moan and suck at the skins. But there were also words, in a voice I knew but had never heard before.

I found the slit between two sections of skin, and put my eye to the gap.

First Wife was as I had never seen her. Her long hair was unbound, hanging down around her face and shoulders. I was startled to see grey at the roots, when just the other day her straight middle parting was as black as mine.

Her face was unpainted, her golden earrings, necklaces and finger rings all gone. Behind her, the ancestral shrine she kept to Sarik was covered over with a shroud. She wore a plain wrap, the kind we swaddle corpses in, and she knelt above the body of her youngest son, one hand on his forehead, one on his knees. A knife lay before her, and there were red blood stains across her chest. Her hands were stained with ash, and she was rocking and calling on Ai Nakota.

As I watched, Tsomak seemed to revive. His eyes stopped rolling beneath their lids, and his mouth opened, his lips forming words I could not hear. Immediately, First Wife crouched over him, her left hand feeling for an earthenware cup. She gathered him up, tipped his head back, and forced him to drink. Within moments, he succumbed again.

She picked up the knife, pulled back the wrap, and brought the blade to her chest. She made a cut, and I saw at that moment that it was one among many, that there were new cuts and old scars side by side.

I have never forgotten the words she said.

Wanderer! Find the missing shade of Tsomak, my greatest treasure, and lead him back to me, whole.

I was terrified. Grown and ready to serve in the horde in less than a year, and the sight of that indomitable woman cutting herself over the broken body of my childhood hero filled me with fear. I burrowed out from between the layers of horse skin, and sat shuddering in the night air.

I knew those born under the sign of Ai Nakota were said to have gifts.

After what I'd seen, I knew that First Wife was like me. No one else was allowed to call on the Wanderer that way. Like me, she'd been born on Gamlig's night. Like her, I was allowed to treat with Ai Nakota. Like her, I would have to pay.

Tsomak emerged a few days later. He was formally presented to my father, as though the interruption had never happened, and he had ridden through the gates like any other son or daughter of the clan. He had all the dignity you would expect of a young warrior newly freed from a decorated service.

I watched him, and for the first time in my life I had that feeling of staring at two people at once, as the memory and the flesh melted into one. I felt like I was seeing my brother after only ever hearing about him.

Tsomak was handsome, yes, but where before that had been something people told me, now I saw it for myself. A strong, noble profile, long, narrow eyes, brows that turned up at the outer edge like wingtips, cheeks a little hollowed but broad and bearing the summer's kiss of sun and wind. He bowed to our father and First Wife, and joined them making his offerings to the family shrines.

It was easy to avoid him; he left almost at once. I already knew nothing would be the same.

I wondered what divine jealousy First Wife had sought to avert by covering Sarik's eyes as she begged another god for the return of her son's missing soul.

In the new year, with the first thaw, I travelled south to Bacaeydon too. My service had begun.

I call you, Wanderer, you who pass through
the mansions of the sky and the earth.

In the Moon of Milk, in my eighteenth year, the Kagan died, Enclosed in Jade.

It was my second year in service. The Qesar were not at war, so my first summer had been spent in the north, in a barracks town, guarding *uareh* from Rus raiders. In the new year my company returned to Bacaeydon before heading east along the trade routes, to protect the spring caravans from bandits. It was out in the steppe, just after our company held the mourning ceremony for the Kagan, that my captain called me to him, and explained that my family was recalling me.

"Has my father died?" I asked. It was all I could think of, though as Seventh Daughter my presence at the rites was not needed.

The captain shook his head. "It's for a Great Rite," he said. "You travel bound."

That scared me. Like the messengers carrying important news, it meant I would be buckled to my horse. Even if I died on the way, my body would be transported until it reached the destination, to fulfil my duty even in death. I had no idea what that duty might be.

It's hard to remember those days. I was used to riding, of course, but this was different. This was day after day of galloping, changing horses all along the way, strapped and held in place. I was rubbed raw, bruised, scraped. Pain didn't matter, only duty did.

I arrived in Bacaeydon half a moon later, just before my birthday. It was five years since the day Tsomak had given me the golden figurines. I had them still, hidden in pouches in my belt, along with my knife. They were there, pressed against me, when I entered the Council building in Bacaeydon, overlooking the Agate Sea.

My father was waiting for me. He looked older, but energised. His deep-set eyes were alight in his round face. He greeted me formally, but the pride rolled off him like wine fumes.

He led me to the Council chamber. There were the clan leaders, and the Noyan – I recognised him from the inspection of the troops the year before – all in mourning colours.

And there was Tsomak.

He was apart from the Council. He sat on a throne of marble, raised above the others but outside of their circle.

My mouth dropped open.

My father bowed at the foot of the steps.

"Celestial Father," he said. "Your bodyguard is here."

Day and night are alike to you,
male and female are alike to you.

Walking down from the plateau in the pre-dawn light, my eyes on Torny, it's only once I'm on the flat that I see that our arrival has not only brought out the Negotiator of the Ban Granis Concession himself, but who that is.

"You could have warned me," I mutter to Kizmid, as we approach the water. She just shrugs as she sets Torny down.

A man in formal dress waits by the Concession's ceremonial *uareh*. The ship is painted like a child's toy: bright reds, blues and yellows. It reminds me of the spring boat races on the Great Lake. I always preferred the summer horse fairs, where I could ride and shoot in the competitions. There were fewer ceremonial worms like Uryz at those.

Uryz himself is done up like a toy official for the toy boat. Even before dawn, there's not a hair out of place, and his fine robes seem uncreased by his journey. His face is unlined, but pouchy, especially under the eyes. The last time I saw him was back in the Confederacy, when he was in service to the Kagan.

"Lady Aisulu, Celestial Sister to the Soul of the Clans," he says, bowing.

I wonder if he knows how much I hate him. I can feel Kizmid's crew watching us. Not directly, of course, but the title Uryz used is not one you use lightly.

"It's just Carrier out here, Uryz," I tell him.

Uryz smiles as though he just bit into a sour plum. Maybe my rejection of titles upsets him just as much as his use of them does me.

"Lady Carrier," he says. "An unfortunate misunderstanding has arisen, and we have reason to believe that we may shortly be confined to the Concession at the Emperor's pleasure. Your crew and the costliest goods you carry will enter Ban Granis with us. The *uareh* must be sunk."

A murmur passes through the crew.

"It is lamentably unavoidable," Uryz says. "Your detention at Gallicia occasioned much comment. Best for us all if the same vessel never reaches Ban Granis."

His eyes fall on Torny. I feel my fingers itch for my knife.

"So this is the one," he says. "Funny. She looks like less than nothing, doesn't she?"

For a moment I think he's going to prod her with one beautifully shod foot, but luckily he thinks better of it.

"What's wrong with her?" he says. "Is she sick?"

"She is under my protection," I say.

"Ah." He gives me a thin smile. "Well. Maybe this time it'll work out better. Stow her away."

Kizmid steps forwards to pick Torny up, but I stop her.

"I'll do it," I say.

She's heavier than she was the first time I took her in my arms. The skinny bloody girl who escaped Vellsberg and Durkno has put on muscle, and I feel my shoulders protesting. But I'm damned if I'm going to let Uryz treat her like baggage.

I carry her up the gangplank. The crew have already uncovered the hideaway, the narrow wooden space between the oar benches. Kizmid helps me lay Torny down, and holds her while I shrug off my jacket and fold it under her head as a pillow, then drapes her own jacket over her.

Laid down there, her white hair shocking against her sun-reddened skin, the dark circles under her eyes making them look like sockets, my girl looks like a corpse. Kizmid puts food by her right hand. I reach over and put the waterskin I prepared by her left, under the scar I made on her.

I put my hand to her cheek. Her skin is cold and clammy.

"Forgive me," I whisper. "I should be with you when you wake up. But I'll be right here, I swear."

Uryz coughs. One of the Concession crew waits beside us, holding jackets identical to her own. I take one and shrug it on. It's embroidered and dyed with the kind of colour that sweat ruins. As rowing uniforms, they're expensive and useless.

"Captain, your braids," Uryz says, holding out a hand.

Kizmid's hand goes protectively to the braid at her hip. The thick blue strands map the course of the rivers and their tributaries, the beads marking fords, villages, and hidden moorings. The knowledge of all the waterways in the Southern Empire lies there, under Kizmid's callused palm. They're her status, and her responsibility.

"No oarsman wears such things," Uryz says, his hand still outstretched.

"They'll be hidden," Kizmid says. "Wherever you put me, I am a Captain of the Water Qesar. No one touches these but me."

Uryz folds his hand back across his front.

"I must see to my crew," Kizmid says, walking ashore.

The crew are already in their ridiculous ceremonial uniforms and stowing the goods that can be kept below decks. The Concession's vessel is for pleasure jaunts and official appearances, so it has a silly little brightly coloured awning raised over the oar pits. If no one looks below it to count the rowers, or notices how much deeper in the water she sits, we should be all right.

On shore, Kizmid's giving orders for the sinking of her *uareh*.

I look down at Torny. There's sweat on her brow, but she seems calm enough. I place my hand over her heart for a moment, then step back. Two crew members heave the walkway planks back into place, locking her in darkness.

I look away. This is for her good as well as mine, I know that.

But I also know how it hurts.

Kizmid and her crew are watching their *uareh* sink. I walk down the gangplank to join them, despite Uryz's impatience. They fall silent as I come to stand beside Kizmid. We are not sentimental, but we hate waste. Sinking a perfectly good boat makes none of us happy.

"I want to thank you," I say, into the quiet. "You delivered me and my friends, although we put you in danger. I know we Carriers have a reputation for thinking only of ourselves. Sometimes we work too hard at it." A couple of the crew smile, one snorts. "This is not the end I hoped for."

There's a pause.

"Is it true?" one of the crew asks. "What he called you?"

There's no avoiding it now.

"Yes," I say. "My brother was the Kagan."

They all bow. I don't tell them to stop, because this isn't about me. It's about an idea, a belief, one that binds us together. One that makes us all Qesar.

And I am part of it, whether I believe it or not.

Aboard the ceremonial *uareh*, I take the oar bench as close to Torny's head as I can. I can't be with her, but I'll be just the other side. Not able to speak, or touch, but close.

Kizmid and her crew settle around me, and I feel the new distance between us. It's respect, but it's also a lie.

My brother, the Soul of the Clans. Chosen by the gods, betrayed by his own kin.

Believe me, Torny. I know what it means to inherit death.

Wanderer, show us the paths
that lead from one realm to the next.

Twenty Four

IMMOLATION

EBBA'S TALE

The Bishop's Palace, Ban Granis

e tell Gisla what we think she'll accept.

"You think Berengar of Vellsberg will reconsider the betrothal?" she asks, sittin in her tall-backed chair in the dimness of the shuttered rooms. Her fingers leaf through a prayer book in her lap. After four days an nights shut up with her, I've realised this, like her sternness, is to hide her fear.

"Yes," I say. "Berengar of Vellsberg is honourable. Both houses gain. He's young, but he's had time now to see what would be best."

"You're the reason he refused," Gisla says. "Why should we trust you?"

"Cos I want to go home," I say. "I din't understand what it would mean, stayin with him. I see now it can't work. There's no place for me with him."

Gisla breathes heavily through her nose, her fingers smoothin the pages.

"It's true," she says. "You're wise to see it. Rosamund . . ."

She reaches out her hand, an Rosamund takes it.

Gisla looks at me.

"Neklaus cannot marry her," she says. "You understand? He will be a very bad husband for her."

I pity this woman her fear of sayin the truth out loud, how it has made her dishonest, even with herself.

He'll kill her, you mean.

"I'll help you reach Dagomar," Gisla says.

We know it'll take a miracle.

"This is part of the display," I tell her. "I'm sorry, but it will hurt."

Luckily, that en't one of the things that Gisla's afraid of. Old scars on her back tell me this woman has suffered for her faith many times before.

My curebag, battered an crushed, was brought to the rooms by Neklaus the day before, while I was alone wi the Bishop. Either they don't know what it is, or they don't care. I dig through it, settin aside the broken vials, the remainin bandages.

"Is this it?"

I look up to see Rosamund holdin the box of salve. Her eyes are wide.

"Don't believe everythin you read," I say. "It's good on burns, bites an bruises, an that's about it."

"But you cured the wolf," she says. Clearly that story's bin repeated a few too many times.

My heartstrings tug. What I wouldn't do to have Fetch wi me now. *He'd of bin killed or bin left behind long ago*, I tell myself. *It's better this way.*

"I was lucky," I say to Rosamund.

"You had a lot of luck," she says, "if half of what Berengar said was true."

I'm searchin through the contents of the bag, holdin em up in a bar of light that falls through the shutters to see em clear.

"Have you ever felt the White God?" I ask Rosamund.

She gives me an odd look.

"The Lord," I correct myself, remembering he's meant to be the only one. "Have you ever felt his presence, or heard him?"

She picks at a loose thread on her sleeve.

"Auntie used to tell me the Lord was merciful and he would protect me if I prayed," Rosamund says. "I prayed, Ebba. Every moment of every day, until they put me in a convent, and sent Neklaus away. He called me his bride. I was twelve. I just wanted company. I wanted to feel less alone."

I reach out an gently take her hand.

"I think you wanted more than that," I say. "You deserved more."

She grips my hand hard, our fingers interlocked, an I feel somethin I en't ever known before, a kind of power growin between us. No salve, no drops, no intercession, but I have that same clearness that the light once gave me.

"The White God came to me when I had nothin," I tell her. "But not when I was in it. Not to protect me. He came after, when I was at a crossroads."

Desire overwhelms me. I've bin longin, wi less an less faith, for that calm to come upon me again. I want that warmth, that light. I want that promise.

"I don't know why he stopped," I tell her.

❀ 281 ❀

"Maybe because now you have what you need," she says. "Did you ever think of that?"

Bishop Ormund no doubt meant it as insult an despair to hold his sister an niece without servants or care. Now it saves us. He is blind to our actions. Before Neklaus comes wi the evenin food, I ask Rosamund if she will speak with him. He's the only person allowed to open the door, an I en't eaten properly in days. Judgin by her aunt's weakness, neither has she.

"We have to eat," I tell her. "This is too dangerous for your aunt otherwise. Anyway, we need him thinkin you're comin round."

Rosamund's face pales, but she nods.

So when Neklaus knocks on the door an calls out for us, she goes to the window.

"Salvebearer," he sings, "Answer me. You must be hungry. Talk to me."

Standin by the shutters, Rosamund whispers, "Neklaus, it's me."

"Hello little cousin," he says. The shadow moves across the fixed wooden bars of the shutters towards her. "Where's your friend?"

"She's praying," Rosamund says. Her eyes are on me where I stand up against the wall beyond the door, an I nod to encourage her. "She and Auntie spend all their time praying in the other room."

"Are you lonely, cousin?"

Rosamund screws up her eyes an wraps her arms around herself, like she's tryin to hold herself together.

"I'm hungry, Neklaus," she says.

"Why don't I come in?" he says. "I'll feed you."

I can see her shaking, but she says what we planned.

"What does uncle say, cousin?"

He growls like a dog. The sound of it makes my hair stand up on end.

"He says I have to wait," Neklaus spits.

So I was right. The Bishop does control him.

"Let me touch your hand," he says. "When I open the door, let me hold your hand, cousin. Just for a moment."

She looks at me. I want to blind the bastard rather'n let him see her ever again. But I nod.

"Only a moment," she says.

"As long as it takes to say one *Ave*," he says.

"One *Ave*," she repeats, "but only my hand."

The key scrapes in the lock.

The red evenin light falls through the crack as the door opens inwards, lightin up Rosamund's pale face, her freckles stark against the white skin. Her hair is covered by a veil, her grey dress reaches from throat to wrist. Only her face an her hand are bare.

A shadow blots out the light, an a hand reaches through the openin an grabs her wrist. My stomach drops, an for a moment I think he's goin to drag her outside, but he pulls her hand through the openin an raises it. The angle of the door hides him from me.

Rosamund's eyes are open an blank. Her lips are movin, an I hear the soft murmurs of kirk tongue rollin from em as she recites the prayer that measures out this violation.

"*In hora mortis nostrae*," she says, an pulls her hand away, but he holds it back. I see her eyes flick up to him, wide an scared.

"*Amen*," he says, an lets her go, a basket in her other hand.

The door closes, the lock scrapes. We wait, listenin to his footsteps go along the gallery, descend the stair. Then I move to her side an reach out.

"Don't touch me," she says. "Don't, Ebba."

So I stand beside her, our backs against the shutters, an we do not touch. I match my breathin to hers, an when she sobs I try to breathe slow for her, hoping she will feel it. I din't want to hurt her.

"I'll do it next time," I say.

She shakes her head.

"He doesn't trust you," she says. "You fought him. I never did. It has to be me."

"You know that en't true," I say.

"It's true to him," she says.

We go into the inner room. Gisla is lyin on the bed, snorin the way old women snore, in gasps, her mouth open an her grey hair uncovered. She looks much frailer than the woman I met in the Concession, who drank mulsum an defended her niece's honour against the treacherous outlander.

"Will she be all right?" Rosamund asks me.

Now is not the time for the truth.

"It will hurt," I tell her. "But she will be free, an if she is free she will survive. It's a better chance than she has here."

I do not say what will happen if we don't escape. Rosamund an I both know that if we stay here, in these chambers where Neklaus has the key, that sooner or later the Bishop's hold will break.

Without another word, we latch the inner door, an I lay out the food while Rosamund wakes her aunt.

Tomorrow, I tell myself. *We'll be free tomorrow.*

We begin as the doves start cooin in the eaves.

There en't many black-wax sealed vials in my curebag. I choose one, the wax still glossy an unbroken. Rosamund gives me a metal stylus, the tip wrapped in a strip of bandage. In a small metal bowl I mix the contents of the vial wi water.

Gisla lies on her front, her dress pulled aside. Her skin is thin an white.

I dip the bandaged tip of the stylus in the bowl, an start to cover her back in long, wavy lines.

"I can't feel it," Gisla says, her face muffled against the pillow.

"You won't," I say. "Not till you go into the sun."

"Why do you have something so noxious in your bag of cures anyway?" Gisla grumbles.

"For burnin off carbuncles before they eat into you," I say.

Gisla stops askin questions. Rosamund sits beside her, watchin me work. When I've covered her back, I ask her to turn over. She does it wi the dignity of someone who has not bin seen uncovered by another person for many years. This time she holds her niece's hand an keeps her eyes closed.

"You would make a good abbess, Rosamund," she says suddenly. "A very good one. Whatever happens, you must know that. I am proud to call you family."

I trace the lines over her belly, unmarked by childbirth, up her chest, along her arms.

Gisla prays quietly under her breath.

By the time Neklaus knocks on the door, I'm done.

Rosamund goes to the next room, an I hear her speakin softly through the shutters as I help Gisla dress, one eye on the doorway.

"You are very resourceful, Ebba of Arngard," Gisla says, "but I do not want my niece to become like you. You use deceit to survive. I want her to live virtuously."

If she meant her words hurtfully, she missed her mark. Maybe because she shoots at herself, not me. I am not ashamed of what I do.

"Abbess, if your niece lives, that'll be enough for me," I say, cranin to hear what Rosamund's sayin.

"Auntie's sick," she's sayin. "She's been having dreams. She wants to see uncle."

"The Bishop is busy," Neklaus says. "He has guests."

"I'm worried, Neklaus," Rosamund says. "She says it's him. The Prester."

Neklaus laughs, that beautiful liquid sound. "The Prester is lying dead in the *frigidarium*, cousin," he says. "He's not causing anyone anymore difficulties."

Gisla pushes me to my knees wi surprisin strength, lies back on the bed, an groans loudly.

"Pray," she hisses to me.

I already have my head bent over my clasped hands.

I hear the door creak open, an a heavy step on the boards, then swearin.

"It's that Northern bitch, isn't it?" Neklaus cries, pushin his way into the room. "I told him, she's dangerous!"

He's behind me now, an I clench my jaw as he grabs me by the hair an throws me aside. My scalp tears an burns.

"Cousin!" Rosamund says. "Auntie's dying! We have to get her to uncle! She can't die unshriven."

"What will you give me?" Neklaus says.

I blink the spots from my eyes an look up.

Neklaus stands over Gisla, strong an young, his aunt lyin feeble an weak before him. He en't lookin at her. He's lookin at Rosamund, her back glued against the doorframe. She stares at him.

"She's dying," she pleads.

"How much is she worth?" he asks. His face is alight. When she don't answer, he moves towards her, grabs her veil wi one hand, an pulls it sideways. Rosamund's strawberry blonde hair falls with it, yanked from its pins. He drops the veil, winds his hand in her hair, an tugs. Her head tilts.

"I'll ask uncle," she says numbly. "I'll ask him to give me to you."

Neklaus lets out a long breath. It whistles through his teeth. He tugs her hair once more, then turns to Gisla an scoops her up in his arms.

"Not so strong now, auntie, are you?" he says, barin his teeth in a grin. "No one's getting any beatings today. Come on."

Lyin in his arms, Gisla groans. He turns, an strides out the room. "Come, cousin," he says over his shoulder. "Come and tell the Bishop what you told me."

Rosamund offers me her hand an heaves me up. I grab my curebag.

"This had better work," she says.

We stagger as we go through the door to the gallery. It's a beautiful day, the full sunlight of early summer fillin the formal courtyard. The marble gleams under a fountain throwin jewels of water through the air, an trees so dark they're almost black stand in the planted beds like shadowy sentinels. At the far end, towards the main house, a group of men sit in conference, servants layin food an drink before em, guards standin back under the portico.

I take Rosamund's hand an pull her after me.

Neklaus is only halfway across the gardens when Gisla starts to scream.

Floodbane is a difficult plant, Ma taught me. Handle it wrong in the sunlight, an your whole body will blister.

The heads of the men at the far end of the garden prick up. Neklaus freezes as Gisla writhes in his arms, while her shrieks rend the air. The men are on their feet now, two of em runnin towards the noise, while the others stare. The beds of plants hide em from me as I drag Rosamund along.

Gisla's screams are unholy. I pray I diluted the Floodbane enough as my heels pound the marble. As we get closer, I hear words in her babble:

"*Like an axe he falls . . . like an axe he has two heads . . .*"

My blood runs cold.

"Rosamund," I gasp. "Did you tell her that?"

"What?" she pants.

"*The fire shall mark the sinners, the fire shall spare the meek . . .*"

We come to the sunken garden. Neklaus is strugglin to hold Gisla, who writhes an shakes half out of his arms, her long grey hair torn loose from its veil. Her fingers claw at Neklaus' face an tunic, gougin into the cloth.

"*Prester, anoint my head with oil,*" she cries, fallin, an her foot slips into the marble basin of the fountain.

I drop to my knees an raise my hands. Beside me, Rosamund does the same.

"Have mercy, Lord," I cry out. "Have mercy on your true servant, an in the name of the Blessed Grimulf, secure her from the flames!"

The men have reached us now. I recognise Dagomar's black an grey head, his sharp nose, as he bends over, puffin from exertion.

With him are two guards in Merzen green, who must belong to the Bishop, an standin back, his broad shoulders covered in Ridgeland blue, a white triple knot on his chest, is a tall Northerner wi blue eyes an a nose that's bin broken a few too many times.

"Ebba," Erland says.

The sudden hope of safety makes me giddy. I daren't do more'n meet his eyes, but I see him frown at the traces of violence on my face.

The other men are comin too. Consequence can only keep you sittin so long when a banshee is let loose in your garden. I see the Bishop's tall form stridin towards us despite his robes. He seems astounded to find his sister almost lyin in the fountain.

"What's this?" he demands.

Rosamund is cryin real tears, but she sticks to her lines.

"She's been visited," she says, kneelin an tryin to catch her aunt's hands an hold em still.

Neklaus has given up an laid her down. Gisla lies on the marble, clawin at her dress an moaning. The men stare at her in consternation.

Erland steps forward, lifts her, an places her in the water. Gisla's eyelids flutter, her whites rollin up beneath em.

"She's burning," he says, an before anyone thinks to stop him, he takes his knife, cuts the high neck of the robe, an pulls it away from her skin.

As the sun falls on her bare skin, Gisla screams again, her voice hoarse. I see her eyes roll back an this time she faints. The men pull back in horror.

Her skin is covered in the red welts of flames.

Rosamund lies wailin across her aunt's body.

I look up into a face I last saw in a darkened tent, behind a veil of gold. Dark blonde hair, grey eyes, an a set to his mouth much firmer than I remember.

"Who is this?" asks King Kolrand. "What's wrong with her?"

He frowns at me, then his eyes widen.

"Salvebearer," he says.

Ormund looks between us. I catch a glimpse of his fury before his face smoothes into concern.

"Captain," he says, an both Erland an Neklaus look up. "Take her to the *frigidarium*."

Erland picks up Gisla. "Lead the way," he says to Neklaus. I see the younger man ball his fists at the order. "Salvebearer, you and your friend come too. Your Highness, your Excellency."

"Yes," mutters Ormund. "Let's see this prodigy."

Shakin out his robe, he shoots me a look of pure distrust.

Down in the *frigidarium*, the bodies of Hadric an his men have disappeared. Erland lays Gisla on her back on the first stone table.

"Salvebearer," he says to me, "we need your skill."

"She's the one who's done this!" Neklaus bursts out. "Everywhere she goes, this happens!"

King Kolrand looks at the Bishop. "Visitations?"

The Bishop purses his lips. "Nothing proven."

"Enough to hunt me an hold me," I say.

These men en't used to women speakin. Neklaus makes a move towards me, but Erland's arm shoots out an holds him back.

Gisla stirs, her eyes flutterin open. "*There is a fire in the north*," she says. Everyone looks at her, an I wonder if a chill just went down their backs like it did mine. Her dazed eyes fix on Kolrand. "He is here," she says. Her head lolls sideways, starin beyond him.

The men turn an stare at the second slab, further back in the gloom, covered in a white sheet. Dagomar, who followed without bein asked to, takes a step back.

Rosamund turns to me. "Help her," she says.

The strangeness of it leaves me. Gisla knew Grimulf's body lies here. She tole me herself that Neklaus described Durkno to her an Rosamund. Yes, her body's half on fire wi burns, but she knows how much is at stake. I have to believe she's a talented woman with a strong will.

You're no believer, the Prester says to me. *You've never believed.*

I can feel him wi me.

I've no time for you, I think. *Go away.*

But I think maybe he'll never go away.

Gisla's breathin is becomin harsher.

"I need to wash her," I tell Erland. "Rosamund, cold water. Captain, take em outside."

The Bishop's head snaps back to me. "This girl is in my possession, Captain," he says. "You forget yourself."

"This woman," Kolrand says, "is one of my faithful subjects."

The Bishop stares at the young king in contempt. "Dagomar, the will," he says.

Dagomar steps forward nervously. "The ah, the Prester's will is quite clear on the matter," he says. "Any property reverts to his superior prelate upon death."

My heart sinks.

"The freewoman known as Ebba Rathnasdota was indentured to Berger Sorleyson of Frithberg for a period of two years as surety for the debt of her uncle, Ulf Arfson of Eldinghope. That debt was purchased by Prester Grimulf of Vellsberg last year, and witnessed by myself, Dagomar, merchant."

"And that debt was paid in full by Ulf Arfson," Erland says. "As *I* witnessed."

"Ah," says Dagomar, "but the contract did not agree early release. Ebba Rathnasdota is still indentured for the period remaining, and indeed fled her service upon the death of her master. My Lord Bishop was merely collecting his property after significant delay. One which will have to be added to her total before release. The girl must stay with her master for another six moons at least."

Erland gives me a helpless look. We both know it's true. I was still indentured to the Prester when he died.

"Your Excellency," Kolrand says, steppin forward. "I see you have disbursed much time and effort acquiring what you believe to be your property, and for that I apologise. Had I known your concerns, I would have done my best to assuage them. Prester Grimulf presented this woman to me on the night of the battle that claimed him. He told me that should he fall in battle, she should be freed, and that I should take her into my household. This, of course, I granted."

"You have proof?" Ormund demands.

"I shall fetch it directly," Kolrand says. "Indeed, I'm surprised by this whole business. The deed of manumission was witnessed by Dagomar himself."

Dagomar's mouth drops open, and the Bishop's jaw clenches. He rounds on the unhappy merchant.

I stare at Kolrand.

That night before the battle of Frithberg, the man I met was a puppet, adorned in jewels, mouthin the prester's words. I could never have expected this from him. Clearly, things have changed.

He meets my gaze calmly.

"Salvebearer," he says. "You have work to do."

Twenty Five
CARRIER'S PRAYER

AISULU'S TALE

I call on you, Ai Nakota, as the Carrier of my people,
the one who wears many faces.

The blossom is dying on the branch. Brown and bruised, it scatters across the grass, no longer drifting like snow, but trodden underfoot. Workers moving between the trees cast incurious looks after us, watching the brightly coloured *uareh* with an edge of hostility. I wonder whether it's always been there, or if it's new.

I've got my back to the prow, so I don't see the bulk of Ban Granis growing on the horizon, but I feel the change as we slide within its domain, beneath the weight of its double walls, the scrutiny of its four towers.

Kizmid nudges me.

"You're brooding," she says.

"Remembering," I say.

"Don't think about Uryz," she says.

"He's here because of me," I say. "Exiled."

Kizmid grunts as she pulls on the oar. "Exiled and Negotiator both," she says. "Not much of a punishment."

"I failed," I say. "My ancestors must be ashamed of me."

Kizmid shoots me one of those looks I got to know well on our long voyage from Bacaeydon. When you're in disgrace, people tend to want you gone quick, and Kizmid was on her first captaincy to the Southern Empire, the farthest west you can get. As an adopted member of the Blue Wolf Clan, she could be trusted to keep her mouth shut.

"You're not usually this self-pitying," she says.

I glance over my shoulder. It's full daylight now, and we're close enough that I can see the guards on the river gate. Uryz is reclining on a folding chair up at the prow, looking as disdainful and relaxed as a person can. I have to admit, he's a good deceiver, and right now that is useful, whatever I may think of him.

Uryz's captain strolls the length of the walkway. Suddenly he stumbles, as muffled cries come from the boards under his feet.

Torny's woken up.

As you guide our shades from fate to fate,
so do I move from host to host.

We came to Izoloh in the depths of summer. The grass was tall, tinged with purple. Wild horses roamed the plains, and narrow streams cut through the turf, deep and cold. The Noyan himself accompanied us. One night he found me standing just beyond the light of our fire, staring out into the weald of stars above us.

"My mother rode with you in the Westlands," I told him, gathering up my courage to speak to him in the dark as I couldn't by day, and he laughed. He must have heard such things many times over the years.

"Your father stole her from us," he answered. "She must be very proud of her daughter."

My face flushed in the warm night. It was true, our whole family was intoxicated with delight. We had left Bacaeydon preceded by a parade of horses in fantastical costumes, disguised as mythical beasts, among troops and cavalry. The night before, the Blue Wolf Clan hosted a banquet for the other candidates, and each one stood to pledge his clan's support to the new Kagan. My father and First Wife presided, arrayed like Taghr and Sarik themselves.

I try not to think of it now.

The Kagan sat silent throughout. He was a living god, after all. His fringed headdress veiled his face from the revellers, and what was glimpsed between the red fringes was so handsome that I heard whispers of his unearthly beauty and celestial qualities from all sides.

The Noyan and a small squad of experienced warriors formed the Kagan's guard of honour. I was his personal bodyguard, but I was also a girl of eighteen years. The men and women of the guard of honour had served the last Kagan, and under their guidance I would learn my new duties, duties I had never imagined for myself.

Out on the Sea of Grass, under the blazing stars, I sensed that this might be the last taste of freedom I ever had, and I understood Tsomak's first words to me when my father presented me to him in Bacaeydon.

"I'm sorry, Aisulu."

Tsomak was not celestial to me. He was my brother, and I knew that carved, cold beauty in him came not from divine favour, but from despair.

The day I saw the stone fortress of Izoloh rising above us, the holy source spilling down from a lake that reflected the sky, the rivers cut into the floodplain, lined with carved stones, I knew I stared upon the hidden graves of every Kagan since the first of our people set foot here. A place where sacred blood must never be spilt. I should have known then: *Sunk with the Moon, Enclosed in Jade.*

There was nothing in that beautiful place but death.

> *I call you as the Carrier of my people,*
> *the one who is free among the bound.*

"Shut her up!"

Uryz hasn't moved, but his body in the chair is stiff with tension.

The hammering on the boards grows more frantic. The words are muffled, but I know she's shouting my name. I'm frozen, not knowing what to do.

Kizmid leans across me and knocks twice on the boards beside me.

There's a pause, then more muffled cries. Kizmid nudges me.

I copy her, the same double knock, like a heartbeat.

Instead of calming her, the hammering grows stronger.

Uryz is glaring pure death at me. I know what he's thinking, that I should have bound and gagged her before I hid her, like merchandise.

I knock again on the wood.

Kizmid glares up at the captain from her oar.

"Don't you know any oar songs?" she demands.

The captain stares at her. I can see dark sweat patches forming under his arms.

"We're trying not to draw attention," Uryz hisses.

The hammering is dying down, but still audible. We're only a short way from the river gate and the guards.

"We're Qesar," Kizmid says. "We'll always be unwelcome. Let's shake them, eh?"

She takes a breath and her deep, pleasant voice rises in lament. It's the song about the lovers Roku and Sata, the one we sang around the fire the night Torny put her hand in mine. Kizmid's crew join in, followed less certainly by the Concession crew. Glancing over my shoulder, I see the guards standing up, watching us. I knock again on the wood. The other side is quieter now.

She must have drunk from the skin, I think.

My heart twists. I did not mean for her to go alone like this. I wanted to be beside her. I wanted to hold her, to pray for her, so that Ai Nakota knew who I was sending to them, and why.

Wanderer, Kaerueg, listen to me,
to the one who is like you, who does as you do.

Uryz was also from our clan, his position at Izoloh elevated now to Advisor by Tsomak's selection. He greeted us inside the fortress, bowing very low before leading us to our quarters. We had passed through the lower ring, dedicated to the goldsmithies, and the second where the guards and servants lived. We were now at the peak, where the temples and palace lay.

The Noyan put one hand on my shoulder before we parted

ways. I think he could tell I was dizzy from it all, the views across the boundless plains, the polished stone floors, the sun thrown back from the lake and rivers.

"Go to him," he said. "He'll need you."

My room adjoined my brother's chambers. I set my golden figurines upon the shrine, my heart beating high and fast, splashed my face with water, and went to him. Through chamber after chamber I went, almost running, until I found him on a balcony carved into the cliffs of the mountain itself. He was staring out, his headdress in one hand.

He turned to me and my heart skipped.

I'd never seen anyone look so lonely.

"Tsomak," I said. For a moment I felt ten again, watching him leave, except then he'd been happy. I forgot he was the Kagan, Celestial Father, Soul of the Clans, or that I was a grown up. I ran to him and wrapped my arms around his waist.

"Aisulu," he said, dropping the headdress, wrapping his arms around my shoulders. He buried his face in my hair, and I felt his own long hair brush my hands as it uncoiled from its pins. His shoulders jerked, and I realised he was crying.

"Don't be scared," I said. "I'm here. I'll protect you."

It was absurd, the child comforting the king.

He gripped my shoulders with his hands, his nails digging into my skin.

"You have to understand," he said. "You can't save me, Aisulu."

I pulled back, startled.

"From what?" I asked.

There was a cough from the doorway. Uryz stood there, obsequious and disapproving.

"The priests are ready, Celestial Father," he said.

Over his arm he held a blood-red robe.

We descended through the palace stair by stair, until we entered a circular room. The chill made me shudder. Tsomak's robe glowed in the light from the lit tapers. The priests stood at the edges of the room, around an ornate metal grille in the floor. Taghr's priest was crowned in gold. Sarik's priestess was clothed in blue silk. Gamlig's priest was dressed in black. White lengths of silk lay across their arms, and they each held a bowl in their hands. Smoke curled from the grille, smelling sweet and sickly.

I saw Tsomak shake as he stepped into the smoke.

And still I did not understand.

"In the name of the Daylit King, eat, Celestial Father." The crowned priest offered my brother a bowl of white mares milk.

Tsomak drank.

"In the name of the Sunlit Queen, drink." Sarik's priestess stepped forward and offered him a bowl of firesap.

Tsomak emptied it.

"In the name of the Unlit King," said Gamlig's priest, "remember what you are." His oddly-shaped bowl held ashes.

Tsomak dipped his fingers in the bowl, and drew them over his face. He moaned.

The fumes from below made my head spin. I realised what Gamlig's priest was holding. It was a funerary urn.

I remembered First Wife, her hands stained with ashes as she wailed. I remembered Tsomak lolling across his horse as he rode home, looking like a dead man, and my lessons at First Wife's knee.

Then I understood. Then I knew.

Taghr's favour. The gift of a certain death.

Together, the priests raised their white silk, and in one movement slipped them over Tsomak's head, around his neck. Standing around them, they began to tighten the silk around his neck.

Tsomak sank to his knees and began to choke.

I must have made some movement, because the Noyan was already beside me, gripping my arm, and his hand closed over my mouth before I could scream.

"He's all right," he breathed in my ear as I struggled. "This is the Ceremony of the Soul. He'll be all right."

Tsomak's face changed horribly, red and dark. His eyes bulged and rolled. Spit foamed on his lips.

And then, just as I thought he must die, the white silks were released, and he collapsed forward onto his hands and knees, enveloped in the smoke, his breath like a death rattle in his lungs.

The voice when it came was not his.

I swear that to this day.

"Wound in Silk," he gasped. "In the Moon of Snow, one year from now."

Uryz cried out. The Noyan's hands dropped away from me in shock.

And I ran to my brother, my Kagan, who had divined that his reign should last just half a year.

I conjure and implore you,
I bind and compel you.

We sing as we pass through the river gate. The guards watch us, outright hatred on their faces.

As we pass beneath the shadows of the walls of Ban Granis, into the guarded heart of the Empire, there is one last flurry of pounding from the hideaway. Then nothing.

Tsomak lingers in my mind, but I can't look directly at the memories anymore. There are tears on my cheeks, tears blinding me as I try to tell my lover that I'm here, that I'll protect her.

Always making promises I can't keep.

I wanted to tell Torny about Tsomak, to explain where I come from, but something always stopped me. Maybe it's the way her family seems to begin and end with her. What I know comes from whispers and rumours: illegitimacy, witchcraft, murder, nobility. These are the things that for the Qesar denote destiny. Any family would be proud to have her, whether she was born to them or not, just as Kizmid was adopted by my clan.

But with that comes possession.

My family inhabits me. My mother, my father, his wives, my siblings, our retainers, our lands, our ancestors – I cannot imagine these things belonging to me alone. They are part of me and I serve them, and even on my own, disgraced, exiled, years and years from the last time I saw them, not knowing if I'll ever go home again . . . I serve them still.

Maybe that's why I want her.

I've never known someone who was so totally her own. She defends the borders of herself like the walls of a great city, some island fortress, and I want in.

I think what she sickens from isn't the spirit that possessed her, but the emptiness it left behind. I believe she misses it. Who wouldn't tire of being alone?

It's all right, Torny. I'm here. I will teach you that the dead are family too.

> *Find the missing soul of Torny, my sworn friend,*
> *and lead her back to me, whole.*

Twenty Six
GNAW

TORNY'S TALE

Qesar Concession, Ban Granis

ater laps me. Not the stagnant depths of the Floodlands, nor the slapping salt waves around Far Isle, but soft, warm ripples. I'm glowing throughout my whole body, and the liquid moves lazily across my skin, as slow and heavy as oil.

So this is what peace feels like.

I can't tell if it's a thought or a voice. My lungs drag with each breath. It's not hard to breathe, exactly, just . . . long. My body rises and falls, buoyed up and sinking again. Something is holding my head in place, keeping my face above the surface.

I blink against the golden light. Everything is blurred.

"She's awake," says a deep, familiar voice.

"Let's keep our thanks until we know it worked," says another, also familiar. "Carrier, your friend has come back to us."

A shadow falls across my face, and I feel strong fingers cupping my jaw.

"Torny?"

"Aisulu," I say, but my tongue is thick, and stuck to my palate. My eyes are still swimming, but I can see a dark head above me. The end of her braid tickles my temples. Tears seep out of the corners of my eyes and trickle down the sides of my face. "What did you do to me?"

I feel the others move away.

"I'm sorry," she says, bringing her face down toward mine. I feel her lips against my forehead. "I'm sorry, Torny. I should have been with you."

Her lips are the one touch of cold in all this warmth.

"You're in the Concession," she says. "We got you into Ban Granis. We were just in time."

"What?"

She strokes my cheek with a finger. "The Qesar have been stripped of their right to free passage within the Empire," she says. "The noble houses of the *Regna* have officially petitioned for our removal."

My head is whirling. "Why?"

"This isn't the time," says Kizmid's deep voice. "Uryz wants to see you."

"Can you see?" says the other voice. An ochre blur moves closer, smelling of deep green leaves and white petals.

I shake my head.

"You gave her too much," the voice says. I remember where I last smelt that scent.

"Serke?" I ask.

"Hello, Rus," Serke says.

"Come on," says Kizmid, tense.

Aisulu sits back. Strong arms hook me under my arms and pull me upright, water streaming off me. It leaves an oily sheen on my skin.

"Rub it in," Aisulu says. "It'll protect you."

I want to ask what from, but my head is spinning. I'm naked, but the space around me feels soft and quiet, except for the splashing of water and the flap of cloth as Serke enfolds me in a long towel. Aisulu steps forward, but Serke stops her.

"I'll get her ready," Serke says. "You go with Kizmid."

My eyes are slowly adjusting, but the world is still blurry.

"How did you get here?" I ask Serke.

"Lughambar was attacked by Rus," Serke says. "With luck, I was not there."

I hear how bleak that luck is.

"I'm sorry," I say, taking the clothes she hands me and pulling them on. "Did Varkha—?"

"No," Serke says. "No one."

I think about those beautiful carvings, the sleeping quarters where Aisulu kissed the corner of my lips, the benches where I burned my mouth on chilli lamb, Serke's garden. All gone up in smoke and ash.

I try very hard not to think of Hero, her soft muzzle, the blaze of white on her forehead.

"You did," I say, shrugging on a clean quilted jacket. "I'm glad."

Serke pats my shoulder. "Me too," she says. "I am not ready to stop living."

"Serke." My sight is still blurry, but I find her arm with my hand. "I think maybe I am."

I don't know why I can say it, all of a sudden, or why I choose her. Maybe it's because of Hero. All I know is finally I recognise this feeling that's been in me since winter.

"I've thought about it a lot," I go on, my words coming out in a rush. "I thought it would go away, but it's been a long time now. Months."

Serke laughs.

Of all the things I imagined, I didn't imagine that.

She wraps her arms around me, and hugs me against her flat chest. The woody, sweet scent enfolds me.

"Death is always there," she says. "But you don't want death, Torny. You want peace. That takes longer."

She gives me another pat on the back, a little awkward.

"I don't laugh at you," she says. "You are young. Months are long to you. I know you've seen terrible things. I have too."

"You lived through Prince Shuru's reign," I say. The words seem to come out of some dark hole in my head.

I still can't see clearly, but I feel Serke hesitate.

"Aisulu told you?" she asks.

"I never told Aisulu," I say. *"The looting, the plague. I didn't want her to know."*

Serke's hands tighten on my shoulders.

"Who am I talking to?" she asks.

But before I can ask her what she means, Kizmid reappears.

"Uryz is waiting," she says, laying her hand on Serke's arm.

My sight is slowly clearing. The world is still blurred, but I can see that I'm being led through a stone corridor, the floor paved with large flagstones. It's different to the Concession at Lughambar. We're within the city walls, and the building is in the Southern style. I'm led across a paved courtyard where a canal that leads from the Arauris river through the walls of the Concession ends in four narrow berths for *uarehs*. There's only one moored up, its colours garish to my sensitive eyes.

We pass into another stone hall. I can hear the noise of people going about their days, but it's muted. The ones we pass all wear the same light blue.

The Concession is in mourning . . . but how I know, I can't tell.

Kizmid pushes open a heavy door.

Aisulu stands alone in the middle of the room, her back to us, facing a seated man whose features I struggle to make out. I feel a wave of hatred so strong it nearly winds me.

I know what you did to me.

Serke steadies me. Kizmid bows, and I follow her lead, remembering Varkha's amusement when I gripped her arm. Poor Varkha.

"Negotiator," Kizmid says. "This is the girl."

The seated man stands and walks past Aisulu to me. He reaches out, takes my chin in his hand, and moves my face from side to side.

"Impressive," he says. "It isn't proof of conspiracy, but she will do. It's just a pity you lost the other one. What's wrong with her eyes?"

"She was drugged," Serke says.

I listen with only half an ear. I'm fighting to keep myself in check. My vision is spangled with lines of light and colour around the edges, but I catch details now – swollen pouches under his eyes, slicked back hair, gold thread and red beads patterning his blue robe.

"Uryz," I think, and then realise I've spoken aloud. *"I know what you did."*

The man pulls his hand back from my face.

There's a tense silence.

"Torny," Serke says softly from behind me. "When did you learn to speak Qesar?"

Uryz shouts a lot. He shouts at Aisulu for bringing a spy amongst the Qesar, and letting her accomplice steal the package. He shouts at Kizmid for not keeping the Carrier in line. He shouts at Serke for trying to be reasonable.

He doesn't shout at me, because there's a space around me now, an uncertainty.

"Lock her up," he says finally, still not willing to address me. "No one is to speak to her, is that clear?"

I look to Aisulu, but she stands silent.

"She needs my attention," Serke says.

"Absolutely not!" Uryz snaps. "How do I know you're not part of this, Stahranid?"

"Negotiator," Serke says. "She's all you have."

"Very well," says Uryz, flustered for a moment. "Find out what she knows. Find out how this happened. As for *you*," he says, turning to Aisulu, his anger floods back. "You above all should understand the consequences. You lost your family's honour, and now you're about to lose the Qesar our place in our greatest rival state. I told them exile wasn't enough. You should have been dealt with, once and for all."

Aisulu stands with her head bowed, not moving.

Part of me longs to stand in front of her and protect her, but my body won't obey.

She left me in the dark.

There is an echo to that thought, a numbing aftertaste of horror that I'm not ready to face.

Serke grips my arm.

"Come," she says.

Kizmid takes my other arm, and together they walk me out of the room, down some steps, and into an underground passage. Once we're out of earshot, Kizmid gives a low whistle.

"How'd you do it, Rus?" she asks. "How'd you know to find Aisulu? You and that friend of yours must have been planning it for weeks."

I shake my head. "I don't know what you're talking about," I say.

"You were good," Kizmid goes on. "You never reacted when we spoke. If Aisulu hadn't tried to heal you, you'd have got away with it."

"We didn't plan anything," I say.

Serke says nothing, but her grip tightens on my arm.

I have a vague sense that I should be feeling something, but everything is very calm, very quiet. At the end of the underground passage, Kizmid calls up a guard. We stop at a door with bars set in it. A guard opens it, and Kizmid and Serke take me inside.

"There's no point pretending," Kizmid says, pushing me down onto a bench. "You may as well tell us, Rus. It will be easier for everyone that way, especially Aisulu. Uryz will skin her."

My vision is almost cleared now. Serke lights a small lamp from the taper outside, and brings it into the room. It casts small rings of light about their faces as they look at me.

"I'm no spy," I say. "I don't know how to speak Qesar."

Kizmid sighs. I know her well enough to know she won't enjoy making me talk, but that she'll do it anyway.

"Did you know about the Rus?" Kizmid asks. "Did Ebba send a message when she ran to the gates? Is that why the Lughambar Concession was attacked?"

I'm in danger, I know that. I should feel fear.

All I feel is impatience.

"Do it," I tell her. "I deserve it."

Kizmid looks sideways at Serke. "You should leave," she says.

Serke's watching me. I can see her clearer now, outlined in the light from the lamp, her black curls, her plum-coloured lips, her black eyes ringed with kohl.

"What did Uryz do?" she asks.

The hole in my head widens.

"He fed me to the Hungry Ones."

Serke draws Kizmid out of the room, locking the door behind them. I can hear them whispering.

"You can't believe her," Kizmid says.

Serke ignores her. "Tell Uryz the interrogation will be useless while she's drugged."

"That will only give you an hour or two."

"That may be enough," Serke says. "Can you get Aisulu down here?"

"Uryz won't allow it."

"Uryz doesn't need to know."

"Serke . . ."

"I know what I'm doing. Trust me."

I sit on the bench, staring at the lamp. The halo around it is shrinking, shrinking. I'm a little disappointed. I thought maybe Kizmid could help me let go of some of this weight.

I must be tired, because I sleep.

I watch a child on a patch of grass. The child falls heavily on their seat, rocking and looking slightly bemused. They lean forward and laboriously pull themself onto their feet, then straighten up, their arms outstretched for balance. They're holding something in one hand.

Thoughtfully, they put the arrowhead in their mouth, and gnaw at it.

I should be worried, but I know the child is safe. Or maybe I know the child will never be safe.

Either way, I just watch.

I wake up inside the golden egg of the lamplight.

Someone has stretched a bedroll on the floor, and laid me on it. Serke kneels over my head. Her long fingers are warm and slippery with oil, and she moves them from my shoulders to my breastbone, then my nape, then my temples. The pressure is firm, a little uncomfortable.

"It won't work," I say. "Just let me go."

Serke ignores me, but glances up at Kizmid. The captain is standing against the wall, a tablet of some sort in her hand, and I see her scratching away with a metal stylus.

"How did you find Aisulu?" Kizmid asks.

"She found me," I say.

Kizmid scribbles.

"How did you know about the package?" she asks.

"What package?"

"Who captured Ebba?"

"That guard," I say. "The one from Merzen."

"Why did she go with him?"

"I don't know."

Serke's fingers dig into the soft flesh beside my breastbone with a scooping gesture.

"Where did you learn to speak Qesar?"

"I don't speak Qesar."

Kizmid's stylus hesitates.

"Why are you spying on us?"

"I'm not."

Serke's fingers are splayed across my face, pressing on the hinges of my jaw, the corners of my eyes, the meeting of my eyebrows.

"How long have you known Aisulu?" she asks.

"All my life."

Her fingers release me.

"She's still drugged," Kizmid says. "We're not going to get any sense from her."

"This is silly," I say. "Kizmid, I'm no spy. You know I don't speak Qesar."

Kizmid puts her tablet down, and rubs her face.

"Torny," she says, "we're speaking it now. Serke just spoke to you in Stahranid, and you answered that too."

I look up at Serke's upside-down face above me.

"None of this makes sense," I say. "You're all crazy."

"It makes perfect sense," Serke says. "You're possessed."

I think about this.

"No," I say. "That was before. The Harrower was inside me. But she's gone. She left me empty."

Kizmid shivers.

Serke puts her hand on my forehead.

"Aisulu was trying to fill you back up," she says.

"Ebba tried that at Durkno," I say. I should feel something. Those words should mean something, but there's nothing but that hole. "It didn't work. The Harrower's gone."

"Ebba didn't have anything to put inside you," Serke says, "but Aisulu did. Kizmid, why was Aisulu exiled?"

Kizmid looks uncomfortable. She checks the door, then crouches down beside us. When she speaks, her voice is barely more than a whisper.

"She was accused of killing her brother, the Kagan," she says.

More murmuring beyond the grille. I lie on the bedroll and listen in whatever language this may be. After Serke's touch, I feel very calm and still. My muscles are loose, relaxed.

"Uryz is keeping Aisulu under guard in her chambers," Kizmid says. "He wants Torny interrogated. Properly."

"You know torture doesn't work," Serke says.

"Sometimes it does," says Kizmid.

It sounds like an argument they've had before.

"Not this time," Serke says.

"We don't have much choice," Kizmid says. "After the Rus came up the Samara, the House of Lughambar has sided with Vellsberg and Merzen. The three major houses of the northern *Regna* have finally buried the hatchet, and are going to petition the Emperor for our removal with the support of the church. Without proof of conspiracy, and Qesar presence at all the attacks, he'll have no grounds to refuse them."

"Uryz was going to use Torny as a bargaining chip," Serke says.

"And now he can't unless he's certain she isn't a spy," Kizmid says.

"How much could she have heard?" Serke asks. "On one *uareh*?"

"Ebba took the package, and deliberately allowed herself to be taken prisoner," Kizmid says. "Torny didn't even argue with me to go after her. That's proof enough, isn't it?"

"Ebba? I don't believe that." Serke says. "But if that is the case, then they were working for the *Regna* the whole time. Uryz's only move now is to hand Torny over to the Emperor as a captive anyway."

"Working for the Emperor was meant to protect us," Kizmid says. "If we give him Torny, he can make nice with the *Regna*, and blame everything on the Qesar."

Serke's voice is cool. "He can do that anyway," she says. "He always could."

They fall silent.

"If it's true," Kizmid says a little later, "does that mean the Celestial Father is inside her?"

"I don't know," Serke says. "I don't know much about possessions. Usually it's just a bad-luck spirit making someone sick. This is different. Powerful. She's been a host before, and a Kagan is close to a god." She sighs. "We have to get her to Aisulu, she's the only one who can confirm it."

"Not the only one," Kizmid says. "Uryz . . ."

"If what she said is true," Serke says, "Uryz had a hand in the Kagan's murder. He'll protect himself at all costs. If he finds out, he'll kill her."

"He'll demand an interrogation," Kizmid says.

"Then you have to do it," Serke says.

"I can't," Kizmid says.

"You have to," Serke says.

That night, Kizmid stands guard outside the door. I have not felt the urge to move since they laid me on the bedroll. I dream with my eyes open. The child keeps me company.

It must be late when a guard offers to take Kizmid's place.

"Trust me," she says gruffly. "You don't want this watch."

I listen to the guard's feet tramp away down the passage.

"Kizmid," I say.

"What is it, Rus?"

"I thought Aisulu loved me," I say. "She cut me and everything. But she hasn't come to see me."

Kizmid's face appears at the bars. I can only see her eyes and nose, and her top lip. The rest is hidden.

"Love isn't a cure or a charm," she says. "It's a thing in the world like anything else."

"I'm tired, Kizmid," I say.

"So go to sleep," she says, turning and settling herself against the door, out of sight.

The lamp is burning low, low. The wick smokes, the oil is dark.

"Don't feel bad if you have to hurt me," I say. "I won't feel it."

"Yes, you will," Kizmid says. "Don't say stupid things, Rus."

"I can put myself elsewhere," I say. "It's a trick I learnt. I can go with the wine, under the mountain, into the silver . . ." Images are slipping past my eyes – Galen with his wineskin, Fenn with his collar, Vigdis with her pendants. Beside me the child is playing quietly, gnawing on a knife like it's a teething toy.

"Please help me die, Kizmid," I say. "It's all right. I want it."

In the end, Uryz insists on an interrogation. It takes place in a larger room. A clerk asks questions, makes notes. Kizmid is ordered to keep me in good enough shape that I can be handed over to the Emperor. No broken bones, no disfigurement.

I smile at her before she starts to remind her what I said.

Everything happens as I said it would. The hole in my head is deep and nothing reaches me there. After a while, Fenn joins me.

"Is this you?" I ask, showing him the child. "Will he be enslaved?"

Fenn smiles.

I come back to the room to find they've finished.

"Did it help?" I ask.

Kizmid won't meet my eyes.

Twenty Seven

INTERMEDIARY

EBBA'S TALE

Dagomar's Compound, Ban Granis

rmund is fumin, but the threat of interruption by mad religious women seems to work.

"My niece shall have a chaperone," he says to King Kolrand through gritted teeth. "Captain Neklaus will accompany them."

And so, it's agreed we are to stay wi King Kolrand in Dagomar's compound, under the Bishop's guard. It seems the delegation from Arngard have found themselves under house arrest.

Neklaus is hoverin in the doorway of the *frigidarium*, peekin over Erland's shoulder, his eyes fixed on me an Rosamund as we work around Gisla. He's like a dog starin at a rabbit he'd like to shake to death.

Rosamund's hands shake as she helps me wash her aunt's body. We've hung a sheet across the doorway to hide the abbess, an together we wipe down her body, very gently, tryin not to scrape the inflamed skin. I'm worried for Gisla. The red flames cover her.

I knew floodbane could be dangerous, so I kept it from her throat an face, but I din't dilute it enough, an her white skin has started to blister in some places. The cool of the *frigidarium* is doin her good for now, but if she develops a fever I don't like to think what it might do.

I go to Erland, where he stands at the door wi Neklaus.

"We'll have to move her covered," I say. "The sun will hurt her."

"We have a carrying chair," Erland says. "You and the young lady can ride with her."

"Make sure your men carry it," I say in a low voice.

Erland looks me over. I know he's takin in the remains of my black eye, the faint bruisin on my neck an shoulders.

"Understood, Salvebearer," he says.

Behind him, Neklaus leers at me, but I ignore him. I'll worry about him in the dark, when I find myself alone. I'm more concerned about leavin this dank, watery room, an the unpleasant shape under the white sheet on the second marble slab. The smell of rottin lilies drifts in the air.

The carryin chair turns out to be a sort of covered bed, curtained all around, carried by six strong men. At least four of em are Bearskins from Erland's company, the king's guard. Peerin between the curtains I see grey stone houses an narrow streets covered wi colourful awnins for shade. A square tower looms over us, an I remember the sight of those four towers inside the city walls as Hadric an I rode down the Golden Way between the orchards.

We arrive jolted but safe. Dagomar is with us, worryin at his ragged lips with his yellow teeth, but he scurries off wi the chair once Gisla is inside the chambers. Neklaus moves to enter, but Erland puts his hand on his shoulder.

"You stay here," he says. "Keep everyone away from this door."

Neklaus looks like he's thinkin of cuttin Erland's hand off.

"I see you've found another guarddog, Ebba," Erland says once we're inside. "I think I liked the wolf better."

Rosamund's eyes are huge.

"It was a hound," I tell her, "not a wolf."

Erland nods towards Gisla. "Will she be all right?"

"I hope so," I say.

Erland switches into Northern. "The king wants to see you, Ebba. Without the guard."

"I can't leave the girl," I say. "The guard may rape her, or worse." Erland flinches, but I en't got time for niceties. He needs to know. "He's dangerous, Erland. He killed his own men to stop me reachin the Emperor."

"The bishop's got us cornered here too," Erland says. "We've no means of contacting the Emperor either. Everything goes through Ormund."

"He's plannin somethin on the Feast of Embers," I tell him. "I don't know what it is, but I need to talk to King Kolrand."

Erland looks me over. "You've grown up," he says.

I smile. I know I should be scared, or guilty, or bewildered, but I don't feel any of that. I feel like my mind is workin freely at last, layin out plans, findin the path that will guide us through the flames.

"It's good to see you again," I say. I decide to ask the question that's bin hidin itself inside me since I saw him. "Is Eldinghope ...?"

"Your home is safe, Ebba," Erland says. "I sent Rafe back there when I came south with the king. He was going to stop in Birchhold to see your mother and brother. I hear they're building a shrine there to the Salvebearer and her wolf."

I roll my eyes.

"You can laugh," Erland says, "but there's a reason the bishop wanted you in his power, girl. Your name carries weight in the north."

"It's not my name," I say.

Erland shrugs. "You should take a walk around the compound," he says. "It'll interest you." He sees my eyes flick to where Neklaus stands outside. "I'll spare a guard for you," he says. "Maybe that will keep your wolf under control."

"Don't choose your favourite," I say.

Erland laughs. "These are Bearskins," he says. "They can handle a wolf."

I hope he's right. I send him off with a list of supplies for Gisla's care. An abbess should warrant Dagomar openin his stores. It's not until Rosamund an I are workin over the hearth to make more salve for her aunt that I realise she seems much calmer. I put my hand on her shoulder an squeeze.

"I'm sorry about your aunt," I say. "I din't mean it to hurt her so."

Rosamund gives me a small smile. "I know you called him," she says.

I frown.

"Auntie really has been dreaming," Rosamund says. "For weeks. Ever since the new moon. She's seen a fire raging in the north, and a falling axe, and a girl walking out of the flames. It was you, Ebba."

After Gisla's settled an treated, I pass on Erland's suggestion that we walk around the compound. I'm beginnin to worry about Rosamund. The bishop's had her locked away a long time, an I think it may be makin her ill.

When we leave, Neklaus an the Bearskin Erland promised me are by the door. Neklaus follows us, but I'd rather that than leave him alone wi Gisla while she's helpless. Rosamund tenses, but we're in a big yard, surrounded by people. The sun is still warm an golden, droppin west, an I breathe deep, enjoyin the feel of it on my skin.

The compound is larger than I expected. It's surrounded by stone walls, with an arched gate, an the packed yellow dirt is rutted. Carts are lined up to the right of the gate, an beyond em is a byre for the cart oxen. The stables are at the far end, wi what looks like quarters for the cart drivers beside em. The warehouses lie behind the main house to the left – easier for the merchant to check no one's sneakin goods from him, I guess – an the house itself looks far bigger'n I imagined. There's a well, too, an a dovecote.

We're passin the carts. There are a lot of em – a dozen or so – an the byre is full. I wonder about that.

A bark sets the doves flyin in a wave of white against the late spring sky.

Rosamund grips my arm in terror.

A huge grey beast flies out of the stable an bounds towards us, its pink tongue flappin in the air, drool hangin from its long teeth.

I barely have time to brace myself. Amid Rosamund's squeals I feel the paws hit my shoulders an the tongue cover my nose. I put out my arms, partly in defence, partly in joy.

"Fetch," I shout. "Down, boy! *Down! Sit!*"

The enormous wolf hound lowers his paws to the ground, sits, an continues to lick my face unhindered.

When I see Erland, I think, *I am goin to give him a piece of my mind.*
But I know I won't. I put my arms around Fetch an hug him fiercely.

"Rosamund," I say. "Come meet Fetch."

Gingerly, she steps towards us. I take her hand an show her how to hold it out to be sniffed an licked. She giggles.

"Fetch," I say. "This is Rosamund. I want you to protect her like you'd protect me."

I doubt he understands. I don't say it for him. I say it for her, so I can see the tension ease in her shoulders, an the worry in her face soften.

I say it for Neklaus, standin behind us an scowlin.

An then comes the second surprise.

"Ebba!" calls a familiar voice.

I look up, an immediately feel scruffy. My dress is smudged an not laced properly, since it belongs to Rosamund who's taller an slimmer'n me. My hair is a mess. My hands are wet wi dog drool. My face is pink, cos I'm blushin.

The young man's sleek blonde hair, tied back in a tail, bounces across his shoulders as he jogs up to us. His shoulders are broader still, his green eyes serious. A scar runs across his face, the skin silvery an puckered around it, but despite it, there's somethin different about him. I realise he's smilin at me.

It's a small smile, a bit nervous, but a smile.

That's new.

"Jarle," I say in Northern. "What are you doin here?"

"I'm caring for the king's horses," Jarle says. "And him." He nods at Fetch.

I look into his green eyes, an find I have to look away.

Rosamund's scratchin Fetch's ear an lookin just as pink as I feel.

"I wasn't sure I'd ever see you again," he says to me.

The idea of Jarle thinkin about me at all is enough to knock me backwards. I'm sure I sway, just a little.

"I'm glad you did," I say, then hear myself an cringe.

"Me too," he says.

He nods to Rosamund and jogs back towards the stables. I join Rosamund and we watch him go, both of us pretendin to pet Fetch. That dog has never bin so well scratched. He don't seem to mind.

"Who was *that*?" Rosamund whispers.

"Someone I used to know," I say.

"I'm sorry," Rosamund says, "but tell me again why you chose Berengar?"

We snigger together over Fetch's scruffy grey coat.

Gisla stirs after sundown. By the time Erland comes by with a platter of bread, soup an wine, she's drunk some water an watched me prepare the salve we're usin on her burns. Fetch lies across the door, an growls whenever anyone comes close, but he lets Erland pass with a wag of his grey tail.

Erland helps the older woman sit up, places the platter on her lap, an pours her some wine as Rosamund comes into the room.

Erland's brought food for us too, so we set ourselves on stools an start eatin.

"You two can go eat," Erland says, stickin his head out of the door. "I'll guard the ladies." The Bearskin don't need tellin twice.

"I can't leave them," Neklaus says. "Have your men bring me food."

Erland looks him over an smiles.

"No," he says.

We've all stopped to watch.

Neklaus draws himself up an snarls at Erland. "You're going to be sorry, Northerner," he says.

Below him, still lyin across the step, Fetch gives a low an lazy growl.

"Let me tell you something," Erland says, layin what looks like a friendly hand on the younger man's shoulder. "I'm from Arngard. We do things there that would make you southerners shit yourselves. A murderous toad like you might get respect down here, but I've lived through the two wars, and you don't scare me. So stop trying." He pats Neklaus on the shoulder. "Now, go get some food."

I can see the effort it takes Neklaus to control himself. The thing that made him so terrifyin when there was no one between him an me now looks like weakness. He spits on the ground – Fetch is lyin between him an Erland's boots – an stalks away.

Erland returns to his place at the foot of Gisla's bed an picks up his bowl of soup. Both Gisla an her niece are lookin at him with amazement.

"Haven't you heard?" Erland says with a grin. "We kill our own kings in the north. A king's guard has to be good at his job."

Gisla sets her spoon down.

"I fear, Captain," she says, "that we are shortly to join you in that tradition."

Erland raises his eyebrows, but keeps eatin.

"My brother is planning something," Gisla says.

Erland licks his spoon thoughtfully. "Jarle tells me there have been an awful lot of ox carts with passengers coming through Dagomar's gates," he says. "The quarters are full of hardened men with battle scars. I didn't know ox-drivers faced such dangers."

"Undeclared troops," Gisla says. "I believe Ormund plans to attack the Emperor on the Feast of Embers."

I can tell that sayin it out loud to an outsider costs her. Fetch trots over to me an lies beside me, his head up on my knee. He watches me eat wi soulful regret.

Gisla meets Erland's eyes.

"*Imperium Infractum* is a lie," she says. "The Emperor has no right to our lands. He has no right to deny our people self-government. The Empire is the same as all temporal power. It has risen, and it will fall, just as the powers before it did. We have built on their ruins, as others will build on ours. And this lie will persist: that we are one and the same, that we have always been here. We're not. We haven't."

Erland nods.

Gisla deflates. "It's a lie," she says, "but either way, the cost is too great. If Ormund fails, the House of Merzen will be charged with treason, and destroyed. The Emperor claims our lands anyway. If he succeeds, we have civil war, and it won't be a series of summer campaigns like the Westlands War, or a matter of defending the border. It will be within us."

"Ebba?" Erland says, bringin me back to the discussion.

I wonder how three women an a guard eatin soup turned into a council of war.

"Civil war in the Empire would leave Arngard free again," Erland says, almost off-hand.

I shake my head. "No," I say. "It would weaken King Kolrand, an we'd have another uprisin on our hands."

"We're only on our second king," Erland says. "Before Arn, there were just lords with their warriors. Maybe the north isn't made for kings."

Gisla an Rosamund look aghast at this treasonous talk.

"Was it better back then?" I ask.

Erland shrugs. "Who knows?" he says. "I don't remember. Grimulf used to say—"

"Order an ash," I say. "There's stability, or there's destruction. I en't sure that's true."

Erland frowns. I know how thoroughly destruction has marked his life.

"If the Emperor falls, Dagomar an Ormund will make my home a slaving post," I say. "I en't havin that."

I wonder if all such choices come down to that. Not the greater good, but the one place within us that we cannot bear to see violated.

"Well, then," Erland says. "I'll see what I can do. I'll talk to Kolrand."

He collects the bowls an puts em on the platter. I can see Gisla's strength is fadin. Rosamund an I help her lie on her side as Erland leaves, closin the door behind him, an I fetch the fresh salve for us to dress her burns. Fetch stretches out before the hearth.

"Is this the famous salve?" Gisla asks.

"Near enough," I say. "I don't have all the ingredients, an I've put in some others for burns, hopin it will help. You endured more'n I meant you to, Abbess."

I don't say I'm sorry, an she don't ask me to. We're out from under the Bishop's thumb. I hope she thinks it was worth it.

"The Captain's a good man," she says to me instead.

"He protected me before," I say. "He'll protect you too."

"I am already protected," Gisla says, her voice weakenin. Her eyelids flutter. "He's with me, Salvebearer. I see him. He is a hard man, but his belief—" she draws in a shudderin breath "—his belief is an axe that levels the lies of evil like firewood. He is setting the fire for you, Salvebearer. It needs only a spark—"

The hairs on my back stand up, an Fetch whines. Rosamund looks at me wi wide blue eyes.

But Gisla is already asleep.

That night no one bangs on our shutters or hisses through the door. Rosamund shares the bed with her aunt while I drag the bedding from the other room before the hearth and lie down with my arms around Fetch.

Wi my nose buried in the long guardhairs of his neck, I feel a peace like no other. I fall asleep immediately. I en't sure I've slept properly for weeks.

I wake up once. The embers of the fire cast a soft glow into the dark.

A broad figure in white stands over me.

You have not been truthful, Salvebearer. You use deceit to survive.

I hug Fetch closer.

"An I've survived," I say. "Which is more'n can be said for you."

I close my eyes against the figure, an sleep again.

The next day I take Fetch to get water. Wi the Bearskins watchin Neklaus, I feel easier leavin Gisla an Rosamund alone. I walk the length of the yard in the early mornin sun. The doves are cooin, an there are little mud nests under the tiled eaves. Carts are already arrivin through the arched gateway, an I watch in interest as a shoutin match breaks out over one cart blockin the other in before the oxen are unhitched.

Erland's right. The carts come with half a dozen men each. They unload long crates an carry em across the yard. One of the men caught up in the shoutin steps back, not lookin, an barges into the men carryin a crate. The crate falls, the lid bangs open, an spears slide out.

The same new-made spears we saw in Durkno.

Seems Ormund has bin preparin for a fight in the *Regna* even before the Houses were fully agreed.

I walk on, Fetch sniffin round beside me. I keep my eye out as I visit the well, but the stables nearby are quiet. I fill the bucket an head back across the yard. As I come close to our quarters, I see another cart rollin in, an a slim, dark-headed figure slip through the gates with it. The figure skulks by the archway, not comin into the yard.

One of the men shoutin over the carts catches sight of him, an decides to shout at him for a change. Neklaus, leanin beside the door of our quarters to the right of the archway, perks up.

The figure looks straight at me.

I already know who it is.

Berengar meets my eyes, then takes one look at the advancin Neklaus, turns tail, an dashes back out the gate. Neklaus hurries after him, shoutin at the men on the gate.

I haul the bucket to our quarters. There's no point tellin myself Neklaus won't hurt Berengar, but I do tell myself Berengar's got more sense than to let himself be caught.

Gisla is sittin up, eatin fresh bread an some kind of sweet preserve. I guess there are perks to bein held prisoner by a merchant.

Rosamund hands me a roll an a spoon covered in jam.

"Auntie's got something to tell you," she says.

I look at Gisla.

"The Blessed Grimulf has visited me," she says. "I'm to make ready the way for you, Salvebearer."

I put down the roll an reach out to feel her forehead.

She en't fevered. In fact she's calm, her face is clear of pain, an she's movin her body more freely than yesterday. She pulls back her shirt.

The burns have healed. No scabbin, no blisters. Just the red print of flames across her body.

"He healed me," she says, "the same way he marked me. Through you. You are his instrument."

I step back.

"You have been sent to heal us, Salvebearer."

I shake my head.

"No," I say. "You're strong. The burns mustn't of bin as bad as I thought."

"Yesterday you worried you'd killed me," Gisla says. "Today I am healed."

"No," I say.

"They're gathering, Salvebearer," she says, an her voice is all wrong. "They're coming, just as they did before. I remember how much you hated it then. So I've sent you a helpmeet. She knows how to perform before crowds. She will be your mediary."

Beside me, Fetch is growlin. Rosamund has her hand pressed hard over her mouth.

The doorway darkens.

Neklaus stands there, his cheeks pink from runnin.

"There are people," he says. "Outside, in the street. Dozens of them. What did you do?"

"They're here for me," Gisla says. "Let me speak to them."

You may imagine how quick Dagomar orders us before him, with a crowd growin outside his compound. I wonder if there are more carts out there, loaded wi weapons an men, caught in the swell of people. He must be sweatin blood.

Gisla refuses.

"I'm an Abbess of the Order of the Blessed Hekatera," she says, "I will be bathed and dressed before I go anywhere."

We're escorted from the dust of the compound into the main house, surrounded by guards of all interests – Neklaus in his crumpled green uniform, Erland's Bearskins, Dagomar's hired men – to a tiled bathing room. It's much smaller than the *frigidarium* at the Bishop's palace, but it has the same graceful lines. Gisla allows one female servant to enter, her arms piled high wi towels an bottles. Then she imperiously closes the door, lockin out even Fetch.

The water is tepid, but the servant goes to stoke a furnace, an the room starts to warm.

"You should only wash in cool water," I tell Gisla, so she undresses an enters the water first. I check her over as she does so. The red lines on her upper body have completely healed, only the colour remainin. The skin looks whole an healthy.

You've bin led by the shadow of your dead Da's luck, I think. *You've seen a god in the body of your best friend. Why is this so hard to accept?*

Because those made sense. My Follower wanted to look after me for Da. The Harrower wanted to leave.

The Prester din't heal people.

He used em.

An heresy or not, I know the White God en't the only god.

※ 331 ※

While the servant takes Gisla into another room to be dressed, we bathe in the warm water. Rosamund shows me how they use oil an scrapers to clean themselves after. There's another of those marble slabs she says is for lyin on while you're scraped an massaged, but I remember the Prester's body. Instead we sit on small wooden stools while she does my back.

"I saw Berengar this mornin," I say.

"Was he all right?" she asks.

"He ran off fast enough."

She snorts, but kindly, I think.

"I'm glad I met you, Rosamund," I tell her.

"I am too," she says, pausin before she continues. "Ebba, can I ask you something? When I saw you and your friend together at Vellsberg, I wondered. And then afterwards—" she stops. "I'm sorry," she says. "I shouldn't be asking."

"You can ask," I tell her.

"Were you in love with her?"

I smile to myself as she scrapes the oil from my back. Thinkin about Torny's bittersweet, but I have to trust Aisulu will take care of her, like she did before.

"I asked myself too," I say. "But no."

"And with Berengar?"

My heart tugs.

"Rosamund," I say, "is it normal for boys here not to want to touch you?"

The scraper on my back stops.

"I wouldn't know," Rosamund says. "First there was Neklaus, and after that, no one who knew wanted me."

"I'm sorry," I say.

"If you're a man, it's different," Rosamund says. "But for us . . . you have to be married. Berengar must have wanted to do it properly."

I can tell that care of his pains her, so I don't tell her it pains me too, but for another reason.

He never asked me what I wanted.

Gisla's demands have turned her audience wi Dagomar into somethin much bigger. I feel it as we walk through the main house, dressed in new clothes, the way servants an workers crane their necks to see us, the whispers runnin between em.

The Abbess is dressed in dove grey, her hair covered by a long white veil, same as her niece. Rosamund's skirts swirl around her feet as she walks. I try not to look on her slim waist with envy.

I'm in a clay-red dress, the warm colour like a fire's glow under new wood. Wonder of wonder, it fits me. Even the sheer veil over my hair stays put, pinned in place. Fetch pads beside me, an no one dares try take him from me.

"Abbess," Dagomar says, his eyes dartin between us. "Your recovery is a miracle. I have already informed His Excellency that you will return—"

"No," says Gisla.

Dagomar looks stunned. "No?"

"No."

He's stuck. On the one hand, his patron is Gisla's brother. On the other, she is far above him in status.

"His Excellency, your brother—"

"My brother," Gisla says, "will understand shortly. What I need, Dagomar, is a stage."

Dagomar's eyes bulge. "What?"

"In the compound will be quite sufficient," Gisla says. "I wouldn't dream of imposing upon you any more than that. A wooden stage," she says, "by the well."

"But what for?" Dagomar asks.

"So that the people can see me," Gisla says. "They must be able to see me when they come in."

"Come in?" Dagomar chokes.

"I have seen the light of the Lord," Gisla says, "and it is a fiery light. It burns within me, Dagomar, do you understand? The Blessed Grimulf has shown it to me, and now I must share it with the world."

There's no sound but the cooin doves. Everyone's watchin Gisla.

Dagomar's eyes slide to me, behind the Abbess.

"This is you," he hisses. "The Bishop warned me—"

"Dagomar," Gisla says, an her voice is horrible, deep an cracked. "Do you have so little faith? When you sent me the letter begging for aid, you said you feared the light of faith guttered against the dark."

Dagomar's mouth drops open, his eyes pulled back to Gisla's rigid face. Her eyes are blank, the lines of her face an throat stark against her grey dress an white veil. When she draws breath, it rattles. She raises her hands like claws, an draws back cloth to reveal the red print of flames on her breastbone.

Beside me, Fetch growls deep in his throat. I ball my fist in the long fur of his neck.

"If the fire will not do, Dagomar," she says in that awful voice, "then there is still the axe."

Twenty Eight
BITE

TORNY'S TALE

Qesar Concession, Ban Granis

I sleep in a stone room. Sometimes I see the back of Kizmid's head through the hole in the door, where a curved scar cuts its way through her cropped hair, and sometimes I look out over a wide plain, criss-crossed with water channels, watching the herds of wild horses.

Is this where you came from? I ask.

This is where I should have died.

It's beautiful, I say.

This world is nothing but tears and loss. There is no beauty in it that cannot be reduced to filth and decay.

Show me where you come from, I say.

I can't go back. I failed them. I betrayed them all.

Yes, I say. *I know. Me too.*

Nobody knows this.

Let me see.

A town among fields fills my sight. Dry grey mountains line the horizon, and the buildings are square, made of dusty yellow stone, their flat rooftops lined with plants, hanging curtains and laundry, coops for birds and small animals. The fields are golden with summer crops.

Look.

In the north I see a cloud, heavy with thunder.

That's us.

The cloud sweeps southwards, towards the town. Its shadow keeps pace with it across the land, until I see it isn't a shadow, but horsemen, banners flying, loosely arranged in regiments.

There must be thousands, I say.

Tens of thousands. This is the Horde.

And you're in it?

At the foremost point of the shadowy wave, I see a regiment in black, their intricate tack picked out in red, yellow and blue. They surround a rider in a high pointed helm, a black horsetail streaming from its conical tip. His face is older, lined, his eyes intelligent. His retinue are young men and women dressed in fish-scale armour, spears and bows by their sides, quivers on their backs and saddles, long curved swords in their sheaths.

I see one, close behind the commander's mount. Very young – younger than me – his face still round with puppy fat, a mane of thick black hair flying from beneath his blue helm, his black almond eyes engrossed in the golden hive of the city ahead.

You must have been important, I say, *for the commander to keep you beside him.*

I was the son of an old friend. Great things were expected of me.

I watch the shockwaves toss his hair like a storm cloud over his shoulders, those winged brows turning up at the tips.

This is before you killed, I say, *isn't it?*

The city is growing before them. The crops are crushed under a hundred thousand hooves.

In less than an hour, I will kill my first child.

The world lurches.

Where is this place?

I look around.

The golden crops, the grey mountains in the distance are gone. Instead, black pillars loom against the grey sky, and the slap of waves, the cry of seabirds fill the air. I'm so cold, cold in a way the body forgets once it is free.

Oh no.

The boulders laid in a pattern leading inwards, the central pillar.

That's you, isn't it?

I don't want to look, but an alien curiosity pulls me closer.

I see a tall girl in an undyed shift. Her short white curls are dirtied with soot, and her arms are tied behind her, her muscles standing out against the black stone of the pillar. There's a bandaged burn on her left shoulder, and a shallow, uneven cut across her chest, under her collar bones. Bruises ring her neck, and her eyes are wrong, the pupils huge inside a thin rim of grey. The front of her shift is blotched bright red with blood. Her mouth is open, screaming a name.

The air throbs with a sound that hovers half in hearing, half below.

Don't look, I say.

But the curiosity is turning from my bound body, and drifting towards the sound. An old blind woman stands outside the labyrinth, spinning the bull-roarer overhead with one hand, while her other holds a child.

Please, I say. *Don't.*

Look, my companion says.

I can't close my eyes, no matter how much I wish I could.

Fenn watches me without fear. His dark brown hair ends in a wonky line above his up-turned moon eyes. His mouth is serious. The iron thrall collar lies against his neck. He turns his head, casually bites the old woman's hand and then wriggles out of her grasp. He fixes his eyes on me, and runs.

No!

He ducks a pair of hands, gets within a few feet of the boulders marking the labyrinth. Then another figure steps in front of him, and runs a knife into his chest.

Fenn falls.

I know what happens next. Over and over, I flip between before and after.

Fenn stands beside the old woman, watching me. He's about to run.

Wait, says my companion. **Stop.**

I can't.

Fenn wriggles free. Fenn runs.

But this has already happened.

Fenn ducks. Fenn falls. Fenn dies.

It's still happening.

Fenn stands beside the woman.

Stop him, says my companion.

I can't, I say. *Look at me.*

My body, bound to the pillar, fights and screams.

Not her, he says. **You. You here, you now.**

Fenn wriggles free. Fenn runs.

And I feel myself. Not stuck in my helpless body, but outside it. Cut loose.

Fenn ducks, and I place myself in his way, wrapping my arms around him.

The knife plunges into me instead.

On my knees, my arms around his thin body, I hold him.

It's all right, I say. *I'll be all right. You were so brave, but you don't have to run anymore. You can rest.*

He looks at me, his arms around my neck.

"I wanted to run," he says.

The sun rises. The island is empty, except for my limp body on the pillar. This isn't how it happened, but I sense that something's been disturbed, altered.

My companion is looking my body over: the bruises, the blood. I join him. I see how cold and exhausted this body is, how broken.

Who did this to you? my companion asks.

My mother, I say.

The air is thick with smoke. I recognise it at once, and the sickness turns in my heart like a blade.

But this is not the plateau outside Ban Granis. This is a large tent, lit by a smouldering fire. In the middle of the dim space, her back against the central wooden tentpole, kneels a woman, huddled over a form.

I kneel too.

It's the same young man, but older. His face is gaunt, the puppy fat gone. There are lines at the corners of his eyes, and his hair is matted. He seems unconscious, but one hand is clenched in a fist.

What happened to you?

The same thing that happened to you. I watched them all die again and again, for years.

The woman leans over him, grey roots in her long black hair, deeper lines on her face.

"You can't leave us yet," she says. "Your work isn't done. You owe your family your duty."

Your child is hurt, I tell her. *Duty doesn't come into it.*

But she doesn't hear me.

There's an altar under a length of undyed cloth. I can just make out a golden figure with smiling eyes.

Sarik, my companion says. **The Sunlit Queen of the realm of Living Waters. She looks after mothers and children.**

Why is she covered up?

Because my mother isn't calling on her, he says. **She's calling on Ai Nakota, the guide of the dead. She's asking them to turn my shade back from the Dark Earth, the realm of the dead, so that I can fulfil my destiny.**

Do you want to come back? I ask.

My companion looks down as his mother forces the drug down his throat with ash-covered hands.

No, he says. **There's nothing for me here. All they want is glory and power.**

But there's something else here. I can feel it. I know these words, the taste of this drug.

What's in your hand?

My companion doesn't answer me. I reach out, and touch it.

His fingers loosen. In his dirty palm lies a small golden figure, much smaller than the one on the altar, only an inch or so tall. It holds a bow, and it's reaching back over its shoulder for an arrow.

I look up, my eyes drawn towards a place in the tent where the skins overlap.

Look, I say.

In a slit between the skins, an eye glitters.

My companion and I are standing in the dark between the skins now, one to either side of the girl. She's about fifteen, and even over the soughing of the wind, I can hear her heart hammering in her chest.

She loves you, I say.

I feel my companion take Aisulu's right hand. I hold her left.

You could have let me go, he says. **It would have hurt, but it would have healed. Every tie to the world will hurt you in the end. This is the good way.**

The snow is falling over Gullcroft. The curse pole drips blood into the snow. The horse skull grimaces out across the deserted village, towards the mountains. The gaping ribs clutch the base of the pole, and six iron staffs stand upright around it.

Vigdis stands there in her blue cloak, her silver pendants shining on her breast. Her long white hair streams in the wind. Tatters of horse skin still clinging to the skull on the pole flutter like banners.

I stand frozen, watching her.

My companion stands beside me.

I see we shared the same kind of mother, he says.

I promise you, mine was worse.

Vigdis stands there, staring through me.

They both tried to turn us into gods, says my companion. **They both knew it would kill us.**

Yours cared for you, at least. Mine didn't even tell me who she was.

Yours tried to shelter you from death. Mine sent me into the jaws of it.

Is yours still alive?

My companion shrugs. **I don't know. Because of what she did to me, I've never been able to find my way out of this world again.**

I look at Vigdis. She doesn't seem to see me at all.

Mine's dead, I say. *She never even faced what she did to me.*

Tell her.

I feel his hand in mine. When I speak, there's an echo. Not a single echo. A thousand.

You took me from my natural path. You abandoned me. You used me. You lied to me. You put me in harm's way. You said it would be good for me. You said I was strong. You did not protect me. You handed me to my enemies. You let them do what they wanted to me. You made me do it alone.

I hate you.

We're in the fiery ruins of the city among the golden fields. Darkness has fallen. There are screams, and the sounds of things breaking. Hooves thunder through the streets. The air smells of blood and burning.

A cart, one axel torn off it, lolls drunkenly in the street.

Is this the battle? I ask.

No, my companion says. **The battle's over. This is the looting.**

A small group of warriors in fish-scale armour are going house to house. I recognise one of them from his rounded face. Their arms are full of the kind of trinkets people have.

There's a shout from a doorway near the cart, and from it a couple of warriors drag out two boys, brothers.

"Who needs to increase their favour with Gamlig?" one of the warriors asks, laughing. "Here's an easy offering. Tsomak! You're low on bodies today."

The round-faced warrior freezes. "They're too young," he says. "Let them go."

The lead warrior smiles at him. "Oh, I suppose you're a mighty general, now? One battle down and you're a hero, eh?"

"No," Tsomak says. His voice shakes. "The law says—"

"The law," sneers the leader. "Recite it then, since you know it so well."

"The eleventh precept," says Tsomak, fighting not to look at the boys, "says that children not higher than a cartwheel may not be killed in war."

His eyes flicker to the broken cart as he speaks. I watch as he realises what he's done.

"Well then," says the leader. "Isn't that convenient? Let's do this by the law, as Tsomak insists."

The two boys are dragged against the cartwheel. One is taller, one shorter.

The leader runs the taller one through almost without looking.

The smaller one begins to sob.

The street is empty. The cart still stands there, but the air is quiet, and there is no smoke, no thunder of hooves, no flicker of flames.

Only Tsomak.

I walk up to the young man. He's a boy really, even younger than I was when I was bound to the black pillar on Far Isle.

I'm so sorry, I say. *What was done to you was unforgivable. You were so young.*

I killed him, Tsomak says. **I killed the boy.**

I don't have an answer for him.

Let me show you what I did, I say.

We stand before the walls of Hellingap. The town rises above the dunes on its tongue of grey stone. Under the low winter sun, the walls are hung with bodies like bunting.

I did this, I say. *All of it.*

The world wobbles, like a spinning top that's hit a bump.

All of it? my companion asks. **I don't think that's true.**

Look.

He turns me round. The walls are empty, the sun is high. On the flats before the town, an army of hundreds is massed.

I made them do it, I say.

My companion stares across the hundreds of faces, the bared teeth, the brandished blades.

Is that what they told you? he says.

Wait, I say.

We're back before the cart, the child sobbing, the warriors watching through the smoke.

The scene goes back to the way it was before. The warriors drag the boys from the doorway.

You didn't kill him, I say.

I killed his brother with my stupidity and my words, says my companion. **I couldn't save him.**

You were a child, I say. *You shouldn't have had to save him.*

I watch the leader push the children towards the cart.

Do it now, I say.

Tsomak steps forward. He kills the leader with a single blow. Then he guts each and every one of the watching warriors.

Precept twenty-six, he says. **A murderer must be put to death.**

Your people put that twenty-sixth? I ask.

Deliberately, he wipes his blade clean. **Technically he could have ransomed himself,** he says. **But I decided to leave that part out.**

We sit on the green grass in the sun. A child is playing beside us. She's sucking on an arrowhead.

That should hurt, I say.

Tsomak smiles. **I blunted them for her,** he says.

I'm sitting next to a boy of about eight with a chubby face and almond eyes under winged brows.

Where is this? I ask.

We look down the hill and across the grasslands. Large round tents made from horse skins stand inside a wooden stockade, and between them are corrals for animals, fire pits, a central space with what looks like a painted shrine at its head.

This is where I came from, he says. **Before I couldn't go back anymore.**

He holds out his hands, and the child waddles into them. She sits down heavily and looks me over. My heart sinks.

She's going to go through what we went through, I say.

I thought I could protect her, Tsomak says, **but I couldn't.**

The Arauris river flows swiftly between wooded hillsides. Merzen guards lie dead on the springy green turf. Aisulu and I are on the *uareh*. Ebba sprawls on the grass, looking down at the young soldier.

Why did she choose him? I ask. *He's no one. He's a stranger.*

Tsomak is studying Ebba's face with interest. He watches as she looks up towards the *uareh*, then back down to the soldier.

Because he needed her, he says, **and you didn't anymore.**

I shouldn't have let her go, I say.

You let her choose, Tsomak says.

The moon is almost eaten up, just the thinnest of slivers left. It rises above a spinney of trees growing among the shelter of the rocks at the top of a small hill. The trees and rocks stand up dark against the snowy plains. Two horses stand beneath the trees, and there is a new stump, the white heartwood glowing, an axe beside it. Not some woodsman's axe, but a double-headed war axe, the kind warriors carry.

The last night of the Moon of Snow, Tsomak says. **I should have died on Taghr's Night, when it was full, two weeks ago.**

There's a horse skin shelter beneath the trees, the new cut firewood piled beside it, and a fire burning before it. Aisulu ducks out from under the skins, takes a large stone from beside the fire, and wraps it in an old, soot-stained jacket.

Inside the tent she presses it against Tsomak's body. He's much thinner than he was even under his mother's hands. He's muttering, and sweat stands out on his skin. His embroidered clothes are dirty, falling to pieces.

Aisulu takes another stone, grown cold, and wearily takes it out to the fire to warm it again. I can feel her exhaustion, her despair.

"You're going to live, Tsomak," she says in the darkness. "I won't let you die."

I want to hold her. I want to tell her she's not alone.

But she is.

At last she lies down beside her shivering brother, and falls asleep.

What's wrong with you? I ask.

Tsomak, my companion, takes my hand and presses it to his living self's forehead.

And I feel it all. Some of it is familiar – the mist, the cold, the sedated horror – but there is something I never felt in my time with the Harrower. It gnaws at me like rats, scratching me raw.

He cursed me, Tsomak says, and his voice gnaws too. *Because I failed them. Because I betrayed them all. When Aisulu made me run from my fate, he called them, and every lost, corrupted soul came hungering for me. This world is nothing but tears and loss. There is no beauty in it that cannot be reduced to filth and decay.*

I pull my hand away.

I watch as Tsomak crawls from the shelter. Aisulu is so deeply asleep she barely twitches.

Tsomak drags himself to the stump. He hauls the axe upright, unnatural strength in his knotted muscles as they balance the axe against the edge of the stump. He lays his head sideways on the white splinters, his arms quivering as they fight to hold the haft in place. The blade hangs over him like the moon.

He lets it fall. There's nothing graceful in it.

The sounds bring Aisulu tumbling out of the shelter.

"No," she says, staring. "No!"

The blood arcs patterns across the snow.

Aisulu tears handfuls of fine material from the shelter to staunch the bleeding, but it's no use. He dies in her arms, wrapped in silk.

That's why she was exiled? I ask. *Because she tried to save you?*

I was the Kagan, Tsomak says. *I should have died when I was meant to. My blood must not be shed, even in death. I wanted her with me, to help me bear what I knew would come. Ever since my first battle, I knew I would die. I hoped it would come early, but my mother dragged me back from the Dark Earth and bound my shade to me. I was trapped. So I became the Kagan, because the Kagan can choose the time of his death. I betrayed my family, my duty, because I longed for death. And then she betrayed me.*

She believed you could live, I say.

I didn't want to live, Tsomak said. **There's no use in living.**

But you're still not free, I say. *Why?*

He turns towards me, and his mouth is all wrong. It's full of needles.

I'm so hungry, he says.

I awake with a start, sitting upright violently.

Kizmid turns, her face half-lit through the grille.

"You're awake," she says. Her voice is a strange mix of relief and pain. "At last."

My heart is pounding.

"I have a spirit inside me," I say. "He's called Tsomak. He's very sad, and he has a mouth full of needles."

Her eyes widen.

"Captain," says a voice that sends the spirit in me hissing and champing. "The girl is to be brought to the Emperor. I will deliver her."

Uryz, the needlemouth that was Tsomak says. *You **did this to** me. I've been looking for you.*

Twenty Nine
REVELATION

Dagomar's Compound,
Ban Granis

en't never seen anythin built so quick in all my life before. The stage goes up amid hammerin an shoutin, driven by panic. Before sunset, Gisla orders the gates opened.

I have to be there. I en't got a choice. I can't leave Rosamund an Neklaus alone together, so me an Fetch go with em, an stand behind the stage an watch as the end of the compound fills wi people. The crowd is tense an excited. When Gisla steps up onto the stage, people fall silent.

This en't the ritual I know. This is exhortation.

Gisla talks about a land in the north where the faith of believers is still new an keen. She says faith there burns so brightly cos it must survive. She says the belief of the few becomes a bonfire of righteousness through which the faithful tread, that springs gush beneath the staff of the believer, that the light of the Lord enters those who repent. Again, she draws back her dress to show the mark of the flames. It burns, she says. It saves.

I grit my teeth, ball my fists, an keep one hand in Fetch's fur. It feels like I barely breathe the whole time.

It's dark by the time she finishes an blesses the crowd. We wait until Dagomar's men drive em all from the compound before returnin to our rooms by the gate. I fall exhausted into bed, Fetch stretched out beside me.

I wake in the depths of the night. The broad figure stands over me again, an the glow of the fire plays over his face.

The boy wouldn't touch you because he sees you as you are, he says. *You are filth and mire. Your sin contaminates all it touches. Decent women know this. Decent women contain their sin.*

"And what about Rosamund?" I ask. "Her virtue did not protect her."

All women are sinful. The sin in her invited the sin in him.

"That's not true."

Your love is a trap. You will never live virtuously.

"But I will live," I say.

Day after day, it goes like this: the crowds outside, the gates opening at sunset, Gisla's sermons, the night visits. Neklaus hovers outside our door, but he seems cowed. The crowds grow bigger. They grow noisier, too. An it's not just their cries for salvation we hear. With em comes news of the city.

"The Qesar are confined to the Concession," Rosamund tells me one day. She's pettin Fetch while I clean. "Some Merzen soldiers were found dead, killed by Qesar arrows, and now their expulsion is almost certain."

"Arrows?" I say. "Rosamund, I bet they were Sergeant Hadric and his men."

"Yes" Rosamund says, her lips thin. "That would serve my uncle well. I wonder where he got the arrows? There's already been one suspected Qesar mobbed to death inside the city walls."

"When will the Emperor answer?"

"At the Feast of Embers," Rosamund says. "Two days from now. Whatever my uncle's planning, it will happen soon."

"Right now I'm more worried about what Gisla's plannin," I tell her. Gisla spends most days locked up in the inner room, prayin, but she's tole me she wants me with her tomorrow.

"Tomorrow is the Day of the Blessed Hekatera," Rosamund says. "We'll fast and we'll repent. They say a single Ember Day can wipe clean your soul. Gisla just wants to help as many people as she can." She smiles at me. "It feels good, Ebba," she says. "Why don't you do it with me?"

I don't want to, but Rosamund's eyes are bright. Her voice is warm when she speaks of it. An I think if she likes it, it can't be so bad.

So that's why I wake at dawn on the day before the Feast of Embers, eat a breadroll before sunrise, an join Rosamund an her aunt in prayer. At first my thoughts rattle between worries, but Rosamund tole me to let em pass.

"We mediate on the Blessed Hekatera," Gisla says as we settle ourselves, "whose bravery and perfection placed her among the saints."

I remember the picture of the woman wreathed in blood an flames. My mind won't linger there, so I think instead of the gold splashed across the page, the richness of it, the light.

The light hovers in my mind, a white heart surrounded by gold.

It en't the same as the light that came to me back in the Northern winter. This light is one I've conjured myself, but still, it warms an sooties me. I feel my body unlock, an after a while, I can hear its voice. My hands itch wi the impulse to labour. My head is loaded wi the thoughts that run through it. My limbs are willin, eager, but my heart is so heavy.

The light hovers by my breastbone. I can't tell if it's over or under my skin, but the gold of it is both inside an outside me. I breathe in light, an as I do it grows.

I understand there are things wi limits, an things without. There are things that reduce, an things that multiply.

When evenin comes, I feel strangely clear-eyed an calm. Even when Gisla leads us out into the compound, my heart don't jump the way it has before. The yard is already fillin up, people pourin through the gates, an this time Gisla leads us straight through em.

People draw back. They're starin at Gisla, but I feel eyes on me too. This time though it en't unbearable. They don't weigh me down. This time they stream off me, like shadows from light.

Gisla leads us up onto the stage, leavin Neklaus down among the crowd.

I en't never bin up here. It's high enough that I'm lookin over people's heads, all the way to the gates. Hundreds of faces turn to us, the settin sun behind us, their eyes an faces alight. The compound is full of urgency, of belief. Among em I think I glimpse a crow-black head wi wide hazel eyes.

The light in me falters, an I look away.

There's a stand on the wooden planks. It holds a flail.

I fasted and repented with my family. I'm free from sin. It was such a relief.

Suddenly I see it all laid out before me. I see Gisla's sermon, the eyes reflectin fire back to me, I see how she'll display me to em like a puppet. I've already heard her tell my story, night after night, and not once was it true.

I see how these hundreds of eyes protect her from the hand of her brother.

I see how they feed the thing inside her.

I see how Rosamund welcomes what she believes will save her.

Like a litany, her words echo inside of me.

She was scourged, but she felt no pain. The king tried to burn her, but she walked through the flames. Finally she ordered him to cut off her head, because she was ready to meet God.

Everyone who saw it was converted.

It makes me sick.

The light has all but died.

I turn on my heel, an I climb down from that stage as the crowd starts to cry out for Gisla, its priestess, its prophet. I push my way to the stable door, slide through it, an close it, my chest heavin wi silent sobs. Fetch, ever beside me, nuzzles my hand.

"Ebba?" says a Northern voice.

I look up.

Jarle comes up to me. The taper in his hand throws golden light across his face. His long blonde hair is down for once. He looks me over, silently hands me the taper, an heaves a heavy wooden bar across the door.

"Come on," he says, takin the taper back an puttin his arm

around my shoulders. "You'll be safe here."

I tug on his arm. My heart feels like it's stopped.

"Wait," I say. "Jarle, I need to know."

He turns back to me, an before he can ask the question I see on his lips, I reach up an kiss him.

It is not a perfect kiss. The wind does not surround us like a live thing, the stars do not tremble. The stable smells of hay an a bit of manure. Somewhere nearby a horse snorts.

But Jarle himself smells like grass, an his hair where it falls against my cheek is soft an clean, an when I stop kissin him, he smiles at me.

"That was nice," he says.

"Not sinful?" I say.

He raises his eyebrows. "You've been in the south too long, Ebba," he says.

He holds out his hand, an I put mine in his.

"I've got some food," he says. "You look like you need something to eat."

"Can I kiss you again?" I ask. My heart has remembered how to do its work, an it's hammerin inside me to make up for stoppin.

Jarle bends down an does it for me.

I'd imagined the hay an the horses. Of course I had. Jarle was the stable boy back in Frithberg too, so those long daydreams were quite detailed. I din't imagine me sayin, "Is that all?" halfway through, an him laughin so much he set me off, so that we have to wait until we both stop gigglin.

"There's a bit more to it," he says when he's caught his breath, an then he shows me.

An this is a sin? I can't help thinkin. *This is what Berengar was so scared of, what he had to whip himself clean of?*

Why?

Jarle asks me things I never thought of. "How does that feel?" "Do you like this?" "Where feels good?"

Sometimes it's all so new, I en't got an answer yet.

"It feels better the more you do it," he says, an I give him a sceptical look that makes him smile again. "I don't mean just with me. With whoever you want."

I don't say so, but I like the way he laughs wi me just as much as the way he touches me. An then there are the times when he's starin up into my eyes an I can't think of anythin but the way his lips look, his body under mine, how it feels fillin in the spaces my mind could never quite imagine, no matter how hard I tried.

"So, what do you think?" he asks me afterwards, when we're layin together, my head on his chest, his arm around me.

"I like it," I tell him. "It's not how I thought it would be."

"How did you think it would be?"

"Passionate," I say. "Overwhelmin."

"It can be those things," he says. "It's different with everyone, you'll see. Are you hungry?"

We sit in the hay an eat hard cheese an bread in companionable silence.

"You've changed," I say. "I never thought I'd hear you laugh."

To my delight, he blushes.

"You didn't know me that well," he says. "You barely spoke to me."

I remember the way him just lookin my way left me breathless. Guess I can't argue wi that.

"Oh," I say, screwing my face up. "I din't even ask about the wayhouse."

"Sorleyson's given it up," he says, "so Aud's running it. She's even more of a terror than he was, of course. Kelda's married the silversmith's son. They're still replanting the fields after the fighting, and they're rebuilding the kirk. There's a shrine to the Salvebearer and her wolf at the foot of the kirkrock."

I look down. I don't want to think how fresh those scars still are.

Then he asks me a question I really don't want to answer.

"What about Torny?"

I think about what Rosamund tole me, about the Qesar being confined, about the person who was mobbed. It's bin half a moon since I arrived in Ban Granis, an this is where the *uareh* was headed too. I hope they're safe.

"I think she's in the city," I say, "but I don't know."

A noise that's been on the edge of hearin suddenly swells. It's the roar of a mob. Both Jarle an I bolt to our feet, draggin clothes back on, scrabblin for our shoes. Some part of us knows that's the kind of noise that means you might have to run.

It's just as well. Erland jogs between the boxes, his sword out.

"Ebba," he says, "here you are. Thank God you're all right."

"What happened?"

He shakes his head.

"That Abbess," he says. "She whipped them into a fervour. She's sent them to the Bishop's palace to get back Grimulf's body."

My mouth drops open, but he en't finished.

"Dagomar's men have armed up an moved out too," Erland says. "They tried to barricade the king, but we fought them off.

One of them told us they plan to take the Emperor captive. We have Rosamund safe, but we have to go."

There are poundin footsteps on the flags.

"I found her!" Erland shouts. "We're here. She's all right."

Berengar, his blue tunic pulled askew, his sword in his hand, skids round the corner.

"Ebba!" he cries, but pulls up and glares at Jarle. Jarle smiles back, a little too smugly I think.

"What are you doin here?" I say.

"I've been trying to reach you for days," he says. "I've been in the crowd every evening, trying to find you, but that guard from Merzen was always there."

I look at the pink in his cheeks, his bright hazel eyes, his crow-black hair flopping over his face.

"It's good to see you," I say. I mean it.

"The houses of the *Regna*," he says, "they're going to rise up against the Emperor."

"We know, lad," Erland says. "The Merzen ladies explained it."

Berengar frowns. "Lady Rosamund," he says, "she said we would find the Emperor in the hypogea."

We stare at him. Erland asks what we're all thinkin.

"Where the hell is that?"

Thirty
HYPOGEA

TORNY'S TALE

The Emperor's Palace, Ban Granis

 here is a big grinning hole where my head should be.

That's him, says Tsomak inside me. ***That's the one I want to eat!***

I smile pleasantly. Kizmid gives me a wary look.

"We're coming in, Rus," she says. "Stay down, d'you understand?"

"Oh yes," I say.

Kizmid's eyes narrow.

"What's taking so long?" Uryz fusses, out of sight behind the door. Inside me, the needlemouth that was Tsomak gnashes its teeth at his voice.

"You stay there," Kizmid says. I don't know if she means Uryz or me. She comes in, crouches, and ties my hands together.

"Who am I talking to?" she asks in Northern.

"Torny," I say.

"Is *he* there?"

"Oh yes."

I can feel her recoil from me.

"You slept the best part of a week," she says.

"We had a lot to talk about," I say.

I have never seen Kizmid so rattled.

"You're going with Uryz," she says. "Torny, if something happens to him on the way, the Concession will be levelled. None of us will make it out. Do you understand?"

"Nothing will happen to him," I say, "I promise. He'll be very safe with me."

Uryz steps into view behind her.

Like a cat arching its back and hissing, I feel the needlemouth coil inside me, flaring out its teeth like a spiked halo.

I smile. My mouth feels wider than usual.

Uryz takes a step back.

"What's wrong with her?" he demands.

Kizmid gestures me out into the corridor.

"Interrogation," she says shortly. "She got hit a bit too hard."

"You damaged our bargaining chip?" Uryz snaps.

Kizmid looks down her nose at him. She's a full head taller.

"She'll be fine," she says. "Stay behind her at all times. I'll keep her quiet."

"You won't be coming with me, Captain," Uryz says.

"I'll do it," says a voice.

The familiar thrill runs through me, sharpened around the edges with anger and a love far deeper than youthful infatuation.

"Aisulu?" Kizmid says.

"Negotiator Uryz wants me to report my failure in person," Aisulu says. Her eyes linger on me.

I want so much to *take her by the shoulders and shake her hard—*

No.

Uryz smirks. He points us down the corridor and into a store room. At first it looks like a dead end, but there's a heavy metal grate in the floor, a drain. The sight of it makes me shudder, although I don't know why. A vision of a metal grille in a stone cavern flashes across my mind, smoke spilling upwards, something choking me.

I blink. The vision is gone. Aisulu stands beside me, tense, while Kizmid levers the metal grate up and sets it aside.

Uryz gestures to the dank hole in the floor.

"After you," he says.

Aisulu goes first. She lowers herself into the hole, hangs by her fingers, then drops. I wonder how I'm going to manage it.

"Come on, Rus," Kizmid says. I sit on the edge of the hole, my legs dangling down into the blackness. She hooks me under the arms and starts to lower me down.

I feel strong arms wrap around my waist, hugging me tightly as Aisulu takes my weight. Tenderness rises through me like a tide.

"Remember your promise," Kizmid murmurs to me, before letting me go.

"Aisulu," I whisper in the dark, and I don't know who says it.

Then a light is lowered, and a metal step, and Uryz climbs down, a moue of satisfaction on his lips.

We're in a sandy tunnel, the ancient stonework of the walls lined with floodmarks. The drain itself lets into a kind of hollowed-out niche, not part of the original structure.

"The *cloaca* of ancient Ban Granis, *Aquae Granatae*," Uryz says.

"They thought I was crazy when I told them to dig."

"How did you know this was here?" Aisulu asks as we start to walk. She's beside me, Uryz behind us giving directions. We follow the tunnels uphill.

"I studied," Uryz says. "Not the trash you Three Clans children are taught. Those of us born to the Fourth Clan can't afford to ride around playing the noble nomad. I spent time in cities all around the Marble Sea. I learned the language of the ancient empires, I read their histories, their treatises."

I imagine biting off his finger, *the bones snapping between my jaws, the skin in shreds, the crunch of the nail.*

Stop it.

The needlemouth withdraws, grumbling.

"Where are you taking me?" I ask.

"The *cloaca*," Uryz says, "runs under all of *Aquae Granatae*. The ancient killing grounds had no use for them, but they did have holding pens for both men and beasts. When the palace was built, those tunnels became a catacomb. It holds the remains of holy men and women sacred to the Empire. The Emperor goes there to pray."

"And you found a way in," Aisulu says. She sounds impressed.

"Every request we lay before the Emperor must be done in full court," Uryz says, "under the scrutiny of our enemies. This way meant we could offer . . . other services."

We walk on in silence. The tunnels are changing. They're wider, and in places the walls have been deliberately broken through. I glimpse dark caves beyond the stonework. We criss-cross through several underground rooms where the air lies heavy, unmoving.

We wind our way through a narrow series of turns. Uryz's

memory must be astounding, or else there are markings I haven't noticed showing the way.

We enter a large, low space. Uryz douses the light. There is a glow, a long way off, but visible. It flickers, like torchlight. Uryz nods us on.

The space is lined with open stone shelves and grander carved boxes, longer than a man.

"Sarcophagi," Uryz says. "For those who could afford the privacy."

I look at one set of shelves as we pass by. A desiccated body, barely more than leather and bone, grins back at me, its arms crossed, hands on its shoulders.

"They're so old, they don't know who they are," Uryz says behind me, "so they put them all here, in case some of them were holy."

The ceiling is supported by blunt columns, and although there are no walls, the columns, shelves and the sarcophagi form a kind of labyrinth, cutting off the line of sight and leading us by winding ways towards the glow.

It takes a few minutes to reach the centre, but then I see him.

A man kneels amongst what must be scores of candles, before an ornate stone tomb. For a moment I think there's someone lying on the tomb, but then I see my mistake. The sarcophagus is topped with a statue of a woman, her torso propped up on one elbow, her body swaddled in finely carved folds of cloth. Her free hand holds what looks like a carved whip.

"Your Majesty," Uryz says, gesturing for us to stop.

The man bows his head, then rises to his feet and turns.

The Emperor looks us over.

I expected a tall man, a man whose bulk and stature matched the weight his empire lays upon the world. Instead, I realise he is a few fingers shorter than me, his build strong but unexceptional. He's wearing a tunic and hose in deep red, with a short, heavily embroidered cape pinned at his right shoulder. His hair falls to his shoulders in light brown curls, lined with grey, and his full beard holds a flash of white over his chin. His eyes, over his thin lips and long hooked nose, are intelligent and dispassionate. His skin is pockmarked, and brown from the sun. His belt, wrists and fingers all glint with gold and precious stones in red, yellow and black. A beautiful sheath lies against his thigh, a decorated hilt resting easily under his hand.

Uryz prods Aisulu and me in the back, and we bow.

"Negotiator Uryz," The Emperor says in Southern, and his voice is clear and pleasant. "You've left delivery until the last possible moment. I was just asking the Blessed Hekatera here to hurry you along."

Uryz bows even lower.

"My apologies, Your Imperial Majesty," he says. "We were regrettably beset. Here is the Carrier to report on her work."

He pushes Aisulu forward.

"Your Majesty," she says, head still bowed. "I went north as I was ordered. I established the hagiography did indeed contain heretical content. The Rus were amenable to our agreement, and the agent at Vellsberg was able to open the gates to them and secure the book. However, the Rus reneged on our agreement, and assaulted the lord's hall. I was able to kill them before capture, but it seems the Rus are decided to continue their attacks on the northern *Regna* in retaliation for the removal of their hunting grounds. As you know, they have already attacked Lughambar on the Samara."

"Indeed," the Emperor says to Uryz and Aisulu, "And now the houses of the *Regna* join against me and demand the expulsion of your people, Carrier. These are not the results I hoped for."

Aisulu keeps her head down.

"In addition," the Emperor continues, "I understand you have lost the book."

"Yes, Your Majesty," Aisulu says, looking up. "But I doubt it would have helped. I bring you something better."

Merovec tilts his head.

"Your Majesty," Aisulu says, taking a breath. "This is Torny Arnsdota. She is the bastard sister of King Kolrand of Arngard, the leader of the rebellion in the north, and the person who killed Prester Grimulf."

And there it is. That is the prize I was for Aisulu, the reason she took us with her, the cause for her protection and care.

I was of use to her. By caring for me, she could fulfil her duty.

My left hand curls, the fingertips rubbing the scar on my palm.

The Emperor looks me over.

"All that," he says, "and all you need to restrain her is a rope around her wrists?"

He knew about me. Someone, probably Uryz, told him what to expect. There's no surprise, only curiosity.

"Tell me, girl," he says to me, "after you killed Grimulf, your army fell apart. You had the advantage, but you relinquished everything and fled. Your own people seem not to be sure whether you even existed."

I smile.

"I wasn't doing it for the kingdom," I say. "Your sources seem inadequate. Haven't you heard? It was a devil murdered Grimulf, not a girl."

"Negotiator, Carrier," the Emperor says, his eyes still on me. "This is sufficient. Go back to your Concession. Tomorrow I will announce your orderly and protected withdrawal from these lands."

"But—" Aisulu protests, before Uryz grabs her and yanks her back.

The Emperor looks at her. "Your incompetence has solidified an alliance against me that now threatens the safety of the empire," he says. "The Rus are emboldened in the north. I have a new cult running wild in the *Regna*, and now on the streets of Ban Granis herself, fed by your actions. You lost me the other girl, the one whose presence enflames the cult, and the book. The Qesar stand accused of murder, sabotage, and espionage. The point of being a spy, Carrier, is to get away with it."

Aisulu's face is flaming red.

"Be thankful you will have imperial protection," the Emperor says. "Without it, none of you would make it out alive."

"Thank you, Your Majesty," Uryz says. "While the outcome was regrettable, it has been a pleasure doing business with you."

Holding Aisulu firmly by the arm, he draws her away.

The needlemouth within me squirms and thrashes, wanting to follow its prey. I clench all my muscles, overriding it.

Finally, Aisulu looks at me. In her eyes I see what I couldn't before. Her desperation, her shame. I remember the girl standing between the dark layers of skin, terrified for her brother.

"You can't protect me, Aisulu," I tell her in Qesar.

My voice has an echo.

Her eyes widen, but Uryz pulls her away among the sarcophagi, lost among the shadows and the dead.

As their footfalls fade away, the Emperor turns to me.

"Enough of the poetry," he says. "I have no interest in devils. I deal in people. You have a claim to the throne of Arngard. Do you want it?"

"Less than anything in all the world," I say. "Do you know what happens to our kings?"

The Emperor bares his teeth in a grin. "Oh yes," he says. "In fact, I count on it." He sighs. "It's a pity," he says, "you do look remarkably alike. It seems a waste."

"What will you do with me instead?" I ask.

"Announce that we have caught the heretic who led a rebellion against the righteous," the Emperor says. "You will be exorcised, tried, and executed. That should calm this sudden fervour for the new saint."

I raise my eyebrows. "Will that be enough for the *Regna*?"

"The *Regna*," the Emperor says, "are a bunch of greedy local lords out for their own gain. They may have temporarily united, but it won't last. Once I remove their Bishop, they will fall. The costs of treason are high. One way or another, those lands will come to me."

He narrows his eyes.

"If he supports me," he says, "I'll grant your king the right to take you back to your own kingdom, and kill you there. That should help him decide his loyalty."

He's watching me again.

"Doesn't that scare you, girl?" he asks.

"It should," I say. "I know it should."

The Emperor shakes his head. "I've known warriors like you," he says. "They'll do anything, and they feel nothing. It's all very impressive, but they make bad soldiers. They risk too much. You'll be more use dead."

"From what I've seen," I tell him, "death is rarely the end of things."

"You won't be going where the rest of us go," the Emperor says.

"No," I say. "I think I'll be stuck here. And that means all of this will keep going."

The Emperor frowns. "I don't think you understand," he says. "You're going to die."

"Give me your hand," I say, offering my two bound ones.

Warily, he places his left hand between mine.

I let the needlemouth free.

It rises up under my skin, hungry for something, even if it's not its prey. It fills up my face and my hands, opening its mouth to *bite*—

The Emperor snatches back his hand.

"What was *that*?"

"*Poetics*," we say. I see his eyes light up with something he gave up on long ago. Belief.

Yes, there are devils in the world, and gods. They *hunger*.

"Heavenly Father," the Emperor mutters, "protect us, now and at the hour of our deaths—"

I smile, and an arrow whips past my head.

I slam my body to the floor, dragging him with me. He stares at the arrow as it shatters and clatters across the stonework. Another follows. I crawl behind the sarcophagus, hauling him with me.

"Where are your guards?" I ask.

"Upstairs," he gasps, "but no one knows how to get here!"

I hold up the arrow. It's Qesar.

"Uryz does," I say. "He has a history of disposing of kings who no longer serve him."

The Emperor's eyes widen. "He wouldn't," he says.

"Just like the *Regna* wouldn't?" I ask.

There are people coming through the labyrinth of the dead, lots of them. I risk a glance over the carved woman's hip, then duck down again.

"They're Southern," I say. "Looks like your lords have decided the costs of treason are worth it."

The initial shock has passed. The Emperor's eyes narrow.

"Can that devil in you help?" he asks.

I see how he's kept grip on this Empire of his.

The needlemouth's hunger is closer to the surface than it was before. I can feel it yearning.

"Yes," I say. "But not if there's going to be exorcisms and trials at the end of this."

"If you get me through this," the Emperor says, "you'll be on my personal guard. I swear."

"Then free my hands, and give me your sword," I say.

He opens his mouth to voice doubts we don't have time for. I grab his hand, let the remains of Tsomak shrill in his ears as well as mine. I need him to understand. A needlemouth isn't a tool or a ploy, it's an appetite, an obsession. I'd already told him: I'm not doing this for a kingdom.

Mute, he unsheathes his sword, saws the bindings free, and hands me the blade. We must be nearly surrounded. I can hear the echoes of footfalls as the attackers try to move quietly between the tombs, edging nearer to us.

Let me lead you, the needlemouth says. ***The dead are dear to me. I can show you the way.***

And just like that, I see the lines of the labyrinth, laid out in desiccated bodies in their stone beds. I slip to the right, around shelves of exposed bones, and the regal sword slides effortlessly forward between the ribs of the first assailant. I kick his sword around the shelves for the Emperor, turn another corner, and dispatch a second man. This one gurgles.

You're doing this, I say to Tsomak.

How do you know? he says.

Because it's too easy.

Do you want me to stop?

No. But you can't take me over completely.

You'll tire, he warns me.

Still.

I take the attacker's bow and quiver, and head back to the sarcophagus of the Blessed Hekatera, stringing an arrow as I run. I round the shelves just in time to see the Emperor hamstring a man as he turns a corner, and then I loose my arrow into the chest of another emerging from the mess of tombs. I hear shouts.

"They'll rush us," the Emperor says as I hand him back his sword, and take the one from the fallen man.

"Can we fight our way to your guards?" I ask.

He gestures in the opposite direction to the one Uryz brought me. "There's a ramp," he says. "If we can get there, we can get out."

I stand, alerted by the needlemouth's senses, and my next arrows bury themselves in a man's side, another in the shoulder of the man behind him. I duck back down as a third man shoots at me.

"If they rush us here, we'll die," Merovec says. "Look out!"

Another man has come around the shelves to our right. I launch myself at him, and hear another arrow clatter behind me. I slash at the man's face, driving him back, then cut down and round, towards his side. He batters my sword away, steps back, then spins forward. At first I think it's an attack, but an arrow is sticking out of his back.

The needlemouth keens even before I look up.

Aisulu stands there, her chest heaving. There's a bump on her forehead, and blood trickles down her temples.

"Tsomak," she says, "is that you?"

It's all I can do to keep the needlemouth under control. It gnashes and writhes inside me, caught like a worm in salt.

"Get away from me," I tell Aisulu, pointing. "The Emperor! Protect him!"

She looks bewildered.

"Help him!" I shout. "Do it!"

She hurries past me as I bare my teeth and try to force the needlemouth back down. I know why it's gone crazy. Everything hurts. Uryz is simple enough – the needlemouth knows what to do with him – but Aisulu awakens a horrible cascade of visions, and I can't stop them. Instead of the child playing safely on the grass, I see her in terrible pain, lacerated by the needlemouth's anger. But the visions bring no relief. Her pain and punishment hurts, because under the anger is a terrible love, a love that must override all fury and envy, all resentment.

She's your sister, I tell him. *You can't hurt her. You have to stop.*

I stagger around the next corner, and catch the attacker's sword descending on my blade. It's the same lock that nearly floored me back in Vellsberg, but the weeks of practice with Aisulu have given my muscles the memory they need. I kick out, breaking his knee, and impale him as he hits the ground.

I am not alone.

There is mist among the shelves and tables of the labyrinth.

No! I think. *I thought this was over! I thought I was done with you!*

The mist coalesces around a slight figure, dark haired, with upturned moon eyes. There is blood on his chest, and his neck, which in life bore a rough iron thrall collar, is ringed with gold.

Fenn smiles at me, and beckons.

"You're dead," I say aloud.

He shrugs and smiles.

I feel the labyrinth of the dead, mapped out around me. At last I understand.

"You're here to guide me," I say, "aren't you? You've been trying to guide me through the mist all along."

He nods. I feel an indescribable weight leave me.

"I'm ready," I say. "I'll follow."

The mist thickens. The dead, holy or otherwise, form lines of light. I know how this works. You get certain powers, but in return, you are more easily caged. In the mist I can see the shape of the leech within me, slithering under my skin, between organs.

"He's hungry," I say to Fenn's shade.

Let him feed.

No one has to force me this time. No one has to tie me up, or tell me it won't hurt, or promise me a future they know I can never have. I don't have to say I'm sorry for not being what they wanted me to be. I am exactly what I have made of myself. Maybe there's no name for what I am, or maybe there's many: *Staffbearer, Spirit Walker, Wanderer*. I don't care. Here and now, I am needed.

I stalk through the mist between the lines of the dead, and it is filled with bodies. I hack my way through them, the movements of my muscles familiar, repetitive. The needlemouth's appetite drives me, Fenn leads me.

It's not like being the Harrower. This time, my sword arm gets tired.

I find myself back in the candlelight. The Emperor leans against the carved tomb, while Aisulu binds his arm with a bandage ripped from her shirt. He stares at me. There are drops of sweat on his forehead, and his decorative cape lies ripped on the floor, its hem trailing in blood.

"Where have you been?" he asks.

"I think I cleared them out," I say.

"Did you find Uryz?" Aisulu asks, not meeting my eyes.

I shake my head. "He give you that?" I ask, nodding to the bump on her head. She nods.

"This Bishop," I say to the Emperor. "Is he the type to leave anything to chance?"

"No," he says.

"Do you trust your guards?" Aisulu asks.

The Emperor is silent. The attack in this shrine has shaken him.

"Who can you trust?" I ask.

"The houses of the *Corda*," he says. "They have nothing to gain from my death. But they are all practising penitence before the Feast of Embers."

There are shouts and footfalls.

"We have to go," I say.

Aisulu scoops up two quivers from the nearby corpses, and the Emperor leads the way. I jog beside him through the twists of the catacombs. The mist has thinned to almost nothing, but I still see a faint golden nimbus ahead of me. When we pass the first body, the Emperor shoots me a look. After another two, he keeps his eyes resolutely turned from mine.

Aisulu grunts behind us, and I hear the twang of her bow and the thunk of an arrow as she looses. They've found us.

"Go!" she shouts.

We round a corner, and I see the ramp leading up and out of the catacombs. I can feel the dead lying above us too, haphazard.

"I think someone surprised your guards," I say.

The Emperor nods grimly. "The ramp leads to the chapel," he says. "The throne room is adjacent to it. From there a corridor leads to my chambers. There's a hidden passage to a safehouse. That will take us close to one of the great houses of the *Corda*. They'll protect me. Get me there and you can have whatever your heart desires."

I look back towards the opening between the tombs. There are cries and running feet, but no sign of Aisulu.

"Come on," I say.

We creep up the ramp. I go ahead, looking around me. The needlemouth can sense the dead, but the living are invisible to it. That's what it needs me for. But there's something odd about the room above us. The dead guards are easy. Someone left them in a pile at the head of the ramp, two more a little further away, where I guess the door must be.

The rest of the room flickers weirdly in my senses, a messy

pattern of arches and lines made up of innumerable dots. I shake my head to clear it, and almost miss a man in a guard's uniform as he lunges past me at the Emperor.

I use my leg to trip him as the Emperor parries his blade and thrusts his own sword at the man's chest. He curses as the sword skitters over the metal scales sewn on the leather jerkin, but the guard has lost his balance and as he slams into the ramp, the Emperor jabs his sword into the exposed flesh at his neck.

"One of mine," he says, his face sour. He looks at the bodies at the top of the ramp. "They've been executed or turned."

I hear the bitterness in his voice at the same time as another guard lunges out from behind a column. Again, I nearly miss him, barely getting my arm up in time. The Emperor steps forward and engages him, but as I try to take him from behind I find my sight clouded.

It's like I'm going blind.

"What's wrong with you?" the Emperor yells. "Help me!"

An arrow zips past me, knocking the guard back, and then Aisulu pounds up the ramp, a curved sword in her hand. She lunges in and cuts under the man's jerkin.

"Torny," she says, putting out a hand to steady me. "What is it? What's wrong?"

I yowl. Where her hand touches me, the needlemouth starts to thrash and blister.

"She's an abomination," says a voice from the grand entrance of the chapel. "In the house of the Lord she cannot fight. Is this what you are reduced to, Merovec? Witches and devils?"

A tall, pale man stands framed by the arched doors, guards to either side of him. The painted walls spin, the air filled with a heavy, cloying scent, the glitter of the golden altars and decorations overlaid with the searing white light of the dead – but in pieces, in tiny, uncountable parts, all blazing.

"It's a trap," I say.

"Torny," Aisulu says, "there's nothing there. It's just a room."

"No," says the Emperor. "It's the relics."

Buried in chalices, hung from crosses, set in figures, in boxes, in altars, even walled up in the stones, I feel them – skulls and fingerbones, teeth, patches of skin, vertebrae, joints and femurs, toenails, half a pelvis, a hank of hair, an eyeball, a vial of blood. The dead surround me, dismembered, divided. Some of them retain the echoes of their deaths, and what deaths. Griddled, boiled, impaled, battered, torn apart. Others are the peaceful dead, but all caught up, all meddled with, all set apart and gazed on, prayed to, kissed and caressed and cherished for their pain, for their horror.

"She cannot withstand their purity," the pale man says. "Their holiness is anathema to her."

I sway, sick and dizzy to my core.

"It's over, Merovec," the man says. "Your unnatural helper is overcome. Surrender."

"And what, Ormund?" the Emperor asks.

The pale man spreads his arms.

"I didn't want to kill you, Merovec," he says. "Only make you see sense. But now I find you the consort of demons. I don't have much choice, do I?"

"No," the Emperor says, irony in his voice. "I suppose not. Well, Bishop. Come and get me."

The guards advance. The Emperor grips his sword. At the head of the ramp Aisulu draws her bow, and shouts a warning.

And then I see him, hidden behind the Bishop.

Uryz!

The needlemouth screams in rage as the chapel fills with mist. People shout and stumble, but there is only one concern in my whole body.

The thing that was Tsomak launches me towards its prey. I'm not sure, but I think I throw myself to all fours as I dash towards him. Among the dancing light shards of the relics I see the Bishop draw his blade, but my eyes are fixed on the man who did this to me, and I dodge the Bishop and fling myself on Uryz, knocking him full-length.

I bite into his neck, and rip.

I know I should be horrified.

I know the blood leaping over my face and tongue should disgust me.

But I feel peace.

I feel the snow falling among pines, and the axe like the weight of the dying moon, and the vast loneliness of the snow-covered grasslands. I feel the rocks, ages old, and the horses, huddled nose-to-tail, and there, curled among skins and silk, I feel the determined thud of a heartbeat that will drag me with it, no matter what.

This is one edge I cannot blunt, Aisulu. This is the blade we all live on, and I lost my balance long ago.

Please, let me go.

Out of the mist I rise, my face streaming with tears, my jaw and throat coated with blood.

Aisulu cries out and runs to me, and now her arms around me don't burn. Now her arms are the rocks and the grass and the horses and the moon, and I see in her the one I was denied so long.

"*Ai Nakota, Wanderer,*" I say. "*I have been searching for you, the one who is free among the bound. Lead me through the mansions of the sky, into the Dark Earth, where I will be at peace. I'm ready.*"

Slowly, while the men stutter through their ugly dance around us, she draws an arrow from her quiver. I see it is her last.

She takes the sharp edge, and draws it lightly across both her palms. Red lines spring up, and then she grips my shoulders.

"Depart, brother," she says. "Thank you for caring for me. I release you."

I feel the glare of the holy dead dim, the mist boil off like ether. Out of my bloody mouth slips the last shreds of Tsomak, Celestial Father, Soul of the Clans. Like smoke, he rises.

There is still a hole inside me. I think there always will be. As I breathe again, it starts to seal, but I know it can be reopened and filled. As the mist disappears, I feel Fenn's closeness, like a small hand in mine. It seems I have a guide now, too.

Aisulu steps into the circle of my arms, raises her face to mine, and kisses me. I know we will have to talk, she and I, about how to love without scarring one another, about the pain we carry, how not to take it with us. But that comes later. For now I kiss her until she pulls away.

"Welcome back, Torny," she says, her lips red with blood. "We have work to do."

"We have help," I say.

Through the grand doorway burst fresh troops. These are dressed in red, and at their head is a big man with a broken nose. They fall upon the guards, freeing the Emperor from his dance.

Behind them come Ebba, Berengar, and a slim figure in black, his dark blonde curls mussed, his dagger held to the neck of the pale Bishop.

Our matching grey eyes meet.

"Brother," I say. "We meet at last."

Epilogue
LIMINA

❧

Ebba's Tale

t is hard enough to meet the half-sister who nearly rent your kingdom apart, whose mother caused the death of your parents, without her bein covered in blood at the time. Even kings may not know which greetin to use in such a case. I'm quite impressed that Kolrand simply nods to Torny.

"Your Majesty," he says. "We caught Bishop Ormund trying to flee."

An that is when I realise that the short, bearded man wi the bloody bandage on his arm an a nicked sword in his hand is the most powerful man in the Southern Empire. He leans on a pillar, tryin to catch his breath, an his torn tunic is stained wi sweat under his arms. He glances down at the gory remains of another man on the tiled floor.

"Bring the Bishop to the throne room," he says.

"What happened here?" Berengar demands. Jarle leans over to see, an makes a face.

I look at Torny an Aisulu. Torny twitches the corner of her

mouth up. Whatever happened, she seems all right. This time she din't need me to bring her back. When I realise that, the relief is like fresh salve on a burn.

She don't need me like that anymore.

I push Berengar an Jarle after the others.

There are dead guards in the throne room too. Erland an his men check the whole room, pilin the dead in one corner, makin sure there's no one hidin. The Emperor sits wearily on his throne, his sword still in his hand.

"Are there more of you?" he asks Ormund.

But the Bishop won't speak.

"Tie him up," the Emperor orders, "and come here, all of you."

He looks us over.

"Not one of you from the *Corda*," he says, lookin down the line. "*Regna*, Qesar, *Limina* . . ." He stops at King Kolrand. "I was not aware you had arrived in Ban Granis," he says.

Kolrand bows his head. "Bishop Ormund kept us under guard at the merchant Dagomar's compound, your Imperial Majesty," he says.

"How did you know to come for me?" the Emperor asks.

"The ladies of Merzen, Abbess Gisla and her niece, risked their lives to tell us," King Kolrand says. "As did Ebba Rathnasdota, also known as the Salvebearer."

The Emperor's eyes run over us again, an stop at me.

"Your capture was reported," he says. "I ordered you to be brought to me."

"The Bishop found me first, your Imperial Majesty," I say.

"You're the one who took my book," he says.

I glance at Aisulu. She has the decency to look ashamed.

"It's doesn't matter now," the Emperor says, lookin at Ormund. "Where are these ladies to whom I owe so much?"

"They went to the Bishop's palace," Kolrand says. "They were searching for Prester Grimulf's body."

The Emperor rubs his face. "This cult," he says. "Saints and devils, everywhere."

I wonder if anyone else notices his hand shakes just a little as he lowers it.

"You," he says to Berengar. "You're the Vellsberg boy, Theogault's cousin? Nephew? Never mind," he says as Berengar opens his mouth. "Go through that door to my chambers. In the far room you will find a dressing room. Open the smaller chest. It will reveal a passage. Follow it until you reach the city. The house before you belongs to the Lord of Masila. Tell him I need him and his men, quickly."

Berengar bows an hurries off.

Aisulu steps forward an bows. "Your Imperial Majesty," she says. "My people at the Concession will be wondering where I am and what must happen to them."

"Don't forget," snaps the emperor, "that it was one of you who betrayed me!"

Torny steps forward. The Emperor flinches a little as he looks at the blood dryin on her.

"We had a deal," Torny says. "What do you say?"

I wince at her bluntness.

The Emperor opens his mouth, an shuts it again.

"I suppose," she says, "a Holy Patriarch probably shouldn't employ anyone who carries devils inside them, should he? Give the Qesar your protection, and I will consider your vow fulfilled."

The Emperor looks at Aisulu. "The Concessions must go," he says. "They've been used to hide fugitives."

"Fugitives who saved your life," Torny says.

"Still," the emperor says. "I know what you're capable of."

"Because you asked us to do it," Aisulu says.

The Emperor wrinkles his nose. "You may keep the trade counters," he says. "And your ships may trade using the waterways. But the Concessions go, and so do the Carriers."

Aisulu nods stiffly. "May I go and tell my people?"

"You won't be safe," the Emperor says.

"I'll take the tunnels," Aisulu says. "Torny?"

Torny nods to the emperor. Then she looks at me an smiles. With a last glance at Kolrand, she leaves with Aisulu.

Once she's gone it's like the whole room breathes out.

Beside me Jarle murmurs, "She's not changed then," an I have to bite my lip to stop a hiccup of laughter from escapin.

"Who are these men?" the Emperor asks Kolrand, waving a hand at Erland and his soldiers.

"Bearskins, your Imperial Majesty," the king says. "They're my personal guard. Captain Erland here is their commander."

"Your Imperial Majesty," Erland says, "have you considered guards unaligned to the lords of your lands? The Bearskins are all baptised, they are loyal believers, and many of them only speak Northern."

The Emperor looks interested. I roll my eyes an step back, drawin Jarle away from the discussion. I don't want the Emperor gettin any ideas.

Lord Masila arrives, accompanied by his guards an Berengar. Bishop Ormund is taken under guard to the dungeon.

Arrangements are made with Erland an his men for Dagomar, though if I know that toad he's probably fled. Erland beckons Jarle an sends him off with em. The Emperor is surrounded by courtiers fussin, guards lookin imposin, an I am startin to feel the toll of a day without food an a night without sleep.

An then Berengar is at my side.

"Ebba," he says. "Will you come with me? I want to talk to you."

I follow him to the chapel. The bodies have already bin moved, but there are still blood stains on the tiles. We step over the one at the door, an he leads me inside the glitterin room.

"I'm sorry," he says. "This is all my fault. If I hadn't been so arrogant, if I had kept my mouth shut, if I had faced my family – none of this would have happened."

We are all alone in the chapel. There is no one to see us but God.

I put my arms around him an hug him.

"It's all right," I tell him.

"No!" he says, "It's not! That brute, he caught you!"

I think about everythin that has happened since Vellsberg.

"Berengar," I say, "I love you. I really do. But I can't marry you. An I don't think you can love without marriage, can you?"

He looks at me sadly.

"I don't think so, no," he says. "It feels wrong. It feels like a block between my God and me."

I take his hand an squeeze it. "Then this won't work," I say. "Cos the God I believe in don't care."

He opens his mouth, ready to argue, an then shuts it. The cry of *heresy!* stays silent this time.

"That's it?" he asks.

"No," I say. "It don't have to be. If you want, we can be friends."

He smiles, shyly, an I'm reminded of the boy who took soup from me, back in Frithberg, in the wayhouse yard.

"I would like that," he says.

"Me too," I say. "An you might want to reconsider Lady Rosamund. Her family's difficult, but she's very brave, an I know she likes you."

He leaves me there, among the relics an the blood stains, an I cry a bit, for the sweetness we had, an that first kiss under the stars. I wish Fetch were here, but he's back at the compound guardin Rosamund.

"Salvebearer?"

I look up to see King Kolrand.

"Sire," I say.

"Kolrand," he says, "please."

I raise my eyebrows. If he sees my eyes are red from cryin, he's too polite to mention it.

"What will you do now?" he asks.

I take a deep breath.

"I think I'm goin to go home," I say. "I tole my family I'd be back by Walpurgis day, an here it's nearly midsummer."

"I'm glad to hear that," Kolrand says. "Erland told me I should not let you go, and I agree with him."

"Really?" I say.

"He has definite views on the subject," Kolrand says. "Did you know there are shrines to you, Salvebearer? Birchold, Frithberg, even some of the southern towns. They seem keen on Grimulf down here, but in Arngard, it's his disciple they remember."

"I en't sure remindin em of what the disciple's really like is a good idea, Sire," I say.

Kolrand looks at me. "She helps people," he says. "She heals people. She's resourceful, brave, she risks her life for others, she does what she has to. I think she's an excellent person to remind Arngard of what we need now."

I can feel the blush in my cheeks.

"Ebba," Kolrand says, "I lost my father the same way you lost yours. Erland told me," he says as I begin to ask how he knows. "We both came under Grimulf's control. You knew him. You know what he was like."

I imagine that man as my regent, my foster father.

I shiver.

"Plenty of saints are never martyred," Kolrand says. "They're queens, princesses, abbesses . . ."

I snort. "Like Gisla. Ormund's lucky the Emperor's locked him up."

"Ormund will be tortured, tried, and executed," Kolrand says.

Oh yes. Rulers do that sort of thing.

"If you want an advisor," I say, "I'll need an income."

His eyebrows rise.

"An another thing." He looks at me. "Eldinghope will not be a slavin post. In fact, I think there might be changes to be made to the law regardin thralls. Bloodprice, treatment, terms of indenturement, things like that."

Kolrand's startin to look hunted.

"Still want the Salvebearer by your side, Sire?" I say.

He smiles weakly.

"We'll have a long journey home," he says, "even going by sea. We'll have time to discuss all these things." He takes my hand. "I'll be glad to have you with us, Ebba Rathnasdota."

The city lolls under the mornin sun like a drunk who stayed out too late. The Bishop's palace was set on fire, it seems, an Gisla is holed up in one of the churches conductin masses over the sacred an incorruptible body of the Blessed Grimulf. Someone's goin to have to try to stop her, but since she has hundreds of passionate worshippers doin her biddin, an since everyone who's anyone has daughters an sisters in the Hekateran convents, no one much wants to be the one to do it.

Good for her, I think. Somethin tells me Gisla has had enough of bein the one locked away.

I sleep for several hours in the compound, Fetch stretched out beside me. No visitor interrupts my sleep. Maybe now he has his followers, Grimulf will leave me alone.

I know some part of him will always be in me. It's a bit like Torny – I let him into me, through my fear, through my obedience, and once someone's in, well, it's hard to get em out. But that also means he is not alone in me, but part of a chorus. Used to be that chorus was made up of people who made me suffer.

That en't the case no more.

In the evenin sun, Rosamund puts her head around the door. "I'm going out," she says. "Can I take Fetch?" Fetch's tail wags lazily against the blankets. I tell him to go with her, an he trots off happily enough.

I get up an wash. I go through my curebag, layin out the meagre remains of my stores, grouped by type. I've almost nothin left. I must get Ma to teach me more. When I travel again I'll need to know how to restock.

I think about goin to the stables, just to see if Jarle's around.

There's a happiness in my chest I can't remember ever feelin before.

There's a tumult of shoutin outside, barkin, then a horrible snap an high pitched whinin.

The door bangs open.

Neklaus stands there, his blonde hair knotted an greasy, his gorgeous face twisted in a rictus of rage. He has one hand wrapped around Rosamund's throat, an the other holds a knife to her breast.

"You," he growls when he sees me. "*You!* This is all your fault!" He kicks the door shut, an leans against it. "You did this. You killed the prester, and you killed my father!"

Rosamund is strugglin, chokin. I can hear shouts outside, but there's no way in except the door. That horrible whinin must be Fetch.

"I'm going to kill you both, you *bitches*," Neklaus spits.

No one's comin to save us.

He slams Rosamund face down against the table, scatterin my vials. "I'll do her first," he says. "Watch carefully, Salvebearer. It's your turn next."

The world seems to slow.

"Neklaus," I says. "Neklaus, listen to me. I'm more dangerous than her. You should get rid of me first."

"Shut up!" Neklaus snarls, but he looks at me as I edge towards the fire. "Don't move!"

I reach for the iron poker, and as I do, Neklaus loosens his hold on Rosamund.

She twists up, her hands full of the black-stoppered vials. She tears the stoppers from em, an empties the lot into Neklaus' face.

Neklaus screams like nothin I've ever heard on earth before. The knife drops from his hand, an as I drag Rosamund away from him, he claws at his face, diggin his nails into the blisterin flesh, tryin to spit the noxious load from his open mouth.

Rosamund an I stand locked in one another's arms as the man who tortured us both falls to his knees, his eyes blind, his face twisted horribly, parts of it burned, parts swellin. Rosamund turns away an buries her face in my shoulder, but I watch.

I hate to say it, but part of me is interested to see what happens.

In less than the time it takes to boil an egg, Neklaus of Merzen, the bastard son of Bishop Ormund, lies dead at our feet.

We leave Ban Granis, with its four square towers, its churches full of believers, its catacombs full of the dead. We take the Arauris down through the green fruitin orchards, headed south to the Marble Sea. At the dock we leave Berengar an Rosamund, both wavin us off wi promises to visit in Sunacre next summer.

Rosamund has her hand tucked under Berengar's arm. I try not to look, but she sees an smiles. She makes a fuss of Fetch, his leg splinted from the break Neklaus gave him, before he lopes three-legged aboard the barge takin us south.

We reach the sea the next day. The Qesar from the Ban Granis Concession are already there, havin left in the night to avoid attention. The violence has died down, but it's an uneasy peace.

I stand on the docks lookin out to sea.

"It's blue," I say. "Shouldn't it be grey?"

Serke covers her mouth an tries not to laugh. Kizmid just snorts.

"I can't believe you're going back north to that gods-forsaken place," she says.

Serke smiles at me. "Your family will be so pleased to see you," she says. "Give my respects to your mother."

"*Sta hada siyati*," I say, "right?"

She nods. "It means 'sit down with happiness,'" she says.

I like that.

The *uarehs* are bein made ready for sea-travel. The wings at the sides are bein lowered to give em more stability. They'll stick to the coast, so it's goin to take em a long time to get where they're goin. I en't exactly sure where that is.

"We'll look after Torny," Serke says, guessin my thoughts.

"We'll make sure she behaves," says Kizmid.

Aisulu comes to tell em the wings are down. Ceremoniously, she hands Kizmid a new bunch of beaded braids. These are white. Kizmid removes the blue braids from her hip, hands em to Aisulu, an fastens the white braids in their place.

"White for the Marble Sea," she says, winkin. "Time to board."

I watch her go.

Aisulu lingers. "Ebba," she says. "I'm sorry—"

But I don't want to hear apologies from her. "Just look after her," I say. "All right?"

Torny jumps down from the *uareh*. She's wearing Qesar clothes, an her hair has bin shaved short at the sides, like Kizmid's.

"They're calling you," she says to Aisulu, squeezin her hand. "I'll come in a moment."

Aisulu nods to me. "I will," she says.

An then it's just me an Torny. The sun shines in her tangle of white-blonde curls, an her grey eyes meet mine.

"Oh Ebba," she says, an wraps her arms around me.

I wrap mine around her waist, an I cry into her shirt without tryin to stop myself. I can feel her tears on my shoulders.

She's goin half a world away. Not the world I grew up in, where across the mountains was the furthest I could imagine, but the world my mother knew, a world so vast you might only ever cross it once. No matter how I travel, or where I go, I doubt I'll ever see Torny again.

"I wish I could know what you're goin to be," I say between sobs. "I wish I could get to see that."

"I already know what you'll be," Torny says. "You'll be powerful, and you'll be free. I'll never forget you, Ebba."

An then it happens. Our fingers unlock, our bodies move apart. I kiss her cheek one last time. An she walks away.

Partin is a kind of death.

I wave until I can't see her anymore.

Jarle slips his hand in mine.

"I know," he says. "It was hard to leave the horses in Ban Granis."

I aim a kick at his shin, half sobbin, half laughin. Fetch lollops up on my other side, his fur stiff wi salt. His long pink tongue licks the tears off my chin before I can stop him. A shadow falls across us.

"Come on," Erland says. "Let's go home."

✦ ACKNOWLEDGEMENTS ✦

A second book is not like a first book. The question of the first book is "Can I do it?" The question of the second book is "Wait, how exactly did I do it, again?"

The answer is the same as it was before: by sitting down and doing it, it gets done.

These are the people who encouraged, helped, and, in certain cases, required me to sit down.

Thank you to Hazel Holmes, who believed in Ebba and Torny's stories in the first place, and who patiently negotiated a delivery timeline when Covid-19 bulldozed the first. Also to Sandra Sawicka, my agent, who was the calm centre when unstoppable forces seemed headed for immovable objects.

A big thank you to the staff at UCLan Publishing, and to the MA in Publishing students who came up with ideas for the design. Special thanks to Becky Chilcott for the final cover design, and to Joe McLaren for another beautiful cover. An extra helping of thanks to my editor, Kieran, who literally worked wonders. The editing process is reputed to be painful, but Kieran made it quite the opposite.

Thank you also to my colleagues, who accommodated regular leave so that I could finish my book as well as having a career I care passionately about.

I'm lucky to have a family that supports and loves me.

My parents, who bore being talked at about such historical phenomena as unauthorised saints with great patience, considering I never let them read the drafts. My brother and his partner Roydon, both of whom I have missed a great deal, and not only for tea-and-chocolate provisioning reasons.

My partner Devon has admirably taken up the baton and has cooked and cared for me through multiple crunch times (it turns out just one deadline doesn't work for me). I'm so lucky and happy I get to share my life with you.

Devon's family, who have welcomed me wholeheartedly, and taken pride in my books in a way that is truly warming. My many cousins – Annie, Flora, Tabs, Alice, and the rest of you, you know who you are – and uncles and aunts and grandparents, here and not here.

My friends, in whose company I have come to understand things greater than myself, and who find their way into my stories in bits and pieces, because I learn the world through you. Special thanks to my friends from the Creative Writing MSt at Oxford University, who understand the pain. Except Andy. Piss off, Andy.

Finally, thank you to every single person who buys, reads, and reviews *The Harm Tree* and *The Ember Days*. It's a privilege to get to share these stories with you. The labyrinth is long, but there is always a guide. Keep your eyes up.

ROSE EDWARDS

This whole
kingdom floats
on a sea of blood

Plough the fields
and it comes
seeping up

The

HARM TREE

"A rich, compelling epic" MELINDA SALISBURY

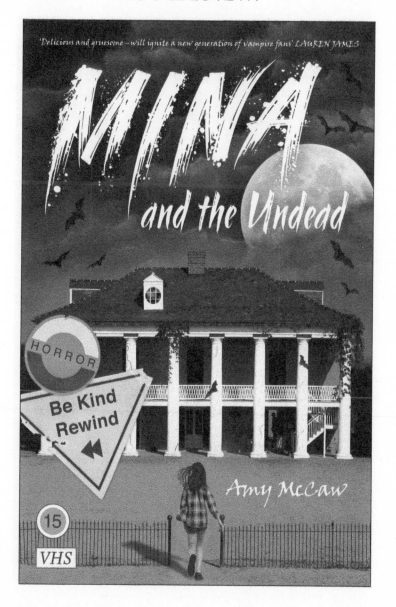

'Delicious and gruesome – will ignite a new generation of vampire fans' LAUREN JAMES

MINA
and the Undead

HORROR

Be Kind
Rewind

Amy McCaw

15

VHS

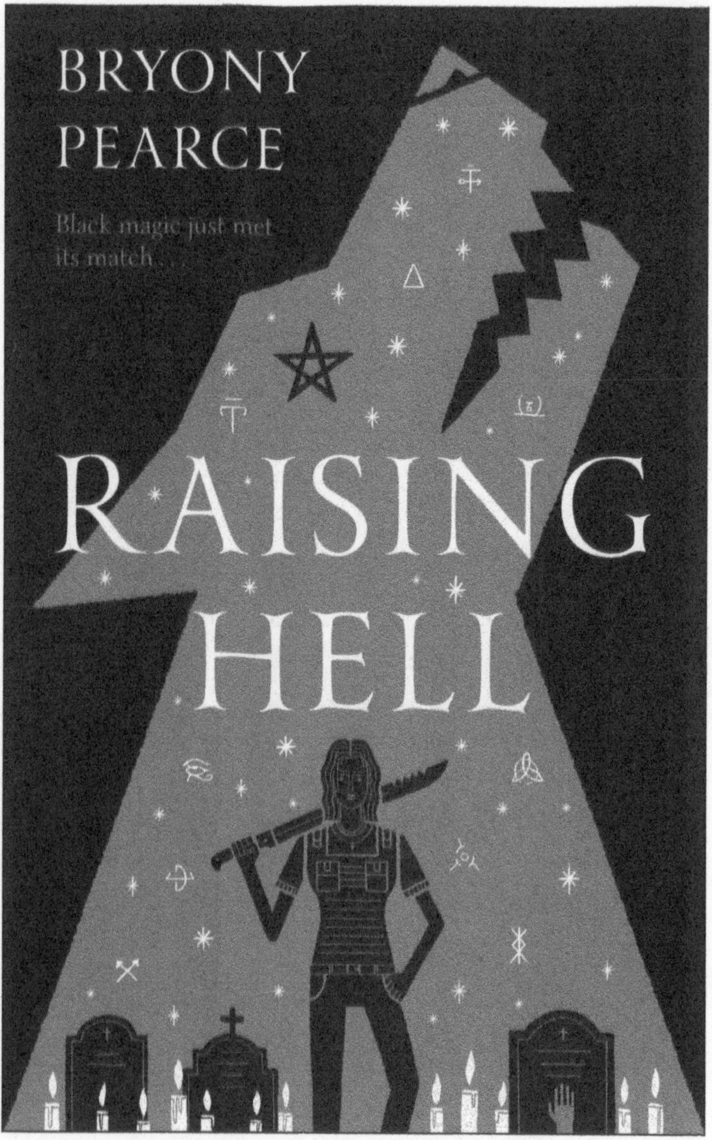
BRYONY
PEARCE
Black magic just met
its match…
RAISING
HELL

EXIT
New York Times
bestselling author
A. J. HARTLEY
IMPERVIOUS

C. G. MOORE

FALL

OUT

The
Witching
St👁ne

I don't believe in witches!
I don't believe in witches!
I don't believe in witches!

Danny Weston

HAVE YOU EVER WONDERED
HOW BOOKS ARE MADE?

UCLan Publishing is an award winning independent publisher specialising in Children's and Young Adult books. Based at The University of Central Lancashire, this Preston-based publisher teaches MA Publishing students how to become industry professionals using the content and resources from its business; students are included at every stage of the publishing process and credited for the work that they contribute.

The business doesn't just help publishing students though. UCLan Publishing has supported the employability and real-life work skills for the University's Illustration, Acting, Translation, Animation, Photography, Film & TV students and many more. This is the beauty of books and stories; they fuel many other creative industries! The MA Publishing students are able to get involved from day one with the business and they acquire a behind the scenes experience of what it is like to work for a such a reputable independent.

The MA course was awarded a Times Higher Award (2018) for Innovation in the Arts and the business, UCLan Publishing, was awarded Best Newcomer at the Independent Publishing Guild (2019) for the ethos of teaching publishing using a commercial publishing house. As the business continues to grow, so too does the student experience upon entering this dynamic Masters course.

www.uclanpublishing.com
www.uclanpublishing.com/courses/
uclanpublishing@uclan.ac.uk